Praise for *The Last Whaler*

"Cynthia Reeves's *The Last Whaler* is an accomplished and magnificent novel. Meticulously researched and fully imagined, it is the story of a couple's sojourn at an Arctic whaling station in the late nineteen thirties. Told in two distinct and vibrant voices through letters that dramatize daily threats and accomplishments, it is a gripping tale about a marriage under extreme stress as a man and woman, already grieving for a lost child, separately find their peace in inhospitable conditions."

—Megan Staffel, author of *The Causative Factor*, *The Exit Coach*, and *Lessons in Another Language*

"*The Last Whaler* reimagines the tropes of Victorian and Romantic novels through a uniquely feminist environmentalist lens, rendering a classic story as timely, contemporary fiction. As Tor Handeland reflects on his years hunting beluga whales in the Svalbard archipelago, the reader travels alongside him to the winter that Astrid, his impetuous wife, demanded to accompany him. The clash between a self-determined woman and the traditional male hierarchies of the whaling trade escalates against the backdrop of formidable, stark beauty as the Arctic winter sets in, stranding Astrid and Tor in the 'mørketid'—'the time of darkness.' *The Last Whaler* is a raw, beautiful novel you will not soon forget."

—Tanya Whiton, author of *Two for the Road*

"*The Last Whaler* reconciles the boundless beauty of the Arctic with a frozen hellscape of grief in this skillfully rendered story of a couple living and working at a whaling station on Svalbard, and struggling to survive the death of their son. Cynthia Reeves's writing is riveting, evoking the shadowy boundary between physical and spiritual realms through such details as the lingering stench of trying blubber or the ghostly grace of a wedding gown. As suspenseful as it is profound, Reeves's novel finds harmony in a perilous landscape that seeks balance between life and death, wonder and danger, joy and sorrow."

—Elizabeth Mosier, author of *Excavating Memory: Archaeology and Home*

"While war rages in Europe, a beluga hunter sails Norwegian seas, taking his wife with him to distract her from mourning the death of their son. After seafaring adventures Jack London would have envied, they become stranded and must try to survive a long polar winter. *The Last Whaler* is gale-force with narrative and unforgettable images: a graveyard of whale bones, a fox embryo in formaldehyde, a polar bear scarfing down the last meat reserves stockpiled for humans. The prose is an overlap of ancient tales and modern insights, a meditation on the fleeting beauty of earthly love and existence, and an inquiry into how we best live with ourselves and other creatures."

—Helen Klein Ross, author of *The Latecomers, What Was Mine,* and *Making It*

"*The Last Whaler* is a deeply moving novel that meditates on the effects of grief and guilt following the loss of a child. The narrative unfolds through two overlapping perspectives: a mother's letters written to the lost child, and the father's responses to the letters ten years later, at the time of the summer solstice. This dual narrative structure reveals how time can be both suspended and cyclical, where personal and historical memory diffuse into the present. The desolate beauty of the remote Arctic shore becomes a powerful metaphor for a struggle to survive inner turmoil and overwhelming grief. Through deep research and luminous prose, Reeves meticulously recreates life in a remote archipelago during the times bracketing World War

II, and she offers a richly drawn portrait of resilience in the face of stunning hardship."

—Beth Castrodale, author of *The Inhabitants*

"*The Last Whaler* is survival epic, nature poem, and mythic history of a land few of us will ever visit. But above all it is a fearless novelistic investigation of the ways in which individuals and entire societies can gradually succumb to madness. Cynthia Reeves's depiction of a couple struggling to move past the incomprehensible loss of a child as war laps at the borders of their world is clear-eyed and deeply compassionate."

—Pamela Erens, author of *Eleven Hours* and *The Virgins*

"This is a hell of a book! Every moment is an urgent conversation between the past and the present, a meditation on the dance between what is ephemeral and what cannot be changed. The landscapes of *The Last Whaler* are at once metaphysical, emotional, unknowable, and all too real. Questions asked of the silent dead mingle with a couple's daily struggles to survive in a frozen world in which darkness reigns. A masterful storyteller, Reeves replicates grief's unique power to demolish clear distinctions between time and place, between love that heals and love that destroys, and in so doing she has written a memorable, necessary *tour de force*."

—Robin Black, author of *Life Drawing* and *Mrs. Dalloway: Bookmarked*

THE LAST WHALER

Cynthia Reeves

Regal House Publishing

Published by
Regal House Publishing, LLC
Raleigh, NC 27605
All rights reserved

ISBN -13 (paperback): 9781646035083
ISBN -13 (epub): 9781646035090
Library of Congress Control Number: 2023949033

All efforts were made to determine the copyright holders and obtain their permissions in any circumstance where copyrighted material was used. The publisher apologizes if any errors were made during this process, or if any omissions occurred. If noted, please contact the publisher and all efforts will be made to incorporate permissions in future editions.

Cover images and design by © C. B. Royal

Regal House Publishing, LLC
https://regalhousepublishing.com

The following is a work of fiction created by the author. All names, individuals, characters, places, items, brands, events, etc. were either the product of the author or were used fictitiously. Any name, place, event, person, brand, or item, current or past, is entirely coincidental.

Regal House Publishing supports rights of free expression and the value of copyright. The purpose of copyright is to encourage the creation of artistic works that enrich and define culture.

Printed in the United States of America

For the whales

…I saw with a new eye
How nothing given us to keep is lost
Till we are, and immortality
Is ours until we have no use for it
And live anonymous in nature's name,
Though named in human memory and art.

~Howard Nemerov, "The Pond"

And everywhere was the silence that broods ceaselessly about the lands that approach the Pole.

~Seton Gordon, *Amid Snowy Wastes: Wild Life on the Spitsbergen Archipelago*

SVALBARD

NORDAUSTLANDET

•GRÅHUKEN

VEST SPITSBERGEN

•NY-ÅLESUND

•PYRAMIDEN

•VILLA FREDHEIM

ISFJORD

•LONGYEARBYEN

•BARENTSBURG

•SVEAGRUVA

BARENTSØYA

EDGEØYA

STORFJORDEN

BELLSUND

•KVITFISKNESET
•HAVEN

BELLSUND–VAN KEULENFJORDEN

Gnomonisk projektion

VAN MIJENFJORDEN

BELLSUND

VAN KEULENFJORDEN

•CALYPSOBYEN

•KVITFISKNESET
•HAVEN

FLEUR DE LYSHAMNA

•PITNERODDEN

•KAPP TOSCANA

•**KVITFISKNESET**

•**HAVEN**

SPRING

Even on this desolate stretch of stony Arctic shore, on the archipelago Svalbard halfway between the northern coast of Norway and the North Pole, I must tell you there are consolations. Here the sun shines day and night from mid-April to late August. One can be fooled into believing summer will never end. Yet the summer solstice, the day of no night, is also the moment the sun begins its retreat. Only the seasoned Arctic dweller would notice the minute differences in the sunlight's quality on either side of the solstice, the fulcrum upon which the season turns. Time and space converge, balance for a moment, then reel apart.

Norwegians celebrate Midsummer's Eve by lighting a bonfire around which we dance and drink and sing. But like everything else in life, our joy comes tempered with the knowledge that sadness nips at our heels. Always. The bonfire reminds us that the sun is once again slowly sinking down. That in time, we'll endure the companion days of no day. Perhaps if, on that evening by the bay, Astrid and I had thought of this precarious balance, this tipping point between the sun's ascension and declination, we would have felt the undertow that foretold the time to come.

I want to relive that moment on the beach, the evening of our first Arctic Midsummer's Eve celebration, 23 June 1937. To reach into time and space and wrench us back. To go forward from that instant and retrace with these words—mine and hers—the journey downshore from this whaling station to our private retreat at Haven. I want to add my thoughts to the weathered leather folio I hold in my hands—held together with fraying navy grosgrain, bulging with Astrid's letters to our son Birk written in her elegant cursive—to bind my words to hers, present and past counterpointed.

As if words themselves will finally solve the riddle of my wife.

As if black marks on these white pages could bring her back. As if a wash of ink will absolve me of my sins.

And so I've returned to my old whaling station on Kvitfisk-neset, to the cabin I once thought of as nothing but a temporary harbor. Does everything in this life circle back to where it started?

I've brought along the essentials. Food and drink to sustain me. Talismans for the coming Midsummer's Eve bonfire. A rifle for protection against polar bears. And, of course, Astrid's wedding dress.

Her wedding dress. Let me explain.

On that June afternoon, we covered the four-kilometer trek from the whaling station to Haven, away from the stinging smoke and foul odor of trying blubber. It was a Wednesday, normally a day of hard labor. But after a morning's work, I'd given my whaling crew the rest of the day off. They had plenty of ale and food to celebrate while we escaped downshore to Haven. My name for it. Astrid called it The Leaning Tower because, after years of shifting foundationless in unstable permafrost, the old hunter's hut pitched ever so slightly sideways. Many of these huts dot the archipelago, belonging to no one and everyone, refuges from the sudden unexpected—storms, impenetrable fog, polar bears. Itinerant hunters keep these cabins stocked with essentials for communal use and leave the doors unlocked to house anyone needing shelter.

Despite Haven's slight lean and the bare trappings of its interior, it was in other ways a perfect jewel. Clad in weathered shingles, the hut boasted a large south-facing window that infused its single unfurnished room with light. Unlike our cabin at the whaling compound, the ground surrounding the hut was clear of offensive detritus. No animal skins dried on racks, no flayed polar bear or Arctic fox carcasses hung from wooden posts, no piles of discarded beluga bones bleached in the sun.

Clusters of yellow Arctic poppies and wood rush and a riot of purple and white saxifrage dotted the scree, as if a garden had been planted by some invisible hand. Astrid could name each flower: phylum, class, order, family, genus, species. She was, after all, a trained botanist. She'd earned a degree in biology at the university in Oslo, studied botany under Hanna Resvoll-Holmsen, and sketched Arctic specimens for her mentor's definitive catalogue *Svalbards flora*. After graduation, she'd worked in Oslo's Natural History Museum, assisting with collection curating in the fall and winter months when her family's dairy farm outside Sandefjord presented fewer demands. Like so many women, she'd put aside her vocation to marry me and raise our children. She rankled when her girlfriends asked about her *hobby* as they passed their ordinary lives with their ordinary husbands. No doubt jealousy was involved. In small part, she'd accompanied me to the Arctic thinking to show them how wrong they were.

That Midsummer's Eve was bright with sunshine. Astrid picked seven different species of flowers, a solstice tradition. She waved the bouquet in front of my face, taunting me that she planned to place it under her pillow that night because, if you honored the tradition, unmarried girls would dream of their future husbands.

"And who might you dream of tonight?" I asked.

"Oh, Tor," she said. "A handsome young prince, naturally."

She arranged the flowers in a chipped porcelain mug, then hugged me. A warm embrace, warmer than anything I could remember her giving me the past year, a year of turning away, of faraway looks, of cold between us like a glacier riven with unbridgeable fissures.

But that afternoon, the old Astrid came back to me.

"My prince," she'd whispered into my neck.

If I close my eyes, a decade vanishes in an instant.

She's here. We build the bonfire together, a ritual we honored that evening as we had all our lives. Norwegians believe that lighting a bonfire will banish illness from animals and increase the fertility of everything living, everything upon which our family depended for our livelihood. Beluga whales and dairy cows and pigs and hens.

We had our share of superstitions. What harm in indulging them?

First comes the base of birch bark kindling, then the pyramid of driftwood. Tradition demands that we use nine distinct kinds of wood. Driftwood isn't native to Svalbard, just timber and flotsam swept in by the sea from as far away as Siberia. I couldn't tell one ash-gray stick or log from another. Astrid might have named the species, found nine unique specimens. I never asked. Was that my mistake?

I kneel to ignite the kindling. Flint on stone, the sharp cracks echo the crash and shatter of glaciers calving into the bay. A spark erupts, the fire catches, a rush of orange wavers against the bleached wood it's consuming. Overhead, curious birds, red-throated divers, *kah kah kah* in unison.

Astrid removes a dried toadstool from her pocket, its cap marked by concentric red circles. This mushroom, too, is part of the ritual, meant to ward off the evils of trolls and witches, ghosts and spirits who emerge from the forests and mountains on Midsummer's Eve. She'd brought the poison mushroom all the way from home especially for this celebration.

"*Lactarius torminosus,*" she says. "Woolly milkcap. It's not deadly."

"Not deadly, no," I say, though I knew from a bad childhood experience that eating it raw could cause blisters on the tongue. "Why don't you go first?"

She pretends to take a bite and offers it to me, Eve to my Adam. I bring it to my lips, kiss it, and toss it into the fire. It flares, brilliant for a moment, then disappears as soon as it touches the flame.

The weather's on the brink of freezing, but fortunately there's no wind. A calm evening. I stand behind Astrid, my arms wrapped around her waist, my face buried in the woodsmoke smell and soft fur of her hooded anorak.

In time, I don't know how much time passed in that moment. A day, a month, a decade.

She frees herself from my embrace and steps away from

me. Quiet at the edge of the shore, she slides off her mittens, one by one, gracefully, as was her way with every movement. Then, toeing each heel of her *komager*, summer boots made from sealskin and stuffed with plaited sennegrass, she loosens and slips off each one without bending over. She pulls back her hood, frees her long blond hair from a navy wool cap, and combs it smooth with her fingers. Her eyes, crystal blue, mirror a small iceberg dancing behind her in the bay.

She heaves her anorak from her shoulders and lets it fall to the ground. Underneath, incongruously, her wedding dress. How hadn't I noticed that she'd slipped on the dress and tucked its skirt into her snowpants before we left the whaling station? The dress is pure white, beaded with small clusters of *liljekonvall*, lily of the valley, with its delicate stems and tiny bell-shaped flowers. She'd insisted on traditional white, hidden the fact of Birgitta in her womb, barely a pinprick. We'd risked scandal, but we were hardly the first couple to make a "mistake." What was said behind our backs, I don't know. Living on a farm insulates you from the most hurtful gossip.

She'd brought the dress all the way from Sandefjord. The lilies would remind her of our home in southern Norway, she'd said.

I reprimanded her. "Bring only the essentials."

"The dress is essential," she said.

She imagined, I suppose, that we were to have a romantic adventure in the High Arctic. Maybe she even planned this celebration about to unfold.

In any case, she was adamant. In the end, she prevailed.

Undoubtedly, the dress was pure indulgence, but I must admit I was grateful for her whimsy. It was the most beautiful thing in this magnificent wasteland besides my wife.

Ten years later, I lift the wedding dress by its shoulders and unfurl its full length. Once bright white, the fabric has yellowed with age, but the translucent beads have withstood time. They catch the light streaming through the cabin window and sparkle in varying shades of a white so white they're almost blue, miniature pearls of ice. I slip my right arm down the back of the disembodied dress, raise the wrist edge of the right sleeve with my left hand, and pace out a three-step waltz across the cabin's kitchen.

My bride. Yes, she's here. She sways in this very dress, rotating her hips, motions me to join her. Arm in arm, we march round and round the fire. And in the curious way time expands and contracts, the two of us, ghost and me, are thrust further back in time to our wedding day two decades ago, when we, newly married, strode down the aisle of Sandar Church. Two become one, we light a single candle before we exit the sanctuary.

Three moments in time, separated by twenty years, unspooling in parallel.

But it's the middle moment that draws me in. We ring the fire one last time, then Astrid pushes me down gently onto the sealskin I've laid on the ground. Around the flames blazing orange into blue sky, she dances three slow, oh so slow, counterclockwise revolutions, and finishes each circuit with a leap across the driftwood pyramid's base. On the last vault, the hem of the dress sparks, singes, and blackens, but doesn't catch fire.

There's a Scandinavian folk tale in which a young woman disappears into the kingdom of elves because she's violated tradition and circled a church clockwise instead of counterclockwise on Midsummer's Eve. On any other evening, direction—west to east, east to west—wouldn't matter. But on solstice, the story goes, one must not tempt fate.

I remind Astrid of this. "Careful," I say.

She smiles. To spite me, she rounds the fire the wrong way. *Widershins*, we call it. In the direction contrary to the sun's course, west to east.

Facing me, she reaches to unfasten the pearl buttons at the nape of her neck and draws the sleeves down her arms. The dress falls to the gravel at her feet. She kicks the gown away, then stands, frozen for a moment in her woolen underwear. Shivering though the fire blazes, she strips the last of her undergarments—chemise, long johns, socks—until all that's left is the gold locket necklace she never takes off.

Faint silvery stretch marks on her stomach remind me of our other life, the one we left behind for these few short months. But I'm not thinking right then of our daughter, Birgitta, safely home with Astrid's parents. I'm not thinking of the days my wife cried from exhaustion, nursing Birgitta and four years later our son Birk, around the clock, nights blending into days until she'd often reached her limits. I'm not thinking of how she felt to be abandoned during the long summers I spent up here harvesting belugas while she carried on with the dull routines of managing her family's dairy farm. I'm not thinking of the past year, a year of grieving Birk's death, a year of silent accusations. I'm not thinking of that final scene of separation: Astrid's mother, Marit, grasping Birgitta's right hand and pulling her back as she cried and reached for Astrid with her left; Marit telegraphing her disapproval of this "escapade" with a look; Astrid blowing a final kiss, then turning away and sobbing only when we were safely aboard ship.

I'm thinking instead of my own long unmet needs, of Astrid's skin, bathed pink and gold in firelight and summer sun. Skin and nothing else.

But what comes next surprises me.

"Count down from thirty," she says. "After that, you'll know what to do."

She turns away and runs down to the water, the calm, frigid water. She strides in but then stops suddenly, no doubt from the shock. I've seen that shock kill some men who weren't prepared, who thought themselves immune to the hazards of an ice-pocked sea. Recovered, she moves forward and immerses herself up to her shoulders, then turns to me. I rise to follow her, but she holds her hands up to stop me.

I start counting to myself at twenty-five, having lost critical seconds reining in my fear.

More quickly, not letting each second have its second's breath, I continue, *Fifteen, fourteen, thirteen.* She dips and surfaces, dips and surfaces, the white moons of her bare ass and then the curves of her calves breaching. Her feet are joined together like flukes slicing the water, propelling her outward.

Ten, nine, eight, seven, six. Too far, I think, *too deep.*

She stops again. *Fivefourthree.* Her head cants backward, a sign that she's about to drown.

Skipping the final seconds, I strip and run to the water. I'm used to that first icy jolt, having plunged into seas colder than this. I swim toward her in broad, powerful strokes. Today the water feels as it always does, as if it's penetrated my skin and entered my veins. As if the blood itself is solidifying into crystals, my circulatory system carrying ice shards to my heart.

Astrid paddles weakly, erratically. Seconds now to reach her before she disappears. My muscles cramp, my heart stutters. Time slows, suffocates the space in which I struggle to keep moving. Numbness replaces pain in my extremities.

I catch her from behind and lock my arms around her waist just before she slips under. I'm a foot taller than my petite wife, tall enough to find purchase on the stones that slip and slide beneath my feet as I make my way to shore. There, I lay her down on the sealskin by the fire. Her skin is the alabaster of fine marble, the firelight pink and gold snuffed out. She coughs, shivers violently as her body fights to warm itself. I nestle her in the anorak she'd tossed so carelessly aside. Rub her feet until they glow pink again, pull on her woolen socks, and lie down behind her. I cover us with the clothes we'd left in a pile, and over top of all fling the wedding dress.

I open my eyes. Astrid disappears. Through the cabin's kitchen window, I survey the fjord. The water beckons. Somewhere in its depths is the solace I seek.

One last time, I close my eyes. Her body cupped in mine, I clasp my arms around her waist and wait for signs of dry drowning. None come.

The bonfire burns down to red-hot embers. More time passes. At long last, her shivering stops as her body regains its equilibrium.

Our pulses coursing together through our skin, I enter her from behind.

This was the beginning of our undoing.

૭

Kvitfiskneset
19 June 1947

Forgive me. I've gotten ahead of myself. Let me start over. Everywhere stillness envelops this Arctic landscape, my empty home. A sacred place. No, not sacred. Hallowed is a better word. Yes, this is hallowed ground. I've been gone almost a decade. Where does time go? It disappears, leaves an echo in its wake. Or maybe, just maybe, the past unwinds parallel to the present. Maybe the dead live in that twinned world. I'm not crazy to think so.

Why have I returned to these godforsaken shores? To rebuild my life. That's what I tell myself. I've left my family behind for the summer on our farm in southern Norway and joined a construction crew that will see Longyearbyen—a town that passes for civilization on this rugged outpost—literally rise from the ashes the Germans left behind when they retreated during the war in 1943. The gaping mouth of Mine 2a still belches red flames. Even the church was destroyed, but its restoration will have to wait. Faith takes a back seat to business. The business is coal mining and with it, reconstruction of the industrial infrastructure, miners' barracks, and a workers' canteen.

To mark the Midsummer holiday, I asked for time off and sailed south from Longyearbyen to Kvitfiskneset. When the gods cooperate, it's a six-hour trip. And the weather was fine. I've brought everything necessary to mark the solstice in the proper way. That is, to ward off bad luck. To engender the good. To acknowledge the realm that exists parallel to the material world, one composed of belief and memory and spirits.

Astrid believed in such a world. That much is clear from her letters to Birk. But once again I'm getting ahead of myself.

Arriving at the cabin, I was surprised to see how little had changed. True, the siding had weathered. True, the shutters hung from their hinges and loose tarpaper flapped in the breeze. But the cabin itself stood stalwart. A single-story, rectangular structure, the cabin is covered with tarpaper battened down with vertical wooden strips, grayed in years of twenty-four-hour sun, and winds that swelled to gale force and then subsided in sudden, unpredictable rhythms. A whetstone, veined with moss and scarred by years of sharpening head spades and axes, boarding knives and mincing knives, stands mute under the kitchen window. Weather-beaten logs, pitched at thirty-degree angles, ring the cabin, buffering it against blizzards that sometimes threaten to blow the foundationless building north into the sea or south against the mountains. Points of long, rusting nails protrude outward from the front door and window frames, a feature meant to ward off polar bears.

Northwest of the cabin lie two storehouses, one used for provisions and perishables, the other for stowing cutting spades and gutting tools and seine nets from my days of slaughtering beluga whales. Farther up the beach are the decaying remains of the sleeping quarters the whaling crew called The Hotel. My first and second mates, Odd Christiansen and Anders Svensen, slept in the hovel that summer of 1937. (I'd heard Odd had been killed by a woman not his wife. I thought it a fitting end for a man who'd betrayed me. Anders, on the other hand, had become a logger and married a lovely woman with whom he'd had two children. His upbeat letters were a bright spot during the long world war.)

Farther along are two stone platforms upon which try-pots once rested. All that's left of the try-pots themselves are rusty shadows. Beyond these are three rowboats bleaching in the grit- and salt-flecked wind that buffets the beach. Two are now piles of wooden planks that hardly resemble boats. But one lies largely intact. It's the rowboat in which Astrid and I had taken refuge one August day, during the worst of her morning sickness, upwind from the stink of boiling try-pots turning blubber to oil.

The rowboats demarcate one border of the station beyond which is the narrow strait where we whalers cast our seine nets. I can almost feel the weight of those nets, the way they cut into my fingers as we lashed them, beluga full, to the rowboat's side. To the east is the landscape's most striking feature—the graveyard of whale bones. Thousands and thousands of beluga bones, the ruins of hundreds of whales. The bones are piled in mounds, blanched and set against the gray and brown scree that covers the beach. From a distance, the white mounds seem part of the natural setting, as if they were vestiges of snow and ice from the previous winter. But close up, you can distinguish vertebral discs imprinted with patterns like radiant starfish. Skulls with their empty eye sockets and narrowing, pointed snouts that belie the belugas' dome-shaped heads. Tail bones shaped like the small trolls I collected as a child—their cylindrical tops resembling the toy figures' wild shock of hair, the bodies like armless, broken dolls.

You may judge me by these bones. When autumn arrives and perpetual light fades into endless night save for the hours of the full moon, and snow blankets every dead and living thing, these bones disappear beneath the pristine white surface and the world can forget, at least for a time, that harvesting belugas created this cemetery. Hundreds of belugas, none mourned in the proper way. Souls I hadn't honored with the indigenous tradition of feeding a piece of each whale's bladder to the sea. I once thought of that ritual as the superstition of pagan Arctic natives. One of my deepest regrets is my arrogance.

I foraged a vertebra from one of the piles and put it in my pocket.

When I arrived at the cabin and turned the handle to the front door, my first thought was *I'm home*. Home. How could this be home? Wasn't home the farm where I'd spent the better part of two decades? Wasn't home where my family lived?

In truth, the cabin is now no more than it was during my

whaling days, a rough-hewn three-room shack. Back then, Astrid had sewn cheerful yellow curtains, scented the air with fresh-baked bread every morning for the hungry whaling crew, and transplanted flowers from the hills and valleys to a garden in front of the cabin in a vain attempt to offset the sight of festering whale carcasses. No, this was never meant to be a proper home, but that year, starting in the late spring of 1937, it had felt like one.

Opening the door, I passed through the dark anteroom into the kitchen. The air was heavy with dust and permeated with peculiar odors. Not the stink of whale oil but something like the stink of life. Lingering smells of cooking, burnt wood, unwashed bodies. Squatters had been free to take refuge here, per Svalbard custom. I opened the windows and shutters and inhaled salt air as I gazed at the blue-green sea and the mountains beyond, brown bluffs striated with rivulets of snow. The crags reminded me of my wizened arthritic fingers, relics of years spent whaling in ice-cold waters.

Next task, crucial in the High Arctic, lighting a fire in the stove. Too tired to climb to the roof and unclog the stovepipe, instead I tested its draft with a piece of newspaper. An invisible current sucked the flame upward, so the pipe seemed clear enough. I filled the stove's belly with kindling and small logs, and, by the grace of God, the fire caught without incident. Then, trained by Astrid's penchant for cleanliness, I straightened the room, dusted the surfaces, and swept the floor.

As the room warmed, I sat down in the rocker I'd fashioned from driftwood as a Christmas gift for Astrid. The gentle back and forth, the warmth, the familiarity of objects surrounding me—yes, this *was* a home of sorts. Astrid called this room the parlor. No doubt she thought of the kitchen in the European way, a multi-purpose room in which to entertain guests with exquisite canapes and mulled wine and boisterous song. She had a beautiful voice. *Summertime and the livin' is easy*, she'd sing (in perfect English, no less, mimicking Billie Holiday) as she went about tidying the cabin or cooking meals. Why that song?

Well, it *was* summertime, even if the Arctic temperatures hovered near freezing. And the jazz singer's version was so popular it had crossed the Atlantic to play hourly on mainland radio. Big bands performed up-tempo versions in Europe's dance halls, and we'd danced to it every night on our sail north from Oslo to Tromsø. But mostly, I think, Astrid sang it to the baby growing in her womb. Lyrics hope-filled, intended to soothe. *There's a nothin' can harm you with daddy and mammy standin' by.* But the words are also tinged with melancholy. *Then you'll spread your wings and you'll take the sky,* the lyrics go. Yes, someday you'll die, but not quite yet.

Rocking in that blessed chair, I closed my eyes and there was my wife, standing by the stove, humming "Summertime" under her breath, kneading dough for the dozen loaves of bread she baked every day for the whalers, that raucous crew. Entertainment never embraced the civilized conviviality of celebrations at the farm. Whatever singing there was revolved around liquor (rationed though it was on these islands) and loose women and sailors gone down with their ships. The parlor played host to drinking games Astrid abhorred, as it meant putting up with the crew's crude language, their incessant tapping of metal tankards in codes they mimicked, and the mess of sticky beer and vomit that she was expected to clean up afterward.

Yet I did try to make the cabin home for her. I built a shelf to display family photos and treasured knickknacks and laid an enormous sealskin rug over the timbered kitchen floor. The room also boasted an elaborately carved cuckoo clock, weatherproofed against the cold and damp with insulating layers of polar bear fur. The cuckoo paced time when time seemed irrelevant in twenty-four-hour daylight or twenty-four-hour night.

The clock had been a gift from my former friend, the German geologist Wilhelm Dege, who'd shared these close quarters with me one summer before the war. Dege later exploited his knowledge of Svalbard, gleaned from "friends" such as I, to provide the Germans with essential weather data during the war. I'd left behind the clock in the chaos of my departure nine years ago. Left behind in its snug polar bear wrap. Nothing suggested that the clock still worked. Nevertheless, I reset the mechanism by pulling down the pinecone weights. Force of habit. The minute hand had stopped at Roman numeral XI, the hour hand near VIII. I tapped the face, as if that gesture would awaken the cuckoo bird and the little boy and girl who dwelled inside.

The world passes by through the open kitchen window. Black-legged kittiwakes swoop underwater and surface with prey. As the birds disappear against the distant cliffs, fish wriggling in their beaks, a sudden gust lifts Astrid's threadbare curtains bracketing the window. I imagine the whir of her sewing machine as she stitched the yellow fabric. And as I imagine that whir, as if on cue, the clock comes to life. The blue bird pops out of its shuttered door and cuckoos the time. *One-two-three,* the whistles come. Startled, I turn to see the brightly painted girl twirl from the clock's arched doorway, her blond braids spun out from her head. *Four-five-six.* Next the little boy appears, his hand upraised in a permanent wave. *Seven-eight,* the cuckoo whistles, then stops. Eight o'clock. The bird retreats into the clock and the door clicks shut. I check cuckoo time against my pocket watch. 7:30. Close enough.

I have plenty of time, all the time in the world, as they say.

The cabin's bedroom is barely large enough for the wooden bunk cantilevered against the wall where we curled up each night that year. In the corner stood the cradle I made for our newborn Hans, carved from a driftwood log in the manner of the Saami's canoe-shaped *komse.* If luck is with me, I'll find the *komse* at the hunter's hut at Haven where I plan to commemorate the solstice.

Haven was erected in the early days of the twentieth century when prospectors, lured by Svalbard's fleeting promises of mineral wealth, built huts along the shores of these fjords.

Haven was our refuge from the crew's prying eyes. What are the chances that the *komse* hasn't been used as tinder in the past decade? I'll find out soon enough.

Above the bunk is a narrow shelf that runs the length of the tiny room. The shelf is empty. Once upon a time, it had been cluttered with the materials Astrid used to study Arctic flora: lined notebooks for recording her finds; flimsies between which she sandwiched her flora for drying; plant presses buckled with leather straps in which she layered the flimsies with cardboard and left everything to dry; thick sheets of paper for mounting and cataloguing the dried specimens in herbarium books; round metal tins and parchment packets for storing seeds; and small wooden boxes for preserving fungi and lichens.

I'd taken all of it back to the farm nine years ago and arranged the items on her dresser like a shrine. I can't tell you how often I dusted each piece, until two years later I finally found the courage to sort through her things. Untying the ribbon that held one of the herbarium books together, I opened the leather cover and was astonished to discover—not sheets of dried flora labeled in Astrid's careful script—but dozens of letters to Birk. She'd bundled them by season and separated each with thick cardboard. That they were so tidily organized right up to the very last one was a shock.

Fittingly, my discovery came the very day, 10 June 1940, that Norway surrendered to Germany after two months of intense fighting. We were dumbfounded by the news. Marit cried and my father-in-law, Christian, railed against the gullibility of Norwegian government officials who thought appeasement and neutrality were options, as they'd been in the First World War.

When I first found the letters, I considered burning them. My motivations were complex. They contained her secret thoughts, I told myself. And after all that had happened, after all the recriminations I'd heaped upon myself, I didn't want to add to my misery. What difficult truths would I discover by prying open the past? Wasn't the unknown better left unknown?

But the letters called to me. An irresistible call. Eventually, I answered. Sitting on our marriage bed at the farm, I read them alone so that I could smile or weep in private. I turned the pages one by one and relived the year through Astrid's eyes. To say it was a trying task...reading those letters that day, I saw only the many times I failed to see what I should have seen.

Now that the war is over and two years have passed to soften the blow, I've brought the letters with me to Svalbard to walk in the footsteps of her words and relive that year in hopes of achieving a measure of peace. I open the folio to the first letter. Take a deep breath. Begin.

ॐ

Constitution Day
17 May 1937

Dear Birk,

I long for those first blissful seconds of consciousness each morning when I wake to the thought that you're alive, that any moment you and Birgitta will run through the bedroom door and leap into bed with me and Pappa and snuggle under our warm down coverlet. Oh, how Pappa resented those intrusions! Oh, how he regrets that now! Oh, how agonizing that abrupt realization each morning that you are dead.

Dread settles over me as I recall that split second a year ago when my concern turned to terror the moment I understood that you'd run off the Sandefjord pier chasing bubbles—innocent bubbles—while I chatted with Mormor and Farfar not a stone's throw away. Can it be that a year has passed and the pain hasn't even begun to subside? I thought grief would settle into a kind of dull ache. But no. Grief is a thing with talons, seizing its quarry, holding fast.

It's getting harder to live. I'm unable to lose myself in busyness. I find myself reliving that terrible day as if I could rewind the reel to the frame the instant before our carefree lives ended and this long nightmare began.

Constitution Day had always been a celebration for the whole family. But last year, Pappa wasn't there. May had been warmer than usual in the Arctic, so he decided to take advantage of the weather and start the whaling season early. He'd left Sandefjord the week before with his crew, headed for Tromsø to lay in supplies and then on to Svalbard. To soothe his conscience, he'd given you and Birgitta a bottle of bubble soap and a giant wooden wand he'd made as a parting gift.

The seventeenth of May dawned sunny and mild, a perfect day for the festivities. We dressed in traditional Norwegian *bunad*. You wore a bright red vest festooned with a double row of brass buttons, a white shirt and black pants, black boots with gold buckles. You fancied yourself a Viking in that costume. My dress featured a red vest trimmed with a woven braid of interlocking hearts and a flowing black skirt. Birgitta's costume matched mine right down to our red felt caps.

We marched through town in the annual parade all the way down to the harbor, shouted, "Hurrah! Hurrah!" and shook rattles and blew whistles, waved our red-white-and-blue flags. Remember? At the dock, the crowd dispersed to play games, enjoy hot dogs and ice cream. You insisted on going onto the pier, the same pier from which Pappa had departed the week before. With a four-year-old's sense of time, you thought he'd be returning that afternoon. I tried to explain that he wouldn't be back for several months, but what are several months to a little boy? Why not indulge your whim? The worst would be disappointment when his boat failed to appear over the horizon.

So down to the pier we went, munching hot dogs and licking ice cream. I handed you the bubble soap, and Birgitta and you took turns with the wand. It became a competition. Who could blow the biggest bubble? The grown-ups clapped as bubbles floated into the air, iridescent as they captured the sunlight streaming down that day. And then we turned to watch a marching band go by, loud with the blare of the trumpets and the bass drum boom boom booming.

Is that why I missed the splash?

Birgitta tugged on my skirt. At first I paid no attention. I thought it was some childish want—she was, at eight, the demanding one—and the music drowned out her words. When finally I turned to her, she said simply, "I can't find Birk."

I pushed my way through the crowd, asking, "Have you seen my little boy?"

Saying, "He's wearing a bright red vest."

Everyone searched for you. Mormor and Farfar chased after the marching band thinking you'd followed it. Birgitta and I retraced our steps to the concession stand thinking you'd gone for another ice cream cone.

I didn't think of the water, so cold this time of year. So very, very cold.

Where else could you be? Please, God, I prayed, not there. Rescue divers arrived. Where did they come from? Who sent for them? They swam out from the pier in all directions. The sun began to set. The horizon turned orange and red, like the autumn leaves we used to press between sheets of wax each fall. Impossibly beautiful. Why did I think of that?

A diver surfaced. Red vest. Brass buttons. I wrapped you in a white towel. Everything else fell away, everything except the distant bass drum's boom boom boom mimicking the terrible pounding of my heart.

A kind policeman offered that a child drowns in seconds. "All it takes is one small inhalation of water," he said. As if that lessened the anguish.

How long was I turned from you? Pappa says nothing, but his eyes blame me.

Something has to give. I can't go on like this.

ॐ

Kvitfiskneset
19 June 1947

Time passes as it always does. The fire in the stove burns down to embers as I hold Astrid's first letter in my hands. Reading it is almost too much to bear. Even now, eleven years since that horrible day.

Did I blame her for Birk's death? Yes. But I thought I kept that blame well hidden. I didn't say, "How long was he under before you thought to look for him?" I didn't say, "Why didn't you realize sooner something was wrong?" I didn't say, "How could you have been so careless?"

Instead, I left her alone when she pushed me away. Would anything I said have consoled her? Our silence ossified, a bone preserved airless under glass. Astrid wandered the house, disheveled, her face red from almost continuous tears or pallid from lack of sleep. At night she refused my advances, the risk of conceiving another child too much to bear. A year passed without the intimacy that couples should share.

Most of what I knew about that day I pieced together from what little Astrid and her parents told me. That is, until I read this letter. It breaks my heart that I wasn't there; then again, the last memory I have of my living boy is the happy one of him standing on the pier from which I'd departed, waving to me and blowing bubbles.

Should I share the blame for that gift of *innocent bubbles*?

I received a call on the ship's radio immediately before we were to depart Tromsø for Svalbard. I remember clearly that moment just before our lives were cleaved in two. One minute I was standing on the bridge laughing with Odd over a vulgar joke and the next...

I left my mates in charge of the ship and returned home for the funeral. We buried our son in the Sandar Church cemetery. The service was surreal, as if I were lost in a nightmare and simply had to shake off sleep to a different reality. Astrid had chosen to outfit him in his incongruously bright *bunad*. Somehow she'd found the irrational courage to wash and dry the costume before giving it to the undertaker.

Laid out in his child-sized coffin, I couldn't dispel the notion that Birk was sleeping. Neither could Birgitta. She refused to believe her brother was dead. It was a matter of waking him. She nudged his shoulder again and again. His eyes and lips stayed firmly closed, sealed by the undertaker's wax. I lifted her up and bent to kiss his forehead, cold to the touch of my lips. The children's bedroom hadn't been entered since my return. Birgitta slept with us, afraid to be alone. "Death might steal me too," she said. I finally worked up the nerve to visit the children's room, sit on their shared bed, and lift one pillow to my face. Inhaling deeply, I smelled the faint odor of my daughter's lavender shampoo. I'd picked up the wrong pillow. Underneath were seven perfectly preserved flowers, a memory of the previous year's solstice. Astrid had ironed them between sheets of wax and replaced them under the pillow each time she laundered the bedding.

I wondered then about the dream Birgitta might have had that solstice eve the year before. Odd thoughts in my grief. I held the flattened, waxen bouquet to my chest, lay down on Birk's pillow, and drifted off to sleep. When I woke, impossible sunlight streamed through the bedroom window. The sun rose and set, impervious to our grief.

Astrid insisted that I return to Kvitfiskneset. Reluctantly, I agreed. There, the work's rhythms lulled me. Catch and haul, butchering and trying-out. Whaling kept the days bearable, but the nights of endless sun were troubled by recurring visions. The conjured image of my son, lifeless in the diver's arms. The all-too-real image of Birk, bright red vest set against the coffin's white satin lining. I awoke from these nightmares to the sound of Astrid screaming. Of course, I didn't hear the actual, unholy sound of heartbreak.

To counter these terrors, I imagined Astrid immersed in the routines of farm work: planting and weeding, milking and bottling, birthing and butchering. When I returned that September, our home seemed back to its usual order. Crops picked, jars full of pickles and brined cabbage and bean salad lined up in the pantry, hay baled in neat windrows, fields plowed and fertilized. I saw what I wanted to see.

Her parents thought my departure a betrayal, my return a betrayal as well. I wanted to tell them this: Sorry, you don't know the half of it, holding someone when they don't want to be held, don't know they don't want to be held, don't know they want to be held, and it's the holding that matters most in that moment, and then that moment's gone.

છ

21 May 1937

Dear Birk,

Last night, Pappa and I had the most tremendous argument! Strangely, the quarrel was cathartic. It shook me from the stupor I've been in since your death. You see, I've decided to accompany Pappa to the Arctic this summer. I think that a dramatic change of scenery and a return to my great passion—botany—will help me regain some semblance of a normal life. This farm, this town—its ghostly emptiness—I need to get away.

It all started with Christiane Ritter. She and I had been exchanging letters this past year. Though we've never met, Pappa and her husband, Hermann, know each other from their days on Svalbard. Hermann is a hunter based in the far, far north of the archipelago, in a place called Gråhuken. When Christiane heard of your death, she sent me the usual perfunctory condolences. But then she kept sending letters in which she shared passages from a memoir she's writing about her year in the Arctic. Her husband had begged her for years to join him at his hunting cabin, and finally, three years ago, she did. As I began to wonder if I'd ever move on with my life, I received another letter in which she described her early summer days in the Arctic. Some of the simplest lines moved me: *For here there are no days because there are no nights. One day melts into the next, and you cannot say this is the end of today and now it is tomorrow and that was yesterday. It is always light, and the sea is always murmuring.* I began to think of the comfort of sunny days blending one into the next and the sea whispering to me...

Then there was Hanna Resvoll-Holmsen, my dear Hanna. You remember her. When she visited us here at the farm, she'd pick a buttercup and place it under your chin to see if you liked butter. And she'd clap her hands and exclaim, "Young man, you do love butter!" And you'd laugh and laugh from the tickle of that flower while she explained the buttercup's strange powers of reflection. She visited several times after your death, but it's the long letter of sympathy she wrote to me that I cherish. I keep it tucked away in her little book of poems. *In the Course of Time*, she called it. I find this small volume a great solace, though its poetry doesn't rank with Ibsen's.

You see, Hanna had a child, a son named Helge. She'd been unhappily married to Helge's father and divorced him. As if that weren't scandal enough, she accompanied men twice to the Arctic—unchaperoned, no less. She married one of them—Gunnar Holmsen, a scientist who shared her passion for the Arctic. Although Helge's father raised their son, Hanna remained close to him. She nursed Helge through the Spanish flu in 1923, when he was twenty-nine. Nine days she sat by his side. Nine days! A lifetime watching one's own flesh and blood waste away, coughing up blood, coughing up his very being.

I scanned her letter's tidy script. *This, too, shall pass, they say,* she wrote. *Who are they to tell such a lie? At best, you'll come to accept your son's passing. Grief wears down its edges, but the emptiness is forever there. Here I am, thirteen years later, wondering 'what if.' What if I'd been a better mother? What if Helge had been with me in Norway instead of Spain? What if he'd lived? Would he have married? Would he have given me grandchildren upon whom I could dote in my old age? Now my progeny are my books and my collections in Oslo's Museum of Natural History and my work preserving Norway's forests from those who'd destroy them. That must count for something.*

When I worked at the university sketching Arctic flora she'd brought back from her trips to Svalbard, I was impatient with her sorrow. That seems like another lifetime. Yesterday, unexpectedly, she came to the farm to visit. Was it providence to receive Christiane's letter and Hanna's visit within days of each other? She hadn't been back to the Arctic in many years—she was weak from a lifetime of battling rickets—but she spoke excitedly, if a bit wistfully, of botanists who were discovering new species on Svalbard.

With Christiane's letter fresh in my mind, I blurted out, "What if I went to the Arctic with Tor?" "It won't heal, but it might help," she said, patting my hand. "Who knows what you might find?"

And so the seed of an idea was planted. I'd go to the Arctic and discover something new, something I could name after you. Preserve it for posterity and turn it over to the Natural History Museum next to Hanna's discoveries.

At first, Pappa thought the whole idea of my accompanying him preposterous. He tried to scare me with tales of people who'd gone mad from isolation and loneliness, from the cold and constant labor.

I was prepared. "You know that plenty of women have summered and even wintered on Svalbard with their husbands. Why, your friend Hilmar Nøis is bringing his girlfriend, Helfrid, up this year."

Pappa countered that she was untested on Svalbard, and "time will tell" whether she was up to the challenge. "Besides," he said, "the Nøises' hunting compound at Sassen is equipped for year-round living. And it's only a few hours from Longyearbyen on the same fjord. My whaling station is 140 kilometers south of Longyearbyen by boat on a different fjord, a good day's sailing trip in fair weather, much longer overland. No one's ever overwintered there before and—"

"I don't plan to spend the winter there."

"I'm just pointing out that Hilmar's station is far superior to mine. Plus, Hilmar's got extended family with him. And he's spent almost thirty years there. Whereas I've got my crew living on the boat or crammed into makeshift quarters on land. And the main cabin is constantly overrun with men, and the stench of trying blubber, and—"

"Enough," I said. I held up my hand as if to staunch the flow of words, but he wasn't finished.

"Hilmar's ex-wife, Elen, have I told you her story?" He went on without waiting for an answer. "He hardly talks about her, much as he likes to talk. But you can piece together the story. They married in 1913 and had a daughter, Embjørg, the next year. Elen stayed behind in Tromsø, raising her daughter while Hilmar spent most of the year at Sassen. He returned home only long enough to father two sons, one stillborn and another who died shortly after birth. She was alone when they were born.

"The constant separation got to her, so she decided to join him at Sassen in 1921 and leave her daughter in her mother's care. Soon she became pregnant with their third son, Kaps. The following June, a few weeks before she was due, Hilmar traveled to Longyearbyen to fetch a doctor. Dangerous weather delayed him. Or so he said. It took him fourteen days to return. While he was gone, Elen gave birth alone. How she did it I'll never know. Woman's instinct? Afterward, she broke down. In late July she returned to Tromsø on the *Braganza*. I know. I was one of the ship's crew. She was hospitalized then. In a sanitarium.

"But I've heard that this wasn't the source of her eventual troubles. She recovered from that first breakdown and again joined Hilmar at Sassen two years later. I suppose she thought that she'd endured near-death physical suffering and mental anguish, and what more could God have in store for her? And besides, Hilmar had begun construction of Villa Fredheim. A palace compared to the earth and peat shack they'd lived in her first year there.

"She brought Kaps along but again left Embjørg behind. And this is where the story Hilmar's willing to tell ends. Rumor has it she became pregnant. Or thought she was pregnant. Either she had a miscarriage or there wasn't a baby to begin with. The gossip is that she forced Hilmar to make a coffin and bury it on a knoll behind Villa Fredheim. That was the last time she stayed at Sassen. She was out on the first boat in June. They divorced years later, but the marriage was broken far sooner."

"But from what I've heard, Elen recovered," I said.

"What I've heard is that she's in and out of sanitariums," Pappa said. "The point is, Svalbard can break you."

"Or heal me," I said. "Heal us."

Truth be told, Elen's story gave me pause. But she sounds like a fragile woman. Her life was filled with suffering. Her own father had hanged himself when she was ten.

I went on before he could think of another objection. "Women have managed Svalbard successfully. Christiane Ritter was hardly a pioneer. As you well know, before her trip to the Arctic, she lived in a grand house in Austria with a gardener, a maid, and a cook. Whereas I'm used to hard work, forking hay for our horses and milking cows at four in the morning." Pappa opened his mouth to say something, but I went on before he could stop me. "Was Christiane as skilled with a rifle as I am? Had she ever butchered a pig or skinned a deer? Had she dissected worms and frogs, or observed the dissection of a cadaver?"

To which he had no reply. After all, I'd managed the farm and the children without Pappa, summer after summer, tending to the myriad problems that arose with such a large endeavor.

Then I got to my main point—my wish to further Hanna's work. I told him how twice she was dropped off alone on Svalbard for weeks at a time, with only a gun, a camera, her botanical equipment, provisions, and a tent.

"And perhaps I might discover something she hadn't. Or something new. The natural world is never static."

I like to think the soundness of my arguments finally persuaded him. But the real reason was that he's afraid. Yes, afraid. I'm also afraid. I was wrong to force him back to Kvitfiskneset last year. And after he returned in the fall came the loneliest months of our marriage. How long can a marriage survive such loneliness?

The hardest part was the prospect of leaving Birgitta behind.

"What kind of mother abandons her child?" my mother asked when she heard the news.

"What kind of husband leaves his wife, summer after

summer?" I responded. "Christiane and Hanna and Elen left children behind. And upper-class women leave their children to travel abroad."

"We aren't upper-class," she said.

"So what?" It was the response of a petulant child, but it served the purpose.

I wanted one summer with Pappa. Was that too much to ask? To remind myself that, not long ago, I had another life?

The idea has crossed my mind more than once that Birgitta is better off with my mother than me. It's a disturbing thought that I push to the back of my mind. It didn't help that my friends also thought this a stroke of madness. Madness—what would they know? What would they know of the trials of separation? Of reacquainting oneself with a stranger each fall? Of the grief I've suffered? Of the chaos that grief imposes? Not linear, not circular. More like a puzzle that never arranges itself into a pattern.

I assured Pappa that I could handle the killing field and whatever else Svalbard threw at me. He thinks I'm delicate, but that's because of my behavior this past year. Too many useless tears.

Yes, a break from my daily life might prove exactly what I need. I wasn't meant to be confined to a doll's house. Ah, Ibsen!

❧

Kvitfiskneset
19 June 1947

I hated to admit that Astrid was right. Women with far fewer of the necessary skills had carved a season or more on Svalbard under more arduous circumstances than what she'd face. And she was right that I thought getting away from the farm with its bittersweet reminders and Sandefjord Harbor with its tragic memories would heal us.

But if I'd been honest, I would have confessed that I *was* afraid. Afraid of the loneliness that had engulfed us since Birk's death. Afraid that the loneliness would deepen with another season away from her. Yes, afraid that our marriage wouldn't survive the separation. The letter shows she knew, just as she sensed that I blamed her for Birk's death. Is anything truly hidden in a long marriage? None of my insufficient counterarguments could hold up against her logic. Her parents could manage the farm without her. Her parents *were* getting older, but they'd run the farm for years before Astrid and I took over its primary responsibilities. And her brother, Johan, who lived nearby, agreed to help.

There was one more thing. I liked to think of myself as the hero of Astrid's story. Not many men would have acquiesced to her demands. Yes, Ibsen. I didn't want to be Torvald, a weakling who claims to want to risk his life for Nora but can't bring himself to forgive her reasonably motivated deception. In the year after Birk's death, I thought I'd failed. Here was a chance to redeem myself.

Leaving Birgitta was another matter. She was old enough to understand that the separation wasn't permanent, but she was also old enough to understand that four months was a long time. Astrid and I sat down with her to break the news. Although we'd already made the decision, we posed it as if she had a choice.

"You mean plants are more important than me?" she asked.

It was the plaintive whine of a child. "No, no, no," Astrid said, taking Birgitta into her arms and stroking her long blond hair. "It's just that, it's just that—"

"Pappa needs help with the whaling this year," I said.

Astrid stared at me. She could never abide lying, but how could we burden our daughter with the complicated reasons for the separation?

"Hanna wants me to continue her work on Svalbard," she said, offering her own half-truth. "Think how much you love coming with me to collect specimens on the farm and in the forests."

"And then we kill them."

"We *preserve* them so that everyone can enjoy them forever."
She opened one of her herbarium folios and paged through
until she found Birgitta's favorite flower, a branch of forsythia,
the first flower of spring. "See," she said, "we can experience
the beauty anytime we want by opening a book."

Birgitta touched the petals, wiped tears from her eyes, and
looked at her mother. "You promise to come back when the
summer is over?"

"Silly bunny," she said. "You bet I will."

"Okay," Birgitta said. "I'll let you go."

The decision made, Astrid spent a hurried week preparing
for the journey while I altered the sailing arrangements. Odd
and Anders would take charge of the whaling ship while I
booked separate passage for Astrid and me on a cruise from
Oslo. We'd rendezvous in Tromsø and from there, sail on together to Svalbard.

In the days leading up to our departure, Astrid sang along
with the radio while she packed her trunks. Her voice was light
and airy, like cream whipped to a froth.

It was, at last, a respite from our grief.

❧

1 June 1937

Dear Birk,

Pappa insisted on booking passage north from Oslo on this
fancy cruise ship to celebrate our tenth wedding anniversary.
Such extravagance! He called this a second honeymoon. We
never had a first, unless my clipping magazine pictures of the
Italian countryside—fields of sunflowers, acres of lavender,
hills covered by grape and olive vines—counts as a journey into
the Tuscan sun.

It's curious, this indulgence. When we married, Pappa
thought a honeymoon frivolous, and truth be told, we couldn't
afford one. Now we have everything we need. Thank God for
those white whales! Bless the cows and pigs!

I was grateful to avoid sailing from Sandefjord Harbor, but it was still hard there on the Oslo dock, Mormor pulling Birgitta back as she stretched her hand to me, her deep blue eyes filled with tears, her cheeks reddened by crying. I blew her a kiss. She caught it with her hand and smeared it on her wet cheek while Mormor scolded me with a look. So be it.

How you would have loved this seafaring voyage! The ship is like a living thing. It rides the waves up and down, sometimes breaching as whales do, launched by a rogue wave and suspended briefly in the air, freed from the natural forces of time and gravity. The engines speak to us. The ship vibrates; its low, steady hum becomes one with the body. The anchor chain rumbles when it's hauled up inside the bowels of the forecastle and serves as an alarm clock every morning, since we tend to dock overnight and sail at first light. The fog has been dense, so the captain blares the foghorn at all hours. All this noise! But the ship's voice is also comforting. It means we're making steady progress toward Tromsø where we'll meet Pappa's boat. Already his crew is there laying in supplies. For now, we're blessedly alone.

You might find this amusing, my darling boy. I can almost hear you laugh, that rich, full-throated sound that erupted from deep inside and tricked us into thinking that you were so much older than your years. In any case, your father, the great beluga whaler, spent the first day of the trip vomiting. And the week leading up to this great adventure, he was concerned that I wouldn't tolerate the ship's heave and roll.

"I'm not seasick," he insisted. "Must be something I ate."

A whole day of vomiting, and me holding a damp cloth to his forehead. Such a wonderful start to our romantic getaway!

Let me tell you a little about this ship. Inside, its warmth engulfs you. We have a cozy cabin with a porthole, and when the fog lifts, we can view the passing landscape like a silent movie of Norway's western fjords. The towns float by, their colorful houses parading down from the hills to the water. We stopped in Bergen, Trondheim, Bodø. I'd forgotten how beautiful Norway's western landscape is. It makes one glad to be alive.

Meals are served in a large dining room, no expense spared. The wine flows freely in stemmed crystal glasses, the food plated on gold-rimmed china flanked by an array of sterling silverware. The tables are covered in crisp white linen with napkins to match. We enjoy a seven-course dinner every evening with delicacies like Russian caviar and fresh oysters.

An orchestra plays far into the night, a parquet floor set aside for dancing. My favorite song is "Summertime." I must admit it's odd to hear an American song on a Norwegian ship bound for Tromsø. Surprising how the world shrinks in on itself. The song seems appropriate as we steam northward into the perpetual light of the Arctic summer and shed the trials we've left behind. I'd almost forgotten what it felt like for Pappa to hold me close while we swayed to music. A fitting beginning to our new life.

Yesterday morning, we stopped in Ålesund. The guidebooks don't do justice to the town's beauty. Imagine a fire that could wipe out a town, as it did Ålesund on a raw January night in 1904. Imagine brightly painted wooden houses, one by one consumed by flames as the inhabitants fled into the night. Imagine the power of fire, Birk. But within three years, the town was rebuilt in gorgeous Art Nouveau style, in stone, brick, and mortar—fireproof materials.

Leaving Ålesund, I had a bit of a scare. Pappa and I stood on the deck yesterday evening, holding hands. The waves calmly lapped the bow, such a change after that first day's violent storm where the breakers almost succeeded in devouring the ship. We stood without speaking. In that moment of peace, I looked down into the water. Suddenly there appeared, beneath the surface, a white, luminous being. I couldn't help but let out a scream, it frightened me so. White against turquoise—it was a ghostly thing. Pappa was puzzled until I pointed to the writhing phantom. He tried to comfort me—it was only a beluga whale headed north.

"It *is* a bit unusual for a beluga to be this far south this late in spring," he conceded. "Unusual, too, to be alone since these whales usually travel in pods. Let's hope he's leading us north to fertile waters."

I trust he's right. Nevertheless, I couldn't stop trembling. As we approached Tromsø, we had another sign, this one from heaven. The fog lifted and the clouds parted and the sun's light shone on the waves, marking a path into safe harbor.

๛

Kvitfiskneset
19 June 1947

Cruising from Oslo to Tromsø reminded me of the early days of our marriage. Astrid was smiling again as I held her close and danced until the wee hours. We were no longer beholden to four o'clock mornings. There was just that one moment of unease when a white flash caught Astrid's eye. It was a vagrant beluga, swimming alone. I lightened the mood by joking that he was the harbinger of a successful season. I led her inside and thought nothing more of the incident.

She bore the first leg of our journey well, never once succumbing to seasickness, including that first day when a storm rocked the ship so violently I couldn't stop vomiting. I assured Astrid it was something I ate because I, who've spent years at sea, wouldn't confess to the obvious in the onslaught of her teasing.

The storm did produce sources of amusement. Once, we tumbled out of bed and onto the floor, tangled in sheets and blankets, our limbs intertwined. I felt well enough to kiss her as we unwound ourselves from the bedcovers. She complained about my breath and the taste of my mouth and who could blame her? No lovemaking that night, but we couldn't help laughing.

As we lay there on the floor, I pulled her close and told her a story I'd repeated over and over, a story I have yet to finish.

"Once upon a time," I said, "there was a great beluga whaler named after the greatest of the Norwegian gods, Thor..."

❧

3 June 1937

Dear Birk,

Tromsø in the spring. We arrived amidst an armada of welcoming boats tooting their horns. Fishing trawlers and ships bound for regions north and south lined the docks. The hills are lush with hemlock and spruce and birch, and from a distance, flowers add touches of red and yellow and purple. Your father tells me to enjoy the riot of color—Svalbard's spring landscape consists of mud and rock and dirty snow. He's wrong. Over a hundred species of plants grow there and add color to the barren rock.

As soon as we docked, your father became Captain Handeland. He put on that hat you used to play with, the white cap with the gold braid across the brim and the embroidered anchor on the visor. You'd cock that oversized hat sideways as Pappa saluted you and said, "Captain Birk."

The minute Pappa boarded, his first mate Odd relinquished control over the proceedings. He'd obviously enjoyed commanding the ship and ordering the crew around. I could tell by the way he saluted Pappa, clicking his heels together and bringing his right hand stiffly to his forehead in an elaborate gesture.

While Pappa and Odd organized the tasks that remained before our departure, Anders took me on a tour of the boat and introduced me to the crew. First were two of the foremast hands, Oskar and Noah, who were busy furling the sails they'd used on the last part of their journey to Tromsø. Perched on the boom, they shouted *hei, hei* and continued with their work.

I pointed to a young man who shadowed Odd as he moved about the ship.

"That's Tomas," Anders said. "A greenhorn. Very quiet, but he works hard."

We went below deck to the galley, where a third foremast hand, Soren, was busy chopping carrots and peeling potatoes.

"Soren doubles as the ship's cook." He put his hand to this throat and pretended to gag. "We'll all be relieved when you take over those duties on land."

Soren laughed. "Unless you want to live on hard tack for the next several days, I'd wager you best take that back."

"A chef like no other," Anders said, stealing a carrot from the pile.

We made our way along a narrow passage, past a small cabin with a brass plate engraved *Captain*. I looked through the window and spied a tiny desk and a bed that seemed scarcely wide enough for one, let alone Pappa and me. It would have to do.

Farther along were wooden bunks flanking either side of a narrow hallway. "This is where the crew sleeps," Anders said.

"Six bunks for seven men?" I asked.

"Plus three miners the captain's agreed to transport north. It's a tight squeeze," he said. "We don't all sleep at the same time, thank goodness."

In the cramped engine room, we found Halvard, the engineer. His hands were covered in black grease as he ran his fingers along the engine's belts and gears.

"Surprise, surprise," Anders said, "to find you here." He introduced us and then turned to me. "Truth be told, the sleeping quarters won't be so crowded since Halvard likes to sleep with his engines."

"They keep me warm," he said. He extended one greasy hand to me, sheepishly wiped it on his equally greasy pant leg, then offered it to me again.

"So glad to meet you," I said, shaking hands. "I've heard you can fix anything with spit and baling wire."

"Absolutely!" he said.

We made our way topside, and Anders bade me farewell so he could join Pappa and Odd on the bridge.

You're too young to understand how first impressions of some people can be bad. It's that way with Odd. I could tell from that phony salute he gave Pappa. Anyway, it's when he saw my trunks that my intuition was confirmed. One trunk contained the equipment I needed for my work—plant presses, magnifying glasses, notebooks, pencils and charcoals, flimsies and cardboard sheets and mounting papers, metal tins and wooden boxes, and several herbarium folios. Another contained the things I'll need to make the cabin home, including my sewing machine, a lovely yellow chintz for curtains to cheer up the cabin's windows, heaps of colorful woolen blankets to keep us warm, and some family photographs to remind us of home. Two other trunks held clothing and boots—enough, I admit, to outfit the Norwegian Army in winter. Buried in one of these trunks was my wedding dress, frivolous yes, but I have sly plans for it.

"There's plenty of coal on Svalbard," Odd complained as he lifted the heaviest trunk, the one with my sewing machine. "What have you got in here anyway?"

I ignored his question, instead asked him for the list of supplies we were bringing to Kvitfiskneset. I wanted to double-check the inventory to see if there was anything to make meals more appealing and nutritious.

He shook his head, muttering under his breath about my "womanly interference." Grudgingly, he handed me the list— flour, sugar, oats, dried peas, condensed milk, potatoes, salt, baking soda, onions, margarine, yeast, coffee.

"Where are the dried fruits and cream?" I asked, knowing these goods would be difficult to obtain in Longyearbyen. "Where are the little treats to break up the monotony of bread and meat—chocolate, honey, and cheese, cloudberries and lingonberries?"

"There's no room left on the boat for such luxuries!" Odd's face turned a brilliant shade of red, and a vein on the side of his neck bulged.

"We can find room somewhere," I said, countering his anger with the most reasonable tone I could muster. I took perverse delight in his irritation. "It's a big boat."

"So how many whaling stations have you outfitted?"

The answer was none. But did I have to defend the fact that

I ran a dairy farm largely alone in summer, a business at least as complicated as running a whaling compound?

"Look," I pressed on. "What—"

"Dammit, woman, stay out of it."

I realized I'd get nowhere with Odd, so I sought out Pappa and asked him if I could shop for additional provisions. It took more convincing than I expected. *Pappa is captain*, I thought. *What he says goes.* But he also had to consider Odd's feelings, I suppose. Odd was his "most capable mate," never mind that my request was entirely sensible.

"Okay," he finally agreed. "Have the things delivered this afternoon. Odd will be away on an errand, and Anders can find places to hide what you buy."

I hurried off to procure the "luxuries" and returned to the dock ahead of the mountain of crates filled with the goods I'd bought. Aboard ship I found Anders in a rare moment of rest, sitting on a barrel lashed to starboard, sanding away the furrows of a whale's tooth with a rasp. He's so boyish looking, the youngest of the whalers save Tomas, too young, it seems, to have earned the honor of second mate. But he's already spent the past three summers on the crew.

So intent was he in his craft that he didn't hear me approach. Startled, he dropped the tooth, and I picked it up. "Scrimshaw?" I asked, running my fingers along its smooth surface.

He nodded, looking a bit embarrassed. "It's my guilty pleasure."

"I thought that art had gone the way of the right whale," I said, and handed it back.

"My father was a whaler. He taught me. I guess it's in my blood." He rolled the tooth into a kit of carving tools and shoved it in his anorak pocket. "I heard you're adding to our meager stores."

"I couldn't help myself," I said.

We disembarked, and I showed him the purchases neatly stacked by the ship.

He lifted a small box marked *canned cream* and another

marked *cinnamon.* "Looks like we'll be having something besides bread and ale."

"What would Sunday breakfast be without pastries?" I asked.

"My mother bakes the most wonderful *skolebrød.*"

"My son loves those as well. He licks the custard from the bun, then devours the donut." I stopped. Loves. Loved. You loved them. I took a deep breath. "I have all the ingredients. I can't promise anything until I see the stove. Tor tells me it's a bit rudimentary."

"Halvard is fond of sweets as well. He'll make it work."

He winked at me, the two of us conspiring. As if by magic, Anders found space on the boat for the whole lot, secreting the bounty into hidden compartments beneath the galley.

ॐ

Kvitfiskneset
19 June 1947

This past May I sailed from Sandefjord to Tromsø and then on to Longyearbyen for a summer of reconstruction. I forced myself to leave from Sandefjord. The harbor hadn't changed a bit from when I'd last departed eleven years ago. Or maybe it had changed completely. As I boarded the ship for the first leg of my journey, I stopped on the gangway to look back at the pier. The crowd waved and cheered and blew kisses to the passengers already leaning over the railing. Birgitta stood apart, alone, her arms folded across her chest. I wondered if she was thinking the same thoughts as I—the absence that was as palpable as grief. Does everything lead like a trail of tears back to Birk's death?

Sailing north, I asked myself over and over why I was returning. I was done with whaling. I thought I was done with Svalbard. But something drew me back, something besides the promise of rebuilding a town lost to war.

Ishavet kaller, the call of the Arctic. That old ghost.

A decade ago, so much hope. A decade ago, we'd launched

the ship from Tromsø on a fine-weather day, headed first to Longyearbyen to lay in a supply of coal and to retrieve my motorboat from dry dock, then onward to Kvitfiskneset. The seas between Tromsø and Longyearbyen are notoriously difficult, challenging even the most seasick-averse sailors. For Astrid's sake, I'd hoped to have a smooth crossing. Alas, the ship rocked so severely that it was impossible to tell up from down. Astrid spent most of the voyage below deck in our tiny cabin, coming topside only to breathe a bit of fresh air rather than the fetid air of our quarters. I refrained from teasing her, green as she was. Secretly, I thought of her seasickness as my revenge.

The turbulent water didn't cause me seasickness as it had on the sail from Oslo. Could it be that it really was something I ate? Or was it that I wasn't in command of the cruise ship?

The heave and roll also didn't affect the three coal miners I took north because they'd missed an earlier transport to Longyearbyen. Svalbard has its share of high-quality coal. Mines are scattered across the western landscape, in the Russian towns of Barentsburg and Grumant and Pyramiden, in the Norwegian towns of Longyearbyen and Ny-Ålesund and Sveagruva.

I'd always thought of coal miners as a weird lot, so much of their lives spent deep inside the mountains breathing in the black dust that coated every inch of their bodies. Crawling along coal seams. Tugging fifteen-kilo iron jacks through tunnels hardly large enough to pass through. Listening to the mountain for the telltale warning of a rockslide. Monitoring the air for dangerous levels of methane. Facing the risk of explosions sealing them into early graves. Back in 1920, a coal dust explosion in Mine 1a killed twenty-six men. Just like that, their lives were extinguished. You know not the day nor the hour.

In fairness, I guess they thought of us whalers as odd. Slaughtering whales, bathed in blood and blubber, our fingers permanently frozen, our clothes forever stained. And the foul odor that saturated our very skin. Whalers and miners were more alike than I cared to admit. We wanted to earn as much money in as short a time as possible. We soothed the physical and mental strains of our labors with alcohol and occasional fisticuffs. We shared the loneliness of a life without our wives and children. We covered our longings with an outward stoicism that belied our true feelings.

Although our sleeping quarters were stretched beyond limit, the three miners were grateful for the passage. The close quarters on my ship were luxurious, apparently, compared to steerage aboard the colliers.

"Steerage," one of the men scoffed. "More like slave quarters. They house us between decks in a space constantly showered with coal dust. Same place they store the coal when headed south. 'Course, we're black with it anyhow, and used to the grit, but suffocating for three days onboard ship is a miserable experience."

"And our galley is down there. Kitchen, dining room. Nothing separating us from the dust while we eat."

"And one toilet for all of us. Usually stopped up. Overflowing into the gangway."

Time repeats itself. Aboard the ship I took north this past May were three miners heading back to Svalbard for another year's work. Time repeats, yes, but the times are also vastly different now. The war is over. Rebuilding our lives almost as if the conflict never happened is a kind of collective amnesia. We almost forget the evil of which humans are capable.

I tried to be optimistic. The miners' enthusiasm rubbed off on me.

There was the cutter, Fredrik, whose job was to stand at his post seven hours a day guiding a blade into the coal seam, a boring job by his own admission, yet one careless move could create catastrophe. A coded series of rings alerted him to a variety of problems, but the one he laughed about was six rings. *Wake up, asshole!* it meant.

The coal shoveler, Ove, claimed to love the mines. "Where else can you spend your workday lying down on the job?" he said. Translation: the tunnel doesn't allow him to stand up.

Thus, he had to lie prone, shoveling coal away from the cutting machine as it bit into each seam.

And finally, the blacksmith, Johannes, who spent his free hours crafting elaborate candlesticks and figurines out of scrap metal. "Why not make the best of idle time?" he said. At least he got to stand and enjoy the comfort of a blazing fire with which he repaired all manner of metal tools and fittings.

One evening as we drank coffee in the galley, they told the story of a miner in Ny-Ålesund who'd committed suicide on New Year's Eve in 1945.

"They stored the body in a shed at the edge of town while awaiting a proper burial," Ove said. "We've had the devil of a time getting a pastor to come to Svalbard to conduct weddings and funerals."

"I heard the townsfolk would go out of their way to avoid that shed. Superstitious lot. As if the miner's ghost was haunting the place," Johannes said.

Fredrik laughed. "I'd be avoiding the shed myself. No need to tempt fate."

"So what happened to the body?" I asked.

"The new governor, Håkon Balstad, came up to Ny-Ålesund last autumn on business," Johannes said. "The locals prevailed on him to conduct a memorial service. I heard tell that the man's fellow miners carried his coffin to the graveyard, where they'd been able to blast a grave deep enough to cover it."

What kind of despair would lead a miner to take his life on a festive night of celebration, the sky lit up with fireworks welcoming that first year without war? I dwell overmuch on reasons and motivations. I know that suicide isn't the exclusive province of desperate miners.

"How can you stand working underground with the constant dangers and the pall of coal dust?" I asked.

Fredrik laughed. "I remember the first day I went into the mine. I swore it would be my last."

"And how long ago was that?" I asked.

"Thirty years," he replied. "And now I can't imagine my life could have been otherwise. Within the mountain, we're apart from the world. Without, all is madness."

I'd seen photos of the decimation of Dresden, now a pile of ruins. Barentsburg smolders. So many cities, towns, villages, devastated.

And yet we rebuild. Take Longyearbyen. The Old Quay is alive with men moving material, machinery, and equipment. Store Norske Spitsbergen Kulkompani has already raised much of a whole new neighborhood for its workers uphill from the center of town. It's called Nybyen, "new town," with barracks and canteens and offices in the shadow of Mine 2b. There's a buoyancy in people's steps, a roll-up-your-sleeves-and-get-to-work attitude. I'm part of this enterprise. It feels good to hammer nails into wood as a new town rises from the devastation.

But the reconstruction is a kind of cover-up, a kind of forgetting. I'm part of that forgetting.

ॐ

6 June 1937

Dear Birk,

My first impression as we sailed along Svalbard's western coast was that we'd entered a primordial world, elemental, composed of rock, ice, and water. As if hell had literally frozen over. Petrified waterfalls clung to the high peaks of knife-edged mountains capped with snow. Lower down, thin falls creviced rockface and rushed sidelong into the sea. The mountains betrayed their sedimentary layers, counting back millions of geologic years to an age when this icy landscape was subtropical. Seeds of that time are buried in the deepest part of these rocks. Might the great tectonic plates shift once again and return this world to its primeval origins? A land of lush green sifted through with flowers bursting in all colors—deep yellows, bright purples, ruby reds?

We turned into Isfjord, and the water calmed. Such a relief after the turbulent passage north from Tromsø. Spending three days vomiting was my penance for teasing Pappa on the trip from Oslo to Tromsø. There was a moment when I wondered if all those friends and relatives were right. Madness to think this would be some grand romantic adventure. As Pappa's boat wove through the drift ice and small icebergs, I became more than a little nervous. Squeezing my hand, he reassured me that he and Odd and Anders had navigated this fjord many times. To prove the point, he left Odd and Anders on the bridge and led me out onto the deck.

It was then I saw that my first impression was wrong. There *is* life here. Birds by the hundreds gather on the cliffs, their cries a cacophony of discordant music. Rocks stained white with guano enrich the scant soil below, enough to fertilize lush green vegetation underneath. Green moss beards stony outcroppings while sunburst-orange lichen colors white stones dotting the lower reaches. Along the shore, bright yellow Arctic poppies wave their tiny flowers from delicate stalks, purple saxifrage stretches along rocky mounds and sandy soil.

The water, too, quivers with life. Schools of herring and cod skim the surface. The sea whirls and bubbles, as if breathing, and disappears into little vortices created by the currents washing up against small icebergs that the crew calls bergy bits. I'm mesmerized by their colors—various shades of crystalline bluish white, like pieces of broken sky. They twirl around each other, dancing to unheard music. I listen. There *is* music. The jingling of bells, the crash of cymbals, the boom of the bass drum. The larger bergs seem alive, mutating from deep greens to pale blue to pure white, swimming in the currents, losing their balance and tipping over, sending small waves lapping against our hull.

So now I see this landscape has its own enchantments—the deeply crevassed glaciers spilling into the sea, the snow-dusted mountains tinted pink and gold by the sun, the endless sculptures of an astonishing variety of icebergs bobbing in the fjord. As we made our way along Isfjord to Longyearbyen, we passed by one such glacier, frozen white lava spilling from the north shore into the water.

"Nansenbreen," Pappa told me. He raised three middle fingers to block the glacier from view. "This trick guarantees we're far enough away, in case it calves." He then told the story of an ill-fated seventeenth-century whaling ship that got too close to an ice cliff. From high up, a large piece of ice broke away, destroyed the foremast and mainmast, and killed three men.

"But we're far enough away, aren't we?" I asked.

"We could also be caught by a rogue wave brought on by calving."

And as if on cue, as if he ordered the spectacle just for me, a massive chunk of ice slid from the glacier into the sea, sending a plume of snow and ice skyward. Birds disrupted from their perches on floes and pancake ice rose. A rush of noise, like a lion's roar, tore across Isfjord.

"Hold on," Pappa said.

A wave erupted from the mouth of the cave where the ice had been and moved toward us. With one great burst, it crashed into us broadside. The boat rose, then settled. An icy spray washed over us.

Welcome to Longyearbyen, the water said.

The very space in which I live has been altered. Norway seems constrained by boundaries, political and personal, but here the terrain's very vastness makes me think of land indivisible, measureless. It provokes a sense of wonder, yes, wonder. Yet simmering underneath is the feeling that dangers lurk everywhere.

When we docked at the quay and I had a chance to survey Longyearbyen close up, I must admit I was disappointed. Natural splendor gave way to dreariness. Instead of the mainland's colorful homes, the houses and barracks here are uniformly gray. A nod to the utilitarian—why waste paint when the cold prevents the wood's deterioration? Smoke beclouds the sky above the mines; coal dust permeates the air like fine mist. Rising from the dock, the road—if you can call it a road—is grimed with filthy snow. It's really hard-packed mud and grit. To be fair, the daisy-like flowers of Arctic mouse-ear push up through the rocks and mud along the road, a touch of beauty to relieve the ashen terrain.

Marching up the hill is the landscape's most striking feature—triangular wooden structures with gondolas dangling from heavy cables. They resemble ski lifts, except that instead of people, these transports carry coal from the mines to the dock and return uphill empty. The cableways look like the legs of a giant spider, converging on a wooden building that is its body. You know how much I hate spiders!

We disembarked. Pappa's crew headed God-knows-where to enjoy their last bit of freedom, no doubt. Pappa was to meet with his friend Einar Sverdrup, the coal company's director, and afterward with Governor Marlow to discuss the most recent whaling laws. He's known Einar since his first days on Svalbard, before me, before you and Birgitta. I wanted to explore the town, hoping my impression would improve upon closer examination, and to send a telegram home telling your grandparents that we'd arrived safely.

Pappa pointed out the telegraph office and then disappeared inside Store Norske's administration building. Much to my chagrin, there are no shops for outsiders here. This is a company town, run by Store Norske, which provides what the miners need. What few luxuries are available, such as alcohol, are strictly rationed to those same miners through the company store. Now I see why Pappa was so diligent in Tromsø to double-check that we had the necessities to last the summer. But I was glad I'd secured the luxuries I'd demanded.

Much to my surprise, a telegram was waiting. I ripped it open, fearful of bad news.

DEAR MAMMA stop I WAS SO SAD WHEN YOU LEFT stop MORMOR AND FARFAR TOOK ME TO GRÖNA LUND TO CHEER ME UP stop WE RODE THE CAROUSEL ROUND AND ROUND stop AND THE DARK TRAIN TUNNEL RIDE YOU SAID WAS TOO SCARY stop I MISS YOU SO MUCH stop KISSES BIRGITTA

Gröna Lund! Your grandparents had taken the train all the way to Stockholm from Oslo after we departed. Mormor and Farfar had somehow managed to keep their plans hidden from us. We'd been to the amusement park once before, just before you died, and spent a long weekend exploring the city. We thought of making it an annual adventure, but then...

I reread the telegram, imagined my mother coaching Birgitta to write these words. After all, it was Birgitta whose fear of the dark prevented her from riding the Ghost Train. Remember, Birk? You and Pappa and I rode the motorized car over and over while Birgitta and your grandparents watched us disappear into the tunnel's mouth. Even so, it makes me happy to hear that my parents spoiled Birgitta with a trip to the amusement park and that your sister finally found the courage to enter that dark tunnel.

I considered my reply. So much to say, but only a short space in which to say it. It's a miracle to be able to communicate with the mainland at all. Do you recall the story of S. A. Andrée and his attempt to be the first to fly over the North Pole in a hot-air balloon in 1897? How he and his two companions disappeared without a trace other than the buoys they threw overboard that washed ashore far afield from where they started, and the single carrier pigeon that made its way back to civilization carrying a note tied to its foot that claimed *all is well*?

I thought of that pigeon, how unreliable a messenger, how untimely the message! Their frozen bodies were finally discovered in 1930 on the tiny island of Kvitøya, a stone's throw from Nordaustlandet. So close to salvation. Unutterably sad.

By the time your sister receives my reply, time will have passed. But it's better than pigeons!

DEAR BIRGITTA stop THE TRIP NORTH WENT SMOOTHLY stop PAPPA WAS SEASICK BUT HE IS FINE NOW stop ALREADY THE FLOWERS ARE BLOOMING HERE stop BEFORE US IS THE FINAL LEG OF OUR JOURNEY TO THE WHALING STATION stop I WILL SEND YOU A PRESSED

FLOWER IF I GET THE CHANCE stop

Pappa has warned me that radio communications at the whaling station are fickle. Weather, equipment failure, the battery requiring constant charging if it can be charged at all, violent winds blowing down the antenna. Knowing this, I wondered what to add. But what more could I say so early in our adventure?

So I signed off.

I WILL BE BACK BEFORE YOU MISS ME stop BE GOOD FOR MORMOR AND FARFAR stop LOVE MAMMA

After being confined to ships for so many days, I welcomed the chance to stretch my legs. Up the muddy road I went, past the hospital, the post office, the family houses, and the miners' barracks. Across from the barracks were a barn, stable, and pigsty. Horses whinnied, luring me inside. That musty odor of hay and piss transported me to our farm, and I felt a momentary pang of homesickness as I stroked the muzzle of one of the horses.

Outside again, I came to a fork. A side road cut into the low hills; the main road stretched in front of me. Right there at the crossroads, as if in a fairy tale, was an old man sitting on a driftwood stump and leaning on a staff with both hands. He had a long white beard and mustache, skull-like hollows at his temples, and loose skin gathered in deep folds along his cheeks. Truly he made me think of Santa Claus. But he was no Saint Nick.

"And what brings you here, young lady?" he asked, eyeing me up and down.

"My husband, Tor Handeland, he's a whaler."

"I know him. He's arrived then?"

"He's meeting with Director Sverdrup and Governor Marlow."

"Ah yes. Staying on the right side of the law. Paying the piper for the privilege of killing innocent life."

"Making a living," I said, curtly. "Humanely." Who was he to judge how we earned our keep?

"Is there such a thing?"

"Tor has assured me the beluga's death is quick and painless." The old man laughed. The way he laughed gave me the creeps, as you used to say, so I turned away from him. But he wasn't finished. "So he's brought his wife with him this year? He's spoken of you before. He'd hoped you'd come to Svalbard with him someday."

I turned back but kept my distance. "You must be mistaken. It took some coaxing to get him to let me come."

The man flashed a crooked smile, the creases on either side of his mouth deepening. "Whaling's a lonely life with a crew of men. I'm sure you'll help make time pass more…pleasantly."

He said it in a way that hinted of something sinister underneath. He picked up his staff and aimed its muddy tip at me. "I've learned of your tragedy," he said. "As that British poet once wrote, 'the blow fallen no grieving can amend.'"

"It's none of your business," I said, irritated that this stranger would have the gall to allude to your death. He was indeed a very peculiar man, a troll guarding a bridge to nowhere. And where had this shriveled goat heard of Robert Browning?

Credit that he was right about grieving. I'd come across the Browning poem soon after your death, and those words, strangely, consoled me. I'd grown weary of well-meaning friends who parroted that cliché about time healing all wounds. No! Time is the evil stepmother who feigns love while conspiring to rob her stepchildren of every happiness.

He stabbed his staff into the ground and leaned forward. "Let me give you some advice."

Before I could object, for I was feeling unnerved by the man's very presence, he went on. "Confinement will be wicked on your mind unless you exercise outside every day. And never leave the cabin without a gun. Polar bears come out of nowhere, and one swipe of their paws can kill you."

To underscore his point, he rolled back his parka sleeve and showed me a series of raw-looking raised red lines creasing his forearm.

"I was lucky," he said, re-covering the scars. "And lastly, the snow is so dry here that you can roll around in it to remove wetness. If you get drenched outside and don't dry off, you will die."

He made the last three words sound like a threat, each one enunciated.

Christiane Ritter had given me these same three pieces of advice—without the portent of doom—in a telegram she'd sent before our departure. It made me wonder if she'd crossed his path, if this same old man sat here every day, imparting the same advice to every errant wanderer.

I turned away without so much as a goodbye and fled down the hill toward the safety of the boat.

"Farewell," he called after me. "Farewell."

My uneasiness over this encounter lingered far into the night, an undercurrent of anxiety blossoming deep within my body and preventing sleep, even with the gentle rocking of the ship and Pappa spooning me, holding me tight.

෴

Kvitfiskneset
19 June 1947

Astrid inserted Birgitta's wistful telegram into the folio following this last letter. She kept everything Birgitta sent her that year. It's proof that our daughter was never far from her mind.

In my own grief I sometimes forgot how much Birgitta suffered after Birk's death. She spent more nights sleeping with us than in her own bed.

"Why not?" Astrid asked me more than once.

At the very least, I felt Birgitta was a living wedge between us. Now I'm glad she had that comfort, especially when she finally revealed the real reason behind my in-laws' secret trip to Gröna Lund. This was during the war, when she suddenly (it seemed to me) cast off childhood and assumed Astrid's role on the farm. Without being asked, she also cared for Marit, who'd been diagnosed with breast cancer in the middle of the war. Christian took his wife to grueling radiation treatments after the mastectomy, but it was Birgitta who changed her dressings and prepared the bland meals that kept her nourished.

One day, after Birgitta had spent a good part of the morning helping her grandmother bathe and dress, I made an offhand comment about how proud Astrid would have been to see her growing into adulthood.

"Mamma never felt she could be as good a mother as Mormor," I said. "Now look at you."

Birgitta shook her head. "I was angry at Mamma for leaving me. But Mormor was hardly the perfect mother."

And then she told me what happened after the ship sailed—the last day she saw her mother alive. Her grandparents treated her to a long weekend in Stockholm and a visit to Gröna Lund. I'd assumed the trip was their way of soothing Birgitta's sadness. But that was only half the story. The other half was that they wanted to make Birgitta face her fears. On the way to Stockholm, they told her that she wouldn't be allowed to climb into bed with them. They even booked her a separate hotel room, which was surprising given Christian's thriftiness.

"You can't imagine how lonely that first night was," Birgitta said. "I didn't sleep a wink. The next day they indulged me at Gröna Lund with all manner of treats. An enormous cone of cotton candy and a double scoop of strawberry ice cream. We rode the carousel over and over until I was dizzy. We strolled through the Mirror Maze, laughing at our reflections stretched to impossible heights or shrunk to elfin size. And then they pulled the meanest trick. When we stood in line for the Ghost Train, they promised I could wait for them at the exit. But before I knew it, Farfar lifted me up and sat me down between them in one of the cars.

"Off we went, plunging into its dark tunnel," she said. "Ghosts sprang out of nowhere, then faded to smoke. The suddenness of things appearing and disappearing caused my heart to race. I covered my eyes, but the shrieks and whistling wind were enough to frighten me. They were right to force me on that ride. In the end, I learned to sleep on my own. And in a strange way, I learned to welcome ghosts."

She paused. "Ghosts," she added. "Can you imagine?" Then she told me that Birk appeared to her in dreams, and sometimes she could sense he was sleeping beside her in the room they'd shared. It comforted her. "Is that weird?" she asked.

"No," I said. "Not at all."

The cuckoo cuckooed twelve times, waking me from a nap. I must have slept deeply, for I couldn't recall anything except feeling a kind of lightness. Remembering Birgitta's words must have led me into that pleasant world. If Astrid's death taught me anything, it was the foolishness in believing that silence was a cure for sadness. Talking with Birgitta as she got older, while it did not resolve our grief, helped bridge the loneliness that silence bred.

I'd fallen asleep in the rocking chair with the folio in my lap, and its contents had scattered at my feet. I collected Astrid's letters and organized them once again by season and date. The ribbon no longer held the folio together since it had grown fatter with the addition of my musings.

Who's going to read them? I wonder. *What am I trying to accomplish?*

This whole exercise reminds me of something my mother once told me, that lost stories go into the *Glemmeboka.* The Book of Forgetting. Sometimes I think it would be a blessing to leave lost things lost. She also told me that God keeps a book of remembrance, an accounting of our deeds good and bad. If so, what has God recorded there for me?

I wonder if it's possible to balance remembering and forgetting as if on the point of a pin. A perfect equilibrium in which every painful memory is offset by a happy one. Like the equinox, during which the earth achieves perfect symmetry between night and day all over the world at the instant the sun is perpendicular to the equator. Two fleeting moments, one in spring, one in autumn.

Is it so much to ask that God grant us such moments?

My store of firewood in the anteroom ran low, so I slung my rifle over my shoulder and ventured outside to gather kindling and logs from the pile. I scanned the shoreline, alert for polar bears. The sun broke the water into a thousand shards of light. Far out I saw a pod of belugas taking turns leaping and diving. I walked the slight incline down to the water's edge to get a better look and watched them until they disappeared over the horizon.

Turning back toward the cabin, I paused to consider how the station, though deteriorating, had survived the war. At the very least, I had this cabin to return to. I brought the wood inside and stacked it neatly in the storage room.

Yes, the whaling station had survived, marred only by the forces of nature. The Germans had ignored this remote strip of land because it offered nothing strategic. Whereas, when I arrived in Longyearbyen, the sight of the town destroyed by war made me feel as if I'd landed on an alien planet. True, some buildings were spared, among them Sverdrupbyen, the miners' residential neighborhood named as a tribute to my friend Einar Sverdrup. And true, reconstruction was proceeding at a furious pace. The sheer level of activity was a tribute to human resilience.

Nature was resilient too. If Astrid were alive, she'd have prodded me to find beauty amid the ruins. The white petals of Arctic mouse-ear still thrived all along the main road. The changing hues of icebergs still caught the blue of water and the golding of the sun. All manner of birds still nested on the vertical bluffs, their life-giving guano splattering the brown ridges. But try as I might, I found it hard to reconcile the town's present desolation with its past.

My first instinct, customary when I arrived in Longyearbyen, was to visit Einar at the coal company's headquarters. I valued his friendship, yes, but also his advice on keeping to the right side of politics. The Svalbard Treaty had granted the archipelago some autonomy from Norway, and thus its control was beholden to whoever was governor. In the late thirties, Wolmar Marlow held that office. He was a stickler for rules, at least when it came to others, and I dreaded my meeting with him every year, sure he'd find some obscure tenet of whaling law that I'd broken.

Halfway uphill, I remembered that I'd be reporting to Store Norske's new director, Erik Anker. I knew the Ankers, a good lot. Their family was instrumental in the company's growth and postwar resurgence into a viable mining operation, the lifeblood of Svalbard's economy. I held nothing against the Ankers, but it was hard for me to accept that I'd never see Einar again.

On the wall of the reception room were a series of framed photographs—Store Norske's directors, a black-and-white history of the company. And here was Einar, as I remembered him: his hair perfectly parted, his tie perfectly knotted, his shirt perfectly starched. His expression? The creased brow and pursed lips reflected a mind never far away from the extraordinary demands of running the mercurial coal business.

A decade before, I'd found Einar in his office poring over a giant ledger, no doubt contemplating one of the many concerns that knitted his brow. I coughed to announce my presence. He looked up and favored me with a rare smile. "Greetings," he said, rising and extending his hand. "Back for another round?"

"I've nothing better to do," I said, "than return to this godforsaken wasteland. Astrid's with me this time. I thought, well, I thought it might do her good to get away."

After an awkward silence, Einar offered his condolences on Birk's death, paused, and shared a bit of his own history. "I lost a son. Erik. Four days old. During the dark season back in '29."

"I had no idea," I said. Was that loss the source of his perpetually serious expression, the prematurely lined forehead, the sorrowful eyes?

"It's hard. Leif takes away some of the sadness. He just turned three. Three candles he proudly blew out in one breath." I'm reminded of my son's last birthday, a sunny November day, his cake a confection of pink frosting dotted with tiny white meringues. "Make a wish," I'd told him as I lit the candles. He closed his eyes tight, then opened them. He blew. Not enough breath. One candle remained lit.

So much for good luck. That stubborn candle has dogged us all.

Einar volunteered for the assignment that led to his death. His ship, the *Isbjørn*, was cursed. Svalbard was evacuated in 1941, the Russians repatriated to their homeland, the Norwegians forced to sail to Scotland. Expatriation rankled Einar, so it's no surprise that he signed on to Operation Fritham, a reconnaissance mission to retake Svalbard from the Germans and to destroy their critical meteorological bases. As commander, he left Scotland in May 1942 aboard the *Isbjørn*, accompanied by the merchant ship *Selis*. German aircraft attacked the two ships near Barentsburg. The *Isbjørn* sank through the ice immediately, and the *Selis* was set on fire. Einar and a dozen other men were killed.

But here he is, in my imagination, as we share a glass of port in his office and talk about the company's prospects for increased coal production.

"*Skål*," I say, touching my crystal glass to his. "To the success of Mine 2b!"

Quiet for a moment, we each take a sip of the fine liquor. "We hope to bring another mine into production in a couple of years. 1b. Taps the old coal seam of 1a." Einar crosses to the wide window that frames the panorama of town and mountains beyond and points to a barren expanse of muddy ground in between. "There'll be new barracks for the miners there next year. You've probably heard they're naming the neighborhood Sverdrupbyen."

"You deserve the recognition," I say.

He laughs, shakes his head. "I had nothing to do with it."

"I had some miners aboard my ship north. They spoke highly of your administration."

"That's good to hear. Sometimes I wonder what they honestly think."

"Well, they weren't too happy with the limits on alcohol—"

"For their own protection—"

"Or the conditions aboard the colliers."

"I've heard as much. All I can say is it's a short trip. We're working on it, but there are so many competing priorities. A new canteen, a decent road up from town, the mines themselves. Have you seen the new post office?"

I nod, adding, "And the school under construction."

"The cableways running down the mountain from Mine 2b? Next year, a real road and new power lines. Pretty soon, Longyearbyen will rival Tromsø." He laughs, but then he turns grave once again. "Let's pray that nothing sets us back. No matter how careful we are, mining is a dangerous business. One accident, and all this could come to a halt."

How could we know that it would be war and not an accident that would intervene?

"I suppose that's why we have regulations," I say. "As long as they don't get in the way of progress."

I stop to measure his reaction, but he remains silent. The laws governing coal production were at least as onerous as those of the whaling industry, and we'd commiserated in the past about the challenges of adhering to them. I drain my glass. The port is a deep ruby color. Like blood. So much death has passed. But life was sweet then. A bit of liquid courage, a chat with an old friend.

Einar empties his glass and pours us each another drink.

"I must meet with Marlow before we head to Kvitfiskneset. His official letter suggests he's even more serious this year about the whaling laws."

"You can't really blame him. He has to deal with the mainland. So much red tape."

"Red tape, yes. The recordkeeping alone is enough to make me want to quit."

"You? Quit? I can't imagine it. The sea is in your blood. Coal runs through my veins. We'll have to be carried out of here."

"I don't know. This past year, the thought of coming back... with all the difficulties." The port has loosened something in me. "Astrid's parents are getting older. Her brother has little interest in the farm though he's helping while Astrid's away. In some ways, staying in one place, raising cows and chickens and pigs and planting wheat appeals to me. My wanderlust is fading. And I'd have my boat to sail for pleasure."

"Time will tell. My Dagny seems homesick for Oslo. But she understands the sacrifice we make for the good of these islands."

"Your family's with you. That helps."

"You're right. I don't know how different life would be if I had to leave my family behind. I'd find it impossible after a while. As it is, Dagny and Leif have accommodated to life here. It's not forever."

It wasn't to be forever. In four years, Svalbard would be forcibly evacuated. Two years later, almost all that was rising in a frenzy of construction would be leveled by war. And in the intervening year, Einar would lie forever at the bottom of Isfjord.

Marlow was another story. He did nothing heroic during the war. If anything, he was a little too cozy with the Germans. At least that's how people thought of him after the war, a man who kowtowed to the enemy to save his own skin.

Let me tell you a story and you can judge. While Norway was under German occupation, he was party to an incident involving the 1941 hijacking of the *Isbjørn*, the very same ship that was later to be Einar's coffin. Nine Norwegian Resistance fighters tried to commandeer the ship to Iceland, where they'd join forces with fellow Norwegians against the Germans. The hijacking was unsuccessful, and the ship's captain arrested the men and returned to Svalbard.

Marlow had to decide whether to report the incident to the German authorities or to keep it secret. I'll grant you it was a difficult decision. If the Gestapo found out he'd hidden the hijacking, there would have been hell to pay. On the other hand, these men had risked their lives to serve a noble cause. In the end, he reported the men, six of whom the Germans quickly executed, the others imprisoned.

The governor may not have joined the Nazis, but he lacked the courage of the Resistance. Perhaps I'm too harsh, swayed by hearsay and popular sentiment. It's easy now to judge those in power, and those who obeyed those in power. What would I have done under the circumstances? I was a coward as well. I had opportunities to become part of the Resistance, and I demurred. I rationalized that the safety of my family came first. I wasn't entirely passive, however. Like many Norwegian farmers, we shared our bounty freely with those less fortunate, refugees passing through on their way to neutral Sweden or countries farther afield. I did my duty, I told myself over and over.

If the war taught us anything, it was the dangers of excessive government control. And the dangers of being sheep who submit to that control. I'm not comparing the Nazis' evil to Norway's governance of the seas; however, when I was whaling, I thought that the laws were unnecessarily burdensome and saw no reason why I should be *fully* subject to them. One requirement of the laws was to obtain a license to hunt whales. Which is what brought me to Marlow's office. I'd learned from experience to be careful with what I said to the governor.

Bent over a thick book no doubt containing opaque regulations, he didn't bother to look up as he pointed to a chair. Before I finished sitting, he began. "As you know, there's a new International Agreement for the Regulation of Whaling. It starts the first of July." He handed me a sheet that spelled out the key aspects of the new laws. "You'll see that these regulations aren't much changed from those of the 1931 Geneva Convention. The difference is, we intend to do a better job of enforcing them."

I nodded, wondering how he planned to oversee our activity to the south, where few ever ventured.

We'd had a decade of anti-whaling activism, spearheaded by a coalition that included a career politician by the name of Birger Bergersen and the shipbroker and writer Bjarne Aagaard. They were in league with the fishermen, who thought that catching whales hurt their livelihood. An old superstition suggested that whales drove fish into shallow waters, making it easier for them to capture. The fewer whales, the myth went, the fewer fish would be driven into their nets. The truth: whales ate fish, so the fewer whales, the more abundant the fishermen's harvest would be. Some whale populations *were* threatened. In the Arctic, right whales had been hunted to near extinction over the past several centuries. Overhunting in the Southern Oceans had devastated the stock of large whales there as well. Norwegian companies were complicit in both.

Public support was also growing for the "ethical" argument that whales were a higher order of species than any other mammal except humans and that killing them was akin to murder. Zealots suggested that whales should have equal rights with humans. Colluding with a gullible press, anti-whaling activists had succeeded in winning public sentiment to their cause. I found these opinions absurd. Humans have a moral compass that even higher-order animals lack. That morality demands certain obligations. The humane treatment of animals, yes. The balanced use of the resources the earth provides, yes. But also the recognition that humans need animals for sustenance and labor to build civilizations. Besides, my method of killing belugas was more compassionate than those we often employed on the farm. Not to mention that farm animals live their lives penned up, whereas whales spend their lives swimming free in their natural environment.

Government regulations had come to favor the fishermen over us whalers. The treaties were meant to protect larger whale species, but exploitation of those whales affected all whalers. Those of us who caught smaller, abundant species like the beluga were thus affected by the regulations. Unfortunately, the policies were confusing enough that I wasn't positive what my responsibilities were under the new laws.

I looked over the sheet Marlow had given me. "So," I asked, "we're not allowed to harvest females who are feeding their calves?"

Marlow nodded. "The calves also. Forbidden."

I didn't state the obvious, that the lactating female yielded the richest source of blubber. She was the prize.

"Furthermore," he said, "you are to use the carcasses to the fullest extent possible."

The law provided detail on extracting oil from every part of the whale, but the meat, the bones? It was anyone's guess. We kept a portion of the meat for personal use. The rest was food for scavengers. Wasn't I supporting the circle of life? And the bones, which were to be ground to meal? My station wasn't set up for that.

Most demanding of all was the recordkeeping. The new laws required more and more data: complete biological information, including date, place, species, sex, length measured from the tip of the snout to the notch between the flukes, stomach contents, and, if the whale had a fetus, the length and sex of that. And the products of our efforts: the amounts of oil, bone meal—even guano.

As if reading my mind, Marlow said, "Your recordkeeping has left something to be desired. And I'm surprised that your catch fell off so precipitously last year. Forty belugas? Could that be right?"

"Last year...the season...was interrupted," I replied. Hadn't he heard about my son's death?

"There are other irregularities. You have a larger proportion of females to males, to the extent you bother to record such information."

"I think it's better to leave sex out rather than make up the details of the kill later."

"Which is why these details should be provided immediately upon the slaughter."

He pursed his lips at the word *slaughter*, as if the very word left a sour taste in his mouth. Hypocrite! He was an avid hunter and enjoyed his share of seal meat, his ptarmigan and eider duck. And I wouldn't have been surprised if he took the occasional reindeer, forbidden by law to be hunted since 1925. Who was to stop him? To the privileged belong the spoils.

I scanned the papers again, pointed to an interesting bullet point. "I see that the treaty's signatories allow aboriginals to harvest whales."

"They're limited to hunting for subsistence, not commercial gain."

"Why should we allow native peoples to take advantage of the whale and not ourselves?" I asked. "We Norwegians have been hunting whales for millennia."

"And we've been regulating their capture for a thousand years," he replied. "The first law dates to 950 AD."

He'd know such an obscure fact. The whole aboriginal argument now seems to me a kind of cultural imperialism, that those in power can decree what the powerless can and can't do. Back then I didn't see it that way. "The Inuit and the Saami are primitive. They haven't moved into the modern age with its modern conveniences. They harvest whales with spears in their sealskin canoes, for God's sake. How humane is that?"

Marlow shook his head. "You may be right. But we're governed by a different set of standards. I expect those who come to Svalbard to reap the bounty of its resources will honor those standards."

With that, he signed my new license, handed it to me, and waved his hand in dismissal.

As I stood and turned away from him, he cleared his throat. "I should say," he said, his voice hoarse, "I'm sorry for your loss."

જ

7 June 1937

Dear Birk,

I've finally met the famous hunter Hilmar Nøis! Pappa fretted about delaying the start of whaling season by a day so that we could visit Hilmar at Sassen. But his crew was still busy loading coal onto the ship when we departed from Longyearbyen. The excursion gave Pappa the excuse to retrieve his motorboat from storage at the shipyard and test its seaworthiness. Besides, I believe he was eager to show me the possibilities of domestic life on Svalbard. Hilmar brought his "fiancée," Helfrid; his fifteen-year-old son, Kaps; his brother Edvin and Edvin's wife, Anna; and his cousin Karl.

Hilmar took us on the grand tour of "Villa Fredheim" before we settled in for the evening. He's obviously proud of his compound. The setting on Templefjorden is breathtaking. Snow-capped mountains form a backdrop against the shoreline below. The beach is dotted with an array of well-kept buildings—living quarters, storehouses, even an outhouse.

Hilmar's uncle Daniel started the family hunting enterprise in 1909, and the oldest cabin, *Gammelhytta*, dates from that period. Hilmar told us that this earthen hut was constructed in the old way—its outer walls insulated with peat and moss, the roof composed of birch bark, the floors lined with gravel. And the odor! It stank of rotten meat.

"Elen and I lived in this cabin our first year here," Hilmar said.

"So," I said, "this is where Kaps was born."

Silence. A look passed over his face that told me I'd made a mistake. I couldn't imagine living in this hut under the best circumstances, let alone giving birth alone in such rough conditions. Maybe that's why she lost her mind afterward. Madness isn't something to be discussed in public, even among friends, so I bit my tongue as we moved on to a hut called *Nødhytta*.

"Our emergency shelter," he explained. "Fire in the stoves and houses made of wood can be a deadly combination."

Fire, yes. I thought back to Ålesund and the tragedy that wiped out the town. It's clear that Hilmar is prepared for anything. This cabin was testament to that, stocked with food, wood, and a small stove. One could easily live here if forced.

We came to the outhouse, a checkered curtain gracing its tiny window, no doubt one of Helfrid's touches. Outhouses are rare on Svalbard. Even so, the thought of wandering outside with a rifle in the winter cold and dark to use it gave me pause. Then again, I might change my mind after relieving myself in the fjord in full sight of the crew or into a bucket that must be emptied daily. There's a "toilet" in the anteroom of the whaling cabin, a wooden seat with a bucket underneath. At least I'll be able to pee in relative warmth and privacy.

Past beached rowboats and drying racks and scattered driftwood, we arrived at the villa itself. A flag boasting the Norwegian colors—red, white, and blue—waved from a pole behind the cabin. The flag gave me another pang of homesickness. Hospitable as this station is, the otherworldly landscape felt as if we'd landed on a different planet. As we approached, Hilmar's beloved huskies howled and leapt against their wire enclosures. He silenced them with a stern *"Vær stille."* Then he bowed and circled his hand in a downward spiral as if he were a courtier and we were royalty.

"Welcome to Villa Fredheim," he said.

"Villa" conjures trees laden with oranges and lemons and the orderly rows of vines crowned with purple grapes such as I've seen in pictures of the Italian countryside. To think of the difference between those photos and this snow-covered landscape! In contrast, someone had planted a garden of purple saxifrage and yellow Arctic poppies and artfully arranged stones covered with moss and lichen along the foundation. I bent to touch the poppies' yellow petals.

A woman appeared, her substantial frame filling the doorway—Helfrid, I assumed, who was wiping her hands on her apron. *"Hei! Hei!"* she said. "I see you're admiring my handiwork."

"This is lovely," I said.

"I transplanted these flowers from the valley. I'm worried they may not survive being moved from there to here."

"These seem healthy enough," I said, turning the leaves over to examine their undersides. "Arctic flora are my specialty. You're right, however. The change of location might not be suitable."

"The worst is that they'll die," Helfrid said. "But I have hope. The Russians transplanted some of their native species to Barentsburg. They even imported grass to carpet their main square."

"Useful experiments," I told her. "The Arctic forces plant life to the very limit of its existence."

"Animals too," Hilmar said. "I've seen seals eat their young for their own survival."

I cringed at the thought of such a spectacle. "Fortunately, flowers don't cannibalize their young. Though there are plants that'll steal pollen or suck nutrients from another plant's roots and stems."

"I've heard of carnivorous plants but not ones that devour their own kind," Helfrid said.

"Not always the fittest survive," I said. "Rather the most ruthless."

Helfrid grasped my hand and led us inside. We passed through a narrow anteroom into a small kitchen. What greeted us there were the yeasty scents of freshly baked bread and the sweetness of heart-shaped waffles and the aroma of percolating coffee. In the corner was the finest-looking stove I'd seen so far.

She followed my gaze. "Hilmar's surprise gift," she said. "Needless to say, I dropped loud hints in the months leading up to our departure that a decent stove was a necessity if he expected me to come—"

"In other words," Hilmar interrupted, "she demanded it. I could hardly object though it meant putting off some more urgent purchases. The thought of her cakes drove me to it."

Helfrid handed each of us a mug of coffee, and we resumed our grand tour.

The villa is two stories high. Off the kitchen a small bedroom had all the trappings of a woman—freshly painted walls in the same deep yellow as the kitchen's; a beautiful woolen blanket woven in bright colors of red and blue; new curtains that matched the blanket's color scheme; and even a jar of Elizabeth Arden night cream on the bedside table. Helfrid's bedroom, to be sure, and there's no evidence that Hilmar shares it with her. Which is right. They aren't married, and neither has mentioned a wedding. But who am I to judge?

Rumors float as to how they came to be together. Some say they've known each other for years since they hail from the same small town. Others say they met by chance on a ship sailing north from Oslo, she on her way to her family home in Skogsøya and he to Svalbard for another hunting season.

Helfrid dispelled the rumors. "I first met Hilmar in 1928 when I was on vacation in Vesterålen. He captivated me with stories of his adventures in the Arctic and invited me to join him there. But I wasn't ready to leave my life in Oslo behind." She winked at him. "We kept in touch through letters. As fate would have it, years later, we ended up on the same ship bound for our family homes in northern Norway. No mistaking the big, barrel-chested man with a mop of wild gray hair and the Santa Claus beard when he strode up the gangway."

"I invited her for coffee. A perfect setting, the sun shining, a fresh breeze blowing, that taste of salt air," Hilmar said. "I'd known from the start she'd be the perfect queen of Sassen. She didn't see it that way."

"I'd heard of his reputation as a ladies' man," Helfrid said. "I was wary. But over coffee, Hilmar spoke of this place as a castle set among fairy-tale mountains and crystal icebergs in a land of eternal sun. He spoke of peace and quiet and the freedom to be yourself. He spoke of Longyearbyen as if it rivaled the small towns along the western fjords. Nonetheless, I refused."

"She told me to ask one of the other charming ladies on the boat. They seemed eager."

Helfrid rolled her eyes. "To tell the truth, I became bored with life in Oslo, running a tobacco shop. And at home, someone was forever knocking at the door asking for me. Helfrid, Helfrid, Helfrid! My sole escape was the church a block away where I might take an hour to breathe. Evenings on the town became tiresome. I was always pretending. And after I lost Leonard…"

Later Pappa told me that Leonard was her fiancé. I had to force him to tell me what happened, something more than a broken engagement.

"Drowned," he finally said.

"Drowned?" I echoed. The very word was a physical blow.

"An accident," he said, and hugged me. "A boating accident."

That's why Helfrid found herself a spinster at thirty-seven. And inclined to shipboard romance. She's independent yet fully capable of the womanly arts. In a few short weeks, she's turned this remote compound into a home filled with feminine touches.

On the other hand, she was flouting convention, a single woman often alone with her beau.

"It was fate to be on the same ship with Hilmar. My horoscope foretold as much. 'Married at a mature age to a man with children from a previous marriage.' A good Christian woman putting her faith in the stars?" Helfrid laughs. "But Mother used to say that to commit to an idea gives you power. I held on to that notion. It's saved me more than once. The idea of Svalbard, that's what drew me. The freedom to become myself."

She smiled. "Mother thought I'd lost my mind when I told her of my plans. I used her own words against her."

"And here she is!" Hilmar kissed her hand.

Helfrid blushed, then turned to me. "And what's your story?" Helfrid asked.

"Our story?"

"You know, how you two met."

"I'm afraid it's nowhere near as exciting as yours," I said. "Tor was bringing cod to market, and I was hauling crates of bottled milk from our dairy farm. We literally bumped into each other, and wobbling, I dropped the crate at his feet. Broken glass and spilled milk everywhere."

"I helped her salvage the unbroken bottles and rinsed them in the town fountain."

"All the while he sputtered and blustered, hardly able to form a coherent sentence."

"I was bewitched by her beauty and embarrassed by my clumsiness," Pappa said. "And as she swept up the broken bottles, I offered her a fish. Imagine, holding out a slimy codfish as if that made up for the lost milk."

"It was your biggest fish," I reminded him.

"The way to Astrid's heart was through a fish."

Everyone laughed as we passed through Helfrid's bedroom into their parlor. A banquette and long table lined one wall, bunks covered in animal hides another. A small cast-iron stove stood in one corner, warming the room.

"The men's room," Hilmar said. "Kaps and me. Our private domain. He's out hunting with Edvin and Anna."

Helfrid and Hilmar exchanged a look, and in that look, a host of harmless lies. So be it. They're in love. Mainland customs don't seem to apply on Svalbard.

We crossed another doorway and found ourselves in a storage area with a ladder to the second floor. Upstairs, a large room crammed from floor to ceiling with all manner of goods ran the length of the cabin. Tools and skis and wooden crates and Christmas decorations. I picked up a stuffed gnome like the ones we lined our stairs with on Christmas Eve.

"Little Tomten," I said, smoothing the gnome's beard.

"What would Christmas be without him to bring us luck?" Helfrid responded.

"The family used to spend Christmas at Sassen, but in the past few years, I've been alone," Hilmar said. "Alone in Longyearbyen. They put up with me there. Maybe this year will be different."

"Maybe," Helfrid said. There was an alcove in the rear where dozens of pairs of socks hung from the rafters. I reached up to touch one. Hilmar laughed. "I've been saving those for Helfrid to mend."

"He's entirely capable of mending them himself. But I expect I'll find the time after I get this muddle sorted."

"Soon she'll have everything organized alphabetically."

"Such luxury to have a second floor," Pappa said. He turned to me and shook his head. "I hope you won't be disappointed when you see our lowly cabin."

We returned to the parlor, where Helfrid served us roast pork and sauerkraut on a table laid out with white linen and china plates. Clearly, we were honored guests. Not that it's all paradise here. Helfrid claimed that she almost fled on arrival. First, there was the disappointment of Longyearbyen with its few scattered houses, leached of color. Then there was the endless mud and rock.

"Imagine my astonishment when I saw draft horses pulling wooden carts on dirt roads. I thought I'd been transported back to the nineteenth century," she said.

Traveling from Longyearbyen to Sassen, they were given a ride in Governor Marlow's boat *Nordsyssel*. But a storm blew up, and they had to put ashore on the opposite side of Sassenfjord. They took refuge in a hunter's cabin. She claimed the stench was terrible. The hunter who'd occupied the cabin the previous year had used whale blubber as fuel, and the walls and ceilings were covered in rancid grease. The stink had seeped into the cabin's very walls. Imagine such smells lingering like ghosts!

"Right then I was determined to return home," Helfrid said. "But where was I to go? I wound myself in a reindeer-skin sleeping bag made for two, turned away from Hilmar, and refused to speak to him."

Finally they arrived at Villa Fredheim. "The place wasn't fit for human habitation, let me tell you," she said. "Outside there were carcasses of dead animals—Arctic foxes mostly—in various states of skinning and tanning and decay. Most revolting was a polar bear shorn of skin, raw muscle and bone exposed. Piles of rubbish were mixed with useful items like driftwood and skis. Inside was a chaos of crates and barrels and glass jars filled with God-knows-what. One of those glass jars contained a fox embryo floating in formaldehyde. A gift from a German scientist."

"Wilhelm Dege," Hilmar said. "He stayed with me last summer."

"Small world," Pappa said. "He stayed with me two years ago."

"If you two gentlemen are through," Helfrid said. "Well, I made the mistake of opening the jar before I realized its contents. Need I tell you how horrible it was!"

Hilmar put up his hands in self-defense. "But I had that new stove installed before she came."

"*Ja*," she said. "Without the stove, I would've been on the next boat back to Tromsø."

"A stove, not a fish, is the way to Helfrid's heart." He winked at her, pulled a pipe and pouch from his pocket, and tamped tobacco into the bowl.

"I've heard that a good stove is something of a rarity up here," I said.

"And here is one of its fruits!" Helfrid served us generous slices of *krydderkake*, better than my spiced cake, and more steaming coffee. The wonderful aromas made me feel as if I'd been transported to one of Sandefjord's cafés. If I closed my eyes, I could imagine it.

The weather was fine, so we took our coffee and cake out to the veranda. When we finished dessert, Hilmar lit his pipe, sucked on its stem, and puffed smoke circles into the air. You'd have thought him the perfect *Julenisse*, with his flowing white hair and beard, a red scarf wrapped around his neck, the smoke swirling about his head. He offered another pipe and the tobacco to Pappa, who imitated the same ritual, carefully packing the bowl with tobacco, lighting it, and sucking on the stem. But he inhaled too deeply and began to cough. Smoke sputtered erratically from his mouth.

"Greenhorn," Hilmar said, and we laughed. He put down his pipe, pulled a deck of cards from his pocket, and laid out a game of patience on a barrel that served as a table. Seven neat horizontal piles. The rest of us enjoyed our coffee in silence while we admired the tumbled turquoise ice cliffs of Von Postbreen plunging into Templefjorden, and the mighty mountain Templet so much like a ruined castle capped with crumbling crenellations and pocked by arrowslits along its face. They reminded me of the stories I told you every night—of good kings and courageous knights, sleeping princesses and evil sorcerers. You'd imagine, if you were sitting here with me, flaming arrows cascading from those arrowslits to repel invaders landing onshore. Oh, how I miss you! What I'd give to cuddle up with you at night and finish the story of the brave knight I left you with so long ago.

What a difference a year makes! The midnight sun bathed us with its golden light as the tender waves lapped the stony shore. I sipped my coffee and beheld what seemed like a boundless vista of glaciers and mountains whose serrated peaks, like rows and rows of ferocious teeth, were softened by a blanket of white. Once again, I was overwhelmed by the vastness of this odd planet. How insignificant I was in the face of this spectacle of snow and ice and rock!

We'd made the mistake of bringing along newspapers from Tromsø and Longyearbyen. A mistake, I say, because Hilmar put aside his cards to peruse the headlines. Talk turned to the possibility of war. In that instant, even in the company of Pappa and the Nøises, even with the breathtaking landscape before us, even with coffee warming me and the sweetness of cake lingering on my tongue, I felt that peculiar anxiety return, simmering under my skin.

And as if to underscore this sudden shift in my mood, we had

our first scrape with a polar bear. A magnificent beast! Helfrid
and I were in the kitchen cleaning up when it happened. The
huskies howled, a deafening din. Helfrid was suddenly beside
me with two rifles. Instinct over reason, we raced to the veranda. I'll spare you the gory details. Killing something so alive is
done only out of necessity. Death, oh death—it shadows me.

⌒

Kvitfiskneset
19 June 1947

As we sat on the Nøises' veranda, the sun shone brightly; the
single clue of the day's ending was its nearly imperceptible declination over Temple Mountain. If I closed my eyes, I could
almost imagine we were sitting on the porch at the farm as fire-
flies skittered across the lawn, Birgitta and Birk chasing them,
catching them in jars as the sun set late on a June evening.

The evening's peace was short-lived, giving way to unease
and then to danger.

Our first mistake was scanning the newspapers we'd brought
from Longyearbyen. Being isolated made even old news irresistible. Hilmar set aside his cards and picked up an *Aftenposten*.

"So much for a quick civil war," Hilmar said, folding back
the front page so that I could read the headlines.

"At least it's confined to Spain," I replied, putting down
my pipe and picking up a more recent paper I hadn't had the
chance to read. "What business is it of ours to intervene in their
politics?"

How little I understood at the time. Now I see how Spain's
war was a prelude for what was to tear Europe apart once
again. Now I understand that there's no such thing as a war
to end all wars. The thirst for power and spoils prevents it.
When countries around the world took sides in Spain's conflict
or pretended to be neutral while aiding the Nationalists or the
Republicans, many of us clung to the naïve hope that Spain was
unique. Uniquely poor, uniquely fractious, uniquely other. We

even-tempered northerners weren't like them. Leading up to the war, Spain's government had allowed the peasants to appropriate land from landowners, the poor to refuse to pay rent and steal goods with impunity, and the revolutionaries to commit acts of violence without punishment while the right committing the same acts were prosecuted. I must admit I looked down upon those less "civilized" countries to the south, as if the very heat stirred up passions we northerners controlled. Their lawlessness, this turmoil setting compatriots against each other, wouldn't be tolerated in Norway.

We should have known better. Those *temperate* northerners, the Germans, bombed Guernica in April. The consensus wasn't only that more civilians had been killed than the fascists would admit, but also that the bombing seemed less strategic than terroristic. Nevertheless, we assured ourselves that what was happening in the south concerned us as purely a news story. We were eight hundred kilometers north of the northern coast of Norway, and Norway itself was separated from the rest of Europe by the Baltic Sea. If war came to Europe, it wouldn't touch us here. So easy to forget that there was another world caught up in the lure of power and territorial ambitions, a world connected in spirit to this one, a world that knew no boundaries.

Helfrid resisted the urge to pick up a paper. Instead, she finished the last of her cake and began to clear the dishes. "All this terrible news makes me want to stay up here permanently."

Hilmar nodded. "Well, that would be one good outcome of a war."

She turned to Astrid. "I'm going to tidy up. Want to keep me company?"

Astrid rose from her chair and cleared the rest of the plates. "You boys need anything?"

We shook our heads, and the women disappeared into the cabin.

It was getting close to midnight, but time seemed irrelevant. The sun told me it might well have been noon. Hilmar relit his pipe, which had gone cold, then offered the matches to me. Again I lit my pipe and sucked lightly on the tip.

"It's troubling to see how quickly alliances form in the wake of an event that doesn't concern the countries involved," I said. "And troubling that other countries would take an active part in the conflict while pretending to be neutral."

"The leaders have their agendas. They ally themselves with those they think will prevail."

"I hope we've learned our lesson from the First World War. Europe's boundaries are settled," I said. "Re-coloring countries on a map never solved anything."

"Don't forget that some of these same countries fought— still fight—over who owns these frozen lands," Hilmar said. "At least Norway had the good sense to stay out of the Great War. I think our current prime minister has the same good sense."

We sat quietly puffing on our pipes and listening to the gentle lapping of waves against the beach, the occasional crash of icebergs in the bay, and distant ice shears tearing down the mountain. That evening was the prologue to a nightmare. Calm before the storm, as they say, lulling us into a false sense of complacency.

Fair warning came with the sudden eruption of Hilmar's huskies howling in concert. He grabbed a rifle leaning against the siding, cocked his head, and scanned the landscape.

"A bear?" I asked.

Hilmar didn't respond but stepped off the veranda. Unarmed, I was torn between sitting tight or retreating into the cabin.

He pointed to what looked like a yellow speck in the distance quickly bounding closer. I wasn't surprised by the bear's speed, covering the gap between us in seconds. I'd witnessed their movement before. Without a rifle, I felt naked before the bear's sheer power.

The dogs howled louder. The din brought Astrid and Helfrid to the door. Both had rifles. Helfrid offered me hers, but before I could move, Hilmar leveled his gun, took aim, and fired. The bullet struck the monster's neck, and the great beast rose on his hind legs and pawed the air. Blood stained his white coat. The dogs threw themselves against the metal fencing of their cages, leaping high, a frenzy of fur and bared teeth. The bear charged. From behind me, a shot rang out. The blast deafened me. A silent movie unwound in slow motion, frame by frame, as the bullet struck the bear between the eyes. Blood poured from the wound. He collapsed forward and stopped moving. I turned to the women and saw that it was Astrid who'd brought the bear down.

Hilmar retreated to the dog pen, paused to glance at the fallen bear, then opened the gate. The dogs rushed to their prey and surrounded it. King nudged the body, nosed it again. The bear remained motionless.

Hilmar reloaded his rifle and strode out to the kill. He prodded the bear with the end of his rifle. Then he called to us, "Come."

My ears were ringing. Words came to me as if mouthed underwater.

"Nice work," Hilmar said, nodding to my wife.

I took Astrid's hand and squeezed it as Hilmar bent down to inspect the wounds. Her bullet had pierced the forehead cleanly, Hilmar's had opened a larger hole in the bear's neck. "No holes in the chest. Good. Good. The skin should be salvageable."

Astrid laughed. "Better his skin than ours."

"Definitely," he said. He took hold of King's collar, which calmed the other dogs. "I'll have to teach Helfrid how to butcher a bear."

"No, thank you," Helfrid said. "I have enough to do." She wiped her hands on her apron, as if she were washing herself of the responsibility.

When I reflect on that gathering, what's remarkable is how quickly the evening's lightness had passed into darkness, how a tranquil scene had been transformed by talk of war and an unexpected threat to our lives. Only Hilmar seemed undisturbed by the turn of events, content to have another bear so early in the season.

He drove the dogs, one by one, back to the pen. His beloved dogs, the ones he'd be forced to put down during the evacuation of Svalbard four years later, when war finally arrived.

❧

9 June 1937

Dear Birk,

On the last leg of our journey, from Longyearbyen to the whaling station, the sky was cloudless, the wind and waves gentle, the trip so smooth that at least some of my concern over being far from civilization dissipated. What is a few hours compared to the days it took for the treacherous crossing from Tromsø to Longyearbyen?

Entering Bellsund on our way to the whaling station was no different than entering Oslofjord, except for a peculiar light that gilded the water, as if gold dust had fallen as rain from the sky and coated everything. I took it as a fortuitous sign that one day Pappa and I will be buried in gold.

Hardly able to contain my excitement, I dashed up to the bridge. "Tor," I asked, "what is this light?"

Pappa turned to me, annoyed by the unexpected intrusion. Odd and he had been bent over maps, no doubt looking for underwater hazards—shoals and rocks that might ground us or worse.

"I asked you not to interrupt us," he scolded.

Odd smirked. I felt as if someone had punched me in the gut. Pappa must have caught the expression on my face because his voice softened.

"This light is proving difficult is all," he said. "It's making it hard to see very far ahead even with sun goggles."

Chastened, I left the men to their navigation and retreated to the deck. My mood had altered, and as if on cue, the golden light disappeared. Cloud cover—an icy blue mist—rolled in. How quickly the weather changes here! I pulled my coat tighter around me and sat on the deck facing backward in the lee of the wheelhouse. The entrance to the fjord disappeared into the mist, and the boat's white-capped wake trailed us. Squinting, I could just make out Pappa's motorboat behind us, Halvard's lone figure at the wheel, a shadow in the window.

Anders appeared beside me. "Mind if I join you?"

I scooted sideways to make room for him. "Aren't you needed on the bridge?"

"Two's company, three's a crowd."

A look passed between us, and in that look, I read a little of Anders's relationship with Odd. Which confirmed my own feelings toward the first mate.

"I have a few minutes," he said, taking a seat. He pointed to a cluster of buildings on the southern shore. "That's Calypsobyen," he said. "Built right after the First World War by a coal company lured by the promise of surface seams. Didn't work out. Not a rich enough vein."

In the distance I spied a telegraph tower. "Is that operational?" I asked.

He shook his head. "Never was. There are stations at Barentsburg and Longyearbyen, but communication's not all that reliable. The weather and mountains get in the way. It's best to assume we've no way of contacting anyone once we're settled at the whaling station. That way you're not disappointed when messages don't go through."

Pappa had warned me of this possibility, but I refused to believe we'd have a problem. This was the modern age. Andrée relied on pigeons, but we have wireless communications. Suddenly the journey to Longyearbyen seemed like an eternity. I'm determined not to think about it.

Anders pointed to a small cabin on shore. "That's Oli Blomli's place. He's a hunter. I wouldn't want that life, I'll tell you. Polar night sets in and you have to stumble around in the dark, checking to see if a bear has been foolish enough to poke its head in a wooden box for a morsel of seal blubber. Or a fox has tripped the trap that seals his fate."

"You believe animals are smart enough to analyze danger like humans?"

"Don't you?" he asked.

Pappa's ship turned to starboard. "This is Van Keulen-fjorden," Anders said. "It's not far now to Kvitfiskneset. Here's where we cast the seine net. The beluga swims in, and we close the net and haul it to shore in our rowboats."

Just then, a beluga pod coasted by. They're no longer ghosts like the single white whale that provoked my earlier uneasiness. So elegant. I must admit I feel a bit of remorse that many will die at Pappa's hands.

Anders stood up suddenly. "Here we are!" he said.

On deck, Pappa called out to the crew. "Lower the anchor. Prepare for landing."

"I must go," Anders said, and touched his woolen cap in farewell.

Pappa was once again in his element, directing the men in the tasks required to move our possessions ashore. It was a marvel to watch them distribute heavy crates into fragile-looking rowboats so that they didn't capsize.

I waited on board while the men worked. From the ship, I surveyed the beach, which rose gently to a narrow swath of sand, and upward to a larger band of small stones called scree. Beyond were hills covered with golden-green moss, and above these hills loomed snow-capped mountains. But the most remarkable thing, the thing I wasn't expecting, were the piles of whale bones, bleached white in the sun, mimicking the alabaster peaks. I counted the piles—ten enormous mounds of bones. A whale cemetery, Birk!

What did I think Pappa did with the bones? Threw them into the sea or burned them to ash? Or let polar bears carry them to their winter dens? Instead, the bones are evidence of the carnage that's gone on here. I don't know why these bones disturbed me so—I, who've slaughtered my share of farm animals. Maybe it's because we don't leave any trace of that killing behind, flesh and bone gone forever.

I shook off the distressing thoughts and turned to helping the crew. I hoped to win Odd's good graces by hoisting some of the lighter cargo to starboard where the unloading was being carried out by a contraption that was part crane and part rope sling. I'm a strong woman, used to manual labor, but I don't have the strength of these men. Although I'd been on the ship with them for the better part of a week, I suddenly felt overwhelmed by their manliness—and my own place as the lone woman in this group.

Odd didn't seem to notice me as I stood holding a small crate, the one with my wedding dress. Then he looked at me, at the crate, and at me again. Suddenly, he lifted me up, crate and all, as if we were made of paper. Without a word, he fastened the rope sling around me and lowered me to the waiting rowboat. Anders caught the sling, deposited the crate, and lifted me onto the seat beside him.

With a few hard strokes, he steered the boat to shore. There he rammed the prow as far up the beach as he could and offered me his hand. I swung my legs over the side of the rocking boat, first one, then the other, and stepped into the water. The slippery, uneven stones made it hard to wade ashore. Scree covered the sand and mud. What was I thinking? Each step threatened to send me toppling. You would've laughed, dear Birk, at the sound of my footsteps. It's the sound Pappa makes when he passes gas. Two steps forward, squelch, squelch, one step back, two more steps, squelch, squelch, and so on.

Anders held my elbow to steady me. As if to save me some embarrassment—for he must have sensed that I was ashamed to need help walking—he told me the story of a seasoned hunter who lost his footing and slid downhill on snow and scree in the mountains a stone's throw from here.

"As near as they could tell, he broke his leg in the fall," he said. "Now this was early in the winter, the heart of the dark season. He must have realized he had no hope of rescue. He planted his ski poles in the snow, marking the place where he would be buried, so that someone might find him. And they did. The next spring. I try to imagine the peace that came over him in those final moments."

Peace? Instead, I'm troubled. So many ways to die here, un-remembered or lost forever. Is that the source of the disquiet I've felt since arriving on Svalbard? And will it fade, or is the feeling a fact of being here? Perhaps it's better to think of this anxiety as a companion whose prongs prick us to be on alert for danger, reduced almost to animal instinct.

On shore, Pappa was directing his crew as they unloaded the rowboats. When I arrived, he turned over the task to Soren, met me halfway to the cabin, and offered me his arm. As we approached the cabin, the first thing I noticed were the stout logs buttressing the exterior. You see, Birk, this cabin has no foundation, so these logs add a measure of security against the wind. We wouldn't want the cabin to be lifted up into the air and blown into the side of the mountains behind it! They're striking—deep brown, covered in moss the texture of green velvet, and ridged in a way that calls to mind an elephant's wrin-kled legs stamping down into the earth. Crowning the peaks are haloes of snow.

Their natural beauty is a contrast to the cabin. *Oh dear*, I thought, *this is my home for the summer?* The exterior is covered in tarpaper secured with wooden slats weathered to ash. Some of the tarpaper is loose, flapping in the light wind. There's a large whetstone fixed on a wooden housing that looks as if it might collapse at any minute, and a crooked stovepipe jutting from the tarred roof.

As we drew closer, I noticed rusty nails protruding from the door and window frames. I touched one and looked at Pappa.

"To ward off polar bears," he said, and opened the door.

Before I could enter, he swept me off my feet and carried me across the threshold as if we were on our honeymoon and not a decade married with a history of joy and tragedy behind us. A lightless storage room—its shelves weighed down with boxes and cans, its floor crammed with crates, barrels, and tools—featured the promised "toilet."

Passing through this room, a second door opened onto the parlor. Pappa kissed me on the forehead and put me down.

"We need to get your wet boots off," Pappa said, and pulled out a chair covered with dust.

I sat to take off my boots and socks while he disappeared through another door and returned with two pairs of woolen socks and some oversized rubber boots.

As my feet warmed, the first thing I noticed besides the clutter and dust was a peculiar odor—like that of burned fat.

"What's that smell?" I asked.

He inhaled deeply, frowned. "What smell?"

"You don't smell anything?" Again I thought of Helfrid and the first cabin she took refuge in. Now I see what almost drove her back to the mainland.

Pappa inhaled again. "Oh, it's the residue of last year's trying-out. Some of the used, empty barrels are stored in the bedroom." He pointed to the door he'd just come through. "We'll put them out back. That should take care of the odor."

"Let's hope so," I said. "Otherwise, I may have to return to Sassen."

For a moment, Pappa seemed to take me seriously. Then I laughed and patted his hand. "Don't worry. I'm here to stay."

He laughed along with me. "Could you light the stove and cook something easy for the men? There should be some oats and powdered milk on the anteroom shelves."

Before I could answer, he left to supervise the crew. Outside the parlor window, I heard a screeching sound and turned toward its source. Someone was prying open the shutters. The sun had come out again, and light flooded the room. Anders's face appeared in the window. I crossed the room and raised the sash.

"I thought you might like some light and fresh air," he said.

His thoughtfulness was a double-edged sword. The rancid odor dissipated somewhat, but the sunlight revealed a cabin in terrible shape. The dust was actually a coating of soot and grease. Everywhere were boxes and barrels and broken bits of God-knows-what. The tiny bedroom was so full that I couldn't walk from one end to the other.

Anders brought in some wood and added it to a small pile by the stove. "There's a wooden box in the storage room filled with cut logs from last season and a small, watertight barrel I filled with ice. We're working on filling the barrels outside with more ice and wood, and a supply of coal. You'll have to melt the ice for cooking and drinking water in that contraption." He pointed to a large copper urn on the stovetop that reminded me of a Russian samovar, only much larger than any I'd ever seen. It had a spigot that reluctantly cranked open when I turned it, and a few feeble drops of water leaked out.

"Halvard made it," he said, as if the gadget needed explanation. "There's also a freshwater spring about a kilometer downshore. The problem's that bringing a bucket or two of water back hardly makes a dent in the day's needs. And that's assuming that the weather cooperates," he said, and winked at me as he turned to leave.

Until that moment I hadn't thought of the practicalities of keeping a supply of drinking water on hand. At home, we turn on the tap. Here we must find freshwater ice and chop it into small pieces stored outside in barrels. The simplest necessities require planning and daily attention. So much for long days spent collecting and cataloguing flora, let alone reading and sewing.

It was time to prepare a meal. Light the stove, Pappa had said. The very thought frightened me.

The stove is like one of the mythical beasts we invented at bedtime. It has three cooking grates arranged so that they appear as eyes and a nose, the gaping potbelly its mouth. It's a monster looking for food. Step one was to clear the stovepipe. I ferreted through the supplies in the anteroom and found a broken broomstick and piece of lambswool. From these, I fashioned a duster of sorts. I climbed onto the roof in my over-sized boots, shimmying up one of the slanted logs for purchase. I must have been a sight! Holding on to the pipe, I forced the duster down into it and pushed up and down until I felt it was clear.

Inside again, I shoveled the ashes and debris from the bowels of the stove into a tin bucket, then arranged kindling and logs in the belly. "Dear God," I said as I lit a match. The kindling ignited, the flames rose and licked the logs.

Ha! I thought as I warmed my hands. *I've conquered the stove on the first try!*

As if to answer my arrogance, a stream of smoke belched from the grates and stovepipe seams. Soot, enough to make my eyes tear, filled the parlor. When I ran outside to catch my breath and wait for the smoke to clear, Pappa and Anders appeared carrying large crates.

Pappa laughed. "You've been officially baptized."

I looked down at my hands, my arms and chest and legs. I was covered with a fine layer of soot that I tried to brush away. All that accomplished was to smear the soot deeper into my clothing. Another chore, but laundering would have to wait.

After washing my hands in the sea, I returned to the anteroom to scout provisions for a meal. On the shelves, I found tins of oats and powdered milk, some hardened raisins, a jar marked sugar, and a canister of tea. There were two large pots, spoons and bowls as well. I brought them down to the water, scrubbed them with grit, and rinsed everything. I'd read that this is how one can clean dishes in the Arctic—sand and sea. Back in the parlor, I wiped down the copper watermaker and filled it with ice. Soon I'd made a porridge of oats and raisins, and sweetened tea enough for the crew. I called to the men, and they lined up, shuffled one by one to the stove for their portion, and sat down outside on crates to eat.

The oatmeal cured the worst of our hunger. To my surprise, Odd ordered the men to thank me. And they obeyed.

∽

Kvitfiskneset
19 June 1947

I hadn't thought to tell Astrid that Odd and Anders would be living with us in the main cabin. It seemed obvious to me. Otherwise, what use were the beds bunked on one of the kitchen walls? The rest of the men would sleep on the boat or in the lean-to dwelling we called The Hotel, a large, upside-down rowboat banked with peat and warmed with a tiny stove tucked in one corner. Sometimes a man recovering from some passing illness—or drunk and unable to make it back to the ship—would sleep there.

Astrid was on her hands and knees scrubbing the kitchen floor when Odd came in with his rucksack. He shoved it under the bunks, oblivious to the look she gave him. I thought it was that his boots left a trail of mud over the newly washed floor.

As soon as he left, Astrid rose from her knees and confronted me. "He's not staying here?"

"He and Anders sleep in the bunks," I said, too distracted by my checklist to catch the tone in her voice.

"Over my dead body," she said. "They can sleep on the ship."

I looked at her then, her lips pursed in a way that told me I'd made an enormous mistake. "You saw how cramped the ship was coming north—"

"There's plenty of room now that you and I can sleep here and the miners are gone and the supplies unloaded."

Right then, Anders appeared at the kitchen door with his pack. How much of this argument he'd heard, I don't know, but enough to say, "I'll put this in The Hotel," and leave.

Alone again, I pointed out that having Odd and Anders nearby, in case of an emergency or to plan each day's work, was more than a convenience. Didn't she understand that business came first, that these sleeping arrangements weren't unusual? That we had our own bedroom, albeit cramped, closed off by a wooden door? Hadn't she seen such arrangements at Villa Fredheim? And Christiane had written to her that a hunter had lived with the Ritters in a single room at Gråhuken.

"Honestly, Astrid, I hadn't expected a problem."

"I don't like Odd. There's something about him I don't trust."

"So that's it? The whole business must be upended because you don't get along with him?"

"It's not getting along."

"He's my best worker. He's always been trustworthy."

"If you were paying attention, you'd see he doesn't want me here."

What could I say to that? If I agreed, it would reinforce her concerns. If I disagreed, it would prove that I hadn't, in fact, been paying attention.

Just then Odd returned with a trunk containing the rest of his personal gear. He strode across the floor and shoved it under the bunks, leaving another set of muddy footprints in his wake.

"Odd," Astrid said, pointing to the mess. "It's a Norwegian custom to remove your shoes before you enter a home."

Odd sneered. "This is a whaling station, not a home."

If he could have said something more provocative, I don't know what it might've been.

"Odd—" I started, but Astrid cut me off. She held out her scrub brush to him, as if she expected the man to get down on his hands and knees to clean up after himself. Instead, he stomped out of the cabin.

Astrid turned to me. "Let me tell you something. And I'm only going to say this once. Either he sleeps elsewhere, or I return home. It's your choice."

Before I could answer, before I could point out that she was disrespecting my authority in front of Odd, she dropped the scrub brush at my feet, disappeared into our bedroom, and shut the door. I'd scrubbed my share of boat decks before. I knelt, picked up the brush, and scoured Odd's mess from the floor. How was he to know?

That night, I found she'd blocked the bedroom door. Little did she realize that the stove's heat would barely penetrate a closed door. But the weather was mild, the temperature a few degrees above freezing, and the bed was covered in woolen blankets and animal hides, so I didn't worry that she'd freeze to death.

There was no hiding the situation from Odd. Annoyed and embarrassed, I'm ashamed to admit that I was comforted by the fact that she'd discover soon enough how cold that room would become. That first night, Odd and I slept on the kitchen bunks while Anders graciously offered to tough it out in The Hotel.

As I settled down to sleep, Odd had the gall to tell me he wouldn't put up with a woman like mine. He would've broken down the bedroom door and claimed his "rights." Easy for him to say. As far as I knew, he had no woman to "put up with."

I wonder now if Astrid really would've left. There was a chance, oh yes, a chance right then for me to stand my ground and let my mates sleep in the kitchen. A chance she would have left and been spared all that was to come.

15 June 1937

Dear Birk,

Forgive me! A week has passed without my writing. So much has happened, so much to do to settle in. Let me start at the beginning.

I'll admit it was petty of me to shut Pappa out of our bedroom the first night, forcing him to bunk with Odd in the kitchen while poor Anders made do at The Hotel. But honestly, the nerve of Odd telling me this isn't my home! Naturally, I didn't give Pappa the satisfaction of letting on how miserable my night was. The cold stung my nose, causing it to run. Although we'd removed the barrels and aired the room all day, the fetid odor of whale oil lingered. What was more—truth be told—I was restless, impatient to begin my new life here and upset that I'd let my emotions get the best of me. I didn't want Pappa to regret having me along. Was I being unreasonable? The thought haunted me all night as I drifted in and out of sleep.

In the morning, we called a truce. I'd allow Anders and Odd to bunk in the parlor until they expanded The Hotel into more suitable living quarters for two. It was to be a hastily constructed affair since Pappa was intent on getting the whaling season underway. Would I have left if Pappa hadn't given in? I wonder myself. Things said and done in the heat of anger. I wish I could take them back. I could tell it pleased Odd to see that Pappa and I were already having difficulties. Airing our grievances in public wasn't how I'd hoped to start this adventure. Why dwell on what can't be undone?

I thought a simpler life would mean an easier life. How naïve! The chores never end. I wake, stoke the stove, and empty the waste bucket. Breakfast is usually a quick affair, porridge and tea, leftover bread and margarine. The whalers come, eat their meal, and start in on the day's catch or the trying-out. Next, I plan supper. Meat must be thawed, fresh bread baked.

Keeping drinking water on hand is the most tedious chore. Chopping ice into manageable bits and blocks is a task more wearying than splitting wood. The first time I tried it, the ice pick flew out of my hands and barely missed impaling my foot. The freshwater spring that Anders mentioned the first day isn't far from the cabin, but it's not a simple matter of walking there and back. Two buckets for nine people would last about five minutes, and the water tends to be gritty. Not to mention I must bring my rifle. And the weather can change so suddenly. What seems like an easy hike on a sunny day can turn treacherous when the fog rolls in.

I've already learned to expect the unexpected. That the parlor takes hours to warm up after the morning fire is stoked. That wet laundry can't be hung outside or it will turn to ice. That food waste must be stored outdoors in covered metal containers to discourage bears. That milk and vegetables must be secured in animal skin bags and placed under more skins to prevent them from freezing. That potatoes and carrots can freeze only once. I learned the last the hard way losing just a small portion of our store. Now I know to keep a close watch to prevent them from turning.

Add collecting and preserving flora to the daily routine. I

must admit it's a welcome break from the tedium of everyday living. When my chores are done, I read the clouds and the sky for weather. Is this a good day to take a long hike into the valley to collect my samples and sketch the flora I find? Fog and icy mist are my enemies. The fog can descend quickly, obscuring my surroundings. I've gotten turned around more than once already. And the cold damp seeps into my clothing and makes it hard to lie for long on the ground to examine a specimen. Not to mention when I prepare my samples the constant moisture threatens the very specimens I'm trying to dry in the plant press.

If I can't get out in the field for collecting, I circle the cabin for exercise, counting the laps. Otherwise, that old man's words haunt me—move or go mad.

But oh, to be once again pursuing my work! To escape the slaughter and stench of the whaling station! It makes living here tolerable, together with the twenty-four hours of daylight that give me the illusion of warmth. That is, until the frosty air and its metallic tinge greet me.

You'd be surprised by the number and variety of plants here. Some plants grow abundantly in the very short summer season—*Saxifraga* and *Ranunculus*, for example. Today I discovered the yellow-flowered *Potentilla pulchella* hidden behind a rock. Hardy little thing, I must say. I pulled it, shallow roots and all, from the ground. It's the most unusual plant I've found so far. It doesn't grow on the mainland, so it's the first time I've seen the living plant.

It's not the most beautiful flower, thin and weedy looking. At home, I'd pass it by without a moment's thought. But here, every growing thing is precious.

Pappa built a shelf in the bedroom so I can sit on the bunk and work in peace. Remember when we pressed plants together two summers ago? I took you out into the woods near the farm, and we picked whatever struck your fancy. You sat quietly while I recorded where we found each specimen, so patient for one so young. You knew some words to describe the plants—"pretty," "little," "red"—to which I added the taxonomy in my trusty notebook.

Your favorite was the dandelion. Such a common plant, a weed no less. But you saw its beauty. And when one stops to look, really look, something common can reveal uncommon insights. How is it possible to see something worn out by its ubiquity in a new light, through fresh eyes? In spring, we blew dandelion seeds into the air, those fluffy white spheres dense with pappi. You didn't understand the connection between those seeds and the dandelions you insisted on picking and bringing home to preserve.

Carefully, ever so carefully, you laid your prized dandelions between flimsies and layered each in the press separated by blotting paper and cardboard, then strapped the wooden press together and tightened the buckles.

"Dandelion sandwiches," you exclaimed, clapping your hands.

In the week we waited for them to dry, we labeled stiff sheets with all the pertinent data. You watched me print *Taraxacum*, which you thought was a funny name for a dandelion. When we finally unwrapped the press to mount the specimens, you were dismayed to see the flowers flattened and the bright yellow petals faded to straw. I don't know what you were expecting. You placed the dried flowers in a jar filled with water. Every day for a week, you checked on your experiment in regeneration. And when the stems finally bent over the lip of the jar, you angrily ripped up the mounting sheets and threw away the flowers. An ignominious end to the dandelions!

I'd hoped you'd share my love of botany, but you refused to accompany me after the great dandelion debacle. Someday you'd have understood. There's beauty in the two-dimensional specimen, captured at a moment in time. I tried to explain that to you.

"The worm," you said. "What about the worm?"

The worm. I should've realized. You'd brought home a wriggling worm that had been partly crushed by someone's careless step.

"Does he hurt?" you asked.

"A worm feels no pain," I said, though no one has ever proven this. "And besides, as long as the head is intact, it has this amazing ability to regrow its tail and squirm happily into the sunset."

You didn't believe me. You insisted on testing my theory. Remember, Birk? We put it into a glass filled with damp earth and dried grass. Weeks later, you saw I was right. A miracle, the worm's regeneration. We released it into the garden behind our house though your father would have preferred to use it as bait for one of his fishing expeditions.

Oh, Birk, there's more than one way to live on. An unknown plant with your name attached. Is that too much to hope for?

&

Kvitfiskneset
19 June 1947

And so, we arrive back at the moment one life ended and another began. My recollection of that day, Midsummer's Eve 1937, I've already committed to these pages.

Consider: the noxious mushroom she'd brought all the way from home. A good-luck charm but one also capable of inflicting injury.

Consider: her baptism in icy water.

Consider: her wedding dress. So beautiful, so delicate, so out of time and place on Svalbard.

Once again I pull the wedding dress onto my lap and trace the swirls of beaded lilies embroidered on the bodice. The yellowed fabric betrays the years since our wedding two decades ago. I see her then, my bride radiant in white, striding confidently down the aisle of Sandar Church, arm in arm with her father. How young we were! How passionately in love! Our marriage came to be over spilled milk. Translucent cream flowing through shards of broken glass, which caught the morning sun and shone a brilliant blue against the white. Spilled milk, broken glass, and a promise to meet again. What did I miss?

&

Midsummer 1937

Dear Birk,

Cold. Cold. Cold. I measured the water temperature, a breath below freezing.

I think of drawing a bath at home, steam rising from the water as I slip down the tub's cast-iron curve. A luxury not to be indulged here. We bathe, for now, in the sea. These baths are, you may imagine, rapid affairs. We wade to our knees, lather quickly, splash frigid water to rinse the soap away. In the perpetual light, under the spying eyes of the crew, I leave on my woolen underwear.

Remember when you and Birgitta happily splashed each other in the tub? Remember those wooden paddle wheel boats your pappa brought home, their mechanisms wound with rubber bands that propelled the boats across the vast expanse of soapy water stretched out between the two of you? Sometimes you pretended it was Pappa's whaler, taking him to Svalbard. More often, it was a Viking longboat, full of figurines armed with tiny daggers, sinking enemy ships and attacking villages along the Scandinavian coast. Never mind that not all Vikings were marauders.

Birgitta cried as you destroyed those wooden boats, cast them to the bathtub's briny depths. She preferred her fairy tale of Hyperborea, a land beyond Svalbard surrounding the North Pole and buffeted by an ice-free polar sea. A utopia of lush vegetation. Temperate breezes. Constant sunshine. Unbroken happiness. And peopled by a caring race of creatures who dwelt in peace. Some ancient poet wrote of these mythical Hyperboreans: "Neither disease nor bitter old age is mixed in their sacred blood. Far from labor and battle they live." Would that there were such a world! Here, removed from reality, we can almost believe in such things, fairy tales set in a last imaginary place.

No fresh news in weeks. World war might be upon us. Why am I incurious about what's happening to the south?

The sea, too, has had a strange effect. Some days, it calls to me. Is it you calling to me? In one way it's a comfort to hear your voice. In another...it feels inevitable.

Yesterday was Midsummer's Eve. The longest day of the year seemed a good day to begin again, baptism a fitting start. I wanted to test myself, to see what it felt like to be immersed in ice-cold water. Not to my knees, as I'd done to bathe, but fully submerged. I'd emerge cleansed.

Pappa and I chose to celebrate at Haven, a hunter's hut four kilometers downshore from the whaling station. I must say that I preferred its tiny leaning cabin to the larger one I'd tidied and warmed with lemon-yellow curtains. If it weren't so far from the work of the station, I'd much prefer to live here. Haven is tucked away on a particularly beautiful coastline, the water a deep blue-green dotted with icebergs, the scree filled with tufts of saxifrage in shades of yellow and purple. The cabin stands on a slight incline above the foreshore. Outside nothing clutters the ground—no rotting carcasses, no bones, no whetstone screeching its unholy song when blades are sharpened—nothing except a large wooden box filled with firewood left there by an anonymous hunter for an occasion like this. Over the entryway, a storm lantern anchored by a heavy metal ring swings gently in the breeze as if to welcome us. The door leads into an entryway lined with shelves stocked with essentials. The cabin contains a single cozy room outfitted with a rudimentary stove, two small bunks, and a little table with two wooden chairs flanking it. A large south-facing window lets in plenty of light. The cabin reminds me of Birgitta's doll house, ready for miniature people to inhabit it. Pappa must duck to enter.

Yesterday evening, we built the traditional bonfire on the beach. And in the warmth of that fire, in the privacy of that beach, I stripped my clothing piece by piece. I had a surprise for Pappa. Underneath my parka I'd worn my wedding dress, its skirt slipped into my snowpants. Off came my parka and my pants. The dress freed, I swept up its hem and spun to show off. Then I crooked my arm, and Pappa hooked his into mine. Together we paraded around the fire as if we were newlyweds marching down the aisle of Sandar Church.

Pappa sat down on a sealskin while I danced around the fire feeling a kind of freedom I hadn't felt in a long, long time. I admit I tempted fate by reversing course and rounding the fire *widershins* despite Pappa's warning about bad luck.

The buttons at the nape of my neck were a bit tricky to unfasten, but then the dress slid easily down my body. Next came my underwear until there was nothing left but skin. Pappa blushed. I can't believe I'm telling you this, but you won't ever read these intimate words.

I asked Pappa to count down from thirty. He stood as if to come with me, but I shook my head. No, I had to do this alone. It was to be a re-creation of something primal.

Taking a deep breath, I strode into the water, quickly, up to my hips.

That shock! You know what it's like. I gasped. Stealing one's breath—that idea became real. It was as if a thousand needles were pricking my skin. Recovering my breath, I stepped further out. Belly, chest, shoulders. I could hardly feel my numbed feet. I turned to Pappa, saw that he'd stood and begun walking toward me. I held both hands in front of me, a signal for him to stop. He stopped.

I forced my head under, imagined my warm blood losing

its battle to the cold. I swam. My blood felt as if it had turned to ice, my heart beat erratically. Blue replaced red in my line of sight. I thought I was hallucinating, my mind given over to dream. I couldn't breathe and inhaled a bit of water accidentally, instinctively searching for air. It felt like icicles as I swallowed. Salt and something slick, like seaweed.

In that moment, I thought of a story Hanna had told me—a story of caterpillars that freeze solid in the winter and thaw— alive!—in the spring. Why that story? Why at that moment? How the mind works!

All of a sudden, I felt myself being lifted up. It was Pappa carrying me to shore. He laid me next to the fire, wrapped me in layers of warmth, and spooned me. I couldn't speak for what seemed like minutes, but Pappa told me later it was close to an hour. Ice loosened its grip on my heart. The blood reversed its thermal properties, restoring itself to liquid. And then we came together for the first time since your death.

Afterward, as we lay together, I imagined many things. I imagined lifting you from the sea as Pappa lifted me. I imagined wrapping you in a fluffy towel and drying you from head to toe, as I'd done a thousand times. I imagined kissing your damp cheek and the smile that little touch of love provoked. Such ordinary acts.

SUMMER

Night passed, or what passed for night. I slept fitfully on the kitchen bunk, and once again I was awakened by the cuckoo cuckooing. Seven whistles. The kitchen had grown cold, the logs spent, the embers grayed with ash. I stoked the embers till they glowed red, threw on some fresh logs, and watched them flare. While the room warmed, I decided to take a walk. What was it that old man had advised Astrid? Move or go mad. I knew better. Nothing in life is so simple.

Nevertheless, I threw on my parka, hoisted my rifle, and went outside.

The fjord glittered in the sun as if a thousand diamonds speckled its surface, drawing me to the water's edge. On a whim, I picked up a smooth stone, skimmed it across the surface, and counted the skips *one-two-three* until it hit a bergy bit and sank. It was a game from my childhood. A game of stones. I picked up more stones, one by one, aimed each away from the bobbing bergy bits. *One-two. One-two-three-four. One-two. One-two-three.* Absorbed in counting, I didn't at first see the beluga surface. It was the sound that alerted me. I'd heard in my years of butchering belugas the entire repertoire of a white whale's peculiar vocalizations—the pop of a cork from a champagne bottle, the creak of a poorly oiled door hinge, the squeak of a baby's rubber toy, the birdsong of canary-like chirping. This time, it was a markedly human moan.

I scanned the horizon and found the source: an adult beluga with unique coloration. Set against the whale's bright white skin was an unusually dark jet-black edging on his twin flukes flaring out from the tail's median notch. It looked singed. I'd seen that marking only once before. It couldn't be the same whale, could it?

I shook my head in disbelief. This was the stuff of legends—and a chance to redeem myself.

Tangled in the beluga's pectoral fins and wrapped around his snout were the remnants of a seine net. And not any net, but one of mine. Mine were unique, painted blue and yellow and coated with tar, the very kind I'd used to capture belugas. Some things do emerge from the deep after long absence. Let me tell the story. The crew and I had rowed out into the fjord one July day to deploy the seine net. As we'd done a hundred times before, my men tethered the ends to wooden pilings on either side of the channel. We caught, almost immediately, a dazzling white mother and her dark gray calf. The calf was nursing on the mother's underside, oblivious that he'd been captured. But the mother moaned, tried to flip and wriggle from the net. The motion caused the baby to lose his grip on her nipple.

The calf gazed slantwise at me, his eye grooved in the side of his head as if someone had cut into the skin and, over time, the gash turned black. Likewise, his tail was edged in the darkest ebony I'd ever seen on a beluga.

But what I remember most vividly were the garbled sounds that came from the baby's melon. Human sounds. "Heave, heave, pull it in" was the litany we sang to the rhythm of rowing as we hauled in the net. I swore the calf picked up the words. *Heave, heave,* the baby beluga seemed to say.

Although the calf was trapped in the seine net with his mother, he didn't show fear. He didn't understand that he'd be shot, his blubber flensed then rendered slowly into oil in the iron try-pots onshore. That his flesh would be added to our stores or discarded like so much waste. That his hide would be salted, rolled, and cured, his leather prized for its buttery texture and crafted into expensive boots and wallets and jackets or, valued for its suppleness, used to make machinery belts and ski bindings. At least, I told myself then, I didn't impale the whales with exploding harpoons, the method pelagic whalers used. Mine was a humane approach, whales caught in the seine net and shot on sight, a quick and painless death.

The crew dragged the cow and calf onto the rocky beach. The very second I shot the cow, her milk spilled translucent white against the dark rocks, as if the bullet had released something deep inside her. The sight of it made me push the calf back into the sea. If nature were true, the remaining pod would care for him, the other females would nurse him until he could feed himself. Marlow had warned me about killing a lactating mother. But what authority was there here to stop this kind of slaughter?

Rationalization, I understood as the years went by. So, too, that the whale died instantly. Astrid understood. She knew that death wasn't immediate in such a large animal. I'd thought her inured to the killing of animals, resigned to the necessity of butchering belugas. But she was dismayed by this particular kill. It wasn't the blood reddening the scree. Rather, it was that pure white milk splashing against the dark rock that unsettled her.

"I saved the calf" was all I managed to tell her in my defense.

So today that calf had returned, I wanted to believe, grown to adulthood. He kept moaning, thrashing, trying to untangle himself from the net. I returned to the rowboat platformed on two logs near the water's edge, the one I'd used to come ashore from my motorboat. I rolled it into the fjord and rowed out to the beleaguered whale. As I removed the netting from the beluga's pectoral fins, I noticed the scars and blemishes that tattooed his skin. In the moments it took him to realize he was free, I ran my hand along a distinctive scar caused by the barb of an indigenous hunter's toggling harpoon.

Gliding away from my touch, the whale dove and breached, dove and breached, his white body cresting, ashine in the sunlight, his ebony-rimmed flukes undulating as he tested the locomotion of his unencumbered fins. And as if waving goodbye, the beluga raised one flipper, then turned away and disappeared.

⁂

10 July 1937

Dear Birk,

A month into the whaling season, and Pappa's already concerned. After a promising start, the belugas have deserted us these past two days. Our fortunes depend on a plentiful harvest, yet I find the lull a relief because I'm becoming increasingly disturbed by the slaughter. Whereas Odd, when he slays the whales, seems to get perverse pleasure in the sheer brutality of the cutting and the blood. He's less interested in the trying-out—not enough there to remind him of the living, breathing creature, I suppose. I must admit he works hard.

I used to think of whales in the same way I thought of farm animals—there to give us what we need. Now I wonder at my arrogance. Whales are more intelligent, more aware of their surroundings. They even seem to mimic human speech. I'm no longer convinced their deaths are quick and painless. How long does it take for the brain to signal the heart to stop, especially in such a large animal? I used to know such things. But it's not instantaneous.

It's sad to watch the whale rendered to its parts. First, the head is cut away from the body, the skull punctured, and the oil in the melon drained. This is the most valuable of the whale's "products"—more valuable than the oil rendered from the blubber. The first time I saw the crew extract the melon oil, I couldn't help but think that the beluga's dreams were being drained away.

And the flensing! After salvaging the skin, the men cut away the blubber from head to fluke. Imagine peeling an orange, except an orange gives off that lovely aroma, whereas flensing renders a nauseating stink—a fusion of vinegar and sulfur and spoiled fish. Worse, when a carcass has been set aside for days to await flensing, the body bloats with gases until those first cuts cause an explosion of the most malodorous stench imaginable. And that, my dear son, has made me vomit more than once.

If the flensing unleashes its foulness, the trying-out is worse. Like nothing you've ever smelled before—smoke and rancid fat and something else beneath all that—an alchemy that's indescribable. Suffice it to say that the odor permeates everything. It soaks into your clothing and your very skin.

The men get used to it. They rarely bathe or wash their clothes.

"What's the point?" they've told me more than once as I scrub my own clothes in Van Keulenfjorden and keep them thawed on a clothesline over the stove while they dry. I have a rule, however. If the men enter the cabin filthy with grease and dirt, their clothing reeking, I send them outside straightaway. I tell them mine is a civilized table. I've caused quite a stir. In past years, they've been allowed inside no matter what the state of their hygiene.

Pappa's told me repeatedly that bathing is a waste of time. I maintain that a "bath" can be had in a matter of minutes—a dip in the fjord with a bar of soap. He counters that removing the grime that accumulates over the course of a day or a week is temporary. I argue that temporary is better than the black filth that etches the creases in their foreheads, necks, and elbows. Not to mention the possible illnesses that can arise from a lack of cleanliness. But, he says, none of the men has been sick. Which was true. Stalemate.

Only my presence encourages any of them to bathe at all. Anders and his camp, Halvard and Soren, are the exception. I watch them in their underwear splashing each other in the shallows.

I'm afraid I'm the cause of such division. Today Anders came into the parlor to show me his prize—the beluga skull that each member of the crew is awarded during the summer. At least that's what he pretended was the purpose of his visit. What he really wanted was to warn me that some of the men were complaining to Pappa about my fastidiousness.

"A mutiny afoot?" I said, making light of his concern.

"Fru Handeland—"

"Astrid, please."

"Astrid—"

"This is my home. I won't be intimidated." My tone was sharp, more strident than I intended. I was out of sorts, worried that I was pregnant, my period three days late. Plus, I didn't take kindly to being told what to do in my own house. But the truth is, I'm uneasy. Imposing my will on the crew hurts Pappa. And Anders has shown me nothing but thoughtfulness and loyalty. He wouldn't have raised the issue except that he's worried.

After he left, I noticed he'd forgotten his "trophy." No doubt he was distracted by my frank dismissiveness in the face of his well-intentioned advice. I held the beluga skull up to the light streaming through the parlor window. It was a beautiful specimen. Triangular in shape, with a sharply pointed mouth lined with spiked teeth, the skull shone bright white as if someone had polished its surface, marred only by the single hole where the bullet had penetrated. Grim reminder that a being almost human had been killed. Nevertheless, I placed the skull on the parlor shelf, next to the photos that remind me of Birgitta and you, of family and home.

෨

Kvitfiskneset
20 June 1947

The good omen from the trip north—the beluga swimming alongside us before we reached Tromsø—proved false. Partly I blamed the fishermen, who'd been permitted by law to catch too much cod and char, the staple of the beluga's diet. Secretly, I also blamed Astrid. Because of her, the crew wasn't working as harmoniously as they had in the past. The whales could sense the growing tension, I reasoned, and stayed away from our shores. I'd underestimated the effect her very presence would have on the crew, and at best, I'd ill-prepared her for life on Kvitfiskneset. Astrid's letters show that she understood she'd created dissension.

In any case, we plied our craft—the capture, the kill, the harvest. Those arduous days now blur together into one long monotonous toil. Yet one particular day lodges in my memory.

It was a Saturday. Some of the crew had returned to the boat to rest in anticipation of an evening spent drinking and playing games in our kitchen. Onshore, Odd was busy sharpening the boarding and mincing knives we used to flense the whales, his idea of relaxation. The whetstone screeched and sparked as each blade bled into it. Halvard and the greenhorn, Tomas, were working in rhythm cutting logs set on sawhorses with a two-man crosscut. The back-and-forth motion created a sound like steady breathing, soothing compared to the whetstone's shriek. Anders had finished mending holes in a seine net, twining the hemp into a fresh pattern of knots. He'd unrolled his scrimshaw kit, set up a magnifying glass on a makeshift tripod, and busied himself scribing the outlines of a woman's figure into a polished whale's tooth.

The ledger in which I documented kills was spread out before me on a barrel. By mid-July we'd caught and processed twenty whales. I'd already fallen behind on the recordkeeping, and I felt as if Marlow himself were looming over me. One of those kills was the nursing female. Astrid had been so distraught over the sight of the cow's milk spilling along the scree that she'd conducted the barest, necessary conversation for two days afterward. "The watermaker needs ice" or "Empty the slop bucket." That sort of thing.

As we worked, I looked up to see her at the kitchen window, bent to the task of cooking fish stew for supper, the window open to let out the inevitable smoke. Our eyes met. Quickly I looked down again, afraid she might see right into my soul. I'd consoled myself that I didn't know until we shot her that the mother beluga was lactating. In truth, the calf was too young to be feeding independently. I decided a half-truth was better than nothing, so I registered her as female but omitted the fact of her lactation. We'd let the calf go in any case.

Scanning the ledger's neat rows of data, I told myself that I'd at least adhered to the spirit of the law. Who would know? The mother beluga was, indeed, a prize.

"That female we caught the other day," I said. "The richest yield so far."

"They're the ones we should be after." Odd raised the knife

he was sharpening above his head. Its blade glinted in the sun. "Females, the nursing kind, make short work of summer."

The rhythmic sound of the saw ceased for a moment. I caught Tomas's eye as he nodded to Odd. Halvard tapped him on the shoulder, dragged the saw inward, and the two of them resumed their work.

Anders shook his head. "It was an accident," he said. "An accident." He peered through the magnifier, intent on carving some minute detail into the whale's tooth.

"In any case, let's keep it to ourselves," I said.

"The law's shit. The people who make them are idiots." Odd waved the knife in the direction of the water. "Plenty of whales in the sea. How's killing a few more cows going to destroy their numbers?"

Though I agreed, I said nothing. I couldn't admit openly that flouting the law might help balance the books.

Odd pumped the whetstone's pedal and ran the blade against the wheel. Sparks rained down on the open ledger.

"Careful," I said, brushing away the embers and closing the book. I noticed another hole in the seine net, so I pulled it onto my lap and began the tedious process of weaving it closed.

The whetstone's screech of metal on stone grated on Astrid's nerves. I told her there was nothing I could do about the noise. The tools had to be sharpened. Beyond the noise, many other things irritated her—my crew's coarseness, foul language, the filth and odors that seemed impossible to fully wash away. Bathed in beluga blood and oil, soaked to the skin with woodsmoke and coal fire, what *was* the point in scrubbing oneself clean or taking the time to wash one's clothes in the fjord and hang them to freeze in the freezing air? What *was* the point of shaving when a beard helped keep one warm, never mind the crumbs and oil that stuck to the coarse hairs? Even brushing teeth, a chore that required fresh water, seemed an extravagance.

It's funny that something as common as bathing should drive a wedge between the men. Bad habits are hard to break. I

realize in hindsight that some of the crew deliberately provoked
my wife with their baser instincts.

One of those men was Odd. He was my hardest worker,
skilled as a navigator at sea and a whaler on land. I let that cloud
my judgment. I should have seen what was happening between
him and Astrid much sooner, should have understood that his
behavior wasn't inspired by habit, should have read those looks
that passed between him and his cohort—Oskar, Noah, and
Tomas—more deeply. Instead, I half-listened to her complaints.
Odd this and Odd that. I liked to think I was the kind of husband who took his wife seriously and listened when she talked,
whether about a calf in distress or a remarkable birth, a flower
that caught her attention or a problem with Birgitta or Birk.

And what did I ask in return?

What did I ask? An interesting question. As if marriage is
a bargain to be constantly negotiated. At the time I thought
of our marriage as two halves of a whole. We worked hard,
together and separately, to build a life. Now I see I assumed that
we thought alike, that each summer's separation made the marriage sweeter upon my return, that her dreams were my dreams.
There's a great deal of silence in marriage. Silent hopes, silent
longings, silent pain. It's a wonder any marriage survives such
silences.

Odd ran his finger along a newly sharpened blade. Satisfied,
he impaled the knife in the scree beside his chair, a neat row of
tools lined up beside it. My fingers numb, I struggled to fasten
knots across a large hole. Anders seemed unbothered by the
cold. His hands were bare as he scribed his tool deeper and
deeper into the surface of the whale's tooth along the outline
of the female figure.

Odd picked up another knife from the pile by his feet. Then
he told a story we'd heard a dozen times. "Once upon a time
in this goddamned wilderness, there was a changeling called
the Spitsbergen Dog. Now this beast required a sacrifice of
every Svalbard hunting party. So when hunters arrived for their
winter season, they killed a male reindeer and flung it over a

rocky cliff. This cliff was the spitting image of a man's head."

He pumped the whetstone. The wheel spun. "One day, a Norwegian prince, bored with his easy life on the mainland, sails off to Spitsbergen with his mistress for a little excitement. No shock in that. Isn't that why we're all here?"

He touched the edge of the blade to the whetstone and raised his voice to be heard over its unholy noise. "Now this prince practiced the black arts. Each evening, the two lovebirds collected plants he used for his magic. The Spitsbergen Dog was jealous of the two and decided to kidnap the girl. The dog turned himself into a male reindeer and grazed near the shore where the maiden often wandered alone. She approached the reindeer and began to pet it. Stupid girl! He changes into a man and carries her away to his cave."

Odd held up the knife and stroked the blade. I remember this because a streak of blood erupted along his finger, and he didn't seem to notice. "The prince had no idea what had happened to her. Now if it had been me, I'd have counted my blessings. But no. The prince summons the spirits. They tell him about the dog who could change into anything. They tell him he'd find the dog in his cave near a rock face that looked like a man's head. So the prince goes off searching the whole island and finally spies the cliff. Nearby he sees his mistress. She leads him on a merry chase. Before he reaches her, she turns into a male reindeer. The idiot prince stops dead in his tracks. It was the Spitsbergen Dog he'd heard about. He was so astonished that he didn't notice he'd halted under the cliff and the rocks above him were loosening. They fell and crushed him. That's why the cliff is now called 'the Capless Lout's Head.'"

Odd smiled at the prince's grim fate. I tied off the final knot I'd worked in the net. I knew what was coming.

Pointing his knife at me, he continued, "And that's why a man should never fall in love." He set the grinding wheel in motion once again and touched the tip of another knife to the spinning stone. Sparks flew, and the screeching grew louder with each rotation. Suddenly, the kitchen window slammed shut. I looked over to where Astrid had been working. Vanished, like a ghost. Then she appeared in the doorway. "So what happens to the woman in your story? The Capless Lout's beloved?"

In all the years Odd had told and retold the story, it never occurred to me to ask that question. A man dies searching for his love. The end.

"Her?" Odd said, shrugging. "The Spitsbergen Dog devours her? Or worse?" He smirked. "Teaches her not to wander off on her own."

"Spoken like a man who's never been in love." Her voice rose with each word. "For that matter, never loved!"

"Women goddamn well serve their purpose."

"Language, Odd," I said, hoping to fend off another shouting match between the two of them. Once again, Halvard and Tomas paused in their sawing, Anders in his carving.

Halvard coughed, as if to clear sawdust from his throat. "You have to admit," he said, "that Astrid has brought beauty to this place that's otherwise a killing ground."

"I'll admit that the food is better."

"Supper, yes," Astrid said. She turned on her heels and disappeared through the doorway.

I stood and clapped my hands together to restore feeling while Odd picked up another knife and set the whetstone in motion. I thought the drama was over.

But no. Astrid returned with a steaming bowl of bacalao. She held it out to Odd, who reached for it with his free hand. At the last moment, she flipped the bowl over, and the fish stew fell into his lap.

"You fuckin' b-b-bitch!" he said, swiping at the hot gravy soaking through his pants.

When he rose and lunged toward her, I pushed him back down into his chair. "Enough!" I said. "That's enough!"

Odd looked stunned, his mouth agape. The grinding wheel spun ever more slowly, round and round until it stopped. Astrid stepped backward and stood in the doorway.

"My useful purpose," she said, and retreated into the cabin.

❧

14 July 1937

Dear Birk,

Last Saturday, I broke some unspoken rule by standing up for myself against Odd. I admit I've been moody, preoccupied with the ever more likely prospect that I'm pregnant. I'm hiding the news from Pappa for now. The thought of having a baby…it scares me. I can only pray that I'm not.

And if that weren't enough, after working all day on chores around the cabin, I'd slaved over a temperamental stove that refused to stop belching smoke. For Saturday supper, I managed to conquer the stove's finickiness and cooked a wonderful bacalao stew made from cod Anders had caught and salted weeks before.

I had the window open for ventilation, so I could hear the men's conversation as they unwound from the week's labors. As usual, Odd monopolized the talk, featuring a tale about a prince who gets crushed by rocks searching in vain for his beloved. Pappa let Odd ramble on with that horrid story, punctuated by the whetstone's terrible song, until I could stand it no longer. You would have laughed at the scene—me dumping hot fish stew onto Odd's lap, him yelping and leaping up and trying to brush the mess from his pants.

Making Odd my mortal enemy isn't such a good idea. But there are things I know that Pappa doesn't. One evening soon after our solstice celebration, Odd came up behind me, uncomfortably close, and whispered in my ear, "I saw you." Then he grinned. Unsure of what he meant, what he saw, I kept this a secret for the sake of peace. But I'm convinced that he trailed Pappa and me to Haven on solstice.

The way Odd looks at me sometimes gives me chills. My only comfort is that I'm rarely alone. And I know how to use a rifle.

❧

Kvitfiskneset
20 June 1947

Perhaps there is some truth to the Saami's belief that everything, animate and inanimate, houses a soul that must be protected. We know so little of the spirit world. Is there an inviolable boundary between the living and the dead? I'm certain that Astrid and Birk will accompany me on my upcoming journey to Haven. Surely one's being can't be thoroughly extinguished. Surely some essence of the dead exists beyond this life if we look for it, care for it. Is there indeed a record of every thought and memory in the ether that surrounds us, as some suppose?

I had never been a great believer in the spiritual world. I practiced the rituals only to appease my wife, and because religious traditions and family celebrations were a source of happiness. Even after Birk's death, marking his significant days kept him alive, so to speak, however difficult those reminders were.

Religious belief was a different matter. I fell victim to the trap so many do: if there is a God, why did He visit us with so much pain? Whereas, after Birk's death, Astrid embraced religion more passionately. She prayed aloud every night, kneeling by our bed, asking God for forgiveness. Listening to her, I couldn't help but think she'd lost her reason. As the year passed, her prayers became more passionate, her unwillingness to forgive herself more pronounced. And then suddenly, her prayers became silent. It was unnerving observing her soundless vigil by the bedside while I feigned sleep. Sometimes we can perceive a loss before that thing is taken from us.

Unlike Astrid, I'd grown up without the habit of attending church on Sundays or kneeling by my bed to pray at night. My parents embraced Christian values ("Do unto others as you would have them do unto you," my mother chided every time she thought I'd sinned), but they didn't favor grandiose displays of devotion. And both were dead before Birk's passing, spared that agony and wrestling with their own faith.

As much as I wanted to have faith in God and guardian

angels, I found myself eschewing such beliefs. I desperately wished for the comfort faith rendered, especially that there was an afterlife where I'd see my little boy again. On the other hand, turning to prayer in my moments of despair seemed hypocritical. And besides, what kind of God stole a child from his parents? A merciful God? I didn't need Him. I stopped believing altogether.

Which brings me to a late July day when Astrid insisted on accompanying me to Longyearbyen. It was a Sunday, the crew's day of rest. We'd run short of some essentials, and besides, it was a good excuse to get away from the whaling station. I'd trade a twelve-hour roundtrip by boat for a few civilized hours in town, a friendly chat with Einar, and most importantly, some time alone with Astrid.

She wanted to light a candle at Svalbard Church "for special intentions," she said. I could guess what those intentions were—for Birk's soul…and the new baby. I'd noticed she hadn't gotten her monthlies; it would've been difficult to hide the bloody rags in our small cabin. Plus, her bouts of nausea seemed to have increased. I told myself that stress and the extreme environment might have caused her to skip a month. That had happened after Birk's death. And even if she were pregnant, it was very early. Anything could happen. *Anything.* Astrid had told me more than once that the thought of having another baby frightened her. My feelings were mixed, but I, too, was afraid. Thus, I decided to let her tell me whenever she was ready.

At the pier she struck up a conversation with a ship scrubber, the lone female dockhand. It had been over a month since she'd had any female companionship. She urged me to go ahead without her, so I walked up the road to the telegraph station to see if there was any word from the mainland. Indeed, there was. Marit had sent a cryptic telegram saying that all was well, and Birgitta had added her own message that she missed us terribly but could endure until September. *Endure.* I knew that was Marit's word, not Birgitta's, her indirect way of chastising us once again. I pocketed the telegrams, resolved not to show them to Astrid, and asked Knut, the telegraph operator, not to mention them to her should she stop by.

"I'll surprise her with them when we get back to the station," I said, and winked.

My business with Einar didn't take long. We chatted. He gave me access to Store Norske's canteen for things we'd run low on and threw in a couple bottles of my favorite whiskey for good measure.

Heathen though I was, I considered joining Astrid at the church but thought better of it. It seemed clear she wanted that time alone. Instead, I wandered along the main road on my way back to the dock. In front of one house, I spied a Saami woman stoking a small fire. What caught my eye was the colorful costume of her people: her dress made of heavy red wool, its collar, sleeves, and hem edged with stripes of gold, white, and cornflower blue, her neck adorned with an intricately knitted goldwork collar. Drawing closer, I heard her chanting a traditional *joik* under her breath as she wove thin strands of pewter and deerskin laces into an intricately patterned bracelet.

Hey ah no yo na no yo
Hey ah no yo na no yo
Hey ah no yo na na ne ah no yo na na ne ah no yo na no yo
Hey ya, eh yoo
Eh yo—na-ah yoooo ah

She looked up at me, and I smiled without saying anything. She resumed weaving and chanting, occasionally freeing her hand to rock the cradle on the ground next to her. It was a *komse*, a portable, canoe-shaped Saami cradle. The *komse's* interior was lined with a reindeer skin, and snuggled within was an infant fast asleep. I'd known of *komses*, handed down from generation to generation, but I'd never seen one up close. This cradle was made in the traditional style, a wooden frame covered in reindeer leather softened and stretched over the outside. It was crisscrossed with ropes the mother used to carry the cradle across her hip or back. Hanging from the small canopy, which shielded the baby from the wind and cold, was a colorful braid, a talisman meant to protect the child.

It was unusual to see the Saami on Svalbard. Their people dwelled in Finnmark, an area that stretched across the northern coastal boundaries of Norway, Sweden, Finland, and Russia. How had she come to be in Longyearbyen? I asked.

"How did you?" she replied in perfect Norwegian.

"I have a whaling station in Van Keulenfjorden," I said. "In the summer. My home is a farm near Sandefjord."

"Norwegian, then," she said. "I'm Verá."

I nodded. "Tor."

She held out her hand, and I grasped it quickly, startled by its softness. *Uncovered hands, exposed to the harshness as they wove such delicate work, should be calloused and rough*, I thought. On her fingers, below each knuckle, tattooed rings of intertwined triangles decorated the soft flesh like wedding bands.

She leaned toward me, looked to her left and right, then whispered, "My husband. He was a reindeer herder in Russia. The Soviets forced us to collectivize. Many Saami were imprisoned, or worse. We were fortunate to escape. Svalbard offered us freedom. We barely get by, but it's better than the alternative."

She leaned back and continued to weave the pewter and deerskin laces in a series of intricate knots, not unlike the knots I used to repair seine nets. "A whaler," she said. "You must hunt belugas. Summer is the season for it though this isn't an auspicious year."

"And what tells you that?"

"The world is out of kilter. I can feel it. The belugas can feel it." She seemed very definite in her forecast.

I laughed. "Superstitious…" I wanted to say nonsense, but I held my tongue. "It's not been the best year, you're right."

She paused to tie off the weaving, snip the loose ends with scissors, and pin the woven plait to a wide leather strip that would form the bracelet. In swift, deft strokes, she sewed the two pieces together with sinew in a series of minute stitches.

"There is time to set things right," she said. "Time for the world. Time for you."

She spoke in riddles. Was that a Saami trait? I knew a little of these nomadic people who drove their reindeer herds into Norway in summer and retreated to Finland or Sweden in the fall. It was ironic that a people who didn't subscribe to politics—who didn't recognize national boundaries and were allowed to traverse Finnmark without impediment—were nevertheless affected by Soviet policies. During the war, the Saami avoided becoming embroiled in the fighting or pledging allegiance to any of the Scandinavian countries, each with differing alliances. Norway was occupied by Germany though its citizens largely rejected the Nazi cause, Sweden remained neutral, and Finland aligned with the Axis.

She must have noted my puzzled look. "We have little power over the course the world is taking. That much I learned from my husband's experience. But we do have power over our personal dominions." She picked up an ivory-colored button carved from an antler and attached it to one end of the bracelet. On the other end, she fashioned a braided leather loop. Then she gave me some unsolicited advice. "Our brother Inuit believe the whale's bladder possesses the spirit. Bless a piece of each bladder and feed it to the sea. In this way, the spirit will find its way to a new body, and you'll ensure the continuation of the species and an abundant catch."

She looked up then, straight at me. "You've not been honoring the belugas in this way."

Which was right. I clung to the Christian belief that only humans have souls, that animals existed exclusively for our needs. Mind you, I didn't condone indiscriminate killing and abhorred the thrill-seeking tourists who haunted Svalbard to hunt whale or walrus, seal, or polar bear for sport. But neither did I subscribe to the anti-whaling protests of the Norwegian fishermen nor the fanatics who'd taken up their cause and who understood little of modern whaling and of the natural waxing and waning of whale populations.

Belugas were plentiful enough to sustain my harvest. I stored the meat we needed and discarded the rest into the sea. Without blessing, without ritual, without ceremony. The meat was worthless compared to the whale's skin and oil.

As the bracelet took shape, I wondered how Verá could create something so fine with bare hands in freezing temperatures. The small fire was hardly enough to keep her warm. I picked up a stick to stir the embers and fed the fire with a fresh log and the telegrams. She watched me do so without comment.

The silence became uncomfortable. That's what prompted me to fill the void. "I think my wife is pregnant."

"She is." Her words gave me chills.

Verá smiled, rooted through a basket filled with antler beads. She picked one out and held it up to me. On its face was a hieroglyph, a figure that looked as if it were holding a weapon aloft.

"Maderakka," she said. "The goddess of childbirth. She unites the soul with the body at conception." She picked out three more charms. "Sarakka, Uksakka, Juksakka—her daughters, who watch over the child from its first inkling to childhood. They will safeguard your baby if you honor the goddesses' spirits."

She laced the four charms onto one end of the bracelet, clasped it with the reindeer button, wrapped it in brown paper, and tied the package with string. Then she held out the package to me. When I offered to pay, she waved my money away.

"A lost soul has found its way to a new body," she said. "This is my gift to that new life."

❧

26 July 1937

Dear Birk,

Imagine my delight to find a *woman*—her name was Amelia—sweeping the pier when we arrived in Longyearbyen. At first, I thought she was one of the men who worked the docks. She wore the same stained canvas workpants and oversized woolen sweater that was their trademark, and her dark hair was shorn practically to her scalp. But close up, the smoothness of her face revealed that my first impression was mistaken.

"*Hei!*" I said, touching her lightly on the shoulder.

She looked up, a little startled, then smiled broadly. "*Hei* to you too."

I turned to Pappa and said, "Why don't you go on ahead? I'll meet you back here at four." He had the good grace to take my cue and head up the road to Store Norske.

My first question was how she'd come to work at the harbor.

"My father is the harbormaster," she said. "I practically grew up on these docks."

I shared that I was here to pursue my own first love—botany. We chatted about ships and flowers, how busy the docks were this time of year, how plentiful I'd found the plant life on Van Keulenfjorden. And then the subject turned to family.

"I won't be working much longer, I'm afraid," she said. She raised her sweater and patted her rounded belly. "My husband won't let me."

I leaned toward her as if I were imparting a state secret and whispered, "Just between us, I'm pregnant too." There. I'd finally said it out loud.

She crossed her heart and said, "It's our secret."

She went back to her sweeping, and I made my way up the road to the post office to honor my promise to Birgitta to mail her an Arctic poppy, *Papaver laestadianum*. The flowers are unique in that they grow only in northernmost Scandinavia and here. To thrive in such harsh climates, they must be resilient, which belies their delicate yellow or white petals. They're also heliotropes, a fancy word for plants that turn continually toward the sun. A plant with an optimistic outlook, I like to think.

One cheerful errand finished, I popped into the telegraph office to ask Knut if there were any telegrams for us.

"Ah," he said, sorting through a pile on his desk. "Sorry, there aren't any."

Strange, I thought. I guess my parents assumed we'd not be back to Longyearbyen till summer's end.

I had one more mission, the pilgrimage to Svalbard Church. The path to the church is steep. From town, one must cross Longycar River over a rickety bridge that seems too flimsy to bear weight. The church sits on a promontory overlooking the town in the shadow of mountains to the west. Near the church is a little cemetery. White crosses, aslant from the forces of thawing and refreezing earth, mark each grave. Names are etched on black backgrounds, one for each lost soul. Here are buried eleven coal miners felled by the Spanish flu in 1918. Ironic that they escaped the hazards of mining coal and fighting a world war only to become victims of an epidemic that traveled across the desolate sea to this place.

The world was too much with them, as Wordsworth would say.

Before me as well are the twenty-six coal miners killed in a coal-dust explosion in 1920. I wondered at their courage, or foolhardiness, undertaking a profession that has danger written all over it. Those three miners Pappa took north from Tromsø told us harrowing stories about near-death experiences escaping cave-ins and explosions. Not to mention breathing in coal dust all day. How many lives will be cut short to supply us with coal? And yet how else would we heat our homes and power our factories? We forfeit their lives so that we can enjoy ours.

I bowed my head and prayed for the souls of these dead, my way of acknowledging their sacrifice. Some of the graves were decorated with red and white carnations. I've been told that supply ships from Tromsø bring things as frivolous as these flowers to Longyearbyen. What's more remarkable is that decades later, some friend or relative still treks uphill to place carnations on a grave. Doubly odd, these bright flowers are foreign to this landscape—transplants from distant soil.

Farther and higher along the road is the church, a one-room shingled structure with a modest bell tower. The church is always open, and I chose a seat at the very front. On the altar were a pair of silver candlesticks—a gift from King Haakon and Queen Maud, according to a plaque engraved with their names. To the left of the altar were a turquoise and gold baptismal font and a wrought-iron candleholder, one votive alight and flickering in a draft.

I took a hymnal from the seat next to me and leafed through its pages until I found my favorite hymn. Softly I sang the line that comforts me: "No one is so safe from danger as the little child of God."

I touched my belly, imagining the quickening that will confirm the new life growing there. *It is a new life*, I reminded myself as I sang the final verse: "What He takes and what He gives, the same Father He remains."

I crossed over to the candles, lit a fresh one from the one left burning by some previous supplicant, and placed it in an empty hole. Then I whispered words I only half-believed: "Dear God, You've formed all things from the beginning of time. I ask that You bless this life created out of nothing. I have faith in Your great love despite all the hardships that have been visited upon me. I trust that You've seen in Your great wisdom to grant me a moment of mercy and redemption. I know that suffering is a part of life, but so is this measure of joy."

And would you believe it, at the very moment I stood watching the candle flame waver, the fog and mist cleared, and a bright sunbeam slashed through the window. Pappa would laugh if I told him this is a sign of good things to come. He dismisses the pagan myths and looks down on what he considers primitive cultures. What harm can it do to adhere to traditions but also trust in God?

Pappa accompanies me to services when it suits him. He was a Christmas and Easter Christian, and now he's no Christian at all. God is merciful, I tell him. Hogwash, he says. He indulges my faith but tells me I'm deluded for believing that a world exists beyond this realm. A world where you now dwell.

The idea comforts me. That's why I cling to it.

The church, too, comforted me. The quiet, the cross, the seats lined up as if waiting for a service to begin.

A small notice reminded me to extinguish the candle before leaving the sanctuary. It made me think once again of the tragedy of Ålesund. The church is made of wood, as are the town's houses. I didn't want to be the one who destroyed Longyearbyen. I snuffed my candle, said another prayer, and blew out the one carelessly left lit.

∾

Kvitfiskneset
20 June 1947

It's difficult to explain how not having a body to bury weighs on the mind. It took a long time for Birgitta to accept that her mother wasn't coming home as she'd promised. Even I deluded myself into believing that my wife existed somewhere, unspoiled, consigned to these depths. I know such thoughts are fantasies, that long ago predators made a meal of her flesh, her bones sunk deep in the seabed's sediment or carried away by ocean currents.

Nevertheless, long after rescuing the beluga from my old seine net, I sat on a rock at the sea edge, scanning the fjord. I told myself I was waiting for the beluga's return. That the motherless calf should appear after my lengthy absence, full grown and playful, brought a kind of solace. As time passed, the tide advanced and water lapped the toes of my rubber boots. What possessed me to remove my glove and dip my bare hand into the water? A kind of test? First came the tingling, then pain. I gritted my teeth until my hand numbed—it didn't take long, a minute or two. My hand turned white then reddish-purple. I couldn't flex my fingers, but the pain vanished. It's odd that the body *in extremis* loses its ability to warn the brain of the danger, surrendering feeling to protect itself from suffering. I'd passed the point of recklessness into the danger of frostbite. I lifted my hand from the water and held it up. My cramped, frozen fingers curled into themselves like a claw. I massaged my hand and slowly, the hand reawakened as blood returned from its refuges deep inside my body. With the blood came pain, worse than the initial pain, as if the body were punishing itself for its stupidity.

৵

30 July 1937

Dear Birk,

I've been thinking a lot lately about things out of place. What does and doesn't belong. What's home and what's not. What got me to thinking was the story Helfrid told about the Russians planting grass in Barentsburg. They started mining there last year, though some say mining is an excuse for the Soviet Union to maintain a strategic presence. The Svalbard Treaty established this archipelago as *terra nullius*—no man's land. It's no woman's land either. Anyway, the treaty allows countries that sign it to exploit the territory only for its natural resources. Nothing military. Should the world go to war, we'd be safe here, Pappa tells me. I believe him. Would countries really fight over this inhospitable spit of tundra?

But I'm getting away from the reason I'm writing to you today. Ever since Helfrid mentioned that the Russians created a massive lawn in Barentsburg's main square, I've been curious to see it. To accomplish such a feat, they imported boatloads of soil and grass seed from their homeland. All to bring a bit of home to Svalbard. And there's a new Russian mining town called Pyramiden, east of Longyearbyen on the northern side of the same fjord. The Russians plan to do the same thing there.

We passed by Barentsburg on our way home from Longyearbyen last Sunday, so I begged Pappa to stop.

"Foreigners need permission to visit Barentsburg," he said. True, but he was also anxious to return to the to the whaling station. We knew the weather could change suddenly and prevent our timely return. Something in my expression must have softened his heart, however. We sailed into Grønfjorden and pulled up to the Barentsburg dock. Several men eagerly helped us secure the boat to the landing, yelling "*Privet! Privet!*" to welcome us. So much for protocols. Pappa claimed he was having trouble with the engine. Men being men, the four of them bent over the engine to "fix" the problem while I stole away to the main square.

Helfrid was right. Lenin presided over a lush expanse of green lawn. Oh, how joyful to see such a wonder, especially after spending these past months with a carpet of gray scree and mud as my immediate landscape. I could have happily spent the evening admiring the Russians' handiwork. But I was mindful of Pappa's desire to return to Kvitfiskneset and the lie he told those helpful Russians to give me this moment.

Ever the botanist, I lay on the ground to examine the unusual grass, which sprouts its own baby plants rather than sending out seeds. Eventually these baby "leaves" blow away and become their own plants. I couldn't resist. Looking left and right to be sure I was alone, I bent to pick a few fronds of the grass, babies, roots, and all. I wrapped the specimens in a handkerchief I kept in my coat pocket. I felt like a thief, and I couldn't imagine the mess I'd get into if I were caught stealing grass.

Our trip back to the station was uneventful. I planted the grass in the garden I'd been cultivating with poppies and saxifrage. Despite my admiration for the Russians' achievement and my own curiosity about how their grass thrives in such a hostile setting, I also wondered about the dangers of transplanting alien flora to this landscape. Funny how we're free to move from one place to another, whereas plants are rooted no matter how inhospitable their environment becomes unless we move them. Sometimes the transplants survive, sometimes they don't.

And then I consider how our exploitation of these once

pristine landscapes has changed the very essence of this Eden. Coal mining scars with its cableways and tunneling. The whale cemetery reminds me of the damage we've done to the fisheries and fauna. In his arrogance, P. T. Barnum captured belugas and exhibited them in his American museum. Over and over, they died in captivity. Barnum exploited polar bears and walruses as well, transporting them to artificial habitats unsuited to their natural environment, which killed them.

Was I moved then by the animals' plight as I am now? If I'm honest, I'm guilty too. I want to recreate a home here, my own square of green. I think of Barnum's belugas, his polar bears and walruses. Home is a fragile thing. I don't belong here. But where do I belong? I thought that being away might rekindle my desire to make a home for Birgitta and Pappa. That longing they call homesickness.

Oh, Birk. Will the farm ever be the same without you? When I lost you it was as if the world dissolved around me, and now I live in that liquid world. I laugh at my naïveté thinking that sewing curtains and cooking communal suppers would make this cabin home. I should have found a place where I could stand on my own, like Hanna. Why did I think that surrounding myself with a company of demanding men would allow me to prove my mettle and fulfill my dreams?

I mark time. In two short months, I'll be back at the farm. And there, God willing, I'll feel differently.

Dear Birk, I sound ungrateful. I have precious time to collect and catalogue specimens. I'd almost forgotten the sheer pleasure of examining a plant. When I worked with Hanna, the plants were dried. These are the living things. Sadly, I haven't unearthed that one undiscovered specimen. I'm afraid that others may have found all there is to find. I must persevere. The season is so short. Come September, the flowers will die. I must take advantage of the time I have.

In one of my wanderings, I stumbled upon the remains of a cabin not far from the whaling station, between Kvitfiskneset and Haven. In the detritus of its rotten wood and guano was a veritable field of mushrooms. They are somewhat trickier specimens to preserve than flora as they dry out rather rapidly. I have a small basket with a damp towel for the purpose.

Until I discovered this trove, I hadn't thought mushrooms would be so abundant on Svalbard. They seem out of place here—the weather too dry, too cold for a species that grows best in the warm, moist dark. Yet here they were. I have a mind to rename one of these ugly mushrooms after Odd as Linnaeus named weeds after his enemies.

My first thought was that this species was edible and might be used in a stew. I recorded as much information as I could before I extracted several samples from the soil, careful to keep their bases intact. Their caps were round and white and streaked with brown, the underside scored with lamella, the stipe cylindrical. They smelled of wood and earth, a musky odor not unlike the soil from which they came.

The smell is no guarantee that this one is edible. So many are poisonous and could sicken me enough to induce labor. I'll have to be careful with these. Pappa still hasn't noticed I'm pregnant. There's time for me to consider what to do. If I were home, I'd use worm fern or pennyroyal. But they can do more than end the life inside me. They can kill me as well. So might this innocent-looking fungus.

What am I saying? I must think of Birgitta. Some days I convince myself that I'm a good mother, that your death was an accident, God's will. I must have faith.

I must think of Pappa too. This isn't the place to get sick. Help is so far away.

I dried the mushrooms in a small wooden box. Today I examined one closely through my magnifying glass. Shriveled, it looked innocent enough. I brought it to my nose, inhaled the scent of earth and wood. In the interest of science, I took a small bite of its cap. The taste was so foul, I spit it out.

In my notes, I wrote, *Probably poisonous.*

❧

Kvitfiskneset
20 June 1947

I gave up on the beluga's return, walked upshore, and ducked into the largest rowboat.

Turned sideways, the rowboat offered me shelter from the cold that's seeped into my aging bones. Arthritis, the doctors have told me, brought on by years immersing my hands and feet in glacial water. Enclosed in its wooden hollow, I thought of Jonah being swallowed by the whale. His story reminds me that God is a God of second chances. I want that second chance. I've asked for forgiveness and returned to the faith despite all that's happened. I'm waiting for a sign that I am forgiven.

Sitting within the rowboat's protective embrace brings back the memory of the day Astrid finally revealed her pregnancy. Only after I'd read her letters to Birk did I realize the dark reason for her silence. The poison mushrooms. She knew how to end a pregnancy.

"I can't stand the smell much longer," Astrid had said one August afternoon. To emphasize the point, she threw up into the waste bucket.

I dipped a rag in cold water, wrung it out, and wiped the vomit from her lips. "Let's move away from the cabin," I suggested. "We can take cover downwind in the big rowboat."

"Can you afford the time?" she asked.

Of course, I couldn't. "Of course," I said.

The wind carrying the stench blew down from the mountains as we made our way past the roiling try-pots where the men were busy loading blubber and tending the fires. As usual, they were singing whaling songs in Norwegian and English and cutting blubber to a song's rhythm to ease the burden and boredom of the work.

There's some that's bound for Hvalfjordur,
and some that's bound for France.
Heave away, me Johnny, heave away.
And some that's bound for the Bellsund Bay

To teach them whales to dance.

Heave away, me Johnny boy, we're all bound to go.

As we passed by, Odd held up his hand. The men quieted one by one. I nodded to them, feeling guilty for abandoning them to their labor. My absence would provoke more resentment of Astrid among some of the crew, egged on by Odd, who seemed especially annoyed by my solicitousness. Our production had suffered indulging her wants. Here was proof of my neglect: stealing away with Astrid instead of cutting blubber to the tune of sea shanties.

Odd's solo voice rose, clear and strong, the improvised words of a melancholy Scottish ballad carried on the wind:

Farewell to Tarwathie, adieu Mormond Hill

And the mainland o' Norway, I bid you farewell

For I'm bound out for Svalbard and ready to sail

In hopes to find riches in hunting the whale.

We stopped to listen. Odd looked directly at Astrid as he sang of the faraway lass whose love would outlast his journey. The final notes faded. Quiet descended. Then the men cheered and clapped.

We clapped as well. Astrid bent to me and whispered, "I had no idea Odd had such a beautiful voice."

"Nor I," I said. The whalers' repertoire usually consisted of ribald songs sung in unison. I'd never heard Odd sing solo.

The men returned to their work as we turned away. Something seemed to have shifted. Whether it was the song or the fresh air, Astrid's spirits lifted. She offered me her gloved hand, and grateful, I grasped it. Ahead were the three rowboats, turned on their sides. I lined the bottom of the largest one with a small piece of reindeer fur I'd brought along to soften the wooden cavity of the boat's interior. We scooted inside. The boat enclosed us like a canopy.

"Better?" I asked, breaking a long silence.

She nodded. I drew her to me, thankful to have her close. It's easy now to see that it was a mistake to bring Astrid to the

Arctic. Better that she had held on to her romantic notions of my life on Kvitfiskneset than to witness the grim reality that paid part of our way in the world. Better that she had continued to play the role of whaler's wife, part of a community of wives, in which she shared the burdens and delights of a few months alone directing her own life and dreaming an illusion of crystalline icebergs and mythical narwhals and Arctic poppies piercing their yellow heads through snow and scree.

But right then, sitting with her, I felt content. The feeling didn't last.

"How much longer will this be necessary?" she asked.

I was confused by the question. "You mean the summer's harvest?"

"This summer, next summer. How many summers of killing?"

I hadn't thought of how my time on Svalbard would end. War was far away. More immediate was the prospect of the government passing ever sterner restrictions on whaling that would force us out of business. "These new laws. Ridiculous!"

"The laws don't seem to have much of an effect on you."

"I try," I offered lamely.

She was quiet as we watched the men feeding blubber to the try-pots. The wind carried the odor away from us.

"How long?" she asked again.

"I don't know. In time the laws will probably ban whaling completely. Those fishermen and their advocates have won public sympathy by publishing gruesome photos of dead whales. They have people believing propaganda like that ancient myth in the *King's Mirror*, that whales drive their precious herring and cod and char toward land so that they can easily harvest them."

"But what about the belugas themselves? Regulations came too late to save the right whale. What was it someone said facetiously? 'Why not ban hunting sea serpents?' And now the threats to blues and fins and seis in the Antarctic with those massive floating factories, sailing outside the reach of international law?"

"I see you've done your homework."

"It was easy not to think about consequences when what you did here was in my imagination."

"Could catching a few dozen white whales each season hurt a population in the tens of thousands? And besides, it's brought us some much-needed income."

"The farm could provide everything we need."

"What would you have me do?"

"Why not join the fishermen in Sandefjord? You'd have the sea. You have it in your bones."

"And how is that so very different from this?" I asked, waving my hand over the beach. "On the sea, we kill fish. On the farm, we slaughter cows and pigs. We use horses to ease the burden of our labors."

"It's just that—"

"Humans have always forced our will upon the natural world. We clear forests to build factories and great cities. We mine coal to heat our homes and manufacture crucial things like steel. How much progress could humanity have made without such things?"

"Did you know whales can sing?" she asked. "They are the sea's canaries. I've looked into their eyes. They seem to understand more than cows and pigs. More than herring certainly."

"Ah, so these whales understand that they're being killed?"

"I can't say what they understand." She considered her words carefully. "I've seen how they build a community, take care of their young, play together. I've seen mothers swim between your boats and their babies. I've seen mothers, deprived of their calves, take up a buoy as substitute infant and swim, bereft."

I, too, had seen these behaviors. I, too, had experienced a kind of communication with the whale, sensed its sentience. I chose to ignore those feelings, push them down so that I could shoot the whale, chop off its head, and cut it to pieces.

"Whales have been part of Norwegian culture for a thousand years," I argued. "And didn't God create the world for man to use?"

"Abuse?"

"What would you have me do?" I asked again.

"Come home," she said.

In silence, we observed the tableau before us. The wind picked up, columns of steam rose from the boiling pots and moved horizontally across the beach and into the sea. At the time, I thought my whaling days would go on and on. That the world would remain an endless parade of seasons. That Astrid would return to the farm, her illusions dispelled, our children to raise, the whalers' wives to keep her company. And I would return each year with those same men, harvesting the same white whales, piling beluga bones upon beluga bones, mounds of skulls and ribs and vertebrae.

Odd was leading the men in song, one he favored called "The Cruel Ship's Captain." We couldn't distinguish all the words, but I knew them by heart, about a sea captain who's murdered for abusing his crew. I sang along:

Now all you sea captains who go out a-navying
Take fair advantage by me
And don't abuse your young apprentice boy
Or it's hanged you sure will be.

"Lovely song," Astrid said. "You should be worried." She smiled, then sighed. "I keep thinking of that mother whale. She'd done everything to protect her calf. She lost all regard for her own safety."

"I took advantage of her natural instinct," I replied. "An old trick."

"A cruel trick, if you ask me."

"But necessary."

No, it was cruel. In the years since, I've often thought about that mother beluga whose milk spilled on the scree and mixed with her blood. How long till she realized that the smell was her own blood, that the pain was her own pain, that the whaler's knife had cut out her heart? Might the tragedies that have befallen me, befallen humanity, be attributable to imposing our collective will on the earth? How difficult would it have been for me to feed a piece of each whale to the sea?

"Making the calf an orphan," she said. "I guess that's better than killing him. I can't imagine trying to replace a baby with a buoy."

For some reason, we both started laughing. We laughed and laughed until tears streamed down our faces and crystallized into tiny particles of ice.

She swiped the moisture from her cheeks and turned to face me. "I'm pregnant."

"I know."

She seemed momentarily fazed, then rested her head on my shoulder and sighed again. "A buoy. A baby. A baby boy. How is it possible, Tor? Is it possible? Is it possible to love a boy so much that he goes on living?"

"Birk's alive in our hearts. Our memories, if that's what you mean."

"It isn't enough."

I nodded. She'd borne the worst of the loss, but I felt it keenly too. True, I didn't see the divers remove his body from the sea or deal with his funeral preparations as she had. Once home, however, I could hardly reconcile myself to the fact of his lifeless body in the casket. All this made the loss seem at once more heartbreaking and less real. When I entered our house, I expected him to come bounding toward me, leap into my arms, and wrap his arms around my neck. That was his habit. The silence that greeted me at the front door the day I came home that fall and the days since will haunt me forever.

"Do you want to stay on?" I asked.

She looked straight at me. "Look, Tor, I know I've taken you away from your work. I hear the crew complaining. They depend on a good season for their livelihood. I don't blame them for resenting my presence here."

"Not all of them."

"No, not all," she said. "And there's my work. The reason I came. I've had far less time than I'd like for collecting."

"I was thinking more about the pregnancy. We're on our own here if anything happens—"

"It's two more months. I can hold out until then." She patted her stomach. "And besides, morning sickness never killed anyone."

As I sit writing about that afternoon in the rowboat, I recall an ordinary morning, both of us waking side by side in our bed at the farm. It was dark outside. Astrid rose from the bed, stood silhouetted against the muted yellow wall of our bedroom, and slid off her nightgown. She moved to the bureau, chose a simple outfit—loose blue pants and a white cotton shirt—and dressed quickly. She turned and smiled, picked up the discarded nightgown, and threw it at me.

"Time to get up," she said.

Yes, time. The cows needed milking, the horses feeding, and afterward, breakfast with the children before they headed off to school.

As I said, an ordinary morning. How many mornings like that did we share? How many mornings did I begrudge that early rising, the tedium of the everyday? Was that my motivation for escaping to Svalbard every summer? I think about Jonah swallowed by a whale, God's punishment for his disobedience. We're meant to accept that there's little point in opposing His will. The problem is knowing what God means for us. He may have intended I come to this very place, to suffer the things I've suffered, and to return here after the yawning gape of war.

9 August 1937

Dear Birk,

I never intended to bring harm to the baby or myself. I let anger get the best of me. And I had a right to be angry.

Saturday evenings, the crew enjoys time off. I don't get the same break. I make a special meal and put up with their drinking and foul language and rowdy behavior. This past Saturday night started out no differently. I roasted a passel of ptarmigan that

Soren had shot and shorn of feathers, mixed a salad of bitter greens I'd harvested in the hills, and roasted potatoes from our cache in the anteroom.

The crowning glory of the meal was dessert, *Bløtkake*, one of Birgitta's favorites. I didn't have the fresh strawberries I usually layer with the sponge cake and the whipped cream. I substituted lingonberry jam and topped the creation with meringues baked from eider egg whites.

When I presented the confection to the men, everyone but Odd cheered. That should have been my first clue that the evening's revelry would turn sour. Odd's cohort chose not to bathe or shave that evening. I decided to heed Anders's warning and overlook their thoughtlessness, so the stench in the parlor—between the persistent odor of cooking and the rancid stink of unwashed bodies—was almost more than I could tolerate in my present condition.

But it wasn't until the drinking games began that the evening took its darkest turn. The game the crew favored involved tapping out increasingly complicated patterns with their metal tankards—left hand, right hand, tap the table, right then left, tap the table. Whoever broke the pattern had to take a long drink. Some punishment!

Pappa knew the tapping drove me crazy and never joined in. I steeled myself for the racket together with their smoking cigarettes and pipes and spitting flecks of tobacco onto the floor. I could see why the miners in Longyearbyen had their alcohol restricted by Store Norske. Pappa did nothing to curb the whalers' drinking on Saturday nights. But what set me off more than anything else was this. Odd doused a cigarette in what was left of the sponge cake, raised his tankard, and toasted, "To our wives and sweethearts, may they never meet."

His cronies laughed, raised their tankards in concert, and clanged them loudly all around. Beer slopped all over the table and floor. Alas, Anders joined in.

Drunkenness wasn't an excuse. I took Pappa aside and asked him to make them leave.

"They're letting off steam," he said.

"Make them leave!"

My shouting embarrassed Pappa. The noise ceased for a moment while Pappa and I stared at each other. Then Odd banged his tankard on the table. One…two…three, loud and slow. Tomas and Oskar responded. Bang…bang…bang. I glared at Pappa, pulled on my parka and snowpants, my hat, mittens, and boots. Pappa watched me dress but said nothing. I guess he thought I was going for my usual laps around the cabin. The temperature was above freezing, warm enough. And the sun was out. Perhaps if I had been greeted by biting cold or violent wind, I might have turned back. But I was so furious, I wasn't thinking straight. I'd even forgotten my rifle.

At first without a plan, I tromped down the beach, past the whale cemetery, and up the vertical cleft between the hills. Scree gave way to snow, my progress slow as I slid backward on the steepening slope. I quelled my fury with prayer—Dear God, keep the bears at bay—a mantra to steady my rapidly beating heart. I felt as if it might leap out of my chest. Blood pulsed in my ears.

Higher and higher I went. My breath became labored. I threw up. The green bile stood out against the pure white snow. I thought of Hansel marking his path with white pebbles. My path was marked with vomit. It gave me an idea. I was nearing a precipice. Meltwater cascaded down the mountain, along a ridge of rocks that lined the edge of the stream. After rinsing my mouth and quenching my thirst, I left the bile as evidence of my passage and walked alongside the ridge, imprinting my feet in the pristine snow to make deep, clear footprints, left right, left right, up to the verge. Then I tiptoed across the shallows, placing my feet carefully on stepping stones so that they stayed dry, lay down on the other side, and rolled away from the stream. It wasn't a perfect plan. The flattened snow would give away my secret. But Pappa's initial terror—my footprints going over the abyss—that was going to be my revenge.

Lining the stream were caves. I'd taken refuge in one of

them when I was caught in a squall while collecting flowers. I decided to spend the night in that cave. The entrance was too narrow for a bear to make his way inside. I squeezed through and lay down on a bed of rocks. Exhausted by anger and the uphill climb, I fell fast asleep.

Polar bears weren't the only hazard of my reckless trek. Overnight, snow and sleet fell. By the time I woke hours later, an icy white sheet smothered the entrance. Had my refuge become a grave? I was stiff from sleeping on stone and had trouble getting to my knees. The ceiling was so low it was impossible to stand.

With nothing but rocks for tools, and in that awkward kneeling position, I began to hollow out the barrier. If I could carve a small hole, I could call out through it. Pappa would be looking for me, and he'd track my footprints to this cave. It rankled that I'd have to be rescued, but what choice did I have?

Then I realized the fresh snow would have erased my footprints and the bile. Frantic, I hacked and scraped the white wall with an array of stones. Suddenly, a piece of the wall gave way. Sunlight pierced the opening. I peered out. The snow had stopped. I picked up a razor-sharp stone shaped like an oversized flinthead—a Stone Age tool—and whittled away at the hole until it was large enough to crawl through.

It was then I heard men's voices.

I was to be rescued.

Only I didn't want rescue. My anger had faded, but I wasn't finished punishing Pappa. I retreated into the vault and waited for the voices to fade away. Then I slipped and slid down the steep bluff, retracing the path I'd taken on the way up. Halfway down, my left leg sank deep into a hidden crevice. Here I was, one leg buried high on my thigh, the other bent at the knee and level to the ground. Worse, the snow that filled in the space was granular firn, something like quicksand made of ice, difficult to dig away. I'd scoop large handfuls of the slick stuff to one side and the hole would immediately fill in. What a predicament! I thought about the story Anders told of the man who fell and broke his leg and marked his final resting place with ski poles. I'd brought nothing of the sort, nothing to mark my final resting place if it came to that.

I was being melodramatic. If anything, my fresh footprints would be easy for the searchers to track. But the last thing I wanted was to be discovered trapped in such an ungainly posture. I could just imagine Odd's smirk as he made some comment about how useless women were.

Through trial and error, I discovered that by shoveling quickly on either side of my leg and lifting it little by little as I progressed, I was able to free my leg from its prison. My bulky gloves made for clumsy shovels, so I removed them. Without their protection, the coarse grains scraped my skin, and my hands soon became numb.

My ordeal wasn't over. When I finally extracted my leg, my boot stayed behind. It took another several minutes to dig it out. By that time, I'd lost all feeling in my hands and bootless left foot. My parka was dry, but sweat had moistened my clothing. That old troll's warning came back to me then—if you get wet, you die. I took refuge in a lee under a nearby towering rock, peeled off my sock, and laid it on a stone. Then I rubbed my hands and foot to restore circulation.

"Fool," I whispered as the feeling returned to my extremities.

I dressed and made my way back to the cabin. Its warmth enveloped me as I entered, but my anger welled up again when I saw the mess from the previous evening's revelries. I fixed myself a cup of tea, pushed aside the half-full tankards, the dinner plates filled with ptarmigan bones and congealed fat, and the sponge cake crowned with Odd's crooked cigarette.

I sat down to brace myself for Pappa's return. It didn't take long. As I suspected, the men followed my tracks back to the cabin. Thankfully, the search crew stayed outside while Pappa rushed through the door, breathless. Hoar frost edged his beard, his bangs. He stared at me as if I were an apparition. When finally able to speak, he sputtered, "You have no idea how worried I was!"

"You have no idea how angry I was," I replied, sipping my tea and affecting a calm I didn't feel.

"The baby," he said.

"The baby's fine," I said. "I wouldn't harm the baby." Which was only half true. If I'd fallen into a crevasse or frozen to death in my ice tomb or come face-to-face with a polar bear, both the baby and I would have perished.

Pappa and I had reached another stalemate. I was waiting for him to apologize. He was waiting for me to apologize.

Regaining his composure, he asked, "What do you want me to do?"

"Last night," I said.

"Yes, last night," he said. "It won't happen again."

I took that as "I'm sorry," offered my own "It won't happen again."

I didn't tell him the story of my night in the cave, and for some reason, he didn't ask. In time, I'd reveal the details, and we'd laugh over them from the safe distance of the future.

Sweeping my hand across the parlor, I said, "Teach the men a lesson," I said. "Have them clean up this mess."

With that, I took my tea, crossed over to the bedroom, and shut the door behind me.

෧

Kvitfiskneset
20 June 1947

I'd tried to find a balance between the men's needs and Astrid's. An exquisite equilibrium. My crew deserved a night of carousing after a week of difficult, tedious labor. Our kitchen was the only place we could easily gather. It wasn't the refined entertainment Astrid may have once imagined would grace her "parlor." Did she expect the men to make a ritual of bathing in the fjord, putting on fresh clothes, and reading their Bibles quietly in their bunks aboard ship until they fell asleep? Or having a civilized dinner with cloth napkins and crystal wine glasses and polished silverware while we discussed the finer points of philosophy or politics? I owed her more of an apology. At the time, I thought that she also owed me more of an apology. She didn't fully understand the terror I felt searching for her with my men, imagining her torn to pieces by a polar bear, who'd cast the pinprick of a baby into the scree like so much waste, a snack for an Arctic fox. That was the picture I carried in my mind as we fanned out along the hills and vales.

I also felt diminished in the crew's eyes. I was their captain, and I couldn't control my wife. Astrid's presence had disturbed the season's usual rhythms. Some blamed her for the dearth of belugas, as if she had some mystical power over the sea. Odd called it "Astrid's curse."

Astrid. Odd. How can you know two people for so long only to discover that you really don't know them at all?

Which brings me to the summer's turning point.

Injuries weren't unusual given the dangers of our labors. Razor-sharp knives and gutting tools. Mauls and axes. Fire and scalding pots of oil.

Astrid had become expert with the first-aid kit. The men called her Nurse Handeland when they needed medical attention.

It seemed that some men needed more attention than others.

Thus, it was no surprise when Odd came to her with a knife wound. I realized only later that her version of what happened was the truth.

ॐ

16 August 1937

Dear Birk,

Last Friday. Friday the thirteenth. I should have known it would be an inauspicious day.

I was alone in the parlor, kneading bread dough for the night's supper. In comes Odd, his right calf streaming blood. He claimed to have slashed it accidentally while he was slicing blubber.

I washed the flour from my hands and got the first-aid kit.

I'd treated knife wounds before. I cleaned the area surrounding the cut, then knelt in front of him and pressed hard with sterilized cotton wool to staunch the bleeding. Bent to the task, I could feel Odd's breath ruffling my hair. At first, I didn't think anything of it, so engrossed was I in stopping the blood. *An unexpected place for a self-inflicted wound,* I thought, *low on the back of his calf.* But then again, I'd seen all sorts of unusual injuries—small stones so deeply embedded in a foot that I had to pry them out with a knife and stitch the small gaps with sterilized thread; the tip of a finger sliced off by a rope (there was no saving the fingertip); a forehead blackened by frostbite; and one poor unfortunate, out collecting eider duck eggs, whose arm was raked in a close brush with a polar bear.

I'd managed to treat them all successfully, no infections. I was proud that none of the men lost more than a day's work.

Odd's bleeding persisted. To stem it, I tied off the leg above the wound with a tourniquet. The bleeding slowed. I bathed the wound in iodine and tightly wrapped a fresh bandage of sterile cotton wool around his leg.

When I stood, I felt dizzy, no doubt from a combination of the odd posture of bending for so long and the pregnancy. I closed my eyes to recover my balance.

"I have to stitch the flaps together," I said. "But it's risky. Greater chance of infection. I don't see as you have a choice. I haven't lost a patient so far, but you'll have to get some proper care in Longyearbyen."

Odd nodded, all the while his eyes on me.

I had nothing left to numb the wound, so I offered him either a dose of laudanum or a measure of whiskey. He chose the whiskey.

"So how did this happen?" I asked, handing him a shot.

He took the glass, drained it, and held it out to me. "Another pour." It was a statement, not a question. I refilled the glass, and he downed it in a single swallow.

For a man who loved to tell tall tales, he was unusually reticent in that moment. "The knife slipped," he said finally. "I was cutting blubber. Tern picked the wrong time to swoop in and attack my head. Fuckin' bird."

I knew that terns could be aggressive. I'd been the victim of their territoriality more than once. But there was something in the way he said it that gave me pause.

The tourniquet had done its work, the bleeding slowed to a trickle. I knelt in front of him again, tore some strips of cotton wool long enough to fit around his calf, and laid out a curved needle, scissors, and thread.

"Ready?" I asked.

He sneered. "Do your worst."

I began to sew continuous stitches, pretending I was making a seam in animal skin. But the skins I'd sewn all summer were stiff and dry, not rubbery and wet and etched by pinpricks of blood where the needle ran in and out. I looked up briefly to see how Odd was taking the pain. He was gritting his teeth, but no sound escaped his lips.

I bent again to the task, swallowing the bile rising in my throat. *In-out-pull*, I said to myself. *In-out-pull.* Maintaining a rhythm, I secured the final stitch with a surgeon's knot and swabbed the wound again with iodine.

I hadn't noticed that Odd had drawn his face down to the top of my head. As I snipped the ends of the thread, he grabbed my shoulders and kissed my hair. Startled, I raised my head quickly, too quickly, my head crashing into his face.

The next thing I knew, Pappa was kneeling beside me. Odd was sitting at the table, sipping whiskey from a shot glass.

I pointed at Odd. "He...he," I stammered.

"You fainted," Odd said.

"Liar," I said. "Ask him why his nose is bleeding,"

"Astrid," Pappa said. "Calm down."

"I am calm," I replied, though my heart raced. Still lying on my back, I turned to Odd and shouted, "Get out!"

Pappa cocked his head toward the door. "Let me straighten this out."

Odd stood and hobbled away, exaggerating a limp for effect.

As soon as the front door slammed shut, I told Pappa what Odd had done. "He grabbed my shoulders and kissed the top of my head. I must have blacked out when I tried to stand and smashed into his face."

"He said you fainted."

"How do you think he got the bloody nose?"

"He told me he passed out briefly himself," Pappa said. "Hit his nose on something."

"And you believe him?" I sat up quickly, and a wave of dizziness passed over me. I lay back again and closed my eyes. Pappa refreshed the cloth and placed it over my forehead.

"We can talk about this later. You should rest." With that he lifted me from the floor, carried me to the bedroom, and pulled the covers up to my chin.

"I know what Odd did," I said. "It's time for him to go."

Pappa argued that he needed Odd, that the catch was already compromised, and blah, blah, blah. On and on Pappa prattled, extolling his first mate's virtues, until I interrupted him.

"Odd followed us," I said. "He saw us."

"What are you talking about?"

"On solstice. He followed us to Haven."

"Followed...us?"

"You want a man like that around?"

That question hung in the air. I could tell Pappa was disturbed by the revelation, but even that wasn't enough to make him fire Odd. It took an incident in Longyearbyen to force that decision. They'd gone up to town to get his wound treated properly. Afterward, Pappa and he got into an argument in the miners' canteen. Apparently they made a scene, and Pappa was injured. That was the final straw. Pappa gave Odd money for passage on the *Lyngen*, which was more than he deserved.

❧

Kvitfiskneset
20 June 1947

What I didn't tell Astrid was that I was more than disturbed by her revelation that Odd spied on us. I was stunned. It makes me wonder what might have happened had I not ducked into the cabin to check on his wound. He was sitting at the kitchen table, bent over Astrid's body, his nose bleeding.

I rushed to Astrid's side and knelt down. She was out cold. "What happened?" I asked.

Odd shrugged. "Must've fainted," he said. "The wound and all." He picked up a napkin and pushed it against his bloody nose, then poured himself a shot of whiskey.

Gently I patted her cheeks, hoping it might wake her. It didn't. I rooted through the first-aid kit, which was opened on the floor, found smelling salts, and waved them under her nose. She revived. When fully conscious, she told me her side of the story. Once again, I tried to placate both sides, and once again, I failed.

I took Odd up to Longyearbyen to have his wound tended. The possibility of a blood infection weighed on my mind. What erupted between him and me after the doctor examined him and declared Astrid's stitching "remarkable for someone un-trained in the medical arts" was the culmination of all that had transpired up to that point.

We were having a drink in the miner's canteen, a privilege accorded me because of my friendship with Einar. I was stall-ing, finding it hard to begin. Odd and I had been together for seven summers, and in that time, I thought I'd gotten to know him. Sitting there, I realized I hardly knew him at all. Where was he born? Where did he live in the off-season? Did he have a family?

"What happened between you and Astrid," I started. I took a long swallow of beer. Chased it with a sip of whiskey. "What happened is making it difficult for us to maintain the present arrangement."

"Nothing happened. She fainted. The rest is in her head." He dropped his shot of whiskey into his half-full pint of beer, then polished off his depth charge in a few gulps. "Given her condition, it's not surprising."

"Can't you see you've put me in an awkward position. There have been other…problems between the two of you…as you well know."

"You should've thought of that before you invited Astrid along to collect her plants."

I shook my head. "She's a botanist by training. It's her profession."

"You see what happens when women get fancy ideas in their heads."

One thing I'd learned about Odd was his old-fashioned view of women. "Look," I said, getting down to the business at hand. "I'm asking you to keep your distance from my wife."

He slammed his empty mug down on the table, the shot glass rattling inside. "Asking? Or ordering?"

I placed my hand on top of his to calm him. "I *am* your captain," I said. "You can take it as you will."

Odd stood, his face red. He backhanded his mug so that it sailed across the table and hit me hard in the chest, fell to the floor, and shattered.

The room went quiet. I stood, trying to control my alarm and anger, and jabbed my finger into his chest. "I *am* your captain," I repeated, as if he hadn't already broken the sailor's code. "You'll treat me with respect."

"Aye, aye, sir," he said, mock-saluting me then turning away. I thought that was the end of it. But he spun around and sucker-punched me in the gut. I grabbed him by his jacket and shoved him so hard that he fell backward.

By this time, a small crowd of miners had gathered around us, egging us on. It was cheap entertainment.

Odd rose and lunged at me. We both went sprawling from the momentum. My head hit the edge of the table behind me, and I literally saw stars. Straddling me, he began to punch me in the chest.

At that moment, one of the miners I'd brought up from Tromsø grabbed Odd's arms from behind and pulled him away. I lay there panting, almost breathless. Though I knew whalers *could* be a rough crew, I prided myself on hiring men who were, at the very least, incapable of mindless violence. Or so I thought. Odd was capable of things I'd never imagined.

Odd retreated to the table where not so many minutes ago we'd shared a drink, having what I thought was a rational conversation. I stood, retrieved a napkin, and wiped the blood from my face. My breathing was ragged, causing sharp pain each time I inhaled. I wondered if he'd broken one of my ribs.

My breathing steadied. I reached into my jacket, drew out my wallet, and threw down enough kroner to cover a ticket on the *Lyngen* and then some.

"Find your own way home," I said, barely controlling my temper.

I thanked the miner who'd rescued me and left the canteen. The long walk back to the boat cleared my head and cooled my anger. Whereas I had Odd on the trip north, I'd have to make the return trip alone. Thank God for the endless summer sun and calm waters—perfect conditions for a smooth trip back to Kvitfiskneset.

On the way, I tried to think of an excuse for the bruises on my face and chest. None came. There was no way to hide that Astrid had been right about Odd all along.

≈

24 August 1937

Dear Birk,

These past weeks reminded me of what normal life is like. With Odd gone, the mutinous crew members have lost their will to make my life difficult. The threat of forfeiting their pay might be part of it. Pappa didn't say as much, but they assume that Odd lost his lay. And that the first mate could be so suddenly dismissed gives them pause. It's "yes, Fru Handeland" and "no, Fru Handeland" and more attention to their hygiene. We had supper these past two Saturday evenings in our parlor, but the men took their drinking and their games back to the ship.

The bright spot of Pappa's trip to Longyearbyen and that

nasty business with Odd was that Hilmar had left a wedding invitation at the post office. Why he anticipated that Pappa might be in Longyearbyen to pick up messages is a bit of a mystery, but then again, for all his talk, Hilmar remains an enigma.

When Pappa returned, he showed me the invitation. The wedding was to be the following Sunday, the twenty-second. He spent the morning offering a hundred reasons for why we couldn't attend. "Another twelve-hour roundtrip, plus the ceremony and the celebration afterward. I'll lose a day of whaling."

"But it's a Sunday," I countered. "We could leave after supper on Saturday and be home at the latest Monday morning.

"You're assuming perfect weather," he said. "Not to mention that the men have decided to work Sundays to make up lost ground."

I know he blamed me for losing Odd. As if a woman's simple presence disrupted the station's harmony. As if men were incapable of observing the most basic rules of decorum. And most importantly, as if my pregnancy had adversely affected my mind.

"But what's one more day in the grand scheme of things? Besides, how many times do you get invited to an Arctic wedding?" I smiled, touched his cheek. "An Arctic wedding. What could be more romantic?"

Pappa gave in. It helped that the "night" we left for Sassen was gloriously sunny with very little wind. We'd had days and days of mist and icy fog, but finally the gods smiled on us. The west coast was ice free, the waves calm as we navigated to Villa Fredheim.

Scheduling the governor's assistant to perform the ceremony was a major headache for Hilmar, who kept the plans secret from Helfrid until a few days before. He wanted to surprise her, he said, but I wonder if he also wanted the opportunity to back out at the last minute. That he'd get cold feet, he who wears but the barest of footwear and claims his feet are never cold. Pappa tells me that Hilmar practices the "Arctic custom" of urinating on his feet to toughen them. Can you imagine, Birk?

He's a maverick, that much is obvious. I admire his confidence, how he strides about as if he's the master of the world. Afraid of nothing. Me? I've never gotten rid of that subliminal dread that inhabits the very air we breathe here, something I thought would pass. It's as if we're always on the verge of calamity. But the wedding allowed me to push that feeling aside for a brief time.

Helfrid wore a stylish dark dress—short-sleeved, flared below her knees, large brass buttons down the front, a wide belt cinching her waist. Wearing white wasn't appropriate, but who am I to say? She'd waved her hair and pulled it back in a low bun, blushed her cheeks with rouge, and painted her lips with bright red lipstick. It made me wonder if she were really all that surprised by Hilmar's secret plans. For his part, he'd shaved his beard and cut his hair, and looked dapper in his dark blue suit, crisp white shirt, and tie. I almost didn't recognize him.

Hilmar's family was there, along with Arne Egge, the manager of the nearby gypsum mine, and four of his co-workers. Each of the guests had bathed and shaved and dressed in their best clothes. I felt out of place in my woolen leggings and parka, no makeup, my hair tangled from the boat ride. Pappa had sworn that the wedding would be informal. Helfrid was too kind to say anything. Before the ceremony, I managed to run a borrowed comb through my hair and pinch my cheeks to give them some color.

The ceremony was held in the living room. The governor's assistant, Kjeld Irgens, officiated. He began: "When you marry, two become one but also remain two independent people. It seems a contradiction to say so, but marriage can be a home for love and unity on the one hand, and freedom and self-sufficiency on the other."

A contradiction, yes, I thought. On Kvitfiskneset I'd been living out that grand contradiction. Your father and I had managed to pursue our lives separately and together. What were the chances I'd find a man willing to do that? I glanced at Pappa. He turned just in that instant and took my hand in his.

Irgens continued. "And now, Helfrid, I ask you first. Do you take Hilmar, who is standing beside you, to be your lawfully wedded husband?"

Helfrid turned to Hilmar, joined both her hands in his. "I do."

"And do you, Hilmar, take Helfrid to be your lawfully wedded wife?"

Hilmar nodded.

Irgens whispered, "You must say 'I do.'"

He coughed, then said, "I do."

"The rings, please."

Hilmar fished in his pocket and produced two identical gold bands. He must have brought them from the mainland back in May. I think Helfrid was finally, genuinely surprised.

"With this ring, I thee wed," the bride and groom said in succession.

Helfrid took a moment to stare at the gold band on her finger. It glinted in the light falling through the living room window.

Irgens read from a page in his book: "As you have promised each other—before God and in the presence of these witnesses—to live together in marriage, I now pronounce you husband and wife."

Hilmar bent to kiss Helfrid's cheek. As he did so, Pappa kissed me lightly on my forehead. And right then, I swear I felt the quickening for the first time—bubbles in my womb. Could it be, this early in the pregnancy?

Somehow Helfrid had found the time to cook a pot roast with vegetables and potatoes. Real beef! Such a luxury after all the whale and seal, ptarmigan and duck. Dessert was your favorite, cloudberry cream, plus cakes and brandy. I wasn't ready to share the news of my pregnancy with the Nøises, so I took the glass of brandy and sipped it slowly.

We sat on the veranda having our cake and coffee while Helfrid and Hilmar posed happily on the beach, Temple Mountain and the glaciers as backdrop to the most unusual wedding photographs ever taken. Hilmar, king of Sassen, had finally found his queen. Helfrid was indeed a force to be reckoned with, as if the challenges of living on this isolated hunting station were no more difficult than running a tobacco shop in Oslo.

When the happy couple returned to the veranda, Helfrid told us about something puzzling that had happened the previous week. Hilmar and the men were off hunting, and Anna was visiting friends in Longyearbyen. So she was alone in the cabin, asleep in her bedroom, when she was awakened by footsteps.

"Heavy, thudding footsteps," she said. "I convinced myself it was the expansion and contraction of the walls. The frost itself talking. Another night, I was working upstairs in the loft and heard the kitchen door fly open with a bang, then slam closed. I was worried that a bear had made his way into the cabin. Eerie silence followed. Working up my courage, I crossed to the top of the stairs and peered down. Nothing."

She paused and took a sip of coffee. "Naturally, when you're alone, sounds can play with your mind. I told myself that any number of things could explain the noises. The tapping of ice pellets against the windows. A glacier calving and sending a wave of air against the door, the ensuing vacuum sucking it closed."

"Well, there's also the possibility of a ghost," Hilmar said.

"You can't succumb to superstition, or you'll lose your wits," Helfrid replied.

"But I've heard ghosts myself," he said. "You know the story of the hunter up north, near Gråhuken?"

"Oh Lord," Helfrid said. "We've heard that story a thousand times."

"I haven't," I said.

"Don't encourage him," Helfrid replied.

Hilmar crossed his hands over his heart. "We haven't been married a day, and already she's trying to change me."

We all laughed, and Hilmar continued. "Well, you see, it happened like this," he began. "A trapper stopped for the night at a hut in Widjefjorden. Outside this hut was the grave of a hunter who'd died of scurvy. 'Course, it was deadly quiet that night. He's alone, and the only sound's that of his own breathing. Suddenly, he hears footsteps outside. He thinks it's a bear, and he pulls his rifle to his side. Crunch, crunch, crunch. Crunch, crunch, crunch. Nearer and nearer the footsteps come. He rises from his bed, crosses to the window, grips his rifle tighter. He can't see anything outside, despite the light of the full moon shining on the snow. The footsteps climb the wall next to him, march over the roof, and fade into the distance. He rushes outside, circles the cabin. Nothing. Not even tracks in the snow. When he told this story later, some thought he'd lost his mind. I didn't. I'd stayed there and heard footsteps too."

Helfrid smiled indulgently. "Hilmar also believes Fridays and the number thirteen are unlucky. He rarely hunts on those days."

"Why tempt fate?" he asked.

"Christiane Ritter told me of sounds carrying incredible distances in Svalbard because of the dry air. Sometimes I swear I hear voices at night," I said.

"You must have mental strength to survive a winter in Svalbard," Helfrid said.

"The Nisjas and the Ediassens come to mind," Hilmar said. "Jetta Nisja persuaded her husband to let her spend the winter here with her three-year-old daughter, Ragna. It was 1898, I believe. They were hunters, reindeer and polar bears. The story goes that little Ragna kept a baby reindeer as a pet that winter. Unfortunately, the calf made its way into the flour stores, ate too much, and blew up."

Helfrid swiped at Hilmar with a dish towel. "That's a terrible story."

Everyone laughed except me. That some don't survive the winter made me think of Elen, hovering in the very air of this compound. Ghosts indeed. The contrast between this newly married couple, besotted with happiness, and Elen, possibly alone in a mental hospital, never having recovered from her two Arctic sojourns, struck me as terribly unfair. And where was Hilmar's daughter? Didn't he owe her something of this joy? After all, Kaps got to share in this special day.

"Do you have any happy stories to tell?" I asked, hungry for something to dispel my uneasiness.

"*Ja, ja,*" Hilmar said. "There's the one about the fourteen Russian sailors stranded on the ice after their ship crashed in a remote part of Svalbard in 1743."

"This is a happy story?"

"Wait!" Hilmar replied. "These were resourceful men. They found a deserted cabin, salvaged a rifle, an axe, twelve cartridges, a kettle, and firewood from their ship. They shot enough reindeer to make it through that first winter. Then they made bows out of driftwood and strings from tendons of a polar bear they'd trapped. And from these weapons, they hunted enough game to last through six winters. They drank polar bear blood to ward off scurvy. And they made clothes from animal hides. All of them survived except the one man who refused to drink blood. And six years later, they were rescued by a Russian ship that had been blown off course."

Can you believe this fairy tale, my sweet son? I want to believe it. To survive six years on hope and ingenuity. Imagine the strength of mind that would require!

Helfrid thinks she has the strength that Elen lacked. "I've decided to spend the winter here," she said as a coda to Hilmar's story. "Though I won't be drinking polar bear blood, thank you very much."

We lifted our glasses to Helfrid's pronouncement. "*Skål,*" we said in unison.

"And now for the crowning touch," Hilmar said. "Come inside."

From the storeroom, Hilmar carried a gramophone with a stack of records piled on top. He cranked the machine, selected a record and inserted it on the spindle, and placed the needle onto the opening groove. Guess what came out of the horn, Birk? "Summertime," of all tunes. Where they bought that record, I'll never know.

All afternoon, Hilmar played song after song. Everyone got up and danced. Helfrid taught the men the foxtrot and a particularly vigorous Charleston. At least it resembled the Charleston. Hilmar danced with Anna, and I with Edvin, and Pappa with Helfrid. Then Pappa cut in and held me close, while Edvin paired up with his wife and Hilmar with Helfrid. Karl and the gypsum workers danced with each other since their wives and sweethearts were far away.

We were bumping into each other and laughing so hard that Edvin fell down and Anna collapsed upon him. The ghost stories faded in the merriment, at least for those last priceless moments surrounded by friends in the warmth of that marvelous living room.

૭

Kvitfiskneset
20 June 1947

I was never much of a storyteller. Astrid was the one who was schooled in literature and raised by a mother who loved to tell stories. But here on Svalbard, reticent men become raconteurs. It passed the time, assuaged the loneliness. Stories were handed down from one hunter or whaler or trapper to another. Many were born of the dark season but told in the light.

Every evening, after supper and chores were done and the fire banked, the crew retreated to their sleeping quarters and Astrid and I to our bedroom. We'd lie close together, spooning out of necessity, because of both the cold and the narrowness of the bed. And love too. Yes, love.

There, in the comfort of the marriage bed, I'd add to the stories others told about this place. Lord knows most of these stories were tragic, the victims' names forgotten: a hunter who misstepped into a narrow crevasse, wedged in with his head above ground while the natural heat of his body melted the ice, further entrapping him until nightfall and the inevitable freezing, locking him in an ice tomb; or the self-styled polar explorer who set off alone across Hinlopenstretet, never seen again (and only a fool would travel across that strait in summer, from Spitsbergen to Nordaustlandet, the pack ice deceiving even the most experienced outdoorsman into believing that he has a solid surface to traverse); or the hunter driven mad during the dark season by *Ishavet kaller*, wading into the sea and drowning. Storytelling seemed like an innocuous way to pass the time. It's clear now those stories affected Astrid. So much heartache, so many ways to go mad or to die. Why do we tell such stories to children? Grimm's fairy tales and Mother Goose rhymes— they teach us what? Fear? Resourcefulness? Hard truths? Birk cried when I told him that Humpty Dumpty couldn't be put back together again. He thought everything could be fixed.

ॐ

29 August 1937

Dear Birk,

The summer is winding down. Gone, the eternal sun. Each passing day adds another half hour of darkness, as if the very dark has at long last remembered how to steal back the light. The fast-shortening days remind me that this idyll will soon be over. Idyll, you say? Yes, Birk. Even surrounded by bloodied whales and mounds of bones, even assaulted by the stench of belching try-pots and festering carcasses, even stung by the sting of constant smoke, I find myself dreading the return home. I know I've complained about the never-ending drudgery of keeping the station shipshape, as Pappa would say. A losing battle, but my thriving garden of transplanted flowers and Barentsburg grass offsets in some small way the damage we've done to the environment.

And then there is the paradise that requires only a short trek into the valleys and up the hills to bring me face-to-face with unsullied landscapes—brilliant flowers unique to each nook and cranny, crags crested with lichens and mosses, glaciers riven with dark veins, mountains cut by rivers of snow. Not to mention wildlife that abounds in August. The birds alone are a wonder—the chunky snow buntings, the white-faced barnacle geese with their characteristic black plumage, the ebony-headed little auks and plump gray-and-white sanderlings, pink-footed geese and elegant whooper swans. (I must admit I'm not fond of the terns who've stolen my woolen hats more than once.) I've made friends with a trusting arctic fox cub, too young to be afraid of me. I feed it bits of stale bread when I'm out in the field near his den. The sheer number of creatures makes me feel so much less alone. This is the world into which I flee to collect my specimens. Each time I feel as if I'm reclaiming a bit of my lost self.

Your father says I've become a real Arctic housewife, mastering a whole new repertoire of tasks. He means it as a compliment, but his words remind me how much of the summer I've wasted. What hurts most is that he shows little interest in my work. He's preoccupied with business, fretting constantly about the underwhelming catch. I should be grateful for his industry.

Maybe it's the pregnancy talking. Ever since the Nøises' wedding, I've been obsessed with Elen's story. Hilmar said little about her each time we visited Sassen, as if he could make Elen disappear. But I could feel her presence there. Her life is so different from mine. We've both suffered tragedies, but hers were graver. Her father a suicide. Two dead infants. The trauma of Kaps's birth. The empty grave at Sassen. Plus, she spent most of her marriage alone year-round while I've endured Pappa's absences only in summer. I imagine the spirits of Sassenfjord calling to her. She resisted that call and returned home. Was that her mistake?

In one of Christiane's letters to me, she told the story of a Norwegian woman who gave birth alone during the dark season. She'd accompanied her hunter-husband to Svalbard one year. In the fall, the man rowed across the fjord to set traps but was caught on the opposite shore when ice blocked his return. Months passed before the ice froze solid enough that he could walk across the fjord. In the heart of winter, with her husband gone and possibly dead, she delivered a healthy baby boy. Soon after, however, she lost her mind because of the trauma.

Ritter's version seems like a case of whisper down the lane—
Elen's story transposed from June to winter, bare facts altered
or embellished as time went on. Could there be more than one
woman on Svalbard with the same fate? Would both women
have been better off heeding the call of the water? Easier that
than admit to madness.

That's why I entered the water on solstice. I wanted to prove
my mettle. Water, even water that hovers around the freezing
point, doesn't mean instant death. One has several minutes, and
I had Pappa on shore, counting the seconds like a pulse. There
were greater things to fear. I passed that test.

Now I think, *I won't be like Elen.*

I won't be like you.

ॐ

Kvitfiskneset
20 June 1947

The sun's been kind all day, warding off the chill of Astrid's last
letter. If only I'd known she was writing to Birk. If only I had
been paying more attention to her rather than the whaling. *If
only*…two terribly destructive words.

I'm stiff from sitting in the rowboat for so long. It's long
past supper, but I don't feel hungry. Icebergs dance on the
water. Every once in a while, one flips as its equilibrium shifts.
This movement sends small waves to shore, rushing in, flowing
out. The seascape both calms and disturbs me.

Somewhere out there, I think, and then banish the thought as
soon as it enters my mind. It's time to return to the cabin.

EQUINOX

The cuckoo tells me morning has broken. The fire died overnight, the kitchen gone cold. I lit the stove and crawled back into bed with the folio and hot tea and a plate of biscuits while I waited for the cabin to warm. The day is overcast, with the kind of icy rain typical of June that makes being outside unpleasant. A good day to stay in bed with the covers pulled up.

They say such idleness is the devil's workshop. I say mindless busyness is equally wicked. This rare solitude, especially here where every corner yields abundant memories, where every page forces me to confront all that I've been avoiding for so many years, may finally give my angels their due.

Much of September had passed without Astrid writing a letter to Birk. Not surprising, since we were all trying to make up for lost time. A strange expression, that. Where does time hide when we lose it? And how is time "made up" by working harder? Isn't that simply a way to lose more time? Could I tap my wife or my mates on the shoulder and ask, "Have you seen my lost time?"

In any event, the whaling ledger didn't lie. By the end of August, we'd barely recouped expenses, so the men and I decided to extend the season into September. Lo and behold, in a few short weeks, we caught almost half again as many whales as we had all season. The men were thrilled by our good fortune.

We halted the catch in mid-September and finished the trying-out. What followed was a whirlwind of loading the ship with barrels of oil and beluga skins and the crew's personal gear. In the past, we'd taken the ship and the motorboat back to Longyearbyen, put the boat in dry dock, and proceeded home in quarters even more cramped than on the journey north. To relieve the overcrowding, Anders and I decided that he would proceed directly to Tromsø while Astrid and I took the motorboat back to Longyearbyen to catch the *Lyngen*'s October sailing.

A simple plan. Beyond the practical considerations, the prospect of spending time alone with Astrid influenced my decision—days spent strolling side by side as the sun set over the fjord and enjoying the first light snowfalls over a moonlit landscape. To say the least, the summer hadn't been the second honeymoon we'd envisioned. I knew beforehand that whaling was an all-consuming business, but I'd thought that sharing my livelihood with her would bring us closer and help heal the rift that had grown wide since Birk's death. I'd also thought that the opportunity to study Arctic flora would give her personal satisfaction.

In fact, it had. One of the few bright spots that summer was the time she spent in the field. One day, she rushed in breathless with excitement. I thought she'd found that one-of-a-kind flower that would make the trip (in her mind) worth the trouble. She unfolded a damp towel with the day's find.

"Look," she said. "*Rubus chamaemorus!*"

The Latin meant nothing, but I recognized the fruits. "Cloudberry," I said. "We have that in Sandefjord."

She wrinkled her nose. "Really, Tor, sometimes you can be so thick-headed. It's common on the mainland but exceedingly rare here. Hanna had managed to find only one small patch, and that was on Isfjord."

"So we'll have cloudberry cream for dessert?" I teased, reaching for one of the berries.

She swatted my hand away. "There's hardly enough for a teaspoon of jam," she said.

How could I begrudge her collecting? Her enthusiasm was reward enough, even if it meant some cold suppers. And in an odd way, though she'd spent hours alone cataloguing her specimens and more hours alone on her rambles, there were fleeting times such as these that made it all worth it. We'd even been able to share some intimate moments and now looked forward to another baby. But still, there was that elusive find...

So when I proposed the plan to Astrid, I wasn't surprised to see how willingly she agreed. Her morning sickness hadn't entirely disappeared. The seasickness induced by the turbulent sea voyage from Tromsø to Svalbard weighed on her mind, she said. Nor did she relish the idea of sharing close quarters with the crew aboard a vessel filled with the stink of whale oil.

"Besides," she said, "I'll have some time for collecting before snow covers everything."

Left unsaid: she might still find that undiscovered specimen. There was family to consider as well. "What about Birgitta?" I asked.

She sighed. "I miss her terribly," she said. "But what's a couple more weeks when we've already been gone for months? I may never get an opportunity like this again."

"How about I send a message to Longyearbyen to tell your parents of our plans?"

She nodded. "And don't forget to say how much we're looking forward to seeing them again."

It crossed my mind that the later we pushed into fall, the more difficult the boat ride would be. But I'd motored uneventfully to Longyearbyen three times that summer, and Astrid assumed this trip would be no different. I did nothing to dispel those thoughts. I knew that predicting ice in the western fjords as winter approached was tricky. True, the Gulf Stream bathed the western shores of Svalbard so that the waters often remained navigable well into the fall. The fjords were a different matter. Sometimes they would ice over unexpectedly fast. But what was the worst-case scenario? Getting trapped at the cabin over the winter? I rationalized that if we couldn't make it to Longyearbyen, Astrid's parents were fully capable of caring for Birgitta. We'd get a message to them on the whaling station's radio. The baby wasn't due until March, and by then, it would be just two months before the fjord opened up and another whaling season was upon us. Astrid might even consider overwintering as an extension of her Arctic adventure. Hadn't she argued that she was as competent as those women who'd done likewise—Christiane Ritter and Wanny Wolstad and Berntine Johansen? She could prove her mettle as those women had. She'd return home on the first ship out in May, and I'd look forward to a new season with my crew.

The winter I'd spent in Longyearbyen in '25, working in administration for Store Norske, fooled me into thinking that we could risk being stranded, that the hardest part of overwintering here was to endure months of darkness.

ॐ

23 September 1937

Dear Birk,

Your kind pappa felt obligated to promise the crew what would have been their lay this year even though the whaling season fell far short of his expectations. Buoyed by their good fortune, the crew was especially enthusiastic as they readied the ship for its journey back to the mainland. I was busy preparing another herbarium folio, which Pappa complained had put me far behind on packing and securing the cabin. His petulance was his way of blaming me for the fact that we'd earned practically nothing despite all the hard work. As if he didn't play a part in my pregnancy or prolonging that foul business with Odd.

Pappa's convinced me to stay on—the two of us blessedly alone—for a week or two, a real "second honeymoon," he said. I must admit it didn't take much encouragement. How selfish of me to put off our reunion with Birgitta! She'll be so disappointed to hear of our plans.

The weather's been mild—for Svalbard, that is. These September days have been so lovely, leading to today, the autumnal equinox, a day with equal portions of light and dark. It creates a sense of normality that twenty-four hours of sun don't provide. The transient return of the day's natural rhythm seems to have lessened my morning sickness. I guess when there's no real end to "morning," the body responds to that rhythm. But gradually over the past few weeks, I've noticed that the stench from the try-pots and whale carcasses hasn't bothered me nearly as much. Traveling on the *Lyngen* will be so much better than crammed on Pappa's ship with that vile whale oil. My seasickness on the crossing from Tromsø was bad enough without that added stink plus the lingering nausea of pregnancy.

Because we'd be taking our small motorboat to Longyearbyen, we packed most of our belongings to send ahead with Anders. He's promised to safeguard my treasured herbaria. I stroked them lovingly and offered them to him as if they were rare manuscripts. He took them, placed them carefully on a barrel, and pulled a small package tied up with string from his coat pocket. I opened it and gasped. It was the scrimshaw he'd worked on all summer. Embedded in the polished surface was an intricate figure of a woman, long hair framing her face, and a small bouquet of flowers clasped in her hands.

Momentarily speechless, I turned the piece over to find he'd engraved his initials on the back, then turned back to the figure and ran my fingers over the delicate carving.

"It's you," he said.

"I can see the resemblance," I lied, though I was touched by the detail of the flowers. He was one of the few who had taken my interest in botany seriously. "It's absolutely exquisite. Are you sure you want me to keep it?"

He nodded, then continued with the many tasks of departure.

We bade farewell to the crew and watched as they sailed out of the fjord on a day of perfect sunshine. I said a little prayer for their safety as I waved to Anders and Halvard. After all the turmoil, I felt a twinge of sadness as the boat disappeared. I'm going to miss Anders, especially, who's been so kind to me. I like to imagine you at his age, all grown up, taking charge of a ship.

Tonight, our first night alone, the beautiful day turned into a deep blue evening that held its breath as an almost full moon rose and sprinkled what looked like fairy dust over the landscape. Pappa and I took a leisurely walk along the shore. These weeks ahead promise a respite from summer's labors and our return to the equally arduous work of the fall chores required by the farm. We're blessed.

ॐ

Kvitfiskneset
21 June 1947

Yes, we were finally alone. The try-pots no longer spewed their foul odors, the whetstone no longer screeched its dissonant music, the men no longer crowded the kitchen expecting fresh bread and soup and salve for their wounds. Summer days bled into autumn, and Astrid's morning sickness had mostly passed. There was, at last, the idyll we'd anticipated.

ॐ

30 September 1937

Dear Birk,

The turning of leaves into fiery colors of red and orange that signals fall in southern Norway is missing here. If you look closely, however, most Svalbard flora do respond to the dwindling sunlight as evidenced by the reddish brown that tinges moss and the leaves of many plants. The common saxifrage with its uncommon name—*Chrysosplenium alternifolium tetrandrum*—follows this pattern. Here's a sketch:

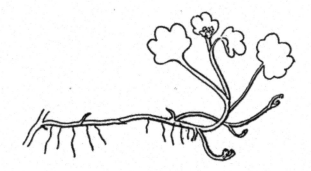

Its leaves and stems are edible, like dandelion greens. I'd added them to salads, but the crew weren't thrilled with the bitterness. Nevertheless, the flowers gave me joy, with their golden-green crowns and fragile green leaves. Now those crowns and leaves are edged with brown and soon will be dormant and covered by snow.

I'd already catalogued the saxifrage, so I passed it by and walked along a ridge I hadn't had a chance to fully explore. The ridge was covered with mountain avens, a species that, like the Arctic poppy, tracks the sun. It was a beautiful day, so I sat for a long time on a rock to watch the movement of its miniature, daisy-like flowers. I bent to pick a cluster cascading from some scree when an unusual flower farther up the ridge caught my eye. Its long, ruby-tinged green runners ended in deep yellow rosettes. The colors had faded slightly with the changing seasons, but enough of the original remained to identify what had once been quite vibrant.

I lay on the ground to record as much information *in situ* as I could, then ever so carefully, I harvested the flower, roots and all. I've tried to identify it, searching the whole of my tattered copy of *Svalbards flora* and methodically tracing the flower's attributes down the dichotomous key. The flower appears to be part of the saxifrage family. Both are five-petaled and long-stemmed, but this one is a distinctively deep gold. I've saved the seeds of this strange species in a metal canister, dried the flower, and filed it into a new herbarium. Could it be I've found that flower to name after you? My hand trembled as I etched a hopeful name underneath the specimen: *Saxifraga birkandrum*.

ॐ

Kvitfiskneset
21 June 1947

On the third of October we motored deep into Van Keulen-fjorden to check on ice conditions and to visit Nathorstbreen, the massive glacier at the fjord's base. As we proceeded east and south, the pancake ice thickened and fast ice swelled along the shore. Nearing the glacier, a frozen cul-de-sac engulfed the southern tip of the fjord. This was uncommon for early October.

Returning home, the difficulty of steering through the field of pancake ice and icebergs increased. For Astrid's sake, I feigned calm and competence. Inwardly, I was alarmed. Worse, as we progressed, the wind picked up and the sun disappeared. By the time we arrived at Kvitfiskneset, the wind had further strengthened. Anchoring the motorboat, we launched the raft, paddled to the edge of the fast ice, and waded ashore, pulling the raft behind us.

The gale that followed was like nothing I'd ever experienced. Winds gusted to hurricane force. We could hear tarpaper tearing from the exterior walls. One of the wooden shutters banged incessantly against the cabin wall. The stove emitted a foul stream of smoke and soot, signaling that debris had blocked the stovepipe. And worst of all, the radio died.

For two days, we hunkered down in the cabin, unable to light a fire for fear of suffocating on noxious fumes. We survived on fish jerky and ice-cold water. Hoarfrost covered the skins lining the walls and ceiling. We smothered ourselves in woolen blankets and polar bear hides, the warmth of our bodies a balm against the cold.

As suddenly as the storm appeared, the wind died, the clouds parted, and the sun shone to reveal the devastation the storm had wrought. The stovepipe lay horizonal, bent where it exited the roof. The radio mast wasn't only blown off its moorings but also broken into pieces, far beyond my ability to repair it. As difficult as communication with Longyearbyen had always been, further transmissions would be impossible. I told myself that the messages I'd sent—one to Marit and Christian informing them of our plans to take the October *Lyngen* and the other to the booking agent for tickets—had gone through, though I hadn't been able to confirm the transmissions. The day I sent the messages, the transmitter seemed to be working, but the receiver wasn't.

Worst of all, ice conditions had become ominous. Miraculously, the motorboat floated in the drift ice as if nothing had happened, but fast ice was increasing along the shore. The open water beyond the widening band of fast ice had turned to slush pocked by a greater number of icebergs and pancake ice. With new urgency, we prepared for departure. We pulled the Jonah rowboat to the edge of the fast ice and rowed to the motorboat, using axes and oars where necessary to clear a lane. Once aboard, I fueled, oiled, and tested the engine—it started after several failed attempts—and removed ice from the anchor line. As a precaution, we carved a wide arc in the boat to see how it would handle under the present conditions. Satisfied, we drove the boat as close to shore as we dared, leaving room for fast ice to form without trapping the boat.

Ashore again, we set about making what repairs we could and sorted through our belongings. Each day, we rowed out to the motorboat, keeping the lane clear of ice, started the boat, and circled the bay. The temperature registered below freezing, but to our good fortune, the ice remained stable.

It was on the third day that we heard the howling. On the horizon we spied dark specks coming toward us—five huskies pulling a sledge and a lone figure outlined against the mountain. As the sledge drew closer, I recognized the lead dog. King, Hilmar's favorite.

The overland routes from Sassen to Kvitfiskneset were a mystery to me as I'd traveled mostly by sea, but Hilmar had spent at least twenty-five seasons on Svalbard and navigated the islands based on his own system of fixed points, reading glacial crevasses, including lidded ones, the way one might read a map. He knew Svalbard's terrestrial geography far better than I, who'd never ventured much beyond the shores of Van Keulenfjorden and Bellsund.

The sea was my domain. I could traverse a field of ice and rocks and shoals in the same way Hilmar navigated his sledge through valleys, across glaciers and frozen fjords. Besides, I never trusted huskies. Last month, a baby in Ny-Ålesund was mauled to death by one. But Hilmar loved his dogs, especially King.

And here is King now, restored to the flesh, straining against the reins as he guides the sledge to my cabin. Hilmar arrives with a flourish, snow spray exploding from the runners and the incessant yelping of the excited animals drowning out his merry *hei, hei*. Despite having traveled a long distance, he's invigorated by the trip. He bounds off the sledge and extends his hand. His clothes show the evidence of past overwinterings: they're yellowed and replete with patches of the fur of different animals, white fox and a square or two of polar bear. Apparently Helfrid hasn't succeeded in separating Hilmar from his coat of many patches. Or the thrift is evidence of her handiwork. A Russian trapper's hat crowns his head, its earflaps pulled low so that they cover his cheeks. On his feet are what look to be woolen socks with some sort of sole composed of animal skin. Given the recent weather, he's surprisingly lightly dressed, but his countless winters here have conditioned his body to the cold.

"Welcome, welcome, *takk for sist*," I say, and call out to Astrid, "Look who's come to visit us."

Astrid emerges from the cabin, an anorak thrown over her shoulders. "Hilmar!" she says, embracing him. "And where's your darling wife?"

He laughs. "Helfrid's busy entertaining. My brother Skjølberg has come to help with the winter trapping. Helfrid persuaded her brother Albert and her friend Guri to come up as well. And my wife is spoiling Kaps. Villa Fredheim has become Hotel Fredheim this fall. You should see the cakes and breads she bakes every day!"

As evidence, he holds up a package, wrapped in brown paper and tied with string, one of her wonderful creations. Astrid takes the package from him as a fleeting frown signals her disappointment. She's been without female companionship since the wedding.

Hilmar throws each of the dogs a piece of frozen meat, which they devour in single gulps. "I heard that you two decided to stay on for a bit. I thought I'd stop by." He makes it seem as if it's no more than a casual jaunt to a next-door neighbor's. "I was out setting traps at my stations. As good an excuse as any to get some time alone."

"So how did you know we were here?"

"Knut told me you booked passage on the *Lyngen's* October sailing." The telegraph office was a hotbed of gossip, so it wasn't surprising that Knut had told Hilmar of our plans. And this was confirmation that at least one message—to the booking agent—had gone through.

"Come in, come in," Astrid says, linking her arm in Hilmar's, leaving me behind. She leans her head on his shoulder. A pang of jealousy passes through me.

Once inside, Hilmar pulls a letter, a packet of newspapers, and a deck of playing cards from his rucksack. I resist the urge to grab the papers, so eager am I for news from the mainland. We've had no word of the civil war in Spain or the ways in which European leaders were escalating that situation. The whole wide world might have fallen apart for all we knew.

Hilmar doesn't seem offended when Astrid opens the letter from her mother. I can only see the date—6 September 1937—scrawled across the top of the page in Marit's beautiful handwriting. Astrid pulls a photograph from the envelope and frowns.

"Is everything all right?" I ask.

"Fine," she says unconvincingly. "You know my mother." Then she tucks the letter into her apron pocket and hands me the photo: Birgitta, transformed in our absence from a girl with pudgy cheeks and long pigtails into a serious young woman with a severe bob framing her face.

Astrid busies herself at the stove, frying up whale steaks and stirring a pot of mashed potatoes. Hilmar doesn't notice, or pretends not to notice, the sudden tension, content to sit by the kitchen window with his well-worn deck of cards, laying out game after game of patience, giving me time to peruse the newspapers.

Finally, he breaks the silence.

"That windstorm was something," he says, pulling aside the curtains and surveying the landscape. "I was caught in Svea to wait it out. I wasn't expecting such extreme weather so early in the season."

He lets the curtains fall back in place and turns to me. "You know, Tor, you really should be heading up to Longyearbyen. Svalbard's weather is notoriously changeable, but October's especially unpredictable."

"We're ready to go. You see, Hilmar, Astrid is—"

Astrid shushes me with another look, this one fiercer than whatever news from home drove her to the stove. I cough, swallow the word *pregnant.* "Astrid's finishing her work. And it's been pleasant carving out some time alone despite the storm."

I wondered then why Astrid didn't want Hilmar to know about the baby. At the time, I assumed she didn't want to remind him of Elen and his own lost children, ghosts from so many years ago. After I read Astrid's letters, I understood that Elen and the "phantom" baby buried near Villa Fredheim weighed on her mind, not to mention the normal concerns that accompany a pregnancy and the memory of our own lost son.

The rhythmic *whoosh* of cards cascading as he shuffles them punctuates each sentence. He tells us of the latest gossip from Longyearbyen and the glass enclosure he's building at Villa Fredheim as a greenhouse. He laments that the price of fox fur has fallen. How is he to make a living under these circumstances? he asks, a momentary darkness passing over his face. Then he laughs and lays out a new game of solitaire.

"You and me both," I say, smiling despite my concern over finances. "This has been the least profitable season in all my years here."

Hilmar's game ends quickly as he's unable to make a move from any of the seven columns or the deck to the foundation piles. He sighs, shuffles again, and starts another game while I pick up a newspaper dated 23 August. "I see that there's a hunt for a missing Russian flier. Levanevsky—the Lindbergh of Russia, it says here."

"They never found him or his companions. Moscow to Fairbanks. Lost after passing the North Pole."

It's disorienting to read article after article about the missing Russian flier and the hope of his rescue while knowing the matter has already played out tragically. "Which reminds me. Did they ever find Amelia Earhart? Last we heard when we were in Longyearbyen in July was that they were searching for her, but hope was waning."

Hilmar shakes his head and sorts through the papers. "Here it is," he says, pointing to one of the headlines. He hands the paper to me.

It's a *Paris Herald Tribune*, dated 19 July, over two months ago. Astrid crosses the room and looks over my shoulder. Her English is better than mine. "'US Navy Ends Search for Miss Earhart,'" she reads. "'Earhart and Noonan are believed dead. The first woman to cross two oceans by plane. The greatest rescue effort ever undertaken for a lost plane. Her attempt to traverse the middle latitudes, a feat never before attempted. It was to be her last major flight.'"

Astrid looks up from the paper. "She almost made it."

"An intrepid woman," Hilmar says. "You have to admire that kind of will."

"Some say there was no value in the flight. Just a publicity stunt," I say. "And would they have launched such a massive search for two fishermen stranded in the Pacific?"

Astrid crosses back to the stove and flips the whale steaks. "It's not a fair comparison, I'd say."

"A life is a life. What if it were me?"

The question hangs in the air. I turn back to the headlines. "Japan still at war with China?"

"That's been the story since 1931," Hilmar says. "It's a regional conflict."

"And Spain? That war drags on?"

"Ah, that one's worrisome. Every world leader taking sides

between the Nationalists or the Republicans. So-called neutral countries. International brigades joining the civil war. Chamberlain's trying to appease Hitler and Mussolini. Italy's outfitting warships. The Nazis are building concentration camps for political prisoners. It doesn't take a fortune-teller to see where all this is heading."

Hilmar sighs. Another game of patience has come to an unsuccessful end. He gathers up the cards, stacks them neatly, and puts them aside. "I'm sorry I brought you bad news. We're better off in the dark. We're better off here, isolated from it all."

"Let's hope Norway remains neutral," Astrid says. She places heaping plates of mashed potatoes and whale steaks before us.

As we eat, the sun sets, and the kitchen grows dark. Astrid lights the oil lamp that rests in the middle of the table. The flickering of light and shadow flutters across her face like sea waves. The warm glow the lamp casts wards off the eerie spell we've created with talk of dead pilots and war. I can see her again in that lamplight, and it's hard to reconcile that peaceful moment with what came after. The Anschluss took Austria by force. Germany invaded Norway. King Haakon escaped to England. My friend Einar was killed in action trying to liberate Svalbard. Concentration camps proved more than holding pens for political prisoners. On and on.

We clear the plates as Hilmar shuffles his cards and lays them out. "So when are you leaving here to meet the *Lyngen?*"

"Soon," I tell him.

He looks at me, puzzled. "Don't let the sudden clearing mislead you. Ice can be tricky. Last year, the north was frozen in by the first week of September. And I was already able to drive the sledge over solid ice—"

I make a cutting motion across my neck to silence him. Astrid's back is turned, bent over the basin washing dishes. Hilmar resumes turning up cards from the deck and lining up the successful ones in neat vertical columns, alternating red and black, eight of hearts, seven of spades, six of diamonds, five of clubs. Aces and kings turn up early, so that he can move cards to the foundation piles. I cross the kitchen to help with the dishes.

He looks up from his game for a moment. "I can take Astrid up to Longyearbyen, just in case," he says.

"In case of what?"

"In case—"

"No," Astrid says. "We'll be fine."

"She's caught the Spitsbergen mania," Hilmar says.

I cast Hilmar a sharp look, not wanting to rekindle the sour mood. Hilmar returns to his game, places the last of his cards, the king of hearts, on the foundation pile, rubs his hands together. A win.

"Spitsbergen mania, ha! Not the worst thing that could happen to a woman," Astrid says. "Or a man, for that matter. You and Tor have a touch of it yourselves. Why else would you come here year after year if not for some bizarre addiction to this frozen world?"

We invite Hilmar to spend the night, and he readily accepts. While Astrid prepares a kitchen bunk with a fresh blanket and a polar bear skin, Hilmar tells a story about Russian trappers murdered in Hornsund back in 1818. Like most of Hilmar's stories, I've heard this one before. Again, I try to warn him off the story with a look, but he's gazing out the window into the almost moonless night. As the story unfolds, Astrid lights two more oil lamps though it's time for bed. It's as if she's trying to ward off the ghosts that Hilmar has conjured. The light brightens the kitchen but doesn't drive away the spell he's cast.

I remember that night. Astrid was especially restless. In the quiet dark, I held her tight.

The next morning, Hilmar readied his sledge, the dogs harnessed through the reins, one behind the other. Without so much as a ho!, the team bounded forward, carrying Hilmar over the ice-covered landscape. We held hands until Hilmar disappeared, until the last of his cries, commanding his huskies right and left around curves and over dips, faded away.

ॐ

9 October 1937

Dear Birk,

Pappa insisted on taking me deep into Van Keulenfjorden to see Nathorstbreen. What a magnificent glacier! Even from the distance that the fast ice forced upon us, the glacier's wall towered above as the sun glinted off its face. The journey back to the cabin proved treacherous. As if to spite us, the weather changed suddenly. The sun disappeared, the wind rose, and sleet pelted the wheelhouse. Pappa navigated the ice field expertly, guiding the boat home. We barely made it inside the cabin when a gale was upon us. For the next two days, the windstorm raged. We'd closed and latched the window shutters, but one parlor shutter broke free, and banged open and closed for hours during the worst of the wind until it tore away. Apprehensive, we waited, spooning under mountains of blankets and skins as the temperature inside fell below freezing. We wondered if the cabin would be lifted from the very ground and hurled against the mountains. Maybe even blown to Oz.

Just as suddenly as the storm erupted, it cleared. What a relief! Outside, we surveyed the damage. The massive logs that held our home in place had weathered the worst of the gale, but several of the wooden strips that secured the tarpaper had loosened, and the tarpaper itself was shredded in places. The window shutter was nowhere to be found, the stovepipe lay twisted along the roof, and the radio mast had broken to pieces. Thank goodness Pappa had already sent messages to Mormor and Farfar and the booking agent relaying our plans.

We felt fortunate that the cabin itself was intact. It could have been so much worse. Repairs took us the past three days. The exterior is a crazy quilt of wood, tarpaper, and animal skins battened down with nails. I swear the skins warm the interior. Why has no one thought of a fur-covered hut before?

Then yesterday, a surprise! Hilmar paid us a visit. That he made it here safely overland during the storm—negotiating several frozen straits across the fjords that separate Sassen from Kvitfiskneset—heartened me. Here was proof that we weren't completely cut off from the outside world.

Hilmar brought with him a pile of newspapers and a letter from Mormor. It might have been better to be cut off from the outside world. As the evening progressed, the letter, the men's talk of war, and the ghosts Hilmar left in his wake revived my disquiet. After he left, I reread your grandmother's letter. Mormor had tucked a photo of Birgitta inside the envelope. In the few short months we've been away, she's changed. Her face has taken on an entirely different aspect. Her smile is gone, her beautiful blond hair cut into a severe bob that frames an un-characteristically solemn expression. Mormor says the haircut was Birgitta's idea. And then she reveals the biggest surprise of all, that Birgitta's now a "woman." I've missed that milestone. I never expected her to cross that threshold so early. My mind fills with all the advice I want to give her.

The broken mast makes sending a return message impossi-ble. Where is Halvard when you need him? I'm afraid Birgitta must think I've forgotten her. I added her photo to the gallery of family pictures, tucked the letter into its envelope, then picked up one of the newspapers and scanned the headlines.

"War, war, war." I opened the stove door and shoved the paper in.

Pappa was suddenly behind me. "What are you doing?" he asked, snatching the rest of the newspapers from my hands. "We'll know soon enough the state of the world."

"You don't have to look at them then. But indulge me. I promise not to share war news with you." Pappa shook his head and stacked the newspapers on a high shelf, out of my easy reach.

He paused. "Why did you keep the pregnancy from Hilmar?"

The newspaper shriveled to embers before I replied. "All those stories full of death," I said. "The lost aviators. Hitler's hate-filled propaganda. The carnage in Spain. I didn't want to bring our new life into it."

That's what I told Pappa. He had to know this was a lie. Talk of war and the ghost stories came later in the evening, after I'd silenced him. But did I know why I was reluctant to share the news of my pregnancy? Was it denial when yesterday morning I felt the first real stirring in my womb? Was it this anxiety I can't seem to shake?

What invaded my dreams that night was the story Hilmar told us at the very end of the evening while I made up a bunk for him to spend the night.

"Well, you see, it happened like this."

Pappa gave him a look, trying to ward off its telling, but Hilmar was staring at his reflection in the window and missed the warning. Here's the story he told:

In the winter of 1818, some Russian hunters traveled to Hornsund to hunt walrus. They never returned to the motherland. Two years later, Norwegian whalers discovered a deserted settlement on the beach and what was left of thirteen corpses buried in shallow graves. As the years passed, a legend grew up around the deaths of these Russian hunters, but no one knew what had happened to them until a Norwegian captain named Stuer chanced upon the site. In the debris that littered the camp was a harpoon with the name Andersen engraved upon it. Andersen, he knew, was the captain of another ship that traveled the Arctic waters. When he returned to mainland Norway, he confronted the man, who denied that he had anything to do with the fate of the Russian hunters. He only admitted to hunting walrus on the same site and claimed to have left the harpoon behind.

Andersen was rattled, however, and became obsessed with getting rid of Stuer. His chance came not too long after when the two ships were hunting walrus in the same area, and Stuer departed his ship alone in a rowboat to scout walrus. Andersen sabotaged Stuer's ship and, when it appeared to be sinking, rescued its passengers. He assumed Stuer was lost.

Unfortunately for Andersen, Stuer made it back to his ship and repaired the damage. He returned to Tromsø to reveal Andersen's crimes. Before justice could be served, Andersen set sail to avoid punishment. According to those aboard his ship, the murderer took his vessel too far into the ice and became trapped. He climbed high up onto an iceberg, hoping to find a lead that would allow safe passage. And to prove there is divine justice, the iceberg suddenly calved. Unbalanced, it tipped over, casting Andersen into the water, whereupon the ice closed over him. He was never seen again.

That story gave me chills. As if that weren't enough, Hilmar told us that this story is what gave birth to *Ishavet kaller* and the madness that overtakes some Arctic dwellers. The parlor grew so dark that the single oil lamp threw eerie, wavering shadows on the wall. Though it was time for sleep, I lit two more lamps. My hands shook, and lighting the wicks was a challenge.

Hilmar and Pappa seemed puzzled by my actions.

"Time for bed," Pappa said, turning down the wicks.

I forced a smile. "To drive away the ghosts," I said, turning the knobs back up.

"She's right." Hilmar laughed. "Drive away those ghosts who overwintered and wandered into the sea, never to be heard from again. Who'll rise from their graves seven weeks before Christmas—"

"Stop!" I said, raising both hands in front of my face as if warding off a blow. I didn't want the baby further subjected to the talk of death and ghosts and souls disappeared into nothingness. Right then, a quickening. Too late.

る

Kvitfiskneset
21 June 1947

It was as if Hilmar's warning controlled the weather. Soon after his departure, temperatures plummeted, fog obscured the landscape, and the wind returned in force, shrieking its alarms.

So fierce were the gusts that I was reduced to retrieving wood and ice from the barrels outside on my hands and knees. Once again, we were trapped.

The *Lyngen* was to sail in a matter of days, and here we were, huddled inside, hardly able to move. Every three hours, I opened the front door and shoveled a path through the drifting snow while Astrid, rifle at the ready, kept watch for polar bears. Visibility was poor in the swirling snow, and I could only hope that if a bear came upon us, she'd have quick enough reflexes to shoot.

What little daylight was left rapidly shrank in on itself, as if time were compressing to a pinpoint. Ten hours of light faded into nine, eight, seven as the days passed. I began to worry about our prospects for a successful trip to Longyearbyen. Our aborted excursion to Nathorstbreen should have been fair warning. Fast ice widened further along the shores of Van Keulenfjorden, and drift ice clogged the bay. Ever the optimist, I thought that if I could make it through the narrow strait where Van Keulenfjorden spilled into Bellsund, the rest of the route to Longyearbyen would be relatively smooth. The sailing charts indicated that Bellsund would remain navigable till at least the end of October. I'd negotiated drift ice before, though my motorboat wasn't the ideal vessel to plow such hazards. I knew that the cold itself could wreak havoc on the engine, and that without a radio, we had no way of sending a distress call in an emergency.

What choice did I have? If we were to make the sailing, we had to leave. I kept my misgivings to myself. Why needlessly burden Astrid? Besides, wasn't I a master of nature, taming it for my purposes and desires, exploiting its bounty? I'd built a station from nothing. I didn't consider myself part of nature but above it.

Such conceit. Ice can outsmart the most experienced sailor. Weather and luck decide almost everything on Svalbard.

We pared our belongings to the essentials we could carry in two rucksacks—binoculars, two blankets, extra clothing, some biscuits and jerky. Reluctantly, Astrid left behind her wedding dress, but she insisted we carry the new herbarium and the tin of unknown seeds.

"It's what I came to Svalbard for," she said.

I could hardly argue. Her pack was full, but I had a little room for them in mine. She watched me slide the folio into my rucksack, saying "careful, careful," then handed me the seeds. She held her breath while I secreted them in a small pocket, which buttoned closed. "Safe," I said, patting the pocket.

"Thank you," she said, and smiled, and kissed me on the cheek. "Thank you for everything." There was a world contained in those simple words.

The weather was promising when we departed on 13 October. Not an auspicious day to begin such a journey, but at least it wasn't a Friday. And at the time, I wasn't thinking of superstitions. I was thinking of getting home.

The sky lightened at eight. We had six hours of daylight ahead, enough time to cover the 140 kilometers from Kvitfiskneset to Longyearbyen. We motored into Van Keulenfjorden, Astrid on the lookout for ice hazards. As we made our way toward Bellsund, the current began to drive drift ice together, forming larger floes that I knew might coalesce into impassable pack ice. Then, as if to mock us, the weather gods stirred the winds. Far across the water, on the north side of Bellsund, stratus clouds gathered over Ingeborgfjellet. Gradually, they formed an unbroken layer that blotted out the sun. Worse, there was no water sky, those blue-gray reflections on the low clouds that would indicate open water ahead. Instead, the yellowish luminosity near the horizon, ice blink, revealed what I feared—an unbroken expanse of ice.

Next, the clouds themselves disappeared as the mist descended further and surrounded us. We couldn't see more than a few meters ahead. *No problem*, I thought. *The compass will guide our way.* I checked our position and noticed only then that the needle was hardly moving even as I steered the boat in vastly different directions. The trouble: tiny beads of moisture had infiltrated the glass housing and frozen along the metal needle.

I should have noticed the broken compass sooner. Again conceit. Who needs a compass when one knows the seas by heart? If worse came to worst, I could navigate according to the direction of the waves. This time, the ice and dense fog rendered such navigation impossible. We crept forward, progress slowed to a crawl as I wove through each lead in turn. The openings would narrow, close, and I'd have to back up to find another route.

I'd been hugging the fast ice along the coastline because, if compelled to lay anchor, we could cross it to shore. The fast ice tongued farther and farther into the bay, forcing me to steer farther and farther away from the shore. More than once I thought to anchor the boat and make our way over the ice. But I worried that the boat would be crushed if left moored in the ice field.

Ultimately, the decision was made for us. The engine sputtered. I opened the hatch to the engine compartment and discovered that the oil had become sludge. We sat motionless as the lead closed around us. I couldn't see a way in or out.

The temperature fell. The wind picked up.

As well as I knew that fjord, the fog had turned the landscape into an undifferentiated mass of white. How close were we to land? I tried the motor. Once, twice, three times. I whispered, "Start, start." Nothing. Might the motor restart if we gave it time, or should we risk traversing the ice? I hid my alarm from Astrid. I assumed she understood our predicament for she'd stopped talking.

"We should head to shore," I said, as calmly as I could. "We aren't that far from where we started. We'll secure the boat, return to the station, and try again when the weather improves. Worst case, we'll catch the last *Lyngen* departure in November."

Astrid nodded.

A narrowing lead had pushed the boat against the fast ice. I cast anchor to keep the boat in place, retrieved an axe from the boat's storage compartment, and climbed down the ladder onto the ice. To test its solidity, I brought the axe head down hard again and again. It seemed stable.

"There's an augur and mooring rod in that same compartment," I said. "Can you get those?"

Astrid found the tools and handed them to me. I drilled a hole in the ice and inserted the rod into it.

"Now for the mooring line."

I lashed the line to the mooring rod and tied it securely. She handed me the rucksacks and a pair of oars to use as walking sticks and climbed out of the boat.

"Will you be okay?" I asked.

"I'm fine," she insisted.

True, she'd been walking every day, through the valleys and along the precipitous paths by crags and glaciers and up into the hills. But this terrain was different. What lay before us was a maze filled with narrow ridges and hummocks, some three meters high, where floes had crashed into each other. The ice field was a scaled-down imitation of the mountainous landscape that hemmed us in on the landward side. With packs slung over our shoulders and using the oars for stability, we tried to discern through the fog the least arduous route across the ice and through jagged hollows between the hummocks.

And just as the shoreline loomed, just when we thought we were safe, a terrible crack sounded an alarm as a lead opened between us. I'd fallen on my ass and scrambled backward from the expanding lead, but Astrid had been caught on the newly formed floe. I watched in horror as she pinwheeled her arms to catch herself. The floe undulated in the turbulent water, and the movement sent her sliding into the sea. Seconds passed, but it seemed like an eternity. I laid my pack on the ice and stripped off my parka and sweater, intending to rescue her.

Incredibly, Astrid surfaced right in front of me.

I knelt, grabbed her arms, and dragged her up onto the ice. Her anorak was soaked, so I removed it and covered her in mine. Rooting through my rucksack, I pulled out dry clothing and a blanket. Astrid was shaking too violently to dress herself. I knelt to help her. It was then I realized her rucksack was missing.

Our ordeal wasn't over. As we crouched together, I caught my breath and took stock of our surroundings. The fog alternated between a solid white wall and an occasional clearing as the wind blew across the landscape. In one of those clearings, I noticed that the boat remained anchored to the floe that had broken away. I hoped that I'd be able to rescue it, assuming by some miracle it remained attached to the mooring and the shifting floes didn't crush it.

The fog lifted once again so that I could glimpse the mountains that indicated we were close to shore. I retrieved a small coil of rope from my pack and tied a length of it to my waist and another to Astrid's. In this way, if one of us fell through the ice again, the rope might save us. Or we'd drown together. I peeled off as much ice as I could from her anorak and clothing and stuffed everything into the rucksack. "Ready?" I asked.

She nodded. I pulled her to her feet, but standing there, she wobbled. I caught her, slung my pack around to my chest, and hoisted her to straddle my back. The ice was slippery, and I regretted not having crampons to gain a better foothold. Who knew we'd be crossing an ice field on foot? Likewise, I regretted not bringing a rifle, but again, who knew we'd need one for a short boat trip?

I followed a break between the hummocks. Ice gave way to snow sprouting dead vegetation that revealed we were, finally, safe on land. We found cover in the lee of a small outcropping of rock. I spread out a dry blanket, and Astrid lay there while I gathered driftwood and arranged it in a pile. I lit the kindling with matches we'd thought to bring. The wood caught slowly and warmed us. We ate hard biscuits and sucked on pieces of glacier ice to quench our thirst.

Sunday Christian that Astrid accused me of being, hypocrite that I am, I prayed right then to God to keep the bears away. The prayer was from my childhood, one that my mother and I recited most nights after she tucked me in bed.

Guardian Angel, keep me safe
Till earth's days are past

When blossoms fade and
Time is fleeting fast
In times of purest joy
Or pain and fear
Guardian Angel guard me
And keep me safe.

I hadn't realized I was praying aloud until Astrid joined in. We recited the prayer again, in unison, and concluded with a resounding "amen" that carried across the fjord and back, echoing in the otherwise soundless air.

❧

21 October 1937

Dear Birk,

Bubbles. Silvery bubbles. Blown glass.

That's what I saw when I closed my eyes.

Bubbles of air trapped in the ice.

My life didn't flash before me in those seconds. Rather, two images flowed by in succession as I peered up through the translucent ceiling of ice—iridescent bubbles rising into the air at the Sandefjord dock and then the cells of a saxifrage stem I'd examined under a microscope long ago.

Pappa told me of belugas who dive deep and become caught under the ice. I was the beluga, nosing the ceiling, tracing patterns of bubbles, looking for a way out. Funny how the mind works. You were trapped under the dock. I was trapped under the ice. I had no idea where the ice edge was. Mere seconds it took for the ice to open and swallow me. Underwater, the world was silent except for the erratic sounds of bubbles. Did you slip under as I did? What did you feel as water replaced air in your lungs? Somehow, you'd turned yourself upside down so that top was bottom and bottom top. There was no sky, no sun to guide you.

My mind reeled. I thought briefly of joining you. How easy that would have been! But then I thought of Birgitta and the wisdom I'd yet to impart. I thought of the new life growing in me, a soul I'd once considered not considering. Only then did I realize I was being pulled down by the pack slung across my shoulders. I managed to free myself. I had to find the floe's edge, but which way was it? There were no white pebbles laid down to lead me out of this forest of ice.

What I remember—the clink and ping of silvery bubbles floating free.

A shaft of murky light penetrated the water near me. I swam toward it and surfaced right in front of Pappa. Panic was written all over his face, as if he'd already lost me. *Good*, I thought. *Now he knows how I felt when the rescue diver found you under the dock and lifted your lifeless body onto the pier.*

How long was I under? Pappa says seconds, but it felt like an eternity.

He heaved me up, up, up. Stripped off my wet parka, dressed me in dry clothes, and piggybacked me across the ice. I've never felt so cold, not even that night of my Midsummer plunge. I drifted in and out. Suddenly there was a fire blazing next to me.

Feeling returned to my fingers, my toes. Stabbing pain.

I turned toward the flames. A patch of snow softened, melted. Water ran in rivulets only to freeze again as soon as it escaped the fire's glow.

I wrote in the snow, *I'm safe.*

I saved myself.

I joined Pappa in prayer. Guardian angels and amen. Amen. The words melted away.

છ

Kvitfiskneset
21 June 1947

The fog lifted before dusk. Taking my bearings, I discovered that we were on the southern shore of Fleur de Lyshamna near Pitnerodden, six kilometers from the whaling station. So little progress we'd made! I used binoculars to scan the horizon for our motorboat and saw that it was tethered to the floe. If by some miracle the ice cooperated, we'd be able to make the return journey by boat. If not, it was a manageable walk. Darkness was fast approaching. Whichever means we chose, we'd have to wait till morning to return to Kvitfiskneset.

Nearby, I recalled, was a hunter's cabin long since abandoned in which I'd once taken refuge. The hut would provide shelter, and if island tradition held, we'd find canned goods to supplement our meager provisions, now reduced by half on account of the lost rucksack. Huddling overnight under the outcropping as the temperature dropped was out of the question. Let alone encountering bears.

Astrid had recovered from her icy plunge. Once again, I hoisted my rucksack and, in that moment, with everything else we had to consider, a ridiculous thought crossed my mind—we'd saved Astrid's herbarium and her precious seeds. Yes, at least there was that.

We hugged the shoreline, heading south, and within a quarter hour came upon the cabin as full dark set in and a half-moon rose. The cabin was a shack, barely large enough for the wooden bunk and stove inside. The door sat askew on its hinges so that a slice of wind blew steadily from its open crack. The single window was shattered, and its shutters banged steadily against the outside walls. But seal blubber stored in repurposed tins and driftwood stowed in a large barrel would keep us warm and the shelter would keep us safe.

I secured the shutters, cleared the ventilation pipe, and arranged wood in the stove's belly. "Please, God," I whispered as I struck a match and lit the fire. God waved his magic wand, and the stove refrained from belching a stream of smoke.

Fog returned that night. Sleet pelted the cabin. Another small miracle: we were dry and out of the weather. We spooned under well-worn skins, wearing all of our clothing.

It wasn't until the next morning that I discovered Astrid's injury. She'd severely bruised her right leg when she fell through the ice. The numbing cold had masked her pain, but by the morning, she was hobbling. At first, she insisted she could walk.

To prove the injury was nothing, she started for the door. Every step was a trial. It was clear we'd have to wait for her to heal.

As if to mock us, the weather turned pleasant, favoring us with the pink-crusted sunrise of mid-October. There was food enough in the cabin, canned beans and pemmican, biscuits hardened to rock that I softened with hot water, tea and coffee, condensed milk, oats. A feast.

Each day I iced Astrid's injury and boiled oats and fried pemmican for our meals. The skies stayed clear, but the temperatures plummeted. A rusty thermometer nailed to the cabin's siding read below zero Celsius.

For two days I used my binoculars to check on the boat and found it bobbing across a wide lead. But on the third day, the boat was gone. The ragged remains of its small wheelhouse perched on the floe, but the hull had vanished. I knew then that we were stranded.

I couldn't bear to tell Astrid the truth. Instead, I told her that too many leads had opened between the shore and the boat to retrieve it, so we'd have to walk back to the whaling station. I thought she'd better reconcile herself to our predicament once we were settled there. The walk would give me time to figure out a plan for our survival. I wanted to put off as long as possible telling her both about the boat and that the message to her parents might not have gone through. And yet if the message had gone through, wouldn't they and the *Lyngen*'s crew assume we'd been lost at sea when we didn't arrive for the October sailing? Or might someone come look for us? Surely Hilmar would hear we were missing and come to investigate? I even had lofty notions of an icebreaker rescuing us, or air reconnaissance scouring the landscape for us. Ha! We weren't an Earhart or Levanevsky, just two ordinary citizens.

These thoughts and more weighed on my mind as we made our way back to the station, mostly in silence, two days later. We spied several polar bears far out on the ice, too busy with seals to care about our presence. Nevertheless, we remained wary, knowing how fast those beasts were.

Astrid seemed wise to the source of my silence. As we passed by the station's broken antenna, she asked how her parents had responded to my message.

I was caught. Not wanting to lie outright, I shook my head.

"They didn't acknowledge?"

I shook my head again. "I...they..."

She gritted her teeth, took a deep breath, and scanned the bay. Temperatures had climbed to the freezing mark and the pack ice had reverted to drift ice. The bay seemed navigable again. Thus, my final deception was revealed.

"At least we have the boat," she said.

For a third time, I shook my head. I was able to utter one word. "Sunk."

"But you said—"

"Crushed by the ice."

She gasped, cradled her belly. "And when were you planning to tell me?"

"I'm hoping someone will come looking—"

"How would they know? Where would they look? We could be anywhere between here and Longyearbyen. And if they'd come looking for us at the whaling station, we'd have been gone."

All thoughts I'd had myself. "There's time. Maybe Hilmar—"

She shook her head. Panting, her words came in broken phrases. "How could you...have risked so much...for those extra weeks...of whaling? How...will my parents cope...thinking we're...dead? How...will we...get home? And the baby..."

She started sobbing, unable to speak. I held her, tried to soothe her with platitudes. "There, there. We'll find a way."

She pushed me away and slapped my cheek. I grabbed her wrist, harder than I meant to, then let go. She turned, stormed into the cabin, into our bedroom, and locked the door behind her.

For hours afterward I sat at the kitchen table, absentmindedly shuffling the deck of cards Hilmar had left behind. That slap resounded in my mind. Anger had gotten the best of Astrid, and I deserved that anger for lying. In waves of self-pity, however, I kept thinking *we*—*we* risked, *we* decided to stay on. Try as I might, I couldn't think of a solution to our predicament. I sat there toting up what we had in our favor. Food, clothing, shelter. Rifles, ammunition. Lamps, coal, and whale oil. A working stove. Likewise, I toted up the other side of the ledger. Depleted provisions. Firewood in desperate need of replenishment. Polar night imminent. And worst of all, even if we *did* survive until the ice broke up in the spring, how would we get to Longyearbyen without a boat or a radio to ask for help?

Just getting through the winter would be a miracle. I'd lived through that single dark season in Longyearbyen, but the town's relative comforts didn't prevent me from struggling mentally, counting the days until the sun's return. The tricks those sunless days play on the mind! Then there were the polar bears and the ungodly weather. On top of all that, caring for the pregnancy complicated matters. Giving birth, even in a modern hospital, had its own set of difficulties. I hadn't been allowed in the delivery room when Birgitta and Birk were born, but how different could that be than delivering an animal? Hadn't I birthed calves and pigs, horses, dogs, and cats? Had that experience given me false confidence when I was contemplating the unlikely possibility of overwintering with my pregnant wife? Was I prepared to deliver the baby alone?

I felt overwhelmed. It took all my resolve to cook a pot of porridge. Astrid refused to leave the bedroom. I left a bowl of oats by the door and knocked softly to let her know supper was served.

Worried that the closed bedroom door would block the heat from the stove, I slept fitfully on the kitchen bunk, rising every hour to feed the fire. In the middle of the night, I checked the outdoor thermometer. It registered just below the freezing mark. The kitchen grew so warm that I began to sweat. I willed the heat to penetrate the bedroom door, and in any case, I consoled myself that there were plenty of skins and woolen blankets to keep Astrid from freezing.

Toward morning, I fell fast asleep and woke to a fire burned down to embers. The kitchen had grown cold. I bolted out of bed and stoked the fire, then ran to the bedroom door. In my haste, I overturned the congealed bowl of oats, which hadn't been touched.

This couldn't go on. I pounded on the door, called Astrid's name. No answer. I considered breaking down the door but thought better of it.

I took a deep breath and said in the calmest voice I could muster, "We need to talk."

Again, I waited for a response. When she didn't answer, I said, "I'm sorry. I'm sorry I got us into this. I should have said something sooner about the boat and the message."

I heard the bed boards creak. She was alive, awake, listening. Finally, I said, "I'm sorry I lied."

I heard footsteps. The door opened a crack. Astrid's eyelids were puffy, her eyes red. She'd wrapped herself in a reindeer skin. "I'm sorry. I'm sorry I hit you." She looked at her offending hand and squeezed it tight, as if she could force it to unslap me. Then she sighed. "I agreed to stay on. Not everything's your fault."

Then she opened the reindeer skin and enveloped me in its warmth. I smoothed her hair and kissed her forehead. We held each other like that for quite a while.

I'd tucked away the Saami bracelet with its four good-luck charms meant to safeguard childbirth and childhood. Admittedly, I didn't much credit the goddesses' powers. I was saving the gift for Christmas, but we needed all the luck we could get. I retrieved the bracelet from my rucksack, knelt before her, and fastened it around her wrist.

"Where did this come from?" she asked, fingering the antler charms.

"Longyearbyen," I said. "While you were at the church."

"Another secret you kept from me," she said, but she smiled and kissed me on top of my head.

I named the goddesses, touching each charm in turn.

"Maderakka, the goddess of childbirth. Her daughters, Sarakka, Uksakka, Juksakka, who watch over the child from conception onward."

"Spirits," she said. "Let's hope *they* know where we are."

I laughed, stood up, and kissed her again. We'd brought our world back into balance, at least for the moment.

◈

24 October 1937

Dear Birk,

We're trapped at the whaling station. Without a boat or a working radio, we're cut off from civilization. Would that we had one of Andrée's pigeons!

Your father is paralyzed by our misfortune. At first, he seemed resolved to our situation. He dug through new-fallen snow to unearth the broken radio mast, then leaned on his shovel and stared at the pieces as if he could put them back together through sheer force of will.

Now he sits for hours at the kitchen table staring out the window and murmuring under his breath. Someone's bound to come looking for us, he says. I'll fix the mast, he says. And strangest of all—I should have fed whale bladders to the sea. He repeats these lines over and over, like an incantation to the spirits. Was he losing his mind? I could hardly afford that. His withdrawal doubled my feelings of isolation and loneliness. I tried to console him. Who could have anticipated what's befallen us? I told him.

We do have a small supply of meat stored in the shed, but not enough to get us through the winter. The law bans reindeer hunting, but the governor would understand our plight. Besides, who's to know? Curious how I can justify breaking some laws while holding Pappa to account for killing that mother whale.

I want to believe in the possibility of rescue. When we failed to arrive in Longyearbyen to meet the *Lyngen*, wouldn't it have raised alarms? That's what I keep telling myself. Then again, where would our saviors have searched? The ice-filled waters that separate us from the town? A bigger boat could make it from Longyearbyen to Kvitfiskneset, assuming someone cares to look. The two of us, insignificant in the scheme of things. If by chance rescuers came while we were nursing my injury at Fleur de Lyshamna, they would have found the whaling station abandoned, our boat gone, and presumed the worst.

What most troubles me is that Mormor and Farfar and Uncle Johan must be sick with worry or believe we're dead. Have they telegraphed Longyearbyen to inquire as to our whereabouts and received the devastating news that we never arrived for the October sailing? And what have they told Birgitta? Are they soothing her with false hope that our return is imminent?

One small consolation is that Pappa's parents are dead. At least they're spared the anguish.

I'll admit I was harsh when I found out Pappa had lied to me that the message to your grandparents may not have gone through and that the motorboat had been crushed by the ice.

But to strike him in anger—can you ever take that back?

So too, I agreed to stay on, denying the risk we were taking against all evidence to the contrary. I knew the weather and the ice were unpredictable and the dangers—frostbite, polar bears, deadly crevasses—were all too real. I lay in bed turning these ideas over and over in my mind till I thought I was going crazy. I realized after a night of punishing Pappa with silence that the only way for us to survive was to work together. I rose from our bed, apologized, and set to work.

First, I inventoried our supplies. In doing so, I found a yellowed scrap of paper tucked under a dusty can of baked beans on one of the anteroom shelves. The paper listed necessities required for one hunter for one year. I have no idea how I missed it when I cleaned the cabin last June. But here it is, written in an anonymous hand:

200 kilos flour
18 kilos margarine
5 kilos rice
15 kilos oats

5 kilos grits
12 kilos coffee
½ kilo tea
5 bottles fruit juice
3 kilos prunes
3 kilos raisins
5 kilos dried potatoes
Salt and spices
12 boxes condensed milk
1 kilo powdered milk
15 kilos syrup
1 barrel sour milk (to prevent scurvy)

I compared this list to our remaining provisions. Thank goodness I dilly-dallied and fell behind in sending things ahead with Anders. Otherwise, we'd have to rely almost solely on what we could shoot. Here are our stores:

30 kilos flour
5 kilos margarine
5 kilos each rice and oats
7 kilos coffee
1 kilo tea
1 kilo each prunes and raisins
12 cans each of fruit, sauerkraut, and beans
1 can baked beans
2 kilos dried peas
10 kilos dried potatoes
4 kilos onions
24 cans condensed milk
2 kilos powdered milk
4 dozen eider eggs
2 kilos syrup
5 kilos sugar
10 kilos salt plus baking soda, yeast, and spices
5 kilos pemmican
2 jars lingonberry jam

4 liters vinegar
1 ham
A small supply of fish jerky, whale and seal meat
4 liters whale's blood
5 bags of coal
small barrel of whale oil

I'd also had the foresight to purchase Redoxon in Tromsø—
our good fortune that I'd not been bullied by Odd. Scurvy kills.
We have enough Vitamin C to last us for a year if it comes to
that. We could also drink the whale's blood (where on earth had
that come from?), but the thought turns my stomach.

I showed the list to Pappa, hoping that he'd see our situation
wasn't as dire as he imagined.

"All we need is meat, wood, and a decent supply of ice," I
said. "We should lay in stores before full dark sets in."

Although I was capable of killing, I handed Pappa the rifle.
A sense of purpose, I thought, *might rouse him from his stupor.*

He took the rifle and dressed in his outdoor clothing. For
the past few days, he's stood at the front door like a sentinel,
rifle butt impaled at his side. He reminded me of those metal
soldiers you played with, lined up neatly, forever frozen in at-
tentive poses. To tell the truth, I worried that he'd stay like that,
vigilant and useless, leaving me alone to cope with the chores.

These islands *are* inhabited in the winter. Coal mining com-
munities thrive in the fjords north and east of us, and hunters
are scattered all across this archipelago. We aren't alone, yet
we're so very alone. Who knows? Maybe Hilmar *will* find out
that we never arrived in Longyearbyen. Maybe he *will* come to
our rescue. Pappa's told me that Hilmar spends every Christmas
in Longyearbyen. Two months from now. Two months. Not
such a very long time. And if not at Christmas, Hilmar is sure to
be in Longyearbyen when the weather improves and hear that
we're missing. Knowing him, he won't be able to resist investi-
gating. Even Pappa said so.

Dear Birk, at least you'll not have to wait at the harbor as the
last ships from Longyearbyen sail into Oslo without us.

෨

Kvitfiskneset
21 June 1947

Foolish of me to think my years navigating between Kvitfisk-neset and Longyearbyen had prepared me for a journey by sea under any conditions.

Foolish to assume the early autumn ice and fog couldn't foil us. True, I knew the shoals and ridges, the depth of the water by feel as Hilmar knew the land. But the vagaries of ice? And in fog without a compass no less? I was no Captain Albrecht Bergersen, the famous ice pilot of Arctic waters.

Foolish to think that a few extra days here wouldn't matter, that adventure was more important than safety, that a good life can't be composed of ordinary moments.

Foolish to think at all.

I spent days torturing myself, brooding over our situation. Astrid got us through those first days back at the cabin. She collected and chopped driftwood, rolled empty barrels stored behind the cabin to the alcove by the front door, and filled them with wood and waxed canvas bags of coal. Ironically, we had plenty of empty barrels because our summer whaling yield had been so compromised.

One thing we lacked was meat. Another foolish thing, wasting whale meat. The Saami woman was right. I should have offered a piece of whale bladder to the sea for the soul of each beluga and conserved the rest for food. Then there were seals. A single seal could provide enough meat to last the winter, but they were difficult to catch under the best circumstances. Keeping them above water after you killed them was tricky. Our crew had caught only one all summer, and we'd exhausted most of that supply. Polar bears I didn't want to contemplate. I knew how to lure them. Set up wooden boxes rigged with sawed-off rifles and baited with meat. I didn't want to sacrifice one of our rifles for the purpose on the off chance a curious bear would be fooled by a morsel of whale. Arctic foxes were easier to trap, but they provided little meat and their taste was foul.

Reindeer were the ideal game. They were easily killed, and a single one would tide us over till spring. To hell with the law. For days I watched the reindeer pawing the ground for the dead vegetation that sustained them through the winter. Each day Astrid handed me the rifle and pointed to the ready source of food. Each day I put on my parka, my hat and boots, and walked outside. I found the rifle almost too heavy to bear. Astrid spied on me from the window. She could have killed the reindeer herself. I see now that she was pushing me from my paralysis. She was right to do so.

On the fifth night after our return, we were lying in bed together, spooning. I had my arms around her belly. She was fast asleep, but I was awake. Brooding. In the middle of that night, something remarkable happened. The baby turned, and a tiny bump protruded. A fist or a foot, I don't know which. I touched that bump, and it moved under my hand, circling left then right, right then left.

I whispered, "I'm here." The baby flipped again, and I cradled him in my palm.

The next morning I fetched a spare shutter to replace the missing one and nailed the shutters in place. With the view blocked, I'd no longer be tempted to sit idly by the window while Astrid worked on our very survival. Those final nails did feel odd—the bang, bang, bang sealing us in. Astrid did look momentarily disconcerted when I said, "Let's hope that keeps the bears at bay."

Not the smartest thing to say.

I drew her close to me. She'd been cooking dinner, and her hair smelled of the salty, musky odor of whale meat.

"Everything's going to be all right," I said, though I didn't believe it.

ॐ

25 October 1937

Dear Birk,

Today daylight lasted but an hour. Tomorrow the dark season begins.

And yet all is not darkness. The sky is filtered with soft clouds, their underbellies lit with a pink froth that reminded me of sugared cake frosting. That's because you insisted on pink frosting on your fourth birthday, frosting dusted with sugar crystals and dotted with tiny white meringues. The sky is lovely, if ephemeral, like frosting itself, when its sweetness provokes such bliss that fast disappears.

Outside, I scan the horizon for the kittiwakes and gulls whose calls used to greet me each morning. They dwell in the cliff-face hollows, overwintering as we are. I almost wish for a wind that would rattle our windows, spin the whetstone, whistle through the cracks in the cabin's weather-beaten boards. I might even welcome the clanging of the try-pot lids, the ripsaw of knives cutting blubber and meat from the belugas, and the crew's boisterous, off-color song.

On second thought, I don't miss those sounds, nor the men themselves. (Well, maybe Anders.) I shudder when I think of Odd. You'll be forever too young to hear the full story. Suffice it to say that he was what you'd have called a "bad man." In your world, there was a clear line between good and bad. So much easier to judge people that way.

The clouds thicken, stealing away that rosy froth.

Funny how one takes the sun for granted until its days number down to nothing. Time is strange, how slowly it passed in the days after your death, how quickly it's passing as we move toward the dark season. Will the days slow again as full dark overtakes us and there's nothing to mark time by other than Dege's insistent cuckoo?

Funny, too, how I've let the days slip by without thinking of you. Your face, your hair, the feel of your warm body against mine when you nursed or crawled into our bed after a

bad dream—all fade from my memory. I open the gold locket around my neck, touch the tiny photo of you, and stroke
the lock of your blond hair secreted there. These relics aren't
enough to conjure the whole of you, but they're all I have. What
remains is the slightest ghost of your softly rounded cheeks,
your stubby fingers, images that aren't enough to blot out that
last fading picture of you on the dock, chasing bubbles. Your
hand reaching up to touch them.

I turned away just for a moment.

Such a simple thing to turn away.

Does Pappa wonder why I never speak of you? Should I
confess that there were days when your demands left me numb?
Your sticky fingers, middle-of-the-night awakenings, and nursing, yes, that nurturing in which other women find deep comfort but I sometimes saw as parasitic? I'd hoped that time away
would give me perspective, recharge me so that I might return
home renewed in my desire to be a good mother, the kind of
mother my own mother is, however flawed. Capable of keeping
her children alive, at least.

Instead, I find myself alternately dreading and anticipating
the coming dark, alone with Pappa, a return to the time before
you, before Birgitta, when heat characterized our marriage,
when there was no shame in a midday tryst, without worrying
that a child might burst through the bedroom door with some
trivial trauma—a scratch on the knee or feelings hurt by careless words. Pappa amused as I swallowed my anger.

But then my selfish heart breaks for Birgitta and Mormor
and Farfar. It's almost too much to bear.

᷉

Kvitfiskneset
21 June 1947

Does Pappa wonder why I never speak of you?

Of course I wondered. I'd see her fingering the locket she never
took off, a necklace now buried in the deep. The gesture showed

that Birk was never far from her thoughts. He was never far from mine either. But I thought *not* talking about the tragedy of his drowning would somehow heal the grief and guilt.

Looking out at the fjord through the icy rain, I imagine what it would have been like to have Birk with me on these very shores. He'd be sixteen now, the same age as Kaps was back in 1937. Poor Kaps. Rumor has it that he has his own demons suppressed with alcohol. Who can blame him? Might Birk have succumbed to the same demons?

I shake off such thoughts. Instead, I conjure the man Birk might have become. Would he have loved science as Astrid had? Would he have come to hate the slaughter of whales as she did? Would he have judged me for my part in that carnage? These questions sharpen my pain.

The cuckoo cuckoos three times. Wrapped up in Astrid's letters and my musings, I'm letting the day get away from me. But curiously, the less I do and the quieter I am, the more I come to understand what happened. One thing I've discovered is that grief and guilt arrive in waves, lapping at the conscience, advancing and receding. Sometimes these waves seem as powerful as those first currents when shock was the only protection against anguish. Certainly, there were thoughts better left unsaid and deeds better left hidden in the long dark.

But we should have talked. We should have held each other. I should have sworn that I didn't blame her for Birk's death. I should have…no. The clock can't be turned back, the cuckoo put back in its cage, the little boy freed from his frozen wave. Alive again.

Why weep into the sea?

DARK SEASON

Dark season. What a fitting name for the polar winter, but also for the darkness that envelops us in our most difficult times. As we entered the dark season far to the north, Birgitta and Marit and Christian waited for us to arrive at the Oslo dock. Astrid's parents never received our message, but Anders had sent word to them that we'd be on the *Lyngen*'s October sailing.

"We watched until the very last passenger disembarked," Birgitta later told me. "We made the steward check and recheck the ship's manifest. Mormor and Farfar stood there staring blankly. That was the beginning of our own dark season."

Afterward, they went to the telegraph office and sent a message to Longyearbyen to see if they'd had word from us. Knut cabled back that the only message to come through weeks ago was the order for passage on the *Lyngen*. Nor was he receiving any signal from Kvitfiskneset. This wasn't uncommon, he reassured them. Svalbard had suffered unusually severe windstorms that may have brought down the whaling station's antenna. And the weather had been colder than usual, he said, the southwestern fjords iced in earlier than usual, making a trip from the whaling station challenging if not impossible.

Thus, they had all manner of reason to hope that we were merely stranded on Kvitfiskneset and would make it out when the weather allowed.

Deep down, Birgitta told me, she had a feeling we were alive. She had a sixth sense about such things. Astrid's parents weren't as optimistic. Whether he believed it or not, Christian tried to reassure Marit that we were alive. She wasn't persuaded. I'm convinced that in their darkest season, the seeds of her cancer were planted.

&

26 October 1937

Dear Birk,

This is the day that night begins. The dark season, they call it. The sky looks as if it's been covered in a gray blanket, creating a world too small for itself, a claustrophobic world without exit. Today Pappa snapped out of his lethargy and ended his vigil by the parlor window. Guess what chore he tackled first? Nailing the shutters closed! The boarded-up windows do keep the wind out and provide an extra measure of protection against polar bears. Nevertheless, as he hammered the shutters into place, I couldn't help but liken the sound to nails securing a coffin lid. Our wooden sarcophagus.

This cabin wasn't designed for overwintering, but here we are. We've insulated every surface with a layer of animal skins to keep out as much wind and cold as possible. We're like Jonah swallowed by the whale, except the skins are outside in. Reconciling myself to being trapped weighs on the mind. What we've saved and what we can obtain from the environment—wood, water, meat, furs—must be enough.

I depend on staying well. The thought that one of us might need a doctor, well, that's something I dismiss as soon as it enters my head. I resolve to be like the women who've come before me, who've overwintered without succumbing to superstition or fear. I'm not the first to bear a child here.

And undoubtedly, children find strength in fending for themselves. Birgitta's tears will be her strength. I have more to do than raise her and tend the dead. You must understand, dear Birk. Had you lived, I might have felt differently, might have let my life be consumed by the everyday. I realize now that I let my dreams fade waiting for Pappa to return each season, summers stretching before me as an unending series of chores.

Pappa assumed I had the companionship of whalers' wives. Ha! It was a club for the forsaken. Not for me the shared anxiety of wondering if the men would return alive and the consuming loneliness that infected us all like a disease. I preferred being alone to that sort of suffocating camaraderie. Many of them admitted to enjoying the break from their husbands' interference, a chance to set the rhythm of their days, and the autonomy to make important decisions without benefit of their husbands' advice. That wasn't enough for me. Now this.

Passing into the dark season, the light doesn't shut itself off like a switch. There's a suggestion of light along the mountain rims, as if to tease us into supposing we won't be left in perpetual night. That night is coming.

The change of seasons has awakened in me some dark urges. I can't believe what I've been thinking, how I rationalize thoughts I'd never thought I'd think. There are those poison mushrooms I harvested and dried and hid from Pappa in a wooden box. Who is this woman who so loved her little boy?

I banish these torturous thoughts with busyness. Diversion isn't hard to come by. There's so much to do to get ready for winter. Plus, I invent ways to draw attention away from our precarious situation. Tonight, I marked the first day of the dark season with a special meal that took most of the day to prepare. The last ham, boiled potatoes, lingonberries. Fresh bread, your favorite *skolebrød* for dessert. The buns are an indulgence since I must ration flour if it's to last until the first ship in May.

As a final flourish, we opened a bottle of champagne to toast the occasion. I drank less sparingly than I should have. Pappa finished the bottle, and the spirits put him in a mellow mood. We could almost forget the encroaching dark.

ॐ

Kvitfiskneset
21 June 1947

There are those poison mushrooms I harvested and dried and hid from Pappa in a wooden box. Who is this woman who so loved her little boy?

Sometimes I wish I'd never discovered Astrid's letters. So many years later, these words haunt me. A hint of madness descending upon her even then? Death was all around us: in the bloody slaughter of the belugas, in the mounds of whale bones, in the reindeer we were forced to kill to live. Those mushrooms were one more way of courting death.

Strangely, these letters also give me a confounding sort of consolation. They remind me that in the months leading up to the baby's birth, joy had been a companion to sorrow, excitement to dull routine, frailty to endurance. In other words, we lived.

ॐ

31 October 1937

Dear Birk,

All Hallows Eve. Superstition has it that this night all the evil spirits disappear into the earth to escape the cold. What a lovely thought that evil might be banished from the earth so easily.

Would that we had such an escape! Instead, we must face winter's cold. I can't imagine how much colder cold could be, as it's felt like winter all along. Seasons mean nothing here. The bleed of light into dark is all that marks autumn's passing. Fall days are short in Norway, but there's a true sunrise and sunset, a window of light from morning to afternoon. Trees turn the shades of our colorful houses—deep reds, bright oranges, sunny yellows.

Here temperatures have plummeted. Only a scant pink and blue light hovers above the mountains for a few hours at midday. The tallest "tree"—technically a shrub—is the stunted Arctic willow, *Salix arctica* to be precise, which grows no more than fifteen inches tall. I admire its tenacity in the face of harsh winds that threaten to tear its roots from the thin soil. Hanna claims that the hardy fellow can live for hundreds of years. In any case, the little willow lies entombed underneath the snow. No fallen leaves paint this landscape, no leaves to rake into piles and bury ourselves in.

Snow obliterates everything—the relentless mud, the endless gray and brown scree, and most importantly, the beluga bones. In that way, pure white is magic. Yet the coating of the landscape is an illusion—those submerged things exist, to be uncovered in the late spring with the melting. What lies beneath the snow provides sustenance. Perennials are only dormant, and some retain their flowers. These plants are the reindeer's lifeblood. I see them pawing the ground, unearthing lichen and browned leaves and dried flowers, eating what they find. The constant pulling and chewing eventually ruins their teeth. Unable to eat, they starve. A sad cycle. Theirs is a constant struggle to survive.

We need to survive as well.

Once Pappa came out of his stupor, we hunted for three days with nothing to show for our efforts. On the fourth day, an enormous male reindeer presented himself to Pappa. At least that's the way Pappa tells it. He says that this deer fairly begged to be shot. I didn't witness the actual killing since I was inside cooking our midday meal. We made the mistake of leaving the dead deer outside while we ate. By the time we were ready to butcher him, he'd frozen solid. What a chore to get him indoors—first cutting the antlers, then the legs, then sliding the body inside. Better inside, despite the mess, than working outside in the strange twilight and freezing cold.

The two of us spent the next morning skinning the poor beast—scraping carefully with the fleshing tool so that no tissue remained. Imagine me, kneeling in a pool of blood, drawing my knife against the hide. I wouldn't have dreamed it when I left Sandefjord so many months ago. I often left the gutting of cows and pigs, the beheading of chickens, to others. Here, I had no choice. We needed food, and we worked together to procure it.

We needed the skin as well, at the very least to serve as an extra blanket or as material to patch our boots and parkas. It's hard to understand how skin so sturdy breaks down so easily, and thus we had to properly tan the hide. Let me describe the process.

We spread the skin flat, flesh side up, trimmed it of the ragged edges at the head and shanks, and coated it with a generous amount of salt. Then we folded it, flesh side to flesh side, rolled and tied it loosely, and hung it to drain. This morning we scrubbed the floor of blood and fat and opened the skin to dry. Pappa prepared a hogshead filled with a solution of borax and water and cleaned the hide. Next came the benzene immersion to render every trace of animal fat. Fearing for the baby's health, Pappa forbade me to help him with the benzene.

"The baby," he called it for the first time.

He soaked the hide, rubbed it with sawdust to remove the grease and chemicals, and beat the skin outside to rid it of sawdust. Even with the doors open for ventilation, the chemical fumes lingered far into the night. I spent much of the day outside sitting on a driftwood stump, stoking a small fire for warmth. The storm lantern cast enough light for me to sketch specimens in my notebook.

We washed the hide one last time and hung it outside on the drying rack to air. It quickly froze. Later, Pappa beat the skin again to dislodge the ice, dried it over the stove, and stored it in the anteroom.

The skull remained. I insisted we give it a proper burial in the whale cemetery. Outside the cabin I held it up to the modest light cast by the storm lantern. The deer seemed to be remonstrating me through his empty eye sockets. On the other hand, the skull is also a thing of beauty, a natural sculpture, like those marble busts we once saw in Oslo's art museum. You remember? I'm sure you don't. You were only two.

With lanterns and a crescent moon to light the way, we carried the skull to the cemetery and placed it among the whale bones. "I'm sorry" was the prayer I offered. Pappa said, "Thank you." Then we walked back to the cabin.

Exhausted, we fell into a deep, sound sleep. Sometime during the night or the day—who knows what time it was—I awakened to Hannah's gymnastics. Hannah, for I'm sure it's a girl. I'm five months along, and she's no longer a pinprick. Her fist or her foot moved down my belly. I lifted my nightgown to watch her trace my womb.

"I'm here, Hannah," I said, rubbing my stomach. Restless, I

rose from our bed and crossed through the parlor to the anteroom. I took down the wooden box hidden behind a large tin
of pemmican, where I'd cached the poison mushrooms. Sitting
at the kitchen table in the light of a single candle, I sketched the
largest one, filling in the streaks of rust and red with my pencils.
I held one up against the candlelight and considered what I'd
once contemplated. Then I opened the stove door and threw
the mushrooms into the hot embers, and for good measure,
burned the wooden box.

☙

Kvitfiskneset
21 June 1947

As October waned and the pink and blue light reflected by
the vanished sun faded, Astrid succeeded in snapping me out
of my doldrums. With new urgency, we tackled the tasks that
needed to be finished before full dark set in. The sheer volume
of everyday chores prevented us from dwelling on matters
back home, the nagging distress that her parents and Birgitta
didn't know of our fate, that they'd assume we'd capsized and
drowned. My dead parents were (thank God) spared that nightmare vision.

The reindeer must have sensed that I'd ceased my vigil by
the window. Where they had been plentiful a week earlier,
taunting me with their slow foraging, now I had to venture into
the valley to search for them. Astrid and I set out each morning,
rifles in hand. For three days, we returned cold and hungry,
empty-handed.

At noon on the fourth day, I was outside fetching coal when
a single male reindeer approached the cabin. His eyes met mine.
I felt a bizarre communion with him, as if he were offering
himself to me. Here, he was saying, is your sustenance for the
winter. My rifle was propped against the siding, and quickly I
grabbed it, leveled it against my shoulder, and sighted the reindeer between his beseeching eyes. I hesitated, then fired.

When Astrid came to the door, I gestured to the dead animal. She smiled. I could tell she was pleased her plan had worked. We wanted to butcher him inside the warm and lighted cabin, but when we dragged him to the door, he was too stiff to fit through the opening.

"Okay, genius," Astrid said, laughing so hard she nearly collapsed. "What's the plan?"

I, too, started laughing. I lit the storm lantern over the door, for the moon was covered in a sable veil. Then I took a saw and cut the antlers from his head while Astrid stood guard with her rifle, alert for bears. Reindeer antlers are hard as stone, so the task took the better part of an hour. By the time I finished, I'd worked up a sweat.

We pulled the reindeer hard, Astrid grasping his forelegs and I his head, but try as we might, he wouldn't fit through the door.

The legs were next. I took the saw to them as well. Another hour passed before we had a legless, antlerless frozen carcass. We maneuvered the carcass through the anteroom and into the kitchen and left it in front of the stove overnight to thaw. The next day, we cut it into pieces, stored the meat and the bones in the shed, and scrubbed the kitchen floor with brushes and lye. We used every bit of that reindeer except the skull.

"Let's go," Astrid said. She handed me a loaded rifle, lit a lantern, and picked up the skull. Side by side we proceeded solemnly to the cemetery. There she held the skull up to the flickering lantern.

"I'm sorry," she said to the skull.

What made her say that? Hadn't she realized we'd done what we had to do?

She looked at me expectantly. My turn. What I saw were the vacant eyes of an animal willing to be sacrificed for our own good. "You've saved us," I said. "Thank you."

Pleased with our little ritual, she placed the reindeer skull next to a whale's skull and said, "There. At least this old bull won't be lonely."

&

6 November 1937

Dear, dear, dearest Birk,

Today would have been your sixth birthday, the cake crowned with seven candles, the extra one for good luck. You'd bend over the cake, make a wish, blow them out. What would you have wished for? I open my locket and examine the tiny photo of you that I took when you turned four. When I think of you, this is the picture I see though this imagined you isn't real. At six, you would have lost your baby fat, the slightly double chin. Your white-blond hair would have darkened a bit, as Birgitta's has. I squeeze my eyes shut and try to conjure your six-year-old self. It's a shadow in my mind, never coming into focus.

It's fitting that today is the day the ghosts rise over Spitsbergen, seven weeks before Christmas. It seems to me that there are more ghosts on Svalbard than the living. So many graves scattered about the islands. Trappers' graves and explorers' cairns and coal miners lost to fires, cave-ins, explosions, and the 1918 flu victims buried on the low slope behind the church.

That may be why, earlier tonight, I swore I heard footsteps outside. Helfrid, intrepid Helfrid, succumbed to similar delusions, as did the trapper who went mad thinking that he heard footsteps across his cabin roof.

But Pappa heard them as well. Why else would he have accompanied me outside, rifle and a whale oil lamp in hand, to investigate? The night was dark as pitch except for the light cast by the storm lantern and the lamp he held in front of him. We made a full circuit of the cabin. Nothing there, not even footprints in the snow. We retraced our steps and saw nothing but our own footprints.

"Your imagination got the best of you," he said.

"My imagination? Look at you with your lamp and rifle."

"To prove you wrong," he said. "I'll keep watch in case the ghosts do rise above Van Keulenfjorden." He raised his arms above his head and made what passed for an eerie, ghost-like wail.

His bravado was a cover. I caught the slight waver in his voice. Why else would he have stood outside for hours afterward, cradling the rifle, in the glow of the storm lantern as it cast its eerie shadows onto the snow? I believe in the rational, but I know some things can't be explained. Those who die in this frozen landscape, unknown and unmourned, may very well rise on this day, hoping to find some relief in our hearing their footsteps, an echo of their existence. Or perhaps, as Christiane wrote to me, these ghosts are reflections of one's own self waiting to be discovered.

ॐ

Kvitfiskneset
21 June 1947

I accused Astrid of letting her imagination run away with her. New moons will do that to you. I'd also heard something unusual, though I pretended I didn't. I thought I hid my alarm well. Her letter attests to my failing.

When we made that first lap of the cabin, I noticed that the axe we kept propped by the front door had moved. I said nothing, not wanting to frighten her. As we circled a second time, I half-convinced myself that I hadn't seen what I'd seen, or that some natural force like a sudden gust of wind or a shifting snowdrift had caused the axe to move. But when we arrived back at the front door, I glanced sideways at the axe and realized that it had moved too far to blame wind or shifting snow.

A curious polar bear? But where were his telltale footprints?

I promised Astrid I'd keep watch. Truth was, I was spooked. Neither of us acknowledged the obvious: it was Birk's sixth birthday. I didn't want to dredge up that anguish. I see now that we were preoccupied with the same heartache. As I stood there, I half-hoped Birk would appear and forgive me for my innocent gift of bubbles. Forgive me for not being there when he died.

By night's end, I took the movement of the axe as a sign that maybe, just maybe, he had.

ॐ

20 November 1937

Dear Birk,

My thirty-fifth birthday. So close to yours, I couldn't help but start the day feeling sad. If you were here, you'd jump into my lap, shout, "Happy birthday, Mamma!" and hug me tight. Let me imagine that hug now. Who would've thought I'd be spending the day in this frozen tundra? Who would've thought any of this? How quickly life changes! Pappa's determined to make this day special. He's ordered me to rest while he treats me like a queen. He's hard at work on my birthday gift—the *komse* that will be your sibling's first home here on Svalbard. I've made the Saami braid, the baby's good-luck charm, and wear it tied around my wrist. Pappa worries the cradle's wood, sanding and smoothing every millimeter, afraid that an errant splinter might hurt the baby. Never mind that the interior will be covered by a protective layer of fur. He promised to have my gift finished today, but perfectionism takes time. It's months before the baby's arrival, so there's no hurry.

Otherwise, we've settled into what passes for routine. We force ourselves to wake at the same time each morning, spurred by the insane cuckooing of Dege's clock. Believe me when I say there's a temptation to stay in bed, where it's reasonably warm and cozy, rather than face the dark and the cold that greet us each morning. Pappa made more oil lamps from scrap metal and hemp wicks, though their light doesn't replace the twenty-four-hour sun. Two days ago, we were supposed to have our first full moon in the pitch dark, but cloud cover obscured the moonlight. Despite the light our oil lamps cast, the constant cold and blackness make me want to sleep till spring. But the fire must be stoked, breakfast prepared, ice collected and fed to the watermaker, clothing washed and hung over the stove to dry. Every day, the two of us venture out into the night to empty the waste bucket, one of us on full alert for polar bears, the other carrying the bucket and lantern to light the way. This last chore is such a bane. How I miss indoor plumbing!

The constant dampness—the effect of cold meeting warmth—accumulates and drips from the ceiling. We'd be bathed in moisture were it not for the skins lining the ceiling and walls. It's a never-ending battle. The skins get soaked, so we must take them down to dry over the stove and replace them with new ones.

The stove is a hungrier beast than I ever imagined. We laid in what we thought was an adequate supply to carry us through winter. We were wrong. Don't fret—we have coal as well, stored in waxed canvas bags inside barrels under the eaves and in the shed. And a small barrel filled with whale oil to burn if we're desperate, though it's mostly for lighting the lamps.

Several times a week we gather driftwood. Ice prevents a fresh supply of wood from entering the fjord, and we've exhausted what lies nearby, so we must wander farther and farther afield of the cabin. We've been fortunate that though it's been very cold, well below freezing, we've had little snow. So if we're willing to travel, we find wood and transport it by sledge. Pappa suggested that if we get desperate, we could dismantle the rowboats and The Hotel and (heaven forbid) the glorious little hut at Haven.

But for now, we hunt for driftwood, and the hunt can be interesting. Driftwood comes from the east, from Siberian forests or the jetsam and flotsam from ships lost at sea or sailors discarding what they don't need—empty barrels with Chinese characters engraved upon them, broken wheelbarrows with rusting handles, even a broom swept in from Russia.

One of the items we scavenged brought back a childhood memory.

When I was young, Mormor would tuck my brother and me into bed, turn out the lights, and tell us a story. Sometimes these stories would be filled with good fairies or benevolent magicians, sometimes (depending on her mood) filled with witches and goblins, ghosts and trolls. Why she chose to scare us with such frightening tales, and in the dark of night, I don't know. What brought this memory back was something Pappa and I foraged among the driftwood. But first let me tell you a story my mother told one night, gleaned from some errant newspaper article about a ghost ship called *Octavius*. I can almost hear her voice spinning this yarn:

Once upon a time, there was a cabin boy who served on a whaling ship called *Herald*. Now this was back in 1775, though the story didn't become known until the boy grew to adulthood and retired from sailing the seven seas. His name was Leif Høyfortelling.

Mormor was particularly good at convincing us that the story was real. All the more to send shivers down our spines. But what were the chances that the boy's name—Høyfortelling, he of the "tall tale"—belies the truth of this story?

I smile at this now, but back then I didn't catch the significance. She was a firm believer in the power of stories to teach children to confront their fears.

She brushed my hair away from my forehead, which had stuck to beads of sweat that had gathered there.

Herald came upon a ship in the seas off Greenland. From a distance, *Herald*'s crew spied a solitary figure at the helm and fired a flare gun to draw his attention. The figure didn't move but remained a sentinel at his post, hands gripping the ship's wheel. As they pulled closer, they saw emblazoned on the ship's prow the word...

Mormor paused dramatically and then whispered, "*Octavius*." My brother reached his hand to mine and clasped it. I remember this because I found comfort in his touch.

Herald's captain, a man named Warrens, took a small crew to the stranded vessel, among them the cabin boy, Leif. They clambered into a rowboat and quickly bridged the gap between the ships. The officer called out to the helmsman, "What ship are you?" He received no reply. Leif threw a rope to a second figure on the deck, hoping he'd catch the line and lash the rowboat to the ship. Alas, the figure failed to catch the rope, not once, not twice, but three times, despite the expertise with which the boy threw the line.

Mormor was so caught up in her storytelling that she didn't notice I'd pulled the bedcovers over my face, as if to ward off the spirits she was conjuring from the past.

The five sailors attached the rope to a wooden spike that protruded from the starboard side and shimmied up to the deck. The officer hailed the helmsman with some salty language, annoyed that the *Octavius* hadn't acknowledged the hail or caught the rope. The helmsman seemed fixed on steering the ship. It was cold and dark, and the officer asked Leif for the lantern he'd carried from the *Herald*. The officer lifted the lantern to the dumb gentleman's face and stared in horror at what he saw. Lo and behold, the wheel was lashed to his hands by ice, his legs frozen to the deck. Leif discovered the reason why the other sailor had failed to catch the rope. He, too, was frozen upright. Despite the dreadfulness of the scene before him, the officer remained calm while the four sailors recoiled. He ordered the crew to follow him below deck, and the threat of punishment induced them to obey.

"And what did they discover below deck?" Mormor asked. "Why, the captain! And what do you think the captain had to say?"

Mormor looked at us then, my brother squeezing my hand so tight that I felt my knuckles bunch. She didn't wait for an answer.

Nothing. He was frozen, sitting at his desk, pen in hand and his logbook spread out before him. The officer held the lantern to the poor captain's face. Green blotches of mold covered his cheeks and forehead and eyes...

My brother and I gasped simultaneously. "Please stop," I managed to say.

"Oh dear," Mormor said, finally noticing my distress. "Let me finish. The story ends happily."

Three of the sailors ran from the scene, but poor Leif became terrified, unable to move. With one hand, the officer picked him up by his collar and with the other swiped the captain's logbook. Close at the retreating sailors' heels, he was afraid that the crew would leave him behind in their fright. He needn't have worried because he found the crew cowering under the thwarts of the rowboat. So hasty was their departure that the officer didn't notice that he'd lost all the middle pages of the logbook. Just a few sheets remained, including the last one, which contained the captain's final entry: "11 Nov 1762: We have been enclosed in the ice seventy days. The fire went out yesterday, and our quartermaster has been trying ever since to kindle it again but without success. His wife died this morning. There is no relief."

"When does the happy part come?" I asked plaintively.

Mormor patted my hand. "Patience," she said. "Patience." Then she continued:

The *Octavius* disappeared from its graveyard near Greenland, but Leif swears that later in his life, on beautiful moonlit evenings, he saw the doomed Ice Ship steering in the wake of his voyages, pursuing the same course. Whenever he saw the ship, a gale rose up as it did on the night they returned to the *Herald* so many years ago. When Leif finally bade the sea goodbye, he purchased a glass ship as a remembrance of his encounter with the *Octavius*. He spent his days sitting by a warm fire, gazing at the glass ship resting on the mantelpiece. Sunlight prismed the glass, casting a rainbow of colors against the walls. When he closed his eyes, he could see every piece of rigging as high as the foreyard swelled to enormous bulk by ice, shining with every kaleidoscopic color. In his mind, the images of the doomed sailors were replaced by the sheer beauty of the ice-covered ship.

Looking back, I believe Mormor added that ending to dispel some of our distress. The story still causes me to shudder. Can you imagine the nightmares I had for nights afterward? I'd wait for Johan to fall asleep, crawl under our bed, pull the covers down to the floor, and leave him to ward off whatever evil came our way.

Thus how extraordinary it was when Pappa and I foraged a plank engraved with three letters. Clearly, it was something manufactured, ripped away from a large vessel. In the dark we couldn't make out the inscription, faded as it was against the weathered grain, but when we returned to the cabin and examined the plank in brighter light, we discerned the letters *OCT*. Perhaps we were eager to read legend into wood. But it stirs the imagination that a piece of that ghost ship might have traveled this far, to this remote beach, and brought me back to Mormor's storytelling nights.

I placed the plank on the shelf of mementos as Leif placed the glass ship on his mantel.

I must go now. Pappa's scrounged some used candles for a lopsided cake he baked this morning. I am trying not to laugh as he lights them.

"Make a wish!" he says.

What I wish for is impossible. To turn back the clock two years, when you stuck your fingers in the buttercream frosting, and I, though secretly amused, clucked my tongue at you.

❧

Kvitfiskneset
21 June 1947

I spent the better part of that long-ago November fashioning a cradle, like the one the Saami woman used for her baby, as a gift for Astrid's birthday. The traditional *komse* calls for a wooden frame covered with deerskin to make it light and portable, but I didn't have the tools to shape the thin wooden strips needed for the frame. Instead, I found an ideal pine log, curved and wider at one end, tapering down to the other.

Each evening during those early days of the dark season, I sat by the stove, stripping the bark and hollowing out the log along its natural curve until I achieved the right balance between lightness and sturdiness. I smoothed the wood with sandpaper and polished it with wax. Drilled holes all along the rim and pounded notched pegs into them from top to bottom. Cut a long, sturdy strip from the reindeer hide we'd tanned and laced it crisscross up the length of the cradle as if lacing a shoe. Finally, I repurposed an old leather belt into a strap that could be attached to the cradle at either end and slung over one's chest to carry the baby.

As I worked on the cradle, Astrid wove a braided band—the traditional Saami good-luck talisman—patterned with a full moon and stars on a blue field. She fringed the braid with red and gold—red for health, she said, and gold for wealth. The weaving seemed like an impossible feat of dexterity and planning. Astrid had worn the Saami bracelet ever since the day I gave it to her, and as she guided the needles back and forth across the breadth of the band, the charms dangling from the bracelet click, click, clicked. I remember that sound because we worked together in silence but for the clicking, and the fire's snap and crackle, and the occasional distant roar of glaciers calving.

Imagine my fixation with sanding away every splinter until the *komse* shone smooth as glass. I was afraid that an errant sliver might injure the baby. So many more urgent dangers lurked. Can you guard against everything at once?

❧

28 November 1937

Dear Birk,

In this dark season, the landscape appears unvarying, but to think so reveals a certain blindness. Last night, a crescent moon rose in a rare clearing of the clouds. This morning, the moon was covered by a solid blanket of white. By afternoon, a rosy tint outlined the mountain peaks as shape-shifting clouds moved across the sky, steel-colored billows to cottony puffs almost blue. In this season's strange twilight, there's enough light to notice such slight changes as the earth turns her slow time. I'd thought that as the days grew rapidly shorter, I'd dread the enveloping darkness. Strangely, I find it comforting, insulation from the outside world. It's an illusion, since the gloom adds to nature's dangers—hides the crevasse and the impassable bergschrund, obscures the approaching polar bear that comes out of nowhere. Windstorms churn and pelt you with icy crystals like a thousand tiny knifepoints, blind you doubly with dark and whiteout.

Every afternoon Pappa offers to come along on my daily walks. I tell him no, I'll be fine. I bundle up, sling my rifle over my shoulder, blow him a kiss. How do I read his face? Anxious? Frightened? I never wander far. Most days, I circle the cabin, counting off the laps out loud. As if my voice will ward off danger. The bears are out there, sometimes disturbing us with their inquisitive paws raking the cabin. Pappa knows I'm a crack shot, but polar bears move fast, up to forty kilometers per hour. And they are patient hunters. A bear could move stealthily upon me before I had a chance to level the gun, aim, and fire. I find myself oddly uncaring of the danger.

It's how I felt on Midsummer's Eve, when the icy sea covered me and I breathed in water like a fish and I wasn't afraid. I didn't struggle against it but let it take me for a moment. And then Pappa lifted me up, straining against the undertow of *Ishavet kaller.*

The landscape calls to me, and I answer. The water calls to me, and I answer. I dip my toes in. Never have I felt such cold.

Pappa lifted me up and carried me to shore, laid me down and covered us with parkas and skins and finally my wedding dress. The fire was warm. It sparked and crackled and its wavery light and smoke blinded me, and numb, I didn't resist him.

Now I walk in the shrinking window of curious twilight, the fruit of that evening growing inside me. If a bear should come upon me, or an unseen crevasse open up under me, or a misstep plunge me into the void, I'd be relieved. Dare I say happy as the world tumbled by, or winked out after a few moments of pain? A new moon is coming. Moonless night. I will embrace it.

❧

Kvitfiskneset
21 June 1947

Funny that when all was light, I wasn't anxious about Astrid's rambles. There she was, off to collect her flóra or just to exercise and breathe fresh air. Why was it that the dark season raised my fears for her safety? Was danger more likely when the sun was hidden?

Astrid's letters reveal that she was aware of my feelings. What she didn't know was that when she paced the cabin, I followed her voice from room to room as she counted off the laps. Her counting reassured me that she was alive.

One day, when I could no longer hear her voice, I paused with my ear against the wall. Minutes passed, the cuckoo cuckooed, and the bird's insistent chirping drove me outside. There she was, down by the water's edge, her back to me. The waning moon provided scant light but enough to make out her silhouette. She bent down, took off each boot, each woolen sock. I held my breath.

She rolled up her pants, then tiptoed into the water.

I took a step toward her.

She stood there, a shadow against the navy sky.

I waited.

Turning back, she retrieved her boots and socks and, barefoot, strode up the hillock toward the cabin. I bundled wood in my arms, preparing my excuse for being outside, and pretended not to notice her bare feet.

"Hello," I said. "How was your walk?"

❧

2 December 1937

Dear Birk,

The aurora borealis—the light you can hear! We've seen those mystic lights for the first time this evening, hissing and popping across the moonless southern sky. Full dark has its rewards. Many myths surround them—the spirits of the dead wandering those wafting veils of color or the play of children lost to time. It would be a great consolation to believe dead spirits live on in such ecstasy. As the lights whirled across the sky, I swear faces appeared and disappeared. Ghosts once again, but happy ghosts. Dare I think that you were among them?

I know these are myths, and the faces merely acts of the imagination. Hanna taught me the theories of Kristian Birkeland, who claimed the aurora was a dance of tiny particles sent out by the sun. Solar wind. No one has been able to prove his theories, and like Galileo, he was ridiculed for his beliefs. In fact, some say his obsession with his work, and the lack of recognition from the scientific community, drove him to suicide. Such is the fate of original thinkers.

Oh, why dwell on his tragic end when providence bestows such beauty upon us! Although Sandefjord has its share of these winter lights, never have I seen such a vivid display, enormous arcing waves of green and red and blue, a slow dance across the navy-blue sky. I'd have missed this spectacle had we returned in September. I could almost forget the distress our disappearance means to Mormor and Farfar and Birgitta.

Pappa seemed equally delighted by the lights. We stood motionless, the night quiet but for our breathing and the odd crackling.

"Do you hear it?" I asked.

Pappa nodded.

"Children speaking to us."

He laughed but didn't disagree.

We listened intently. I held my breath and strained to hear. The noise stopped. I exhaled, the noise resumed. A faint hiss sizzled the air in front of me. *What is that?* I wondered. "Hold your breath and count to three," I said.

Together we held our breath. The noise stopped. We exhaled. Crackling.

"Again," I said. We held our breath, waited, exhaled. Crackling.

I lifted the whale oil lamp to my face. Inhaled, paused, exhaled. And that's when I saw it—the very moisture in my breath turned instantly to tiny particles of ice, freezing in mid-air and falling to the ground. The crackling issued from that precise moment when droplets turned to ice. It wasn't the lights giving voice to ghosts. Rather, the aurora created an atmosphere that enhanced those silenced voices. The lights forced us to pay deeper attention to the universe's mysteries.

I raised the lamp to Pappa's face and said, "Go ahead."

He inhaled deeply, paused, exhaled. His breath crackled in the calm night air, and the ice droplets sparkled in the light.

We laughed. Over and over we amused ourselves with the sound of ice particles freezing and falling to the ground. When we tired of the game, we held hands as the aurora patterned the sky.

I was sad to acknowledge the scientific truth. The crackling wasn't the aurora speaking to us in its idiosyncratic language or playful children chattering. But at least I'd found an explanation for the noise. A minor discovery to share with the world, more easily provable than solar wind. No complicated machinery needed, just the act of breathing, and watching, and paying attention to the infinite.

ॐ

Kvitfiskneset
21 June 1947

Summer's perpetual daylight blinds us to the aurora's presence, hidden but still shimmering, waiting for that moment in autumn or winter to reappear in all its glory. I feel its spirit. Ghost children playing, alive in a parallel world unfolding beside us. I've found comfort in these superstitions as I have in returning to my Christian faith, to ideas of guardian angels and the afterlife. Inexplicable what we will ourselves to believe.

I'll admit that my initial reaction to Astrid's death was to rail against her God, her merciless God, who'd let so many tragedies befall me. I was Job, tested by a purportedly benevolent God, patient in my suffering. Or not so patient. As Job attested, the thing that I'd so greatly feared had come upon me. Twice.

In my empty bed in the dark of night, I'd weep into my pillow and grind my fists into the side of the bed where Astrid used to sleep. Quick to anger, I drove many away, including my in-laws, who kept me at a distance, their own anger channeled toward me. Who could blame them?

I threw myself into the physical labors of the farm, blessedly removed from the worst horrors of war. I told myself I wasn't a Quisling, but volunteering wasn't feasible. I had responsibilities to my children, who'd already lost their mother. I had responsibilities to the farm, which my in-laws couldn't manage alone.

The farm wasn't far from Sandefjord Harbor, but I refused to go there. The sea, former friend, had become my enemy.

On better nights, I spent time praying like the hypocrite I was. "Dear God," I'd whisper, "someday let me see my beloveds again." Some nights, I'd believe He answered yes.

Other nights, I'd despair. I wanted to believe, as Job did, that my Redeemer liveth.

The first Christmas Eve after the war ended, Marit and Christian talked me into attending midnight services at Sandar Church. Marit was dying, that much was clear, and who was I to deny her a last Christmas wish?

It was one of those perfect winter evenings, snow dusting the path up to the church alive with twinkling lights. That night, the choir performed a passage from Handel's *Messiah*. As they sang "I know that my Redeemer liveth," I took it as a sign from heaven that my prayers had been answered. As if this weren't enough proof, when we left the church and looked up to the sky, an aurora wavered there.

It was very cold that night. I drew a deep breath, held it, exhaled. The ice particles, faint crackling. My ghost child speaking to me.

Is death the end of us? I looked up at the aurora, as if its very brilliance bespoke a parallel world in which the dead did indeed live. I embraced the faith again, mainly for its comforts. If that makes me a hypocrite, so be it.

దా

13 December 1937
Santa Lucia

Dear Birk,

The Christmas holidays are upon us, and once again, the happiness that they promise has been marred by unforeseen events. Last year we tried in vain to mark each celebration with the customary festivities—at the very least for Birgitta's sake—but even she lacked the Christmas spirit. Your absence loomed over every moment, large and small, from tromping through the woods on the farm to find the perfect tree to unwrapping ornaments that you'd made each year before your death.

Today we arrived at the first of these celebrations—Santa Lucia—and we find ourselves desperate to fill the emptiness we feel so far from those we love and with you gone. I must resolve that life will never be the same instead of wishing for something that cannot be.

To nourish me on this holiday, Pappa decided to spoil me with an Arctic delicacy—blood pancakes. All our eggs are gone and the adult eider ducks have long since flown south, leaving their babies behind to fend for themselves. So he made do with what we have on hand—flour, baking soda and salt for leavening, a little sugar for sweetness, water and powdered milk. The secret ingredient? Whale's blood. Bloody beluga blood.

I consoled myself that he was trying to help. Your pappa feels responsible for our difficult situation. We're trapped here for the winter—let's hope it's only for the winter—and managing a pregnancy no less. The unspoken between us—he's never overwintered on Kvitfiskneset, only in Longyearbyen where he didn't have to forage for food or fret about the constant dangers. He's projecting confidence in getting us through, confidence betrayed by his earlier paralysis in the face of all that we must endure.

"The blood," he said—which tinges the pancakes a gruesome blackish-purple color, the same revolting color of seal's meat—"will strengthen you and the baby."

"I'm perfectly fine," I told him. "Pregnancy isn't an illness to be cured with whale's blood."

He laughed. I must say he flipped the pancakes expertly, perfect rounds that, without the blood, might have appealed to me. His forehead was smeared with a paste of sweat and flour. What should have been a pleasant odor—the scent of pancakes wafting through the cabin—made me feel both hungry and nauseous. And the purple-black color—so hard to unsee, to pretend these are the sweet golden pancakes I make at home. Nevertheless, I was determined to force down at least one of these delicacies to reward your father for his thoughtfulness.

He laid out plates, margarine, honey and jam, and a stack of pancakes. I hesitated, selected the smallest of the bunch, and cut it into tiny pieces. He looked at me intently as I took the first bite, chewed carefully, and swallowed. Now I know how you felt when I forced you to eat lima beans. At least those are a pleasing color and don't assault your nostrils with an ungodly fishy-gamey odor.

"Delicious," I lied, and forced myself to take another bite. Holding my breath while I chewed kept the worst of the nausea at bay.

Only then did your father serve himself a stack slathered with margarine and jam. I managed to finish that single pancake and sip some reconstituted milk to wash down the rancid taste. Careful not to hurt his feelings, I told him I needed fresh air and hastily threw on my parka. Outside, I retched a bilious brownish bile and covered the evidence with snow.

Pappa wasn't done with the surprises. I woke from a sound

sleep in the late afternoon to find he'd prepared a Santa Lucia celebration. You remember Lucia, the martyr who's depicted holding her eyes on a plate, plucked out by a soldier torturing her for her Christian beliefs? Today's the day we celebrate her feast with a festival of light. Pappa had fashioned a wreath from wispy twigs of Arctic willow, a far cry from the lingonberry branches we used at the farm. He tugged a balaclava over my head, then placed this crown on top. A sideways glance into the mirror revealed I looked ridiculous, but I was touched by his kindness.

"Remember how Birgitta loved being our Lucia wearing a wreath of lingonberry branches alight with candles?" I asked.

"I wonder if my mother has made a crown for her this year."

Right then, I felt a pang of sadness. Santa Lucia is doubly special because it's Birgitta's birthday as well. Last year we went through the motions, performed the familiar rituals. Birgitta walked in the town's annual procession with other girls her age, but she was the only one not smiling.

Would your grandparents acknowledge either occasion today when they're unsure of our fate? I tried to talk myself into believing they could sense we're alive. But I couldn't rid the thought that they consider us perished on our journey home and thus couldn't bring themselves to celebrate.

As if reading my mind, Pappa said, "Birgitta will be fine. Your parents have endured worse."

I forced a smile. I knew he was wrong.

He insisted I dress warmly and led me outside. The moon was three-quarters full, irradiating the landscape. In one of her letters to me, Christiane had spoken of the wonder of the Arctic moon, something about feeling like she was dissolving in moonlight and being drawn into the moon itself. I thought she was exaggerating. Now I know what she meant by "I am moonlight." The landscape looked as if the gods had planted lights like seeds whose tendrils pushed up through the ice and snow. It reminded me of the Striezelmarkt I'd once visited as a child, Dresden's Christmas market luminous with thousands of small lights that made the night almost as bright as day. The granular firn coating the ground sparkled, each tiny particle catching the light like those tiny bulbs.

Christiane told me that Karl, the hunter who'd spent the winter with her and her husband, claimed moonlight might drive her mad. The cure? Seal meat and cod liver oil.

If moonstruck be a form of madness, let me go mad!

To add to the radiance, Pappa had set out a path of whale oil lamps and carved steps into the snow and scree to make the hillock near the water's edge easier to manage. As we stood by the shore, I got so caught up in the night's magic I began to sing the traditional Lucia song. How angels speak to us and their light dispels the darkness. That was true this evening.

He'd rolled a large driftwood log by the firepit and covered it with sealskin. He helped me sit and then withdrew from his pocket some matches to light a small wood pile. Slowly, the fire spread upward through the wooden teepee.

Neither of us spoke for a long time. My thoughts remained with your sister and Mormor and Farfar. I tricked myself into imagining they were celebrating with *safranboller* and spiced hot cider. As if the sheer force of my projection could span the distance that separated us and convince them that we were alive.

Pappa had one more surprise. He'd made a pinwheel "bun" out of a slice of bread swirled with cinnamon sugar. He broke off a bit of the roll and fed it to me. Then he kissed my cheek and whispered, "My Lucia."

చ

Kvitfiskneset
21 June 1947

Norwegians call winter *mørketid*. The time of darkness. That Lucia evening, however, the moon christened the landscape in an iridescent glow that seemed to emanate from below.

I remember that day in particular because Astrid seemed fully recovered from her morning sickness. So much so that she tolerated the delicacy and nourishment of my blood pancakes.

Only upon reading her letter did I find she hadn't tolerated them as well as I'd thought. Harmless little lies buried among the larger ones.

While Astrid napped that afternoon, I shoveled a path from the front door to the water, carved steps in the snow along the hillock that fell to the sea, and arranged a teepee of wood for a small fire. And last, I lined the path with whale oil lamps.

When Astrid awoke, I led her to the kitchen and pulled a balaclava over her head. She was a bit taken aback, wondering what I was up to.

"Happy Santa Lucia," I said, and placed the wreath I'd made on her head.

She gasped, touched it. "How did you keep this from me?"

"It wasn't me," I said. "I found the crown outside our door. The *Julenisse* came down from the North Pole? It's not that far, you know."

She laughed at my whimsy. "Little Tomten who protects us. Little Tomten no one ever sees but for the footprints he leaves in the snow. Another ghost."

"A benevolent ghost."

"Sometimes," she said, then recited, "'Gray he stands at the barnyard door, gray by the drifts of white there—'"

I joined in. "'Ponders—some problem vexes, some strange riddle perplexes'—something, something, something—"

"Something, something, something," she said, laughing. "But it ends so peacefully. 'Cold is the night, and still, and strange, stars they glitter and shimmer. All yet sleep in the lonely grange soundly till morn shall glimmer.'"

She sighed. "A pity we have no candles to light the wreath."

"Come," I said. I opened the front door and led her outside along the path of light.

It's hard to describe the delight on her face when she saw the whole landscape ablaze. We walked hand in hand along the path of light. In the short time I'd been with her inside the cabin, the moon shone brighter and the lamplights leapt higher inside their metal enclosures. The sky was clear, and the stars cooperated. Polaris gleamed from its fixed perch to the north, the other stars seeming to circle around it. Wheel in the sky keeps on turning, as they say.

We stood at the water's edge. Time stopped. Or rather, time counted itself by sound.

I remember the silence into which every tiny noise echoed.

I remember the rhythmic whisper of her breathing in concert with mine.

I remember the cracks and knocks emanating from the field of ice, which spread out before us as if summoning us into the fjord.

Somewhere in the distance came the firecracker shot of a glacier calving. The sound receded, and we held hands in the quiet aftermath.

Astrid had a beautiful voice. She began to sing the festival song:

Black night descends on us
in stall and living room.
Bright sun has gone away,
bleak brooding shadows loom.
Then into our dark home
with lighted candles comes
Santa Lucia, Santa Lucia.

I listened to her sing—I can almost hear her voice now—and then joined in the final verse:

From valleys of the earth
darkness shall soon flee.
Then in words wonderful
the wingèd angel speaks.
Day shall be new again
as rosy skies ascend—
Santa Lucia, Santa Lucia.

What more can I say? I lit the fire, and we sat down to warm ourselves. After a time, I withdrew from my pocket a mock cinnamon bun, broke off a piece, and fed it to Astrid.

It was an almost perfect night. The twinge of sadness Astrid felt? I felt it too, that precarious balance between joy and sorrow. We could never entirely forget that our fate was unknown to those we loved most.

Looking back, I see that evening differently. Was it indeed a night of turning toward the light? Or was it a night that turned us toward the darkness that was to come? If I'm honest, if I stop and close my eyes, I can once again see the happiness on Astrid's face. I can understand that such moments of pure joy are joyful because we have the sorrows to compare them to, just as, without darkness, we wouldn't understand the light.

࿇

Christmas Eve 1937

Dear Birk,

I imagine Mormor and Farfar and Birgitta, bundled against the cold, making their way to Sandar Church for midnight services. Birgitta is wearing the navy woolen hat trimmed with fur that Pappa and I gave her last Christmas. Her rosy cheeks and blond bangs peek from the halo of fur as she walks between Mormor and Farfar, holding their hands, along the curved path that leads past the graveyard with its granite markers barely visible above the drifts. Do they notice the gravestones? Do they stop at Birk's grave? Or do they focus on the golden glow emanating from the open door as the church bells peal and a soprano sings "*Adeste fideles*," welcoming them to celebrate Christ's birth? Pappa smiled indulgently when I told him I could hear the bells of Svalbard Church announcing Christmas Eve service. Was it because I wished so hard to hear them?

Tonight we decorated our "tree." Pappa made it. The stand was two small planks nailed into a cross, the center post a dowel set into the base. The "branches" were birch bark sticks of ever smaller lengths. He drilled holes into the center of each stick and inserted them into the post so that the arrangement tapered to a point. I wove a star out of twigs, made a daisy chain from flimsies cut into strips, and dusted the branches with "snow" of the cotton wool we stuff into our boots. Traditional candles to light the tree would pose a danger of fire. Instead, Pappa lit the lanterns he'd made for Saint Lucy's Day and placed them around the tree. The effect was striking.

From somewhere deep in our storehouse of frozen meat, Pappa procured a ham. I thought we'd exhausted the meat we'd brought from Tromsø, but he'd hidden it away like buried treasure. I'd also stashed treasure—jars of sauerkraut and lingonberry jam. And we had steaming mashed potatoes and cinnamon-spiced grøgg. The pièce de résistance was the traditional rice pudding with the single almond nestled inside. Remember how you loved that creamy concoction? I rigged the game so that you were always the lucky one to get the almond, much to Birgitta's dismay. We have no almonds here, so I tucked a prune into Pappa's portion. Now he's the lucky one!

And what would Christmas be without Santa Claus? Somehow, he squeezed down the stovepipe and left the most useful gifts. Pappa got a new pair of boots made from our illicit reindeer. His old ones had been patched so often that they looked like a crazy quilt of scars. His "stocking" was stuffed with luxuries—a bottle of champagne and his favorite milk chocolate. In my stocking were several homemade bars of cinnamon-scented soap. I turned them over in my hands, wondering where on earth they could have come from.

"The North Pole," Pappa said, and winked.

Pappa had finally finished the *komse*, polished to perfection and gleaming in the lantern light. I unfastened the good-luck braid I'd been wearing around my wrist and tied it to a hook in the cradle's canopy. In his woodworking zeal over the past month, he'd also built a rocker so that, as he said, I'd have a special place to nurse your sister Hannah.

But the biggest surprise was to come. While I was busy cooking, Pappa claimed he needed to organize the storehouse and check our inventory. This evening he rolled a strangely foreshortened hogshead into the cabin.

"Voilà," he said.

At first, I was confused. It looked like the same hogshead he'd used to tan the reindeer hide, only with its top lopped off. Had he shot another deer in secret? Were we to spend the evening tanning its hide? "A bath," he said in answer to my quizzical look. "Cut down and waterproofed." Now I understood why Santa had left me soap and why he'd spent the better part of the morning chipping two barrels of ice while I prepared our Christmas feast. I thought he'd gone mad. While I looked on, he fed the watermaker with ice and filled the hogshead with hot water through a piece of rubber tubing connected to the spigot.

Imagine the luxury of a warm bath and perfumed soap after so many months of sponge baths and icy plunges in the fjord, scrubbing with a bar of lye. Well, the bath wasn't exactly warm. Despite the roaring fire in the stove, the water quickly cooled. And it was a tight fit when Pappa decided to squeeze in behind me. We washed each other, and the water turned murky.

Your father tried so hard. But even with the delicious meal, the warm bath, and Santa's thoughtfulness, sadness intruded on the evening. I'd clung to the hope that Hilmar would spend Christmas in Longyearbyen as was his custom. That he'd hear we'd never arrived there two months ago. That he'd corral his huskies and rescue us. I hadn't realized how that hope had blossomed to the point that I actually listened for his approach, for the yowling of his dogs and the friendly *hei* of his greeting.

But my hope was a dream.

The moon, half full, is waning tonight, and we face two more months of darkness. Pappa reminds me that the days are now lengthening, that the worst is behind us. I nod but keep to myself thoughts of the near future, months more of surviving with what we've managed to hoard or kill, and all of this with the prospect of delivering a baby long before help arrives.

I sat in Pappa's lap with my head against his chest as we rocked in our beautiful new chair beside the tree. I smiled until my face hurt from the strain. I hoped some caroling might lift our spirits, chase away thoughts of joyful Christmases past. I sang:

Silent night! Holy night!
All is calm, all is bright.
Round yon virgin mother and child.
Holy infant, so tender and mild...

My voice wavered, and I swallowed hard. Pappa hugged me tight, and in his rich baritone, he picked up the tune:

Sleep in heavenly peace!
Sleep in heavenly peace!

How is it that the songs we've repeated for years suddenly seem to speak to us? It's as if we mindlessly sing and recite until one day, we finally listen.

❧

Kvitfiskneset
21 June 1947

By Christmas, the waning moon illuminated the landscape, but its magic light was gone. Such a change from Santa Lucia, when the waxing moon approached its fullness, and we bathed in its enchanted radiance. Astrid claimed she heard Longyearbyen's church bells coming over the fjord and the windswept mountains. Sound travels far in the dry Arctic air, but not that far. As the crow flies, Svalbard Church was eighty kilometers away and blocked by mountains. But she swore she heard bells. The ringing of church bells must have haunted her dreams, memories of Christmas Eves past when we made our way up the cobbled path to Sandar Church.

That Christmas season in Sandefjord was altogether different from what Astrid imagined. Birgitta clung to the hope that we were alive, marooned on Kvitfiskneset. Astrid's parents became increasingly pessimistic. Late at night Birgitta would hear Marit crying through her bedroom walls, whereas Christian affected an optimism he didn't feel. They marked Birgitta's tenth birthday by crowning her with the traditional wreath to walk in the town's procession. They celebrated with a cake decorated with eleven candles. She made a wish—"more of a prayer for your safe return," she said—and blew the candles out in a single breath.

On Christmas Eve, Christian and Birgitta tramped into the woods and cut down a Norway spruce. "He let me pick out the perfect tree, cone-shaped and so big we had the horses drag it back to the house. Mormor refused to help, but she did watch as we decorated the tree."

The whole affair was more of a solemn, silent ritual than the festive celebrations we'd had before Birk died. They tried hard to feign normality when their hearts must have been breaking. Dressed for Christmas Eve services, they walked up the snow-dusted path to Sandar Church as Astrid had envisioned, but Marit insisted on stopping to lay a wreath on Birk's grave. Carols wafted from inside the church, but Marit couldn't bear to enter.

"We stood by the grave for what seemed like hours," Birgitta told me. "The bells rang out to mark the end of the service. Then we left."

In Longyearbyen there are no more church bells. All that remains is the idea of a church. And yet, I swear I can hear bells.

ॐ

30 December 1937

Dear Birk,

Another year without you ends. After Pappa fell asleep, I walked outside into utter darkness—a night or two before the new moon—without a lantern, without a rifle. Starlight guided my path. Polaris glimmered, bewitched me. I followed it as the Three Wise Men must have followed it to find the baby Jesus. Before I knew it, I'd crossed the fast ice to the water's edge. The cold soaking my feet broke the spell. Such a foolish thing to do.

ॐ

Kvitfiskneset
21 June 1947

Before I left Longyearbyen, I dropped by the telegraph office to see if I'd had any word from home. The telegraph operator handed me a single telegram with my name blurred by coffee stains. *Tor...land*, it read.

I pretended to chastise him for damaging the message. He shook his head. "Don't blame me," he said. "It was a ghost in the machine."

I laughed. "A caffeine-addicted ghost?"

He grew serious. "You wouldn't believe how one little thing like a smeared address can set people off." He leaned toward me as if he were imparting a state secret. "You know every Christmas, wires arrive by the thousands, and everyone gets at least one. It's a lonely time for the miners here without their families. Last Christmas Eve, a miner refused to open a telegram that appeared to be addressed to him because his name was blurred."

"Spilled coffee on that one as well?"

"No, no," he said, and leaned back in his chair. "As the Christmas season wore on, the miner went a bit mad for he believed he hadn't received a telegram from his wife. He brooded and brooded, wearied his fellow miners with all sorts of wild reasons why his wife, Gudrun, hadn't written. He stopped going to the mines. The townspeople became more and more concerned for his welfare. Finally I took matters into hand, brought the telegram to his room, and forced him to open it. And when he did, the scene was pitiful. 'Oh, Gudrun, Gudrun,' he said, weeping equal parts joy and relief, 'and my children!'"

I know how that miner felt. The telegram he handed me was from Birgitta. I've read it at least a dozen times.

DEAREST PAPPA STOP THANK YOU FOR THE SEALSKIN SLIPPERS STOP I WEAR THEM EVERYWHERE UNTIL FARFAR MAKES ME TAKE THEM OFF STOP HE TELLS ME I WILL WEAR

THEM OUT AND BESIDES WHO WEARS SLIP-
PERS IN SUMMER? STOP FARFAR LIKES HIS TOO
BUT HE SAYS IT IS TOO EXPENSIVE TO SEND
ANOTHER TELEGRAM TO THANK YOU STOP
WE KNOW YOU ARE WORKING HARD STOP WE
ARE COUNTING THE DAYS TILL WE SEE YOU
AGAIN STOP LOVE YOU WITH ALL OUR HEARTS
STOP BIRGITTA

Buried in those words is Christian's refusal to forgive. He
hides it well. It's apparent in trivial things. He *can* afford a second telegram. Will he ever forgive me?

I understand that feeling. When someone dies, people often
channel their bewilderment toward someone or something.
For Marit and Christian, that was me. The further insult of
not having a body to bury made it particularly unpardonable.
Christian's sullenness has hardened since his wife's passing. I
know he thinks their daughter's death hastened her own. So I
have three deaths on my conscience.

I tell myself I came back to Longyearbyen to earn a living.
Then why am I here at Kvitfiskneset, sacrificing a week's pay,
and planning a trek to Haven for Midsummer? Can revisiting
the past finally assuage my guilt?

❧

New Year's 1938

Dear Birk,

The dawn of a new year, and I feel as if we've finally turned
toward the light. The sun stays stubbornly below the horizon,
but by my calculations, we're halfway through this dark season.
The eighth of March 1938—*Soldagen*—will herald the sun's
return. The baby's due then. I have the date marked in red on
the calendar.

After the traditional meal of salted meat and boiled pota-
tocs, we meandered to Haven and stood outside for the longest while, gloved hand in gloved hand. Fireworks burst over
Longyearbyen. A multi-colored glow to the north framed the

utterly dark, new-moon sky. We heard them, their rapid-fire boom boom boom. It made us feel connected to the world to know that not too far away, people were celebrating—dancing, drinking, singing.

Your father couldn't deny the buzzing, hissing, whistling as he did the church bells on Christmas Eve. But to tease me, he pretended I was imagining things.

"Could it be that my hearing is more acute than yours, old man?" I smiled and launched into the theory that plants can hear. "The temple bell stops, but I still hear the sound coming out of the flowers."

He turned to me. "And trees?"

"Trees," I said. "Absolutely. If you listen closely enough, you might hear what they have to say."

"Didn't you once tell me that Darwin dismissed such ideas as a 'fool's experiment'?"

"So you do listen to me occasionally," I said, touched that he remembered this from a conversation we'd had years ago.

We stood outside far into the night, until a last great cacophony, a percussive sound like cannon fire, signaled the end to the celebration. And just like that, I was reminded that somewhere to the south, real fireworks burst inside the hearts of men. Are Japan and China still at war? Does civil war yet rage in Spain? Has it engulfed Europe?

Is it possible to be at peace for one blessed night?

At the stroke of midnight, or what passed for that moment in time, I squeezed Pappa's hand. Then in a nod to tradition, he hoisted his rifle, aimed it high, and fired several rounds. Had the whole world gone up in smoke while we welcomed a new year with gunshot, safe on our faraway island?

Pappa and I turned to each other and whispered the traditional New Year's greeting. *Godt nytt aar, takk for det gamle.* A bittersweet promise for what's to come.

❧

Kvitfiskneset
21 June 1947

Dare I say it was a blessing not to know that the world was moving toward war while Astrid and I held hands that New Year's Eve? In a matter of months, Germany would annex Austria and Europe would fail to act. World leaders thought appeasement a workable solution. Before the next New Year, Germany would destroy Jewish shops, synagogues, and homes in a pogrom called *Kristallnacht*, and finally there would be international outrage. By then, it was too late.

Who would have thought that the war would bring me back here years later?

As I've said, I wasn't a Quisling. Even before that loathsome man sold Norway out to the Germans, I knew he was evil. That Hitler's cause was evil. But nor did I have anything to do with the Resistance. I considered myself a patriot, yet I didn't rise to the heroism of my friend Einar, sailing to his death to liberate Svalbard. In truth, I was afraid. When the Home Front came to recruit me, using the kind of veiled language I could plausibly deny if interrogated, I demurred. I was afraid for my family, my in-laws, my children. I was afraid for myself. The Germans treated saboteurs harshly, with unspeakable tortures, with executions or imprisonment in concentration camps.

The story of Jan Baalsrud illustrates the point. Here was a rightful hero who sailed back from Scotland to Bardufoss in northern Norway with eleven Resistance men to sabotage a German airfield control tower. They were betrayed by a local shopkeeper who, afraid for his life, reported them to the local authorities, who in turn reported them to the Germans. A German warship attacked their boat. One man died during the attack, ten were captured, and Jan escaped. Eight of the captured men were tortured and executed at a mass grave they themselves were forced to dig. Later evidence revealed that some of the men were alive as dirt was shoveled over them. Two others were hospitalized with gunshot wounds and later died of torture and those wounds.

Jan embarked on a two-hundred-kilometer odyssey across
northern Norway to neutral Sweden, rescued along the way by
dozens of courageous Norwegians who risked their lives to
help him. He made it to safety after undergoing unbelievable
horrors of gangrene and starvation and worse, amputating his
own toes to save his life. The townspeople of Manndalen were
especially helpful on the last leg of Baalsrud's journey, and their
reward was to have the Germans burn down their village. I
marvel at those who put their lives and the lives of their families
and neighbors at risk to save a single man. Norwegian goodness
and decency shone through in this and so many other examples.

On the other hand, there were horrors that don't speak as
kindly to Norwegian courage. *Lebensborn* was one that affected
me personally. *Lebensborn*: the Fount of Life. Could there be a
more ironic name for a eugenics program cooked up by the
Germans to create perfect Aryan babies by mating "pure" Norwegian women with SS officers? At first, I thought the rumors
were the product of overactive imaginations. Our good people
would never embrace such a foul notion.

When it became clear that the Germans had established
nurseries in Norway to house such "perfect" offspring, I consoled myself that few Norwegian women would participate in
the scheme. Over the course of the war, however, ten thousand
Norwegian women agreed. Some were no doubt pressured,
but some chose freely. Thousands of babies were born of that
nefarious program.

Birgitta was a teenager. Beautiful, vivacious. Blond-haired
and blue-eyed. A perfect Aryan. She had to be protected. German soldiers were everywhere, occasionally "visiting" what I
thought of as our secluded farm, looking for those of us who
would hide members of the Resistance. At least I protected her
from those soldiers' predations. The threat was all too real.

One day I caught her flirting with a handsome German
soldier decked out in his spotless uniform. He'd come with a
bribe, a tin of coffee, which was nearly impossible for us to
obtain during the war. Coffee was Norwegian lifeblood, and

the Rika we drank was a poor substitute. This young man, his chest adorned with medals that doubtless signified Norwegian kills, was more than I could take. I controlled the urge to shout at him, instead calling Birgitta inside on the pretext of helping Marit prepare Sunday dinner.

The row that erupted between my daughter and me! The shouting and accusations!

"Do you want to whore yourself out to the enemy?" I yelled. I could feel my face flush. I must have looked a sight.

To her credit, Birgitta neither cried nor withered from my verbal assault. She stood there, fists on hips, her face set in a mask of determination—Astrid reincarnated, her stubbornness, her composure when I lost my temper.

My anger escalated in direct proportion to her unnerving calm. "Do you?" I hollered. "Answer me!"

At last Marit intervened. She took Birgitta's hand and led her to her bedroom. There she had the kind of talk Astrid would have had with her. To her credit, Marit must have imparted the kind of womanly wisdom that brought the situation under control. Wary of the soldier's intentions, she supported me. But she did admonish me afterward, reminding me that real men, strong men, could be tender as well.

Nevertheless, I kept Birgitta under virtual lock and key. Rarely was she out of sight. I forbade her from going into town alone. I had her working on the farm from sunup to sundown, or taking care of Hans, or caring for her grandmother as her health failed toward the end of the war.

After the war, she saw I was right. Women who had succumbed to German advances, whether because they believed in the Nazi cause or fell in love with the wrong person or worse (yes, there was worse), were paraded through the streets with their heads shaved. "Shame, shame, shame," the mob yelled. Many threw eggs and fruit at them.

Not only do we ostracize the mothers, we ostracize their children as well. Rumor has it that some of these innocents are incarcerated in mental hospitals. The irony isn't lost on me.

These children, conceived as products of perfect breeding, are now thought to be "poisoned" with German blood. I'm ashamed by our lack of compassion. Of the treason trials, our great writer Sigurd Hoel has asked, "Who among us is so pure that he can stand up in public and say, 'I'm innocent'?"

No one.

My penance was to offer these women and their children some small kindness, bounty from our farm. It's not enough, I know. Not enough.

At least Birgitta has forgiven me for robbing her of any measure of carefree existence during what should have been the most carefree years of her life. But growing up during the deprivations and terrors of wartime, even without the discipline and responsibilities I imposed on her, would have stolen away many youthful pleasures. I know firsthand. I'd grown up during the First World War, though I was spared the worst of it because of Norway's neutrality.

After the war ended and just before Marit's death from cancer, Birgitta came to me as I was preparing for bed. She'd turned eighteen, and I remember thinking that suddenly she was a grown woman. She sat on the edge of my bed, a serious look on her face, and patted the space beside her. I sat down and waited while she gathered her thoughts.

"Pappa," she said, finally, "I want to know how Mamma died."

"She drowned," I said.

Birgitta shook her head. "I want the whole story. I'm old enough to understand. And I can tell you're hiding something from me."

My daughter. She *did* have a sixth sense about these things. So I told her the truth. I told her about the joyful parts and the tragic parts, how I thought her mother was brave and strong and kind but was overtaken by some darkness that no amount of light could drive away. I told her that I loved Astrid with all my heart, that I loved *her* as well, and that I was sorry that she would never really know her mamma.

"I'm to blame," I said. "I'm to blame for her death. I stayed too long in the Arctic. I thought I could—"

Birgitta put her fingers to my lips. "What good is guilt?" she asked. She looked down at her open palm, traced the lifeline there. "You know, I used to blame myself for Birk's death. He wouldn't give me a turn with the bubbles, so I stomped away from him. When I turned back, he was gone. If I'd been a better sister—"

Now it was my turn to put a finger to her lips. What more was there to say? We hugged each other tightly for a long while. Then she kissed me lightly on the cheek and left the room.

The war seemed so much larger than our losses. Young boys a few years older than Birgitta were listed among the missing and the dead. Villagers guilty of nothing more than living in the same place as those courageous Resistance fighters were slaughtered, their towns burned. What a world! Would that Hyperborea existed!

We'd spent the war remaking our family amidst war's desolations. Wasn't that enough?

It wasn't. I found myself drawn back here one last time. Director Ankers invited me to help with the rebuilding, and I said yes without plumbing the depths of my motivations. During the war, Johan had returned to live and work at the farm, and Christian was hale enough to put in a day's labor. They could hire day laborers as needed to keep the farm going. And Birgitta had long since become the woman of the house.

I finally wrestled these thoughts down to this: One can never fully explain one's own motivations, let alone another's reasons for doing things. It's not just what people hide from each other. It's not knowing in the first place. I think of the forgotten ones, hunters and explorers and miners who have disappeared without a trace, frozen for all time in this very landscape. Only those who carry their memory remember. And then *they* die, taking with them all that's known of their ancestors.

That's one reason I've returned. The foolish quest to remember. Someday there will be no one left to remember Astrid.

Hans never knew her. Birgitta's memories are those of a child. Marit is dead. Christian holds on to ghosts. Johan tells me stories of their childhood growing up on the farm, but he is aging and will, like me, someday be gone.

So here I am, salvaging what can be salvaged. As if the sea itself will give up its secrets, summon Astrid's body from the depths a decade later. As if the sea will tell me why I risked it all for a few days more of whaling and being alone with my wife. How was I to see that A would lead to B would lead to C?

It's a form of madness to think I can recover some part of my life by returning here, a form of madness to think Astrid might appear to me because I've returned to claim her.

Oh, she is with me. I love her. Present tense, even as I'm propelled back in time. I can hear those fireworks bursting overhead, the report of those last rockets echoing. I can feel her lips, our tongues touching ever so briefly.

Darwin was wrong on two counts. Flowers can hear, and the fittest don't always survive.

&

6 January 1938

Dear Birk,

Twelfth Night.

Folklore has it that it's bad luck to leave Christmas decorations up past Epiphany, when the three Wise Men ended their pilgrimage to Bethlehem by bestowing gold, frankincense, and myrrh upon the baby Jesus. So Pappa and I dismantled the tree today and fed the wood and the paper decorations into the stove. I couldn't bear to burn the willow star, however, so I stored it in one of my specimen boxes. Next year I'll have Birgitta mount it atop a real tree lush with the scent of pine as we recall this Christmas season spent apart. *Next year.*

Can it be two years since I tucked you and Birgitta in bed on Twelfth Night eve and told you the Italian story of La Befana? That version unfolds as the three magi ask Befana to help them find the newborn Christ. Though she refuses, she houses them for the night. Later she regrets her decision and goes searching for them. Legend has it that she's forever searching. In her endless pursuit, she leaves behind gifts for all good children on Epiphany Eve.

Early the next morning, you'd comb the house for the gifts Befana left behind. How excited you were to discover a chocolate bar slipped under your pillow or a toy soldier in your shoe! In the darker version of the legend, the one I never told you, Befana is a witch. Her little boy dies, and grief propels her to madness. Believing that the baby Jesus was her son, she sets out to find him. It's a fruitless quest, but she persists, circling and circling the earth, clinging to false hope.

Let me purge these dark thoughts. Our last Epiphany together was such a happy one. We took down the decorations, wrapped them in tissue paper, and stored them for the next year. Most precious were the handprints you and Birgitta made each year in clay, each dated and hung on the tree with twine. You placed your hand on the one made the year before. Your palm alone covered the impression there.

"Oh my, how you've grown!" I said. And you smiled, pleased with yourself, as if growing required some effort on your part.

We saved the last of the decorations, the crackers we made every year from rolled cardboard and tissue paper and ribbon, stuffed with candy from the general store. We broke open those crackers and feasted. A marvel that none of us got sick from all that sweetness.

Today the sweetness is gone but for the memory of that happiness.

❧

Kvitfiskneset
21 June 1947

As the dark season wore on, Astrid's letters turned bleaker. When I first read them, I saw that Astrid's melancholy and her obsession with Elen's fate weighed on her mind. If only I'd known that she'd contemplated eating the poison mushrooms…

❧

15 January 1938

Dear Birk,

Can you indulge me in another story?

Once upon a time, a hunter and his wife came to live on an icebound island way up north, very near the North Pole, in the land of Thule. They lived in a tiny house whose walls were made of peat and moss, whose roof was sheathed with birch bark that had floated all the way from Siberia, whose floors were composed of gravel and dirt.

Was there a witch in the house, like in the fairy tales? you ask.

Oh no, it was much too cold for witches. No, this tiny house was empty, not much of a home. The man hoped that his wife might brighten the place with her womanly touch—sew curtains for the window, knit a colorful blanket for the bed, throw animal skins over the gravel floor, warm the living area with the scent of freshly baked bread. And so she did. For several months they lived together in this enchanted land of ice and snow. Then one day, she discovered she had a baby in her belly. During that winter she suffered greatly. She got extremely sick. She was feverish and so tired that she couldn't get out of bed. Because the cabin was so far away from the nearest town, she resigned herself to suffering. She worried about the baby, but what could she do?

Did she die?

Thank goodness, no.

What happened then, Mamma?

By now, the baby had grown inside her. It was early June, and the sun was up twenty-four hours a day. The weather had turned mild. They thought everything was going to be all right. The hunter decided to go to the nearest town to get help delivering the baby. But the weather turned against him. A sudden storm came up—wind and snow and ice crystals pelted the man as he drove his sledge and dog team over the landscape. He was forced to take shelter in an abandoned hut along the way. Some say he was gone for three days, some say he was gone a fortnight.

Did the woman stop the baby from coming out?

Well, once a baby decides to come into the world, there's no stopping it. The woman was brave. She had the baby right there on the floor. Miraculously, the baby boy was healthy. Although she was weak from the birth, she cleaned him, wrapped him in a blanket, and nursed him when he was hungry. And when the hunter returned days later with a doctor, he found his wife lying in bed, cradling their infant son. But the ordeal had taken its toll. She refused to leave the bed, refused to let either man touch the baby. The doctor gave her some special medicine to calm her nerves and left it for the hunter to give to his wife. Eventually she recovered enough to return to the mainland with her son. But she was never the same.

That's a very sad story. I like stories with happy endings.

Not all stories have happy endings, my sweet son.

જે

21 January 1938

Dear Birk,

Why am I writing these letters to you? Those idle gossips were right. Coming here was madness. Darkness visible.

જે

7 February 1938

Dear Birk,

The dark season is starting to wear on me despite the brightening at midday and the promise of the sun's return. As Hannah kicks and turns in my womb, her imminent arrival becomes more real. I'm paralyzed by the fear that we won't be able to deliver the baby. Your father tries to reassure me, but he looks apprehensive when we talk about the practicalities of delivering a baby in this cabin.

We've set up a "kit"—sterilized scissors, iodine, a supply of clean water, rags torn from clothing that has long since worn out, and a metal bucket. I can't help but consider all the things that can go wrong—breech birth, stillbirth, the umbilical cord wrapped around the baby's neck. I try to push these thoughts from my mind, but as I lie awake at night, these nightmares return.

Nightmares. In some ways, I'm better off lying awake than falling asleep. I dwell on Elen's story. The two sons she lost in Tromsø, baby Kaps she delivered alone, the ghost child buried on the slopes above Villa Fredheim.

Last night I dreamed of a funeral. It started in the traditional way with the ringing of the bells. I was thinking of church bells as I fell asleep, how I could swear I heard them coming from Longyearbyen on Christmas Eve. I mentioned it again to Pappa as we lay together last night. He grunted. He humors what he calls my fantasy.

Those bells were ringing in my dreams. And within the bells rose the haunting melody we sang at your funeral. *Her skal jeg vente til du kommer igjen; og venter du hist oppe, vi træffes der, min sønn!*...Ibsen understood. Ibsen understood that death's only solace was the promise of meeting again in heaven. I hear the song, always, thrumming in my mind. It's as if your funeral never ends.

They say time heals all wounds. They lie.

They say grief ennobles, clears away trivial matters, reduces us to concerns for the essential. They lie.

Grief is like walking on an ice floe. It fools you into believing you're standing on something solid, moves imperceptibly beneath you, and carries you into the unknown. It threatens at every step to fissure, to fracture, to open into leads that can swallow you whole.

These were my thoughts as I fell from wakefulness to nightmare.

Sleet pelting the window sounds like earth sifted on your casket. Suddenly I'm at Sassen, or what appears to be Sassen, Helfrid's gaily colored curtains blowing inward toward an empty room, cakes lining the kitchen sill. The wind picks up, speaking to me. I lean into it. I walk toward the slopes behind Fredheim and up a short rise. Before me is a cairn. I lift the stones one by one. Underneath is a small wooden coffin. I kneel in the snow and scree. The lid isn't nailed shut. I lift it. Inside are an infant's bones. I reach into the coffin and touch the skull, slide my fingers to the mandible where the mouth once gave voice to the human. I run my hand down the length of the infant body, sternum to pelvis, femur to tibia to tarsals. Every bone has a name. A child's body has at least three hundred bones. I can name every single one.

I trace the baby's right hand. The thumb's tiny distal phalange breaks at my touch. I put the bone in my coat pocket. That's all I remember.

I wake, shivering. Pappa's stolen all the bedcovers. I can't shake the nightmare.

I rise and pull on my parka, snowpants, and boots, shoulder my rifle, and leave the cabin. Outdoors, everything's quiet. The moon appears as if God has torn its face in half. The clouds move rapidly across it, obscuring the moon altogether. Then it emerges so close to earth it seems I could reach out and touch it. I tell myself this celestial phenomenon must be a sign, a promise, as I wait for my breathing to return to normal, for my heart to stop throbbing in my ears. Oh, Birk!

ॐ

Kvitfiskneset
21 June 1947

What appears to be a most innocuous thing—a desire to be alone with one's spouse, a careless afternoon on a beach, a door left ajar—can alter one's destiny.

It's so easy to see now.

Astrid had gone to the shed to fetch a container of whale's blood. Yes, whale's blood. She'd developed an odd craving for it, convinced the baby wasn't thriving. Her affinity for whale's blood was curious given her earlier aversion to my blood pancakes. She began to add it to everything she cooked. One morning I found her mixing onions and flour and whale's blood and spices into a paste from which she made patties fried in grease. I must admit they were delicious. Other times she drank the blood like a cocktail. Even *I* found the taste of straight whale's blood vile.

The next day, she asked me to retrieve reindeer meat to thaw for the day's supper. That's when I discovered her mistake. As I approached the shed, I saw first a trail of blood, next the enormous tracks of a polar bear, and finally some smaller footprints left by a fox. The door lay askew, torn off its hinges, the iron bolt likewise cast aside. But it was the rock that gave Astrid's mistake away, a rock that lay by the gaping entrance and hadn't been there the last time I'd visited the shed. Inside, not a single piece of meat remained.

I fixed the door on its hinges and picked up the iron latch.

Astrid was sleeping when I returned to the cabin. I shook her awake, pointed the latch at her as an accusation.

"The meat is gone," I said.

"Gone?"

"Tell me what happened."

"I don't know what you're talking about."

Looking back, I can see that she was half asleep. We'd been getting on each other's nerves. She was tired all the time, snapping at the least provocation. I'd lost patience with her testiness. But in that moment, I mistook her reaction as feigned innocence, which heightened my anger.

"A bear broke into the shed and helped himself to our meat."

Astrid gasped. "I couldn't get the door to close all the way. The threshold was choked with ice. I thought a rock—"

"Is no match for a polar bear. Why on earth didn't you tell me?"

"You were out collecting driftwood. I was busy making bread. By the time you came back inside, I'd forgotten. I haven't been myself lately. You see how difficult it's been…" Her eyes welled up, but her tears didn't move me.

I stalked back to the shed with my tools. It took the better part of the afternoon to repair the door, reattach the bolt, and hammer nails around the perimeter. *Closing the barn door after the horse has bolted*, I thought. *Closing the shed door after the polar bear has had his fill.*

By the time I returned to the cabin, my anger was spent. But that night and for two nights after, we slept in separate beds, she in the bedroom, me in the kitchen. The usual punishment. Me lying awake half the night worrying that she'd freeze with the bedroom door closed. As before, I kept the fire stoked so that at least some of its warmth would penetrate the thin walls.

Despite that concern, it was a relief to have those nighttime hours alone. Astrid's belly, the baby's gymnastics, no longer thrilled me. The marriage bed was becoming a kind of prison in which every movement had to be orchestrated.

I was tired, too, tired of being solicitous, tired of the daily grind of chores required to keep us alive, tired of waiting for the sun to return.

Oh, to have back those days! Oh, to see how differently life might have turned out, if only.

ॐ

18 February 1938

Dear Birk,

Pappa's gone on a very dangerous journey.

He left this morning for Oli Blomli's cabin at Calypsobyen. If he skis across the frozen fjord, the trek is a manageable twenty kilometers. But no distance here is ever easy. Leads suddenly open, as I well know. Floes move surreptitiously, carrying you back to where you started. I've seen my own footsteps embedded in ice, broken and rearranged like a crazy quilt, making it impossible to return to the place from which I started.

I fear for Pappa's safety, but what choice did we have? We're desperate for fresh meat. It's my fault we're in this predicament. I left the shed door ajar, protected only by a feeble rock. Ice across the threshold prevented me from closing the door all the way. I thought I'd secured it. As if. In the night, a polar bear slapped the stone away. I could imagine him chuckling at what he considered a pebble, a pathetic irritant. We've seen bears almost as big as our cabin. He pawed open the shed and devoured the meat. The one good to come of it is that the bear left the dry goods untouched.

And the argument that ensued! Two nights sleeping alone. Two nights of nightmares from which I awoke to a cold and empty bed, Pappa's arms no longer a comfort, his soothing words no longer bringing me back to reality.

For three days we waited for a reindeer to wander across our path, but they seem to have vanished. An Arctic fox would sustain us for a few days. Those, too, have disappeared. Are the gods taunting us? Even the polar bears have deserted us. We'd hoped for the thieving polar bear's return, or any bear for that matter, however dangerous that wish. A bear's meat would be all we'd need. Killing a bear is no easy task. Beginner's luck that I killed that one at Sassen what seems like years ago. I bring my rifle whenever I venture outside but pray each time I won't have to use it on those white monsters. In any case, how would I butcher a bear on my own?

I watched your father ski into the white, thinking, *This is madness.* I dispelled that thought by admiring the expertise with which he glided across the snow shouldering his rifle and pulling an empty sledge behind him. And we packed his rucksack full of essentials—a flashlight, a change of clothes, some dried whale jerky, hardtack.

It was a good day for him to try for Calypsobyen. The thermometer registered forty degrees of frost this morning. Cold, but mercifully almost no wind and several hours of lightening around midday. There's a kind of twilight noon now. A pink rim on the horizon. Plus, there's the light of a nearly full moon brightening the snow.

Pappa and I worked out a schedule. Two days out and two days back, he should return by the twenty-second. Sooner if he snags a reindeer on the way out and carries some of it back on his sledge. He left before "dawn," hoping to make it to the hut at Fleur de Lyshamna in the few hours of daily twilight. From there he'll cross the frozen sound and on to Oli's. If Oli's there, he'll welcome Pappa with open arms. He's said to bake throughout the winter—for imaginary guests, I suppose—so he should be thrilled to see another human in the middle of winter. Oli might even help Pappa bring back a sledge full of meat. What a pleasure it would be to see another person! Otherwise, Pappa will have to make do with what he can pull alone.

That's the plan.

Pappa promised me he'd return in no more than a week, mindful that I'm due in three. He laid in a supply of ice, firewood, and coal in the anteroom to last at least seven days. Beyond that, I don't want to think.

I spent the day baking bread, a dozen loaves, which I'll ration. The margarine from the shed is rock hard, and I stab it with a sharp knife. I stab and stab until small pieces break off. I warm it in my palms, smear it on a chunk of the bread with my hands, and lick my fingers, for I don't wish to waste this precious fat. A year ago I couldn't have imagined myself scraping my fingers with my teeth for nourishment. I laugh out loud at my former fussiness, insisting on the crew's hygiene, causing trouble where none should have existed. When was the last time I bathed? Combed my hair, which now is a mass of tangles? Let alone thought of anything as civilized as foundation, blush, lipstick?

There's no end to what one will do to survive. If it weren't for the baby…

I'm tired all the time, my feet swollen, my toes tiny sausages. Sometimes I feel I can't make it through the daily chores, my daily exercise. But when I can muster the strength, I take my rifle, circle the cabin, count off ten rotations, turn around, ten more. *One, two, three, four, five, six, seven, eight, nine, ten. Ten, nine, eight, seven, six, five, four, three, two, one.* My life consumed by counting, minutes cuckooed into quarter hours, lengthening into days.

I don't know what I'll do if Pappa doesn't return in a week. And what if he doesn't return at all?

The wind again. Shrieking. A human sound, like mourners wailing.

❧

19 February 1938

Dear Birk,

Day 2.

A reindeer wandered by our cabin, as if to mock me. The reason for Pappa's journey presents itself, a gift from heaven. If only we'd waited one more day!

Where did she come from? Where was the rest of her herd? Nearby, no doubt. Reindeer travel in packs. This one appeared to be an old cow. She had massive antlers and an equally massive torso. Svalbard reindeer are unique in that both males and females have antlers. So how did I know this one was female? The male loses its antlers in the early winter, while the female retains hers for an entire year, shedding them in June. The bulls need their antlers only in the fall, during the rut, when they're competing for females. The cows use them in spring and summer to drive away the males and build their community of females and calves.

She pawed through the snow to uncover dormant vegetation, poppies and crowfoot and moss, then bent her head to the desiccated fronds poking up from the scant layer of earth. So much work to gather so little sustenance. Confounding that she was plump after a winter of such meager foraging. *Food for us*, I thought as I raised my rifle to my shoulder and worked the bolt action as smoothly as possible. The scrape of metal on metal alerted the reindeer to my presence. She paused, lifted her head, and turned her face toward me. Her eyes had the melancholy aspect of one who'd seen too much in her many years.

I told myself that she was as weary of this world as I. I told myself she'd be happy to give herself to me. Her death would be an honorable one, sacrificed so that three might live. I took careful aim at her head. I didn't want her to suffer. I slowed my breathing to steady the rifle, sighted her right eye down the barrel, and squeezed the trigger. Her front legs buckled, unable to support her tremendous weight. She knelt in the snow as if praying. Her right eye hung from its socket, a gruesome testimony to what I'd done. She leaned sideways, tottered for a moment, then fell to the ground. I bridged the gap separating us, bent to place my hand on her chest, and waited for her heart to stop.

It was then I saw her belly move. What I'd mistaken for a well-fed cow was actually a pregnant one. Her gestating calf would die a slow death inside the womb, so I had no choice but to load the rifle once more, aim, and fire.

I placed my hand on my belly, felt Hannah kick and somersault, alive. I placed my hand on the reindeer's belly where there was only death. I'm sickened by the thought of the pain I must have caused that fledgling calf, but at least it didn't endure drowning in its mother's amniotic fluid. I closed my eyes and offered a prayer for forgiveness. Two more spirits offered up to the Spitsbergen gods.

I can't dwell on what I've done. There's demanding work ahead—skinning and butchering this animal before she freezes. I'll have my fill of her meat, and Hannah will have my milk to drink.

❧

21 February 1938

Dear Birk,

Day 4, the day Pappa should have returned. I push down any thought but that he's delayed.

I didn't have the energy to write yesterday. Cutting up the cow and storing the meat in the shed was arduous work. At first, the natural warmth issuing from her flesh kept my hands warm while I knelt outside and butchered the poor beast. But then the cold got to me. The small fire I kept feeding with driftwood did little to dispel the cold.

In any case, I salvaged meat enough to last the rest of the winter, together with her heart, bladder, and tongue. I'd resolved not to open the womb, but curiosity got the best of me. Inside was a male fetus, larger than I expected. Gently, I lifted the damaged calf from his mother and laid him on the ground beside me. I don't know what possessed me to cut away his toenails. Eight tiny pebbles, tiny buttons, like the charms on my Saami bracelet. I put them in my blood-soaked apron's pocket.

I couldn't bring myself to butcher the little calf. Instead, I carried him to the whale cemetery. Moving some whale bones aside, I laid the body in the hollow and traced a cross on the calf's forehead. I placed the cow's heart on top of her calf and rearranged the whale bones—skulls and vertebrae—over the makeshift grave. A futile effort. A bear or a fox would soon scavenge the remains.

A light wind whistled through the graveyard, animating the whale skulls. I imagined they were saying a prayer to send these souls on their way. Another small consolation. Why shouldn't they join you in heaven? It made me happy to think of you welcoming them, befriending them, caring for them as you did the baby chicks and calves on the farm. Standing there, I thought back to the reading at your burial. My hand trembles as I write this. The pain is almost unbearable.

And Jesus said, "Let the little children come to me, do not stop them; for it is to such that the kingdom of God belongs. Truly, I tell you, whoever does not receive the kingdom of God as a little child will never enter it." And He took them up in his arms, laid his hands on them, and blessed them.

How could Jesus take a child from his mother? How could I?

I knelt beside the grave, hoping that peace would wash over me. How long did I kneel until cold got the best of me? I had trouble rising. Hannah's weight held me down. You would have laughed at my predicament. I tried to lift myself up in the normal way, pushing my hands against the ground. But I couldn't find purchase. Finally, I lay on my side and rolled onto my back. Panting from the exertion, I drifted off. How long, I don't know. But the pause restored my strength. If it weren't for Hannah, I might have closed my eyes forever. Instead, I rolled onto my side again, pushed myself to a sitting position, and used a whale's rib bone to lever myself up.

Pappa had once told me of the Saami woman's advice to offer some remnant of each kill to the sea, so I threw the cow's bladder far into the fjord, comforted by the notion that I'd freed her spirit to reunite with her baby. Then I dragged the cow's remains to the water's edge, a small feast for a hungry bear, but at a safe distance from the cabin.

Back inside, I pickled the tongue, now silenced by my actions. Pappa loves pickled tongue, God knows why. Today is his thirty-eighth birthday. When he returns, and I must trust he will, we'll feast on the tongue and the bounty of reindeer meat.

My final task was to wipe each of the calf's toenails clean of blood and place them in an empty spice tin. I shook the tin, which will make a fine rattle for the baby. My blood-soaked apron fed the fire.

The moon has disappeared behind the clouds. It took what little remaining strength I had to fill the storm lantern with paraffin, light it, and fix it in place on the iron fastener above the front door. A beacon for Pappa's return. I should have done so sooner to guide Pappa home. Careless of me to forget.

Just as I finished, the wind picked up again. Wind so fierce I felt as if it might hurl me against the door. On top of that, a bear ventured onto the shore and seized upon the cow's remains. I lifted my rifle to my shoulder, but fortunately, he had an easier meal and hardly noted my presence.

I backed through the cabin door and secured it with an iron rod as an extra precaution. I dare not venture outside again today.

❧

22 February 1938

Dear Birk,

Day 5.

The windstorm has lasted all day. Picture a wind so violent that it can't exhaust itself, but blows unrepentantly, beats its drum-fire against the cabin as if it might at any moment decide to lift this hut and carry it northward, smash into the mountain on the other side of the fjord. Will the slanted logs that buttress the cabin hold it to the ground?

I was desperate for wood and coal. My store had run out. I'd even burned that prized piece of driftwood marked OCT. Outside, it was impossible to stay upright against the wind, so I knelt in the face of it and stared out at the fjord. A vast expanse of hummocks and crevasses lay before me. Snow drove across the landscape in rolling waves of icy mist, as if the sea had escaped gravity and risen into the sky. It became difficult to breathe. I felt as if I were smothering as the crystal veil penetrated my lungs. I wrapped my scarf more tightly around my mouth and nose to filter the particles.

The wind swirled loose snow and ice upward into spindrifts, which resembled those Spitsbergen ghosts surfacing from the very depths and dancing on the water. I closed my eyes. Beneath the ice, bodies submerged. Floated by. I could see them in the shadow of my eyelids.

I opened my eyes, shook off the hallucination, and crawled inside and out to replenish my store of wood and coal. This chore took the better part of two hours. Or what seemed like two hours. It's hard to say. The cuckoo clock has stopped working. The little boy and the bird are trapped inside; the little girl with the golden braids is motionless outside the wooden door.

Lighting the stove became a battle between the draft that blew smoky miasmas down the stovepipe and into the parlor but also sucked the heat upward out of the room. I managed to cook before the vacuum caused one of my lamps to blow out. I tried to relight it, but the fuel had run out. Too tired and hungry to refill the lamp, I ate by the light of the one remaining. Odd shadows wavered on the wall, rippling over the animal skins. It was as if they'd reincarnated. The movement and the continuous low note played by the wind—yes, they'd come alive. Reproaching me for killing the cow and calf. Ice pellets knocked at the door, against the walls, dirt sifted on your coffin. I covered my ears, to no avail. The noise vibrated in my very bones. It's as if Elen has taken over my body. Yes, I feel utter loneliness. And terror. Her terror? Pappa gone, lost in this very storm, his skis useless in this gale. The baby twisting and turning inside me trying to find a way out.

৵

Dear Birk,

I've lost track of the days.

Relentless wind. Terrible wind. I didn't know wind could be so fierce, worse than the autumn storm that trapped us here.

After my ordeal fetching wood and coal and stoking the fire, I warmed some stones on the stovetop and tucked them into the parlor bunk where I lay cocooned. The stones have long since gone cold.

Night is day and day is night.

I'm hungry, but I can't seem to gather the will to rise.

Sleet sounds like bullets impaling the siding. I could swear I heard a polar bear scraping the outside walls, looking for a way in. And in the distance, the crash-boom of ice calving mingles with a melancholy moan like that of an organ stuck on one low note.

The thermometer registers thirty below, but that doesn't account for the chill the wind undoubtably adds. Inside, the fire has died down, and the cold penetrates under the weight of three animal skins. I must rise and feed the stove with fresh wood and coal. It seems an impossible task, but I must do it. Not for my sake, but Hannah's.

I made up a dozen bottles of reconstituted milk and lined them up on the kitchen sill where the cold that penetrates from the outside will keep the milk from spoiling. I can survive on that and fish jerky and stale bread until Pappa returns. I dare not go out again. I pray that the wind lets up before the wood runs out.

రు

Dear Birk,

More time has passed. Hours, days? Is it still February? Where is Pappa? Clock's frozen in time. It's impossible to tell day from night. The wind, the sleet, the skulls mock me. Then suddenly, the world hushes. Wind quits trying to find a way through the walls. The whale skulls cease their chattering.

I rose from my bed to retrieve wood and coal from the stockpiles outside, but the wind had driven snow and ice against the cabin, blocking the front door. My only escape was through one of the windows. Both were covered by shutters nailed to guard against the very weather that laid its trap for me. I chose the bedroom window since I was no longer sleeping there and could seal out the draft I was about to create by closing the bedroom door. The window itself opened easily, but the shutters were a different matter. I rummaged a spare axe from the anteroom and pounded on them until the shutter splintered into pieces. I tore an opening large enough for me to snake through. The snow had drifted up to the ledge and was covered with a thin sheet of ice, forming a kind of sliding board to the ground.

I had to shovel a path to the front door. Fortunately, the shovel hung high on a hook by the door, its handle barely visible. I piled the snow into a large heap, then retrieved the axe to chop through the ice that coated the threshold. I don't know where I found the strength. I said a small prayer, thanking God that the snowfall itself had been light.

When I finished, I looked up and came face-to-face with a polar bear. He had his head tilted to the side as if wondering what kind of creature I was. I must have looked a fright, coated from head to foot in a thin sheet of ice, just my blue eyes peering out from my balaclava. My rifle was propped against the siding, not more than a meter away, but I worried that in the time it took to retrieve it, the bear would be upon me, rendering the weapon useless. All I had to defend myself was the axe. I'd been warned not to scream or run in the face of a polar bear, but rather to stare straight at him and feign confidence. I inhaled deeply in and out, steadying my breathing, stood up tall, motionless. My stomach roiled and as if in response, Hannah somersaulted over and over.

Did the bear sense that I was prepared to hack him to death with the axe? How gruesome that battle would have been! Instead, in the meeting of our eyes there was the kind of communion Pappa must have experienced last fall with the reindeer. We were two desperate beings trying to endure a brutal winter. I like to think so, but in truth, I may have been too inconsequential to be worth killing. A midnight snack for a hungry bear. After several minutes, he turned from me and loped away.

With my rifle slung across my shoulders, and glancing backward with each blow, I nailed what was left of the broken shutters into place. The flimsy fix had to be enough to discourage the bears. Just in case, I nailed the bedroom door shut as well.

Hours had passed. How many hours, I'd no way to know.

With the fire blazing once again, I filled a mug with hot water, measured out a portion of tea and milk, and sat down at the kitchen table. Wrapping my hands around the mug to warm them, I took a sip. And just then, I felt the first contraction. Was it my imagination? Maybe I'd strained a muscle. But no.

The baby's coming. In the pause between the pains, I lay out the kit with its sterile cloth and scissors, iodine and rags.

I write to you so that Pappa will know what's happened. And if the worst should come to pass, you'll be there to greet me and your newborn sister, there among the clouds, my angel.

ৡ

Kvitfiskneset
21 June 1947

How was I to know that Hans could arrive early? How was I to know it would take me two days to reach the hut at Fleur de Lyshamna, or that I'd have to hunker down for almost a week to wait out the windstorm? And then be marooned for a day when a lead opened in front of me as I crossed the ice? Thank God I'd packed a tarpaulin and ropes to cover the sledge for the return journey. I was able to fashion a tent with them using the sledge as a prop. What a miserable night that was! I was afraid the lead would widen and swallow me whole. Miraculously the lead closed overnight, and I was able to make it to shore unscathed.

My concern for Astrid weighed on my mind. Already gone for longer than we'd planned, I considered returning to the whaling station empty-handed. But how were we to live without meat? I talked myself into believing in her resilience and carried on. When I arrived at Oli's, the cabin was deserted. My luck that he was out tending his traps. Miraculously, his stove was still warm. There were fresh breads and sweets lining the windowsill, and barrels filled with ice and coal and wood in his storeroom. A small shed housed meat and skins from his winter harvest. It was strange helping myself to his bounty without him. Half-starved from my journey, I gorged myself on cakes and bread and meat and consoled myself that he would have happily fed me had he been home.

I waited out the day hoping for his return until my concern for Astrid's well-being overwhelmed me. I packed the sledge with as much as I could safely carry and left a note for Oli promising to replenish what I'd taken.

The saving grace was that the return journey went smoothly, three days to Fleur de Lyshamna and another three to Kvitfiskneset. Dragging the heavy sledge without Oli's help made the going slow. But at least the weather cooperated—the wind was calm and the hours of twilight lengthened with each passing day.

As I skied over the hardened, slippery snow on the last day of my trek, the clouds parted, and the sun edged briefly over the rim of the mountains. Its appearance after so long an absence provoked in me the kind of elation ancient peoples must have felt seeing it peek above the horizon. I knew that the Earth was round, that it revolved around the sun, that the sun's return had to do with the interaction of the earth's tilt and its position relative to the sun. But in that moment, I believed in magic.

SOLDAGEN

Sometime deep in the night, I fell asleep over these pages only to awaken to the cuckooing of the clock at six. What luxury to have spent an entire day in bed yesterday reliving the winter memories, reminding myself that even in our most desperate hours, we persevered. Feeling too close to the person who's died can pull you under. Yet, throughout the relentless dark, Astrid resisted that pull. I still marvel at her ability to deliver Hans alone and keep them both alive in my absence.

It's time for me to prepare for tomorrow's journey to Haven and the rituals of Midsummer's Eve. Brilliant sunshine has replaced yesterday's icy rain, and the temperature has warmed to eight degrees Celsius. I hadn't shaved or bathed in days, and here God had delivered a perfect day for bathing in the sea. The water was frigid, of course, but I couldn't help submerging myself completely as I rinsed the soap from my hair and face and body. The cold water revived me after a largely sleepless night.

Wrapped in a blanket, I couldn't resist looking heavenward and saying out loud, "Do you see me, Astrid?" I stood there waiting for a response. The only sound was the susurration of waves gently lapping my feet.

Far out in the fjord, near the horizon, a pod of belugas surfaced, leaping and diving. *Oh*, I thought. *How bountiful the harvest would have been this year!*

When they disappeared, I stepped back from the water, closed my eyes, and tilted my head to the sun.

The sun. The Inuit believed the Earth to be the center of the universe, flat and stationary, around which celestial objects revolved. The sun, weighed down in winter's heart by cold and snow and ice, disappeared for months. At last the sun was able to lift itself back above the horizon—a cause for celebration.

Norwegians call that fortuitous return *Soldagen*. The eighth of March.

Yet there's no bright line between the dark season and the return of the light. It's more of a yearning as light teases itself over the horizon starting in late January. Winter would soon be left behind, but the cold—the cold was much colder in this cusp time on Svalbard. Many have found March's bitter cold more unbearable than winter's full dark. The sun taunts weak-minded souls with its promise of warmth. Could there be a worse betrayal for those accustomed to the promise of spring?

Soldagen. I'd been away almost three weeks. There before me, finally, was our cabin. My joy at seeing the sun quickly evaporated. The storm lantern over the front door wasn't lit, and the path to the door was blocked by snow. Worse, the bedroom shutters looked broken. Had a bear smashed through the window? As I drew closer, I saw that the shutters, though broken, had been haphazardly nailed into place. That calmed me enough to collect my wits and race to the front door.

Waist high in the drift by the entrance, the snow was soft enough that I could wade and paw my way through it to retrieve the shovel and uncover the threshold. Incongruously, my thoughts ran back to our first day here together, to that romantic gesture of carrying Astrid across this very threshold. Was that a dream?

Or this: I heard a baby crying. Then silence.

I dug faster. My heart raced.

I strained to hear the cry. Nothing.

Was it my imagination?

No. The cry again.

I took off my bulky, sodden glove and grabbed the door handle with my bare hand. My thumb stuck to the ice-cold metal. When I pulled my hand away, part of the skin sheared off. I crammed my glove over the bleeding finger and rushed inside.

"Astrid," I called.

No answer.

"Astrid?"

I opened the kitchen door. The stove had gone out. Frost covered the walls and tiny icicles dripped from the skins that lined them.

But I *had* heard a baby's cry.

The bedroom door was nailed shut, and at first I thought to break through. Then I realized it was nailed on the kitchen side. I heard a coo, another cry, and turned toward the sound.

And there, on the kitchen bunk, covered in heaps of woolen blankets and animal skins, were the outlines of a body.

I hesitated over the humps, my pulse pounding in my ears. Slowly I peeled back the covers. Astrid lay motionless, the baby nestled at her breast, sucking. Empty milk bottles and breadcrumbs were strewn across the bunk.

"Astrid?" I shook her gently. "Astrid?"

Her eyes fluttered open.

လ

15 March 1938

Dear Birk,

Pappa's returned! This past week went by in a blur. Today I feel almost restored to my skin.

Yes, Pappa's home. A split second of terror on his face vanished a moment after I opened my eyes. He told me later he thought I was dead.

The last thing I remember was crawling into bed with Hansel, a loaf of bread, and a bottle of milk. What day was that? I'm having trouble keeping track. Pappa's brought the calendar into the bedroom, crossed off each passing day with a big red X. It says 15 March. I must believe it's so.

He removed the broken window shutters—I hardly remember that day I had to axe my way outside—so that I could see that indeed, the sun has returned. Light slants through the window but barely warms the room. Buried under a mountain of blankets, I hate to leave my bed.

He fixed the clock so that I can hear the passing of each hour, though the sound of that bird cuckooing, cuckooing, cuckooing wears on my nerves. Everything wears on my nerves.

Pappa and I argued over the name I'd chosen. Why hadn't I waited? he asked. Did I need to tell him that many times I feared him dead, fallen deep into a crevasse or drowned under ice that suddenly yielded to his weight? Or worse, torn apart by a polar bear and consumed? No body left to find?

We argued. He'd once suggested Olaf if it was a boy, in honor of his dead father. I'd agreed because I was sure of a daughter.

In those solitary hours, I'd forgotten my promise.

"Crooning his name made him real," I told Pappa. "Not a ghost."

"But a fairy-tale boy?" he asked. "Hansel?"

As he uttered the name, the baby turned his head toward Pappa.

"Hansel," he said again. "Hans." The baby gurgled, staring straight at Pappa. What choice did he have?

Choices. Part of me had hoped that Hansel wouldn't be born into this dead world. Now I look at his face, the eyes' dark pupils responding to the newborn light. He knows no other world. His innocence feels like a bullet to the heart. He's satisfied with so little—warm fur soft against his cheeks, nursing, being held.

I touch his face and repeat under my breath, "You are Hansel. You are Hansel."

We shouldn't be here, the two of us. We're out of time and place, in a kind of limbo from which I'm having trouble seeing the way out. I feel, sometimes, like I'm dying. That Hansel is sucking the very life from me. I have these terrible thoughts, but if I write them down, I'm afraid they'll come true. Just as writing Elen's story made it come true.

❧

Kvitfiskneset
22 June 1947

Those first few days after my return Astrid drifted in and out of rational thought. She'd obviously been living in a land of nightmares.

"Birk, Birk," she'd croon to the baby in her delirium.

"Hans," I reminded her.

"He'll be clever enough to find his way home. Pebbles and crumbs, pebbles and crumbs."

"I hear the church bells chime. I hear the whales shrieking."

"We bury the dead so that they might grow."

Through all the madness, she'd managed to give birth and provide Hans with what he needed. The empty milk bottles were a testament to her will to survive.

I returned to a cabin frigid and in complete disarray. Blood and waste were everywhere, but cleaning would have to wait. The first order of business was to warm the cabin with a roaring fire, then to give Astrid milk and some bread from Oli's cache. The baby was sleeping soundly, so I let him be.

I filled a bucket with hot water from the watermaker and bathed the skinless patch of my injured thumb with iodine, wrapped it in cotton gauze, and slipped on a rubber glove to waterproof the bandage. The last thing I needed was to have the wound become infected. We'd fretted over the dangers of not having medical care. I hated to admit how vulnerable that made us. The least little infection could be disastrous if not tended properly.

The baby woke, so I bathed him with the same water, examined every inch of his body, counted his fingers and toes like a first-time father. I ran my hand over the stub of his umbilical cord, which Astrid had expertly cut. The doctor in Longyearbyen would have been impressed. The orange-stained skin told me that she'd sterilized the stub with iodine. That it was attached meant the baby was no more than two weeks old. I fashioned a diaper from clean rags, then snugged him into the *komse* and covered him with a small patch of reindeer skin. Once again, he dozed peacefully.

I turned my attention to Astrid, who lay mutely on the kitchen bunk watching me. I retrieved the hogshead we'd used at Christmas from the anteroom, fed the watermaker with ice, and opened the spigot to fill the tub. When the bath was ready, I undressed her. She'd lost so much weight that she felt incorporeal. Her breasts were swollen from mother's milk, but her ribs protruded from her chest. It seemed like the baby thrived while she wasted away. As if the baby *were* drawing the life out of her.

I lifted Astrid into the tub. She closed her eyes as her body sank. The water was soon clotted with dirt and blood. She stared at me with a look I can't describe, as if she were someplace far from here.

Her hair had grown long and hopelessly tangled. I retrieved the scissors, the very ones she used to cut Hans's umbilical cord, and carefully cropped her hair into short tresses. When I finished, I poured fresh water over her head and body, rinsing her as best I could. Finally, I held out my hand to her to help her stand.

Instead, she pulled me toward her. "Get in," she said.

Those were her first clear words.

I stripped my clothes and straddled the barrel edge. We'd both lost a lot of weight since Christmas, and with Astrid no longer pregnant, I slid easily down behind her, wrapped my arms around her waist, and rested my head against her neck. We bathed until the water went cold. I climbed out of the hogshead and fastened a towel around my waist, then lifted her over the barrel edge, dried her, and pulled a woolen nightgown over her head. I fashioned a clean rag into her underwear to catch the blood, the normal flow after birth.

After settling her in the bedroom bunk and dressing myself, I turned to the task of storing the haul from Oli's in the shed. Lo and behold, I found reindeer meat enough to last till spring. How was I to know my journey had been unnecessary? Returning to the cabin, my first task was to fix the clock, as if time itself couldn't march on without a working cuckoo. I gathered the empty milk bottles and rinsed them in clean water, scrubbed blood from the kitchen floor, and washed the rags and bedclothes and hung them to dry on the line above the stove. I wrapped the placenta in a rag and fed it to the sea. Finally, I boiled water to sterilize the instruments she'd used to deliver the baby and returned them to the medical kit. It was then I noticed the laudanum, a drug we hardly ever used. I held the brown bottle up to the light. It was full. *In case of emergency,* I thought. I placed it back into the kit, locked it, and hid the key underneath.

Astrid had fallen fast asleep, snoring softly, murmuring. The single word I could make out was "Birk." I thought of Hilmar's experience, tending to a newborn and a woman who'd lost her reason. My previous lack of empathy for him shamed me. I was drained. My whole body ached from the arduous trek and the labor of tending to my family. I boiled some fresh water, fixed myself a cup of tea, and sat down at the kitchen table. And right then, Hans began to cry.

の

19 March 1938

Dear Birk,

Lifting pen to paper seems overwhelming, but I'm determined to return to some sense of normality, if not for myself, then for Pappa and Hansel. Yesterday I managed to fix Pappa a belated birthday supper featuring the pickled reindeer tongue. He oohed and aahed, claimed it was the best pickled tongue he'd ever eaten.

Pappa hovers over me, as if I might break. But he, too, might break. His skin is tight over his bones, his forehead creased with deepening wrinkles. He tries hard to cheer me, to please me. Today, he tells me, is the spring equinox. When he says this, he pats me on the head like I'm a child, and with a flourish, engraves another big red X on the calendar by our bed.

"Twelve hours of sun," he crows, lifting his hand horizontally in the air and moving it ever so slightly side to side as if to demonstrate the exquisite symmetry of day and night. "Twelve hours, Astrid. Soon we'll be back to perpetual sun."

I try to embrace his enthusiasm, but it's so cold that the sun's rays provide little warmth. This past week the temperatures registered well below zero. Pappa was outside chopping ice yesterday, and when he came in, I noticed that his cheeks had turned white—the initial stages of frostbite. We warmed his cheeks slowly and applied a special ointment that heals damaged skin.

I'm afraid it's my fault. I've been useless these past weeks, too weak to help Pappa with the necessary chores. In fact, I haven't been myself, lost to nightmares, crying uncontrollably at the least provocation. The subliminal anxiety I've felt throughout my time on Svalbard has turned to deepening dread that hasn't passed since Hansel's birth. I keep reminding myself this is baby Hansel, not you. He looks so much like you—the same dimple in his chin, the same translucent blue eyes, the way he holds his tiny fists against my breast when he's nursing.

Yes, he looks so much like you, but I don't look like me. You see, Pappa cut my hair. I understand why he did so. Taking care of it is so much easier. It doesn't freeze to my head while it's drying or cake in clumps if I'm too tired to wash it. But when I look in the mirror that hangs above the bunk, I hardly recognize myself. My face is gaunt, my hair a crown of ringlets, my body a thing of bones. *Who is that woman?* I wonder. *Am I a changeling too?*

I try to suppress these thoughts. Despite Hanna's encouragement to pursue my dreams, she warned me repeatedly of the vagaries of grief. She said it wasn't something one eventually left behind, that the past lives in parallel to the present. I opened her book of poems and turned to one that most spoke to me, "At a Son's Deathbed," wherein she seeks to console herself. It begins, "Lay, my child, in the lap of sleep, close your eyes." What comfort to think of death as merely sleep. Sleep in heavenly peace.

I opened her letter I keep tucked in the book and read it once again. My hands began to tremble, the thin paper rustled. *My dear Helge would have been forty-two last 25 February.*

Could it be? Hansel born prematurely. I don't know the exact day. What are the chances? Close enough. Helge reincarnated in Hansel's soul. Would it comfort Hanna to know this? To know that we bury the dead so that they might live again?

Time moves enigmatically on Svalbard, she wrote me. *Sometimes the days slip one into another as if they're a single day. Other times, days stretch into the tick-tock of seconds.*

Yes, here time warps and bends around itself. There are gaps when I don't remember where I am or what I'm supposed to be doing. Time seems so fragile it should be kept in a gilded cage like an unusual bird. Or conserved in a leatherbound portfolio, like a rare flower.

Time, time, time. The time it takes to die. The anticipation of it. Hanna had nine days to prepare for Helge's death. I had seconds. One moment you were happily chasing bubbles along the pier, the next you disappeared. Is sudden loss more painful? Is a mother ever prepared to lose a child? I think of this as I nurse Hansel. I think, *What's the point? What's the point of all this mothering if in the end there's only death?*

I try to embrace the optimism of Hanna's closing words. *The Arctic's elemental nature—rock, ice, air, water, the landscape's purity—affects one's very soul. It seems to me that these elements exist in perfect harmony, as if we've returned to primordial Earth to encounter the ancients' wellspring of peace.*

Harmony. Peace. I want to believe these feelings are possible. Winter rages on inside me. Even with the sun's return, when I close my eyes each evening, my mind turns dark.

My dear, sweet Birk. No, no, no. Hansel. Who are you? Has a troll left his fairy child and snatched you away? Folklore tells us that such demons are afraid of iron, so I hung a knife on the canopy of your *komse* right next to the good-luck braid. Perhaps it's already too late.

So many dangers. How could I have brought you into this world? Either of you. And yet how could I not?

SPRING

To Haven
23 June 1947

The cuckoo woke me at seven. The sun was bright, and the temperature hovered right at the freezing mark as I packed my rucksack with the supplies for the journey to Haven. I slung my rifle and pack across my shoulders and walked down to the shoreline. Toeing the mud and scree, I knew it was ridiculous to think I'd find anything of Astrid there. Logic didn't stop me from searching for something, anything that outlasted time. Her gold locket? A skull? A rib bone?

This is now bone of my bones and flesh of my flesh; she shall be called woman, for she was taken out of man.

Astrid despised that Bible verse, and who could blame her? All that Old Testament nonsense about helpmeets and wives submitting to their husbands. I thought myself an enlightened man, more New Testament than Old. I'm reminded of a conversation I once had with a glaciologist by the name of Alex Glen, who spent '35 and '36 on Svalbard as part of the Oxford Arctic expedition. Our tongues loosened by drinks in the miners' canteen, we waxed philosophical about the meaning of life, the conflicting desires of conformity and the pursuit of the extraordinary, the roles of men and women in a changing society. Later, in his book documenting the expedition, he harkened back to that barroom discussion, asking, *Does woman hold the whip, or does the instinct of man insist on mastery and then despise the slavery he has inflicted?* Yes, we were enlightened men.

Bone of my bones. Would that it were possible to conjure my wife from my bones. To bury a rib bone and let it germinate, as a seed pushes up through the soil and produces a stunning flower. To start marriage over and avoid the sins and errors of the past. To reclaim what was lost.

Impossible. Why bother, why indulge in a place of so much grief?

Ah, but there was joy as well, I keep reminding myself.

Halfway to Haven, I spied the remains of the old shed where Astrid had gathered those troublesome mushrooms so long ago. Amid the detritus was a crate, surprisingly sturdy despite years of weathering. I sat down, picked one of the mushrooms, and stuffed it in my rucksack.

As I rested, a ringed seal surfaced, his head visible. He glided elegantly back and forth and left small wakes that quickly swallowed themselves. And just like that, the calm I'd begun to feel was broken by a memory of another ringed seal.

It was the noise that roused me—Astrid screaming and gulls screeching and what sounded like a baby crying. Where was she? Our bed was warm. The last thing I remembered was the *perrrrrit* of a snow bunting outside the bedroom window and imagining that I was in bed at the farm hearing the symphony of birdsong as the migrants returned from their winter quarters. I'd fallen into a dream of spring in southern Norway. How I missed the farm, the scent that rose from the ground as I plowed the fields, the sun's rays warming me as I drove my tractor forward, creating orderly furrows ready for new seed. On Svalbard, sparse signs of life baptized the earth. Yes, the sun returned, quickly gained time in its arc across the sky so that by early April, a month after *Soldagen*, the sun shone daily for sixteen hours. But its shine was a lie. Its rays failed to warm. The temperatures registered well below freezing. May seemed impossibly far away.

Again I heard Astrid screaming and a baby crying and those wretched gulls. Dispelling the last remnants of my dreams, I checked on Hans, fast asleep in his *komse*, oblivious to the cacophony. But it *was* a baby's cry. Quickly, I jammed my feet into boots and heaved on my anorak.

Outside, the scene before me:

Astrid in her nightgown, no coat, wool socks on her feet. She was slip-sliding on the last of the fast ice near shore, waving a shovel at a swarm of gulls.

On the ice was a baby seal, his deep black eyes set against his pale white face. That is, what was left of his eyes. Blood streamed from one empty socket. A gull swooped in, its beak drilling the remaining eye. Where was the mother seal? Mating season starts soon after the pups are born, and the mothers, after a month of nursing, abandon their children to begin the breeding cycle again. The babies are helpless on the ice, unable to swim for weeks. A blinded seal is as good as dead.

The gulls swarming the pup worked in concert, some distracting Astrid away from their prey by pecking at her head and arms, some working on the baby. Astrid's efforts were puny in comparison to their orchestrated attack.

The pup's fate was settled, but Astrid continued her defense as the gulls swooped and pecked. She, too, had been bloodied.

Retrieving my flare gun, I joined her on the ice and fired the gun into the flock. The flare hit one of the birds, which fell to the ice. I took aim again and fired, missing them all as they wheeled into the sky.

Together, Astrid and I dragged the injured seal up the hillock to the front door. Astrid was weeping, breathing heavily, choking on her sobs. The baby's cries weakened, faded away.

"Birgitta, Birgitta." Keening, she knelt on the ground and cradled the dying seal.

"Birgitta's safe," I said to her. "She's with your mother."

"Where *is* the mother?"

To answer her question, I shook my head, though she wasn't looking at me. Yes, she *was* far away from me and getting farther. I can see that now.

"There's nothing to save a blinded seal," I said. "Let's go inside."

She shook her head, continuing to cradle the pup and croon our daughter's name. She was shivering. I draped my coat over her.

"Astrid," I said, "come back." I placed my hands on her shoulders, shook her gently. Her eyes were opaque, glazed with tears.

The pup finally stopped crying. His body slackened.

And right then, as if the pup's soul rose and passed through the cabin walls to our newborn son, Hans began to cry.

"Astrid," I begged her. "He's gone. Please."

I had to tug the pup from her arms, pull her to her feet, and carry her inside. I sat her down, pulled off her socks stiffened with ice, and rubbed warmth back into her feet. She stared out the window at the dead seal while I cleaned the wounds on her face and arms with a wet cloth, applied iodine, and massaged her hands to restore circulation. Then I dressed her in fresh clothing and draped a blanket around her.

All the while, Hans cried for his mother, hungry for breakfast. Astrid didn't seem to hear, didn't notice her milk had let down and seeped through her shirt. I plucked Hans from the *komse*'s comforting embrace and placed him in her arms. Hans rooted for Astrid's breast through her thin shirt, found purchase, and suckled.

∂

4 April 1938

Dear Birk,

The calendar tells me it's the fourth of April. Is it possible that over a month has passed since Hansel was born? Or are those bloody crosses a lie Pappa tells me so that I won't despair at the slow days and nights until the end of our incarceration? I don't trust him anymore. He's working against me. I prefer to know the truth.

The seal pup was real. I had his blood on my nightgown. Pappa threw the nightgown into the fire, but my eyes didn't deceive me. The gulls were real too. They bloodied me.

I held the pup as he drew his last breaths. I could feel faint puffs of air coming from his nostrils until that paltry indication of life ceased. The fate of a mother's abandonment.

I woke screaming from a nightmare. But it wasn't a nightmare. Birgitta's eyes were empty sockets against her pale skin. My little Lucia, eyes on a platter.

Birgitta is dead. A mother senses these things. I see the dead ranged along the hillsides.

Pappa won't listen. He tries to calm me with his whispers.

Words meant to soothe. "It was the seal," he says. "It's only the seal. Birgitta's safe. She's with your parents."

One by one, my children are dying. What does that say about me as a mother? Does he not see? Does he not hear? Can he not sense it?

Here is Hansel, in my arms. Or is this Birk? Birk, my sweet little boy. You've followed the smooth stones you had the good sense to drop, found your way back to me. Alive. Breathing. You always were a clever boy.

The dead wish to be seen.

I pass my hand over your face to make sure you're breathing like I did so many times when you were little. A mother does these things. Feels for the puffs of air coming from the nose, the mouth. How many times I did that, brushed the hair from your forehead, leaned into the crib to kiss your warm cheek.

A heartbeat is autonomous. Breathing, too, until you struggle for breath.

Hansel will die. I'm helpless before him.

"No, no," Pappa says. "Hans is fine. See, he grows fatter every day. Look! Look at these rolls of fat on his arms, his legs. His double chin." He pinches him there and turns to me.

He's exaggerating. Hansel is pale. I can't feed him enough. I'm being punished for my sins. Punish me, God. Leave Hansel alone.

When Pappa looks at me nursing Hansel, he's not marveling at the bond between mother and child. No. It's the look of a husband searching for the woman he married, the one he thought resilient, kind, rational. He's afraid I'll hurt the baby. But that's not what he should fear. No harm will come to Hansel from my hands. It's me Pappa should fear.

I turned away from you for an instant. That's my sin. And now Birgitta. I abandoned her when she needed me most. The only comfort is that she's joined you in heaven. I know she missed you, know she wasn't whole without you. Two become one. Isn't that the wedding vow?

I used to imagine Birgitta in my wedding dress, someday far

in the future, walking down the aisle at Sandar Church toward her groom. What good is that gown now? Pappa thought he'd hidden it. Is he afraid of what I might do?

When he finally left me alone to inventory our supplies in the shed, I had my chance to search the cabin. I opened the curtains to let in more light, knelt before the bunk in our bedroom, and pulled out one crate after another. In the farthest corner I found what I was looking for—the dress folded beneath layers and layers of yellowed tissue, the very tissue I'd used to repack it last June. Thin ivory tissue, like skin. Before I put it away, I traced the beaded lilies of the valley and tried to remember what real lilies look like. It's spring in Sandefjord, almost time for the lilies to bloom. Their sharp green leaves have begun to push up through the moist earth, white bell-shaped flowers enfolded in those leaves. Church bells.

I can hear them now.

I won't hear them again.

I can feel it, just as I can feel Birgitta has joined you. My only solace is that you're happy again. The two of you will wind the paddle wheel of your wooden boat, a boat big enough for the two of your lost souls. Sail off to Hyperborea. Sail past me and wave on your way to paradise. Blue sky. Turquoise water. Forest primeval.

"You'll never be cold again," I whisper. "Sail on. Sail on."

"Hush," Pappa says. He's come in stealthily, unheard. This is how he moves now. Like a thief. He takes the dress from my hands. "Hush. Hush."

He's there beside me, stroking my cropped hair.

Why can't he sense Birgitta sailing by? Why can't he see that Hansel isn't far behind?

❧

To Haven
23 June 1947

Looking back over these letters, I think that the episode with the seal was the turning point, or rather the precipice from which the inevitable fall began.

I had to get rid of the seal. Those empty eye sockets, staring at nothing. I'd never seen gulls do that to a living seal. They usually thrive on carrion. Easy prey.

I tucked Hans into his *komse* and sat beside Astrid on our bunk. No amount of soothing calmed her. It was then I thought of the laudanum. I worried briefly about the effect the drug would have on her milk, but I didn't feel I had a choice. And besides, didn't doctors prescribe it for "women's troubles"? I left her sitting up in bed and went into the kitchen. There, I fixed two cups of tea. Into hers, I measured two drops of laudanum and sweetened it with extra sugar to hide the drug's bitterness. We sat side by side on the bunk and drank the tea. Then, I eased her down in bed and left the cabin, praying Hans and she would be safe. I couldn't be everywhere at once.

I dragged the seal downshore, past the mounds of whale bones to the last pile. The whale cemetery became a cemetery for this baby seal. The gulls could finally enjoy the meal they'd labored for that morning, reduce seal flesh and blubber to bone.

~

5 April 1938

Dear Birk,

Laudanum. What a lovely drug! Pappa locked it away in the medicine kit and "hid" the key underneath. He thinks I didn't see him. Nothing here is truly hidden. I've taken it when he wasn't around. Blackout sleep. Carefully, ever so carefully, I refill the bottle drop by drop with water.

To calm my nerves after the seal died in my arms, Pappa measured the drug into tea. I saw him through the open bedroom door. I sipped it slowly, as if I were reluctant. The effect was almost immediate. Gone were the nightmares, gone the wicked thoughts haunting me night and day. Lucid dreams drifted before me. Gardens of roses and lilies. A path of stones. Fields of sunflowers swaying in a summer breeze.

The effect was short-lived, my fault for diluting it. Sunlight angled through the window, awakening me. In the distance I spied Pappa standing in the whale cemetery, the dead seal pup in his arms. I dressed quickly, checked that Hansel was fast asleep, and walked to the graveyard.

Pappa startled when I touched his shoulder. He'd fashioned a shallow grave among the whale bones and laid the pup in the ditch.

"Let's pray," I said. We folded our hands and bowed our heads. "May the baby find its way back to his mother's spirit. May she take back her sightless son."

I bent to stroke the pup's head, yanked a whisker from his chin, and put it in my pocket.

"Be on your way," I said.

Together Pappa and I covered the seal with stones and bones, then walked hand-in-hand back to the cabin. It was high tide. The water lapped close to our feet, tempting me. I understand why whalers and hunters might answer that call. It feels very much like the laudanum, that instant underwater when one gives in to the sea. A strange kind of peace.

I wonder if you felt it when you realized there was no way out, the wooden dock blocking your escape. We found your body. At least there was that.

I pray you were at peace. Otherwise, I couldn't live with myself.

&

1 May 1938

Dear Birk,

"It's May," Pappa says, striking another day from the calendar. "We don't have long to wait."

For what? I think. He seems irrationally confident in our rescue. What is there to look forward to but interminable days of eking out our survival?

May used to be my favorite month, flowers bursting forth in earnest, the farm animals giving birth, crops spiking up through the freshly tilled soil. And our wedding: this May marks the eleventh anniversary of our marriage.

But May is now marred by your death. The second anniversary of your death. How could May be so kind *and* so cruel? I long for darkness where before I longed for light. Serenity came from being nestled with Pappa in the cold dark, in the dead of winter, before Hansel, before these nightmares that won't stop. I wonder if this is how the beluga feels, diving deep into the sea, cocooned below the ice ceiling and the reach of light. The white whale can dive to inconceivable depths, some say deeper than any other whale. They can hold their breath for fifteen minutes. The heart rate slows, and oxygen critical for mammals is temporarily drawn from circulating blood.

Imagine the darkness that far below the surface. Imagine holding one's breath that long. Imagine the heart rate slowing, slowing, slowing. Would that humans had the same capacity for surviving underwater!

I think of that nursing beluga calf, so vulnerable. I think of Hansel, so trusting as he nurses, so trusting as he sleeps bundled in the *komse*. Hansel's crying bespeaks a bottomless need I can't fill. Pappa says it's colic. He pats my head. His touch is like an electric shock. I turn away.

I bundle Hansel, walk outside, and circle the cabin round and round, counting the laps. Still Hansel cries, his cheeks redden. His body is stiff against mine as he arches away from me. I'm convinced he knows I killed you. He wants no part of me, yet when he nurses, he sucks greedily. Instinct over reason. He doesn't know the milk poisons him. He doesn't know my secret—two drops of laudanum under the tongue lifts my spirits and thrusts away the nightmares. I'm a dangerous woman.

I like to talk to the whales in the cemetery, pick up skull after skull. The wind carries their voices through the jawbones. Despite missing tongues, they speak. Have you heard them wherever you dwell? The pregnant cows Pappa's killed, the mothers of newborn calves. The calves as well. I tell the skulls I'm afraid of what I might do. And suddenly the voices stop.

This afternoon I left Hansel with Pappa and headed for the whale cemetery. I don't bother with a rifle anymore. Even the polar bears have fled from me.

I picked up a whale skull. So many to choose from! Why do these skulls haunt me so? We all become these bones that speak to us. Each time I visit these graves I pick up a bone and put it in my pocket. My parka pockets are filled with bones. Whale bones are so much like human bones. A vertebra looks like a tiny baby, metacarpals and phalanges like human wrist and finger bones. Some claim these are the last traces of a vestigial hand the flipper now supplants.

"Alas, poor Yorick," I said to the skull. Is there a more poignant scene? A father killed, and a son filled with guilt. Alas, indeed. I laughed; I couldn't stop laughing. "Alas, poor Yorick. I knew him, Horatio."

Remember how you loved to ride piggyback on Pappa, how he pretended to be a horse down on all fours, lifting his arms in the air and whinnying while you held on tight, laughing and laughing and laughing. I remember holding my breath, afraid you might slide off and what?—skin your knee? How silly my worries were then!

Is there no way back from your death, Birk?

At the farthest verge of the cemetery, I came upon the seal pup's grave. Or what was left of the grave. Marauders have desecrated the site, scavenged the meat, and left the bones behind. I picked up the pup's skull, its empty eye sockets staring at me, and raised it up two-handed like an offering to the gods.

"Alas, poor Birk, did I ever know you?" I asked, then placed the skull in my pocket.

&

To Haven
23 June 1947

A gull's cries distracted me from these last two letters and the melancholy ruminations they evoked. The seal glides past me again, eying me while I rest. I wonder what he thinks of this old man, scribbling onto sheets of paper ruffled by the wind. Do seals think? What would Astrid say of the seal's sentience? Yes, that business with the seal should have been fair warning of what was to come. How thoroughly Astrid had changed was never more evident than when Hilmar *did* come to our rescue on the second of May. I heard his dogs first, King in the lead, the others spread out fan-shaped, and behind them, Hilmar riding a contraption that looked like a sledge with both runners and wheels.

Imagine my relief! I literally fell to my knees as he approached. But my relief gave way to embarrassment when I thought of the state Astrid was in. Of all people, though, Hilmar might understand.

"*Hallo!*" I said, waving to him as he brought his sledge to a stop.

He leapt off, tied the reins to the driftwood post, and gave me a bear hug. He squeezed my shoulders and pinched my cheeks, as if to make sure that I was alive.

"I came as soon as I heard that you were missing," he said. "If I'd known! What happened?"

I told him about the disaster with the boat, how Astrid almost drowned slipping from the floe, how we sought refuge in the hunter's cabin at Fleur de Lyshamna, and so on. The words came in a giant rush. I hadn't spoken to anyone for so long except what passed for conversation with Astrid.

At that moment, Hans began to cry.

"A baby?" Hilmar said, arching his eyebrows. "Is Astrid…"

"She's fine," I said, praying that Hilmar's very presence might shake her back to normality. That she'd pull herself together and welcome him to our "parlor," lay out bread and jam and tea. That some deep instinct might allow her to feign such common rituals for a few hours. I suspected that she was using laudanum but attributed the fluctuations in her mood to the natural progression of emotions after giving birth. Illogical hope, I see now.

"It's been…difficult."

Hilmar scrutinized my face, as if he were trying to divine the meaning of *difficult*.

"As you can imagine, Astrid's worn out by the long winter, giving birth, and taking care of a newborn," I said. "Come inside."

Hilmar retrieved a package from the sledge, and together we entered the cabin. The package contained Helfrid's handiwork: three loaves of bread, jam and biscuits, and a sponge cake. Apparently, he and Helfrid assumed we were alive. Or that the gifts themselves would magic us to life. I offered Hilmar some coffee, lukewarm from breakfast, set out plates and forks and a knife and margarine.

Hilmar sat down at the kitchen table and sliced off a large hunk of bread. Hans continued to cry, though the bedroom door muted the sound. I excused myself, took a deep breath, and opened the door. Hans was punching the air with his tiny fists. Astrid lay on the bed, her eyes wide open, but she made no move to pick up our hungry son.

I peeled away the bearskin covering her, pulled down her nightgown, and laid Hans next to her breast. He latched on and began to suck.

"Astrid," I whispered, brushing her bangs away from her forehead. "Hilmar is here."

Her eyes remained glazed, staring straight ahead.

"Astrid," I said again, gently nudging her. "Hilmar is here."

Her eyes finally registered my presence. "Helfrid?" she asked.

I shook my head.

"I can't," she said.

"Can't what?"

"Can't come out."

"Okay," I said. I admit I was relieved.

I left her with Hans sucking and closed the door behind me.

"Astrid's feeding the baby," I said.

Hilmar nodded as if that explained the tension that hung in the air like a fog that wouldn't lift.

I sighed. "There were times I wasn't sure we'd make it through the winter."

"I'm sorry I didn't hear sooner," he said, wolfing down another large hunk of bread. "I wasn't in Longyearbyen this Christmas as usual because my whole family was at Sassen this year."

"I should've listened to you last fall," I started. "I thought I knew how to navigate autumn ice."

"In any case, you made it through. That's something for a winter greenhorn. And a baby to boot."

We laughed.

"The first boat is coming later this month, assuming Isfjord thaws. June at the latest. I can take you all up to Sassen for now. Helfrid's there with my uncle and son. You're welcome to stay—"

"No." Astrid was suddenly at the bedroom door, holding Hans to her bare breast. Her nightgown hung down her arms.

I leapt to my feet and crossed over to her, my back to Hilmar to block the spectacle of my half-naked wife.

"Astrid," I said.

She raised her voice. "I won't."

"Astrid," I said again, as if my vocabulary had been reduced to that one word.

"The babies are all buried here. I can't leave them." She started crying. "The babies, the babies…"

I lifted Astrid's face to mine. "Your babies are safe," I said. "Birgitta, Hans. Look. Hans is in your arms."

"I won't leave them."

"I know you won't. But we have to get home. Your parents must be worried sick."

I took Hans from Astrid's arms, covered her with her nightgown, and sat her down on the kitchen bunk.

Behind me, Hilmar cleared his throat. "I can send a message in Longyearbyen that you're safe. Alive! And the baby—your parents will be thrilled to be grandparents again."

"Astrid," I said, "if you really want to stay a little longer,

I can send for Anders. There should still be time for him to gather a crew and outfit the boat. Then I'll bring you and Hans up to Longyearbyen in June after they arrive."

She nodded, and I turned to Hilmar.

"It's settled then," Hilmar said, rising quickly. "I'll be on my way for now. But I *will* make sure that Anders arrives safely. Otherwise, I'll come back to get you myself."

"You're welcome to stay," I said, though my invitation lacked conviction.

He shook his head. "Better that I get word to your in-laws and Anders as soon as possible."

I laid Hans on the bunk and scribbled a note with our plans for Marit and Christian and Birgitta, another for Anders asking him to oversee the provisioning and sailing to Kvitfiskneset, and one for Knut asking him to book passage on June's *Lyngen* for Astrid and Hans. While I was writing, Hilmar heaved on his parka and left to feed his dogs and secure them to his sledge.

Outside, I handed him the notes, and he promised to give them to Knut as soon as he got to Longyearbyen. It would take him days, but I was sure he'd make it. Legends don't die.

I watched Hilmar until his sledge disappeared. I felt abandoned. And yes, ashamed. So unlike his last visit, when Astrid and I held hands as his figure receded and we anticipated a second honeymoon.

I found Astrid as I'd left her, sitting upright on the bunk, the vacant look returned to her face. I grabbed her shoulders and shook her, as if shaking her would release her from her trance.

"Wake up! Wake up!" I shouted. "You're alive and so am I! And since we're alive, we must live! You're Birgitta's mother! You're Hans's mother!"

My yelling started Hans crying again. Anger had gotten the best of me. I released my grip, picked Hans up, and took deep breaths to calm myself.

Astrid looked up at me and whispered, "I am no one's mother."

Her words chilled me, but at least I'd gotten through to her.

"There, there," I said, patting her head. I laid her back on the bunk, nestled Hans beside her, and covered them both with a bearskin. The fire had burned down, so I went outside to retrieve a fresh supply of logs. Outdoors all was calm, the water gently lapping the shore, the wind shushed. Present is past. Time is memory. Looking downshore, I can almost see Hilmar and his dog team fade away. The imagination plays tricks. His dogs are ghosts.

&

In mid-June, Anders arrived with a crew for the start of another whaling season. I asked him how he'd made it on such short notice.

"I had a feeling you were alive," he said. "And your credit was good everywhere."

We got to work, and it seemed as if the previous summer's rhythm had been restored. Hans was thriving, and the men honored Anders's example, respectful in Astrid's presence. Soren had joined us again, and he took over the cooking duties as he had in the years before Astrid.

Among the supplies Anders brought was a new medical kit, and with it, a bottle of laudanum. This I administered to Astrid. I decided to leave the kit unlocked, wanting her to know that I trusted her even though I now knew that she'd been using it on her own. She'd stopped replacing what she'd used. The drug helped. Or appeared to. She was able to sleep under its influence.

Astrid seemed buoyed by Anders's arrival. Ever thoughtful, he'd brought fresh supplies for her botanical collecting. She whisked them to the bedroom and spent her final days at Kvitfiskneset in there with the door closed. I assumed that she'd returned to her great passion and was busy mounting the specimens she'd dried in the fall. Only later did I realize it was Birk's letters, not flora, she was painstakingly preserving.

Now I chide myself: What did I miss? In moments of light, like an errant sunbeam that suddenly illuminates a room or falls unexpectedly through an opening in tree branches or a break between clouds, I see that we were too often cocooned in clothing and animal skins, fighting the cold dark that enveloped us, measuring each other's breath, the rise and fall of our chests rhythmic and synchronized, the baby turning and turning in her womb. I thought we were bound together by Birk's death and our love. I was wrong. His death made us strangers to each other. We couldn't have been more distant than if she'd made it back to Sandefjord and I'd spent the winter at Kvitfiskneset alone.

I've come to understand that grief and love are intertwined. You can't love and be spared the pain of loss. That is the unbearable beauty of grief.

Unexpectedly, suddenly, another dark day arrived. Anders burst into the cabin, breathless.

"Captain," he said, "come quick."

I checked on Hans, sleeping in his *komse*, and put on my parka. Astrid was in the whale cemetery, at the site of the seal pup's grave. One could hardly call it a grave anymore—bones were scattered everywhere. Astrid had no coat on, just light clothing and a canvas apron to keep her warm. She didn't seem to notice the cold as she paced the area, picking up bones and arranging them as a skeleton, a skull where the head should be, vertebrae and ribs, metacarpals and phalanges. It was a partial skeleton, mostly whale bones but also reindeer and seal. A puzzle she was trying to solve.

I took off my parka and draped it over her shoulders. Anders graciously took his leave.

"I need proof," she said.

"Proof of what?" I asked.

In response, she picked up a tiny bone and slid it into her apron pocket. I hadn't noticed her obsession with collecting bones until that moment. Before I left nine years ago, I found a cache of bones—whale bones and the pup's skull and some tiny black disks that at first I couldn't identify—in a wooden box she'd stashed under the bed.

She piled rocks over the skeleton, lifted a whale's skull to the heavens, and recited a verse over and over from a poem I didn't recognize at the time but later learned was "Echo":

Yet come to me in dreams, that I may live
My very life again though cold in death:
Come back to me in dreams, that I may give
Pulse for pulse, breath for breath:
Speak low, lean low,
As long ago, my love, how long ago.

Kneeling there, I took up the verse like a prayer, hoping to comfort her. As we chanted, sunlight caught the skull just right and shone through its empty eye sockets and jaw. A strange phenomenon. I saw it as an answer to our ersatz prayer.

She laid the skull on top of the newly arranged stones and rose from the grave. Turning to me, she looked relieved. I took her hand, and together we walked back to the cabin.

ॐ

21 June 1938

Dear Birk,

I'm finally at peace. The laudanum makes everything clear. My life stopped two years ago.

I thought I could gather up broken pieces and organize them into something meaningful. I tried. God, I *did* try. I put myself back together, but the whole was different. Like those jigsaw ice floes and those animal bones. One could rearrange the pieces a hundred times and a hundred times create a different self.

Now I see how I can make things right. I can right time. I can see you again. Pulse for pulse, breath for breath.

I've catalogued my letters in the new folio Anders was kind enough to bring me. Someday, they'll explain everything to Pappa, to Mormor and Farfar, to my Birgitta.

Dear Birgitta, you'll be in better hands than mine. Dear Birk, you won't be alone anymore.

❧

To Haven
23 June 1947

And there it is. Her last letter.

❧

I pretended not to notice that the laudanum was disappearing. With it, both Astrid and Hans slept deeply. Such blessed calm the drug produced! Everything would be all right once they were headed home, I told myself.

As I sit here writing out my thoughts, I find consolation in the fact that Astrid didn't live to see the war. It's a bizarre notion. The rest of the family suffered. Marit died. Christian carried on, a lonely, bitter widower. Birgitta shouldered too much responsibility, mourning her mother and filling her shoes, watching Marit die. What did Astrid say? That children who face challenges are stronger for it, a lesson passed down from her mother? No. I believe that displays of outward strength are covers for holes that can never be filled.

The war is everywhere still, in the fire that burns in the mouth of Mine 2a, in the devastation of Dresden and so many other cities, in the mass Jewish graves scattered throughout Germany and Poland and Austria, in the Norwegian women and their children shamed and ostracized for their fraternization with German soldiers. No matter how furiously we work—covering over the war's destruction by raising shiny new buildings, seeking justice by imprisoning and executing war criminals, and voicing empty platitudes about the world uniting behind a noble peace—simmering underneath is the knowledge of our capacity for evil.

We're all, every one of us, irrevocably changed by the war. Our hearts beat in a different rhythm, our breaths poised between inhalations and exhalations. It's as if our flesh is tattooed by the shadow of evil as those Japanese whose skin was tattooed by radiation imprinting the designs of the kimonos they wore at the moment the atomic bomb obliterated their cities. *We're all changed.*

That's what I was thinking when my old friend Hilmar approached my living quarters in Longyearbyen right before I left for Kvitfiskneset. I hadn't invited him. In fact, I'd been avoiding him, which was difficult in a town this small. Why? To be honest, he reminded me too much of myself.

"*Hei der*" came his familiar greeting. He looked so much older than his fifty-seven years. His gait had slowed, his breathing was labored. Yes, his very breath had changed. I opened the conversation by apologizing for not having him over sooner. He waved me off. "It's good to see you again," he said.

We shook hands, and I offered him a seat on my porch. Taking a pipe from his pocket, he filled the bowl with tobacco, lit it, and offered it to me. *A peace pipe*, I thought, though he and I had never been at war.

We passed the pipe back and forth as we talked. We began by exchanging the usual pleasantries—how was the family and so forth. He avoided telling me that his daughter Embjørg had died, but I'd heard. News like that travels. Our conversation eventually turned to the war, its ghosts hovering in the air even as new construction rose around us.

"I was finally doing well," he said. "Helfrid and I had stored several years of provisions at Villa Fredheim. Eight hundred kilos of fine Canadian wheat alone. We'd put a little money aside for our retirement. Then came the evacuation."

Governor Marlow had signed the decree mandating Norwegians' evacuation to Scotland in the fall of 1941. There was no reprieve. British and Norwegian soldiers destroyed everything in Ny-Ålesund and Longyearbyen that might benefit the Germans—substations, radio masts, and telegraph equipment, mining infrastructure and entrances, and all the coal stores. What wasn't ruined during the evacuation the Germans mostly burned down two years later when they fled before the return of Norwegian forces.

Hilmar sucked vigorously on the pipe, and clouds of smoke

swirled above his head. "We were limited to fifty kilos each during the evacuation. Fifty kilos! All our hard-earned bounty left behind even though there was plenty of room aboard the *Empress of Canada*."

His bitterness was palpable. "There were my huskies." He coughed, handed me the pipe, coughed again. "My Greenland huskies. No animals were allowed aboard the *Empress*. Those were the orders. Pigs and horses were slaughtered. I'd killed my share of bears and reindeer and foxes. But the dogs?

"I had a friend put the dogs down. You'd think with all the animals I've killed—I couldn't…King was last. His tongue hung out. The trust in his eyes."

My friend looked away. His eyes teared. Six years had passed, and still.

"Then exile in Scotland. All those wasted years. I tried to enlist in the merchant fleet. They wouldn't have me. At least Kaps and my brothers managed to enlist. Eventually Helfrid, who found work in Edinburgh tending to Norwegian soldiers, prevailed upon the Norwegian consulate there to find work for me. I became a janitor at the Edinburgh Depot. A janitor! But I proved competent enough to ascend through the ranks, eventually becoming quartermaster of the entire repository. At least it was something to keep me busy."

I told him then of my own time during the war tending to the farm, as if the war were being fought in some other place. Of course, there were shortages, German atrocities against the Norwegian Resistance, and the destruction of towns and villages as the Germans abandoned them when defeat was imminent. Mercifully, our little farm remained unscathed.

I returned the spent pipe to Hilmar. He emptied the remnants of tobacco onto the ground, refilled the bowl, and relit the pipe. His hands were scarred, the skin almost translucent in places, the veins protruding. "To think I trusted them."

"Who?" I asked.

"Those German dogs. Dege and Ritter. To think I hosted them at Sassen."

I'd heard both men were drafted, Ritter to Greenland, Dege to Nordaustlandet—that vast island of ice in northeast Svalbard. Each was assigned to build a weather monitoring station. The Arctic is the origin of most weather in Europe, and predicting it was critical to the Germans' attempt to subjugate the world to their corrupt schemes.

Svalbard was thus one ideal location for monitoring the weather. Operation Haudegen, Dege's base was called. He and his fellow meteorologists were the last Germans to surrender in September 1945, four months after the war in Europe ended, not because they were passionate about the Nazi cause, but because they'd been forgotten. Dege sent desperate messages to anyone who could hear, and it was a Norwegian sealing vessel that finally came to their rescue.

Ritter set up a station in Hansa Bay but was captured soon after by a Danish ski patrol. He ended up a POW in America for much of the war. There were rumors that he'd "allowed" himself to be captured rather than participate in a war for which he had little stomach. There were also stories that he, a staunch Catholic, refused to kill the enemy unless he was threatened with death himself.

Then again, both men were recruited for their knowledge and experience in the Arctic. Both men supplied the Wehrmacht with maps. Guilty as charged?

"We should have realized sooner what was happening," I said. "I mean, we knew that Hitler was planning unspeakable things, carrying out his barbaric ideas. I try to put myself in the Germans' place with the choices they had to make. With the loyalties they had to their country. Remember, they were just men like us."

"No. Nothing like us." Hilmar paused, the pipe resting quietly in his hand. "On their last visit here, Dege's wife, Liselotte, said, 'We return to Germany to teach our children to build trenches.' And Helfrid said, 'You Germans always seem to be preparing for war.' And Liselotte said—I'll never forget this as long as I live—'But this time we'll win!'"

I understood his bitterness, but we were all complicit. We Europeans were playing some kind of game, winners and losers. A vile game of patience, where the crucial cards are hidden from view until it's too late. Frau Dege's prophecy, thankfully, proved wrong.

But we all lost.

"Dege had the gall to write to me afterward. Told me how he saved Villa Fredheim. The Germans were ordered to burn it to the ground. My brother Skjølberg was with a small Norwegian security force at Sassen when Dege arrived. The Germans chased the Norwegians away." He sucked on the pipe and offered it to me. I shook my head, and he continued. "I expect I should be grateful Dege ordered his company not to destroy my compound. But nothing's the same. That's why I'm in Longyearbyen, not there."

Hilmar emptied the bowl once again, wiped the stem and tip with a handkerchief, and shoved the pipe in his pocket. "Listen to me go on. I never thought I'd become an angry old man."

"I try to tell myself the past is past," I said. "But it's hard to put aside all the things we might have done differently."

Hilmar nodded. "I should have stayed at Sassen. I'd have liked to confront Dege myself."

"And what would you have done?"

The question hung in the air, another ghost hovering. From our perch on the hill that overlooks Longyearbyen, the water shone a brilliant shade of blue. Everywhere were signs of new life.

"Let's stretch our legs," I said.

We rose together and walked down along the road until we reached the docks. Above us, gulls streaked across the sky in a perfect V. Across Adventfjorden, the mountains were etched with snow, and lower down, the valleys were dotted with bursts of yellow and red and purple, Astrid's beloved flora.

"It's hard to believe that long ago Svalbard was a tropical paradise," Hilmar said. "Before we evacuated, I'd found a primordial fish fossil in one of the mountains. The government promised me ten thousand kroner if I could retrieve it. But then the war intervened. I went back up into the mountains when I returned but couldn't find the fossil. It was as if that world, too, had completely disappeared."

A world gone to ash, I thought. "The things we might have done. If we'd had the courage."

"We had the courage to survive. What's that saying? You can't kill an old fox."

We turned toward town and in companionable silence strolled up to Hilmar's place.

"Some good did come out of our time in Scotland," Hilmar said. "We adopted a little girl. Else-Marie. She's the light of our lives. It's why Helfrid chose not to come up to Svalbard with me this year. Else-Marie softens the blow of losing Embjørg to *them*." Hilmar's lower lip quivered. He looked down at his hands, then straight at me. "Not that one child can replace the other, as you well know."

I nodded, speechless for a moment. The barely contained anger against Dege and Ritter, and at the Germans in general, was understandable given Embjørg's death in Oslo at the hands of the enemy. When had Hilmar revealed so much of himself? Had age stripped him of his reticence in personal matters?

"You did get my letter?" he asked.

I nodded again. "Things were…difficult…chaotic. I'm sorry I didn't respond."

"No need to apologize," he said. "I can imagine."

What's left unspoken. *She was afraid of what she might do.* Elen's madness. Astrid's. We don't discuss such things. Mental illness is shame. The world has little compassion for it. Easier to say such madness is a woman's inherent weakness, if one says anything at all. But polar madness has overtaken the strongest men. Was it polar madness? The accumulation of losses?

In the years since Astrid died, doctors have begun to investigate an illness, a special kind of depression that overwhelms some women after giving birth. Now as then, people don't talk openly about such things. Is it better to pretend that some women are weak, or don't love their newborns, or didn't want the child to begin with?

Astrid fought that rising tide. Her letters tell me that. She was struggling but enduring in the months leading up to Hans's birth, I lie to myself. It was only afterward that her mind wavered.

Tucked into the folio is a scrap of paper with lines scribbled from who knows where:

She turned about but rose not from the ground,
Turned to the sun, still as he rolled his round,
On his bright face hung her desiring eyes,
Till fixed to earth, she strove in vain to rise.

Fixed to earth, yet she became untethered even as the sun returned the days to their natural rhythm of light and dark. A different kind of love coursed through her. A need to be with Birk, to protect Hans from her worst impulses.

How did I miss the signs? Was I too focused on the moments of joy, like the night of the glorious December moon and Astrid's face alight with happiness? "Santa Lucia, Santa Lucia" rang in my ears when I sought relief from the grief in those months after her death.

With all our talk, Hilmar avoided speaking of Kaps and Elen. Is his silence a testimony to his guilt? Rumor has it that Kaps has fallen into the kind of heavy drinking that leads to dissolution and early death. And Elen, poor Elen. Perhaps it's easier for him to pretend Kaps is fine or to erase Elen from his memory though she lives, if you call incarceration in a mental hospital living.

But I'm as guilty as Hilmar.

I'm the man who told Astrid's parents that she fell through the ice and drowned because I believed that the lie was easier than the truth, that thinking it was an accident, not suicide, would lessen their grief. Birgitta kept my secret.

Astrid's death hastened Marit's own. For that, too, I bear some guilt. After all, I *allowed* Astrid to come to Svalbard, as Marit once told me.

"What was the point of collecting flowers in that godforsaken place?" she'd asked.

But Astrid was adamant. And who was I to give her *permission* to come? No, that wasn't the mistake. We survived the months alone. We had a baby, a healthy son. We had so much. Hadn't the worst of the trauma from Birk's death passed? I didn't understand then the nature of grief, that it doesn't fade away but loops endlessly. The death of a child, all that long, unlived life. How naïve I was!

I left Hilmar in front of his lodging. He didn't invite me in but stood outside watching me walk up the main road. I turned once, and he waved, and I waved back. From a distance, he looked small, as if time had curled him into himself. This man whom Helfrid had once described as a force of nature, who once ruled as king of Sassen.

I passed through the town center, and what should I hear but the same rhythmic chant, the same *joik* humming across the square that I'd heard a decade ago:

Hey ah no yo na no yo
Hey ah no yo na no yo
Hey ah no yo na na ne ah no yo na na ne ah no yo na no yo
Hey ya, eh yoo
Eh yo—na-ah yoooo ah

What were the chances? Or does all of time wheel back on itself through eternity?

Sitting outside her home was the same Saami woman from whom I'd bought Astrid's good-luck bracelet years ago. The scene wasn't precisely a hiccup in time. The *komse* was gone. In its place, a young boy sat carving a design into a reindeer antler. And instead of a bracelet, she was busy weaving a pattern of interlocking antlers into a *grener*, the Saami's traditional woolen blanket in shades of gray, white, and black—the natural colors of the wool.

She looked up as I approached. "Hello, Tor," she said.

"Hello, Verá."

Funny after so much time to remember names. She hadn't aged. Her bare hands worked two shuttles through the warp, hands as yet unwrinkled by time.

I stood watching her weave. Finally I said, "It's good to see you again."

"And you." She paused. "I was sorry to hear about your wife. I'm sorry that the charms didn't work their magic."

"How did you—"

She smiled her enigmatic smile. Longyearbyen was a small town. Everyone knew everyone's business.

"Her loss wasn't the charms' fault," I said. I pulled back my sleeve and showed her the bracelet, the pewter still shiny and the leather soft as butter. Astrid had stashed the bracelet in the box of bones, and I'd worn it ever since I found it there. I like to think she left it behind so that the charms would continue to protect the living. They clung to the leather loop, which I'd repaired a dozen times. I shook my wrist, and the beads clicked.

"Your loss, yes," she said. "And the war. The idea of one people conquering another is foreign to the Saami. So much tragedy as a result." She tied on a fresh strand of yarn and plunged the shuttle through a gap in the row of strings. "And what did anyone gain?"

She let the question hang in the air, then continued. "There's a myth among my people that when the last days are here, Faavdna, the hunter in the sky, will shoot down the North Star, Boahje, which supports the dome of the sky and around which all the stars reel. Afterward, the heavens will fall down and crush the earth, the world will be set on fire, and everything will be destroyed."

She looked up at me. "We thought that time had come."

"But we were spared."

"Spared?" she said. "Yes, the world didn't end. We pick up the pieces."

She rooted through a leather pouch at her feet and pulled out another charm.

"Rana Neida, daughter of the earth." She fixed the talisman to my bracelet with a piece of yarn.

"A remembrance. Your wife loved all things of the earth, no?"

I thanked her, fighting back tears, then made my way back home.

The sun's angle reminds me that the day is passing into mid-afternoon. I've sat here scribbling far too long. The seal surfaces one last time, reminding me that I must be on my way.

He's an elegant creature, wet fur sleek against his body, his coat dotted with black spots. What a prize his skin would be, stripped of its flesh and tanned. But there's already been too much death on these shores.

MIDSUMMER 1947

Haven
Midsummer's Eve
23 June 1947

And so I come to the end of this *Glemmeboka*.
I arrived at Haven in the late afternoon. Like me, the hunter's hut has assumed the posture of an old man bent slightly to the infirmities of age. Remnants of a fire remained in a stone ring by the shore. I sifted a handful of ash through my fingers. This was the very place we lit our solstice fires. Little changes in the Arctic climate, but this ring of stones and charred wood can't have lasted a decade.
Someone had nailed a wooden plank across the hut's front door. Propped against the outside wall was a rusty axe. I put aside my rucksack and my rifle and picked it up, pried the nails from the barricade. A crude tool, but effective. As I grasped the door handle, a tremor erupted from deep in my right shoulder and traveled down the length of my arm. The last time I'd been through this door was when Anders and Halvard pulled me away, carrying Hans close to my chest.

Solstice arrived, the longest day but also the day (as I've said) that turns the earth toward darkness once again. Astrid had talked me into spending the day at Haven, "to mark our year in exile," she said. A celebration. An answer to my prayers.
Once again, I gave the crew a half day off. Once again, Astrid and I packed some food, a rifle, and the wedding dress. Once again, we trekked to Haven, gathered driftwood, and built a fire to warm ourselves on this cold tongue of land.
The difference this year: Hans in his *komse*.
In the late afternoon, she put Hans down for a nap and emerged from the cabin in the wedding dress, its lily-of-the-valley beads sparkling in the sun. I see her now before me, rouge dusting her cheeks, her hair parted neatly to the side. She looks more like herself than at any time in the past several

months. She carries a bouquet of seven native flowers, her
blessed Svalbard flora. I take her in my arms and kiss her. She
returns the kiss. Arm in arm, we march down to the water's
edge.

"Sit," she says, and hands me the bouquet. "My prince."

I inhale the flowers' faint scent, place them on a rock, and
stoke the bonfire. Then I sit, happily anticipating what comes
next.

Astrid dances the same dance around the fire, *widershins*, per-
forms the same tease down to the last bit of clothing. Naked
but for the gold locket necklace, she steps away from me and
smiles. I smile back.

She runs into the water (*thirty, twenty-nine, twenty-eight*), dives
(*twenty-one twenty nineteen*), surfaces briefly (*fifteenfourteenthirteen*),
dives again (*tennineeight*).

She hasn't reappeared (*sixfive*). My first thought is that she's
struck her head on the rocky bottom. I strip off my parka and
boots and race down to the water. Underwater is so dark I can
see but a few feet in front of me. The bottom seems bottomless, the last rays of the sun too weak to penetrate the dark. I
surface, gasping for air. It's then I see her. She's swum far, far
out. Away from me and swimming farther. I swim as far out as
I dare.

The sea swallows her, then forgets.

All these many years later, nightmares linger, after-images in my
mind's eye. Anders and Halvard arriving at Haven to find out
what had delayed our return. Scouring the beach, fanning out,
searching and searching for her body washed up on shore.

"She's gone," Anders said, over and over. *Gone. Gone. Gone.*
Ghost word that haunts me.

The trek back from Haven to the whaling station plays like
the stuttering unreeling of a silent movie. Halvard feeds the
baby with a "bottle" he's engineered from a foraged Mason jar
and thin tubing. Hans spits out the foreign-tasting milk until

hunger and thirst get the best of him. Anders and Halvard
flank me, each holding on to an arm so that I don't collapse,
my legs rubbery and insubstantial. Someone snugs Hans inside
my parka. He's fast asleep, oblivious to the tragedy of moth-
erlessness that has befallen him. Halvard carries my rucksack.
Astrid's wedding dress protrudes. Its translucent beads catch
the sun and shine as if lighting the way to Kvitfiskneset. Who's
thought of retrieving the dress from the pile of clothes beside
the bonfire? Anders? Halvard? Me?

But the *komse* is left behind.

Yes, life unreels in bursts. Anders and Halvard wave goodbye from the Longyearbyen dock, the last time I see them. I'm
standing on the deck of the *Lyngen*, the sea rushing by. Hans
squirms in my arms, rooting in vain for mother's milk. We arrive
at the Oslo dock, Astrid's parents' faces blank with grief. Marit
snatches the baby from me. Birgitta, poor Birgitta. Bewildered.

"Where's Mamma? Where's Mamma?" she asks, pulling
aside the blanket shielding Hans from the wind. She raises her
hand and hits him across the cheek. I grab the offending hand
(too hard) before she can strike him again.

For nights afterward, when sleep came grudgingly, I awoke
to the image in my deepest nightmare—Astrid with her golden
hair transformed to seaweed, her body bloated, her arms and
legs eaten away by sharks.

At Haven's door, I turned toward the water. Somewhere out
there lay Astrid's bones. If I'm honest, her bones have drifted
as flotsam drifts, caught up in unseen but powerful westerly
currents, far from here. She's followed the Vikings or Nansen's
Fram to Greenland. Or floated to Birgitta's Hyperborea.

It's a peculiar sort of preoccupation that overtook me, led
me here, the culmination of fixation borne of not having a
body to bury or a grave to visit. It reminds me of a story Astrid
told me once, the strange case of Anna Charlier, fiancée of
Nils Strindberg, one of the three men lost on Andrée's balloon

expedition. The accidental discovery of their bodies on Kvitøya in 1930, thirty-three years after they went missing, created a sensation. Newspapers around the world covered the story for months afterward. Astrid wasn't as intrigued by the men's tragic end or the many theories of how they died, mysteries that were never solved. No, she was captivated by Anna's decades-long fixation over her dead fiancé. Interviewed after the bodies were discovered, Anna revealed that she'd clipped every article about the doomed flight and bound each into leather scrapbooks. She'd waited a dozen years hoping for Nils's return or some idea of his fate before marrying in 1909. And strangest of all, she made her husband promise to remove her heart when she died, transport it from their home in Torquay, England, and bury it beside Nils's grave in Stockholm.

I understood such obsession only after Astrid's passing.

Stalling worked only so long. Inevitably I needed to enter the hut. I grasped the knob again and opened the door. Haven's interior was as I remembered it: the blackened cast-iron stove, the bunk tucked beneath the pitched ceiling, animal skins folded neatly on the bed slats, shelves stocked with cans of pemmican and beans, salt and sugar, a tin of tea.

And miraculously, here was the one thing I'd come to Haven hoping to find—the *komse*, intact, right down to the braid (now faded) hanging from the canopy. I wonder what hunters seeking refuge here thought of this mysterious cradle. That a baby had been born here? Or a young family had lived here for a time?

That the *komse* lies untouched reflects the communal spirit that abides on Svalbard. I'm surprised that some desperate itinerant hadn't used it as firewood. Maybe there *is* hope for the human race.

I unfastened the braid from the canopy and tied it on my wrist alongside the Saami bracelet. (You can never have too much luck.) I wiped the accumulation of dust from the *komse* with the edge of my shirt until the woodgrain came alive.

I imagine Hans dozing peacefully in his *komse* on that solstice, after Astrid nursed him to sleep. I imagine Astrid pulling her wedding dress from the rucksack, placing it over her head, fastening the three pearl buttons behind her neck. I imagine that fleeting twinge I felt then, a kind of contentment that we'd gotten through the worst of times.

Hans sleeping, Astrid dancing around the fire and then stripping off her dress, me ready for another icy plunge. Me counting, counting. *Thirty...twenty-nine...twenty-eight...*

The *komse* gleams in shafts of light.

I've brought to Haven an odd assortment of items. Two tins, one containing the seeds of the flower she discovered and the other the reindeer calf's toenails. A box filled with the animal bones she surreptitiously collected in her final days. Nine species of wood. Anders's scrimshaw. The wedding dress.

The trek here has tired me. Writing this has tired me. The day was waning, and I had much to do. Within the ring of stones left by a previous wanderer, I built a pyramid, kindling at the base, then small logs, and finally a teepee of larger logs. From my rucksack I removed the small pieces of wood I'd brought all the way from Sandefjord. Nine distinct species. I can name them all now—chestnut, ash, oak, beech, walnut, sycamore, maple, birch, and in a nod to this place, the lowly Arctic willow. I arranged them at the teepee's base, then lit the kindling.

Flames and smoke spread upward into the blue sky. I sat on a driftwood log (perhaps the very one I'd sat on nine years ago) and rummaged through my rucksack for bread and salted cod. I ate my fill and threw bread crusts to the gulls that glided above my head, handsome birds with their tan-speckled feathers. They fought each other over the meager meal.

Again I dug through the rucksack and pulled out the mushroom I'd harvested earlier. I touched it to my lips, licked it, and tasted its foulness before I threw it into the fire. It whispered itself to nothing.

Finally, it was time. I spread the wedding dress across my lap, fingered its delicate beading, and traced its singed edge. Rising,

I slid my arm around the dress's waist, held up the wrist of one sleeve, and danced clockwise around the fire. Then I began to sing.

"Summertime and the livin' is easy."

The words blended with the *kah kah kah* of the gulls winging overhead.

How beautiful the world is!

"Summertime," I sang again, "and the livin' is easy."

The birds swooped and soared, swooped and soared.

"There's a nothin' can harm you with daddy and mammy standin' by."

I sang and sang. "Then you'll spread your wings and you'll take the sky." If anyone had seen me, they'd have thought I'd lost my mind.

Yes, the world is dangerous and sad and beautiful. There is no equilibrium, no careful balance between joy and sorrow. There is now, there is then, there is whatever may come. And no guarantee that You mete out only what we can endure. Write that down in Your book of remembrance, dear God.

I danced around the fire once more, then leapt across the edge of the flames. The dress trailed into the flames, caught fire. I stopped. The beads melted, the delicate fabric turning to ash.

Why not? I thought. I threw the dress into the fire and watched until all that was left were black flakes rising into the air, floating away.

Stay with me now as I finish the story.

On a hillock above the shoreline, I arranged stones in stepwise rings until all that remained was a small hole at the top. Inside, I laid the box of bones and the tin of toenails. I covered the cairn with a final stone, then placed the scrimshaw on top. A poor substitute for a body. Will I ever be reconciled to its absence? No, a thousand times no. But at least her spirit will have a place to alight.

The seed tin emitted a pleasing rattle, the sound one of the few things that soothed Hans in those first months after we arrived back home. It's labeled in Astrid's lavish script, *Saxifraga birkandrum*. Hanna had renamed the new flora after her mentee, *Saxifraga Birkia astridii*. I opened the tin and buried the seeds in the mud and scree around the cairn.

"Dear God, let these precious seeds take root," I prayed aloud. "Let Astrid's spirit rise from the sea and find its way to this eternal resting place. Amen."

I returned to the bonfire and piled fresh logs upon it. Then I sat, basking in its warmth. A light fog descended over Van Keulenfjorden, swirling briefly above the water, skimming toward me like an apparition. *Fog*, I thought, but I could almost believe Astrid was right. The dead do long for us to see them again.

Close to shore came an orange flash, appearing and disappearing, like Morse code. SOS, SOS. The flash was a small buoy fishers use to mark their nets. Carrying the buoy was a bereft female beluga. Behind her was an enormous pod of belugas, more belugas than I'd ever seen in one place in all my years here. And in the rear, the same whale with the ebony-edged flukes I'd freed days ago. Together they breached, spraying water from their blowholes.

Wonderful, I thought. *Let them be! Let them thrive!*

Wanting to join in their merriment, I stripped off my clothing, left it in a pile by the fire, and waded into the sea.

Thirty, twenty-nine, twenty-eight, I counted to myself as I strode into the fjord.

Nineteeneighteenseventeensixteenfifteenfourteenthirteen. I dove underwater and swam through clouds of silvery bubbles, their soft clink and ping whispering to me. I closed my eyes and listened. She was there.

I believe that my old pal was portent, deliverance. That he nudged me to shore and watched my naked body being carried up and down by the gentle waves. I could swear I heard in my last moments of consciousness a song within the music of bubbles, high-pitched as birdsong. *Heave, heave.*

Fitting requiem for the last whaler of Kvitfiskneset.
I woke, shivering violently. The fire burned bright. I crawled
to it and warmed myself.

Yes, you can't kill an old fox.

Slowly I dressed myself, stood unsteadily, and scanned the
horizon. Farther out in the bay, my friend breached one last
time, then lunged across the surface until he disappeared.

ॐ

Kvitfiskneset
24 June 1947

Water edged up to the smoldering fire and lapped gently at its
base. The flames winked out, the spent logs sizzled. I picked up
my rucksack and headed back to Kvitfiskneset, worried that I
was already late. In my haste, my feet slid in the mud and scree.
I fell once and had trouble getting back on my feet.

I've become an old man like Hilmar, I thought. *How did that hap-*
pen? We believe ourselves invincible until we're not.

As I approached the whaling station, I realized that, like
Longyearbyen, it needed attention. I resolved then and there to
leave the whale cemetery untouched, partly out of vanity, silent
witness to my industry. But it would also stand forever as testimony to the kind of destruction with which we scar the earth.

What of the rest? The rowboats, beached like white whales,
their broken staves like so many rib bones. The cabin itself, a
relic of time past. The shutters askew, never fully repaired after
Astrid took an axe to them. The stovepipe, aslant on the roof.
The crazy quilt of animals' skins long ago nailed to the siding,
frayed and flapping in the breeze. Perhaps I should wrap the
outside in hides. Hadn't that been Astrid's idea? Covering the
exterior with polar bear skins, the cabin itself an animal hun-
kering down. What might a polar bear think coming upon such
a sight, a mirror image of himself? Why had no one thought of
such a shroud before?

Such whimsy would have to wait. There were more important tasks to finish, and little time to finish them. The Hotel's walls had collapsed, and two of the old rowboats were long past usefulness, their stove-in hulls yawing Os. The Jonah boat had (surprisingly) defied nature's attempts to destroy it. All were relics of my past life. As with all human-made things, these relics would inevitably return to dust, traces of those who came before us erased. Eventually nature reclaims what was once hers.

I fashioned a torch from a long driftwood stick and a rag soaked with kerosene and lit the head with a match. First, I ignited The Hotel and watched the fire consume the structure. Passing the platforms where the try-pots once stood, I came to the three rowboats canted on their sides. Sentimentality spared the Jonah rowboat, but the other two I set aflame. As the fire flared, I pulled the folio from my rucksack. What good would it do for my children to read it someday? What harm? No. Better they have what little they remember. I threw the folio into the conflagration and watched the past burn.

৵

Kvitfiskneset
24 June 1947

This entry is the beginning of a new *Glemmeboka.*

My signal fires shone bright against the shadow hills that framed the flames. The wind shifted, blowing down from the mountains to the sea, passing through the whale cemetery. Downshore, I could swear I heard the whale's skulls whispering as the gusts moved through their jaws. Songs pulled inside out.

I scanned the horizon. It was growing very late. My impatience turned to apprehension.

As if my very thoughts summoned a mirage into existence, a motorboat approached. There at last was Birgitta, holding Hans's hand. Birgitta. So much like Astrid, her short blond hair fanned around her face, her body erect, ready to face any challenge.

Birgitta and Hans waved furiously as the boat drew nearer to shore. The pilot came as close as he dared, cut the engine, and cast anchor. Together the three of them lowered a small boat and rowed in unison until I caught the prow and pulled the boat onto the beach.

My sweet children clambered out and gave me fierce hugs.

"*Hei*, Pappa," they said in unison. "*Hei, hei, hei.*"

I held them close, so close, and joined in their *a cappella* hymn.

"*Hei, hei, hei.*"

ACKNOWLEDGMENTS

I am deeply indebted to the people who helped inspire and shape this novel: to Aaron O'Connor and the Arctic Circle organization for providing the residency aboard the *Antigua* in June 2017 that gave birth to the story's central idea; to Hamish Robinson and Hawthornden Castle for giving me the space to write an early draft; to Jan Martin Berg and Daria Khelsengreen at Galleri Svalbard in Longyearbyen for the residencies and the invaluable access to the library there; to Nancy Lowe for the Art of the Climate residency; to the administrators at the Scott Polar Institute in Cambridge (UK), who provided access to their unique library of all things polar; to Tanya Whiton, whose close reading propelled the book to its final form; to Carleen Sheehan, fellow ice- and whale-bone-obsessed traveler; and to the artists, scientists, and crew aboard ship whose conversations enriched the novel's development.

I am also indebted to the writers whose work illuminates the lives of women in the Arctic. Christiane Ritter's *A Woman in the Polar Night* (Jane Degras, English trans., *A Woman in the Polar Night*, London: Pushkin Press, 2019) gave me insight into the particular joys and difficulties of women on Svalbard. In addition to the quote "For here there are no days because there are no nights…," Ritter is the original source of the story of the Norwegian woman who gave birth alone on Svalbard and later went mad, though versions of this story appear elsewhere. Background on other women who forged lives on Svalbard comes from a number of sources, including *North of the Desolate Sea* by Liv Balstad (London: Souvenir Press, 1958); *Polarheltinner* by Sigri Sandberg Meløy (Oslo: Gyldendal Norsk Forlag, 2012); and *Home Is a Tent* by Myrtle Simpson (London: The Camelot Press Ltd., 1964).

Background on the Nøis family comes from the following

sources: *Ishavskvinne: Historien om Helfrid Nøis* by Tor Jacobsen (Oslo: Gyldendal Norsk Forlag, 1979); *Nøis, der Grossjäger von Spitzbergen* by Odd Berset (Wiesbaden: Eberhard Brockhaus, 1955); *Hilmar Nøis: Storjegeren fra Svalbard* by Odd Berset (Oslo: J. W. Eides Forlag, 1953); and John-Eldar Pedersen's website containing the Nøis family history (www.nordpol.no/index. html).

As to the unique aspects of Svalbard's botany, I found a rare copy of Hanna Resvoll-Holmsen's *Svalbards flora: med endel om dens plantevekst i nutid og fortid* (Oslo: Cappelen, 1927) in the library at Galleri Svalbard, where I spent two residencies, one as Longyearbyen entered the dark season and one as the town came into the light of *Soldagen*. The botanical illustrations contained herein were first published in Resvoll-Holmsen's guide. Other books consulted for information on Svalbard's flora include *A Naturalist's Guide to the Arctic* by E. C. Pielou (Chicago: The University of Chicago Press, 1994); *Arctic Plants of Svalbard: What We Learn From the Green in the Treeless White World* by Yoo Kyung Lee (Cham, Switzerland: Springer, 2020); and *Longyear Flora: A Basic Field Guide 3rd Edition* (Haugesund: Longyearbyen Field Biology Association, 2017).

Among the many books I consulted for information on Svalbard and the Arctic include the following. Gordon Seton's *Amid Snowy Wastes: Wild Life on the Spitsbergen Archipelago* (London: Cassell and Company, Limited, 1922) provided one of the novel's epigraphs. A. R. Glen and N. A. C. Croft's *Under the Pole Star: The Oxford University Arctic Expedition, 1935-36* (London: Methuen Publishers, 1937) was an invaluable resource for what life was like on Svalbard in the 1930s. The book is also the source for the quote "Does woman hold the whip, or does the instinct of man insist on mastery and then despise the slavery he has inflicted?" (161). Methuen no longer holds the rights to the work and does not know the whereabouts of the rights holders. Other key works include *No Man's Land: A History of Spitsbergen From Its Discovery in 1596 to the Beginning of the Scientific Exploration of the Country* by Sir Martin Conway (Cambridge:

Cambridge UP, 1906); *Arctic Dreams: Imagination and Desire in a Northern Landscape* by Barry Lopez (New York: Vintage Books, 2001); and the *Cruise Handbook for Svalbard* by Kristin Prestvold and Øystein Overrein, edited by Bjørn Fossli Johansen (Tromsø: Norwegian Polar Institute, 2011). The most valuable sources for the history of whaling are the two volumes of William Scoresby's *An Account of the Arctic Regions, with a history and description of the Northern Whale Fishery* (Edinburgh: Archibald Constable and Co. and London: Hurst, Robinson and Co., 1820). The source for the Saami pictograph of Maderakka is the website *Godchecker* (godchecker.com, 12 May 2019), edited by Chas Saunders and Peter J. Allen. The pictograph for Rana Neida is widely available on the web.

Background regarding Norway's role in World War II comes from general histories as well as biographies and autobiographies of those mentioned within, including *Norway and the Second World War* by Johs. Andenæs, Olav Riste, and Magne Skodvin (Oslo: Johan Grundt Tanum Forlag, 1974); *War in the Arctic* by Olav Farnes (London: Darf Publishers Ltd., 1991); *The German Occupation of Norway* by Paul G. Vigness (New York: Vantage Press, 1970); and *Master Race: The Lebensborn Experiment in Nazi Germany* by Catrine Clay and Michael Leapman (London: BCA, 1995). Two biographies that contain the remarkable story of Jan Baalsrud are *We Die Alone: A World War II Epic of Escape and Endurance* by David Howarth (Guilford, CT: The Lyons Press, 1999) and *The 12th Man: A WWII Epic of Escape and Endurance* by Astrid Karlsen Scott and Dr. Tore Haug (New York: Skyhorse Publishing, 2017). Wilhelm Dege's autobiography, *War North of 80: The Last German Arctic Weather Station of World War II*, translated by William Barr (Calgary: Calgary UP and Arctic Institute of North America and Boulder, CO: Colorado UP, 2004), gives his account as leader of Operation Haudegen.

Poets, lyricists, and writers whose work is quoted herein and lies in the public domain include Pindar's lines from the fifth century regarding the Hyperboreans; Robert Browning's line from "Childe Roland to the Dark Tower Came" (published in

Men and Women, Boston: Ticknor and Fields, 1856, p. 97); Christina Rossetti's "Echo" (Christina Rossetti and William Michael Rossetti, ed., *The Poetical Works of Christina Georgina Rossetti*, London: Macmillan and Co., 1904, p. 314); Viktor Rydberg's "The House-Goblin: Tomten" (found in *Anthology of Swedish Lyrics from 1750 to 1915*, Charles Wharton Stork, trans., New York: The American-Scandinavian Foundation and London: Oxford University Press, 1917, pp. 114-17); the line "Lay, my child, in the lap of sleep, close your eyes" from Hanna Resvoll-Holmsen's "*Ved en sons dødsleie*" ("At a Son's Deathbed") from *I tidens løp* ("In the Course of Time") (Oslo: Some & Co. Forlag [now defunct], 1930); the slightly altered closing lines of "Solveig's Song" ("*Her skal jeg vente til du kommer igjen; og venter du hist oppe, vi træffes der, min sonn!*") by Henrik Ibsen and Edvard Grieg from *Peer Gynt* (1875); and George Scroggie's "Farewell to Tarwathie," written around 1850 and whose lyrics I've adapted within. The earliest versions of the shanty "Heave Away, Me Johnny, Heave Away" date back to the 1850s. The song has no known original authorship. I modified the lyrics that the whaling crew sings from widely available versions of this song. Likewise, the ballad "The Captain's Apprentice" (also known as "The Cruel Ship's Captain" and "Captain James") is part of the oral tradition of songs passed down through generations. Elizabeth James asserts that the earliest printed version was collected by Ralph Vaughan Williams in 1905 based on events that occurred in 1857 involving the murder of a ship's apprentice and the subsequent hanging of the ship's captain guilty of the murder (see Elizabeth James, "*The Captain's Apprentice* and the Death of Young Robert Eastick of King's Lynn: A Study in the Development of a Folk Song," *Folk Music Journal*, 7:5, pp. 579-94). The lines from Ovid's *Metamorphoses* (Book IV, Verse 109)—"She turned about but rose not from the ground…"—are adapted from the translation by Sir Samuel Garth, John Dryden, et. al. (Dublin: S. Powell, 1727). "The temple bell stops, but I still hear the sound coming out of the flowers" is a haiku by Matsuo Bashō.

Many versions of the story of the ghost ship *Octavius* exist, though not all name the ship. My primary source lies in *Invisible Horizons: True Mysteries of the Sea* by Vincent Gaddis (Radnor, PA: Chilton Book Company, 1965, pp. 104-08). And finally, special thanks to the mapmaker Keenan Boscoe of the Topo Gallery in Camden, Maine, for the illustration of Svalbard contained in the novel's front matter.

Any factual errors contained in *The Last Whaler* are my responsibility.

I would like to thank Regal House Publishing, and especially Jaynie Royal, who shares my fascination with the Arctic. I would also like to thank the many people who supported me during the writing of this book, especially Carolyn Grashof, Beth Kephart, Margaret Luongo, and Elizabeth Mosier. And as always, special thanks to my family, my husband, Douglas, and my children, Elizabeth and Christopher.

PERMISSIONS

Book Club Questions

1. Birk's death is the precipitating factor in the couple's decision to spend the summer together at Kvitfiskneset. In what ways do Tor and Astrid reconcile themselves to the vagaries of grief? Why do you think Astrid chooses to channel her grief by writing to her dead son? Why does Tor finally decide to bring her letters to Svalbard?

2. Why does Tor feel compelled to return to Svalbard to resolve his guilt over Astrid's suicide? Why can't he come to terms with his culpability at his home in Sandefjord?

3. How do the events of World War II—the precursors to the conflict, the war itself, and its aftermath—deepen the themes underpinning the novel?

4. The lives of little-known historical figures are woven throughout. How does the presence of these figures—in particular, Hanna Resvoll-Holmsen, Christiane Ritter, the Nøises, and Einar Sverdrup—contribute to the story's authenticity? In what ways are these characters critical to Tor's journey of self-discovery?

5. Mental illness underscores the lives and attitudes of many of the characters. How does lack of empathy and understanding of mental illness play a role in Astrid's suicide and Tor's coming to terms with his guilt?